Dark Sun

DARK SUN

Christopher Nicole

$$\overline{\underline{C}}$$

CENTURY
LONDON SYDNEY AUCKLAND JOHANNESBURG

This is a novel. Except where they can be identified his-
torically, the characters are invented, and are not intended
to depict actual persons, living or dead. However, most
of the events in the story are based on fact.

The right of Christopher Nicole to be identified as the author
of this work has been asserted by him in accordance with the
Copyright, Designs and Patents Act 1988

First published in Great Britain in 1990 by
Random Century Group
20 Vauxhall Bridge Road, London SW1V 2SA

Century Hutchinson South Africa (Pty) Ltd
PO Box 337, Bergvlei 2012, South Africa

Random Century Australia Pty Ltd
20 Alfred Street, Milsons Point, Sydney, NSW 2061
Australia

Random Century New Zealand Ltd
PO Box 40–086, Glenfield, Auckland 10
New Zealand

British Library Cataloguing in Publication Data
Nicole, Christopher, *1930–*
    Dark sun.
    I. Title
    823.914 [F]

ISBN 0–7126–3669–2

Phototypeset by Input Typesetting Ltd, London
Printed in Great Britain by
Mackays of Chatham PLC, Chatham, Kent

Prologue

The first hint of dawn brought the mists swirling from the turgid surface of the Yalu River. There was no wind, and the only sound was the running of the water as it flowed towards the Bay of Korea.

The river was a mile wide here, and the far bank was invisible in the darkness. Kitachi knew there were border guards over there, soldiers of Marshal Chang Tso-lin's motley army. They showed no lights. But then, they did not show themselves during the day, either. In this year of 1927 the Marshal, perhaps the most powerful of the many warlords who had seized vast portions of China since the collapse of the once-eternal Manchu Empire, had no wish to provoke an incident with the Japanese army of occupation in Korea.

Kitachi Tano also knew the Marshal was only buying one more year of peace at best. He, personally, had never crossed the Yalu, but intended to do so one day. Manchuria was Japan's natural hinterland. It would belong, soon, to Japan.

He put away the field-glasses with which he had been peering into the darkness; they were useless in the gathering mist. Now it was a matter of listening. His men understood this too; they crouched in the reeds bordering the river, silent, alert, tense.

They were little men, in green uniforms, with small, soft green peaked caps and green leggings over their brown boots. Each man was armed with a rifle and a bayonet. Kitachi himself wore breeches and black boots, brown leather cross- and waist-belts. His face was small and composed, with rounded rather than flattened features; some said there was Ainu in his ancestry but his face was clean shaven. His rank of captain was designated on his shoulder straps, and he was armed with an automatic pistol and two samurai swords: the small sword hung on his right beside the pistol holster; the long sword was suspended on his left. Both were in brown leather scabbards. These swords were not regulation dress, but any Japanese officer who possessed a sword, and had the right to wear it, might do so if he chose.

The order, the state pensions, the overweaning power, of the samurai had been ended by the great Emperor Mutsuhito, some twenty years before Kitachi was born. But how could a man forget his ancestors? This long sword had spilt blood, in the hands of Kitachi's grandfather, and there was every prospect of it doing so again in the near future.

Kano, his sergeant, touched his arm. The two men had an intimate working relationship, and although Kano would never have dared touch him in public, now he was doing as his captain wished; they could not risk even a whispered word of warning.

Kitachi listened, and heard the sound of booted feet squelching on the river bank. He could feel the tension in his men. They had found where the rowing boat was hidden during the night. Since then it had been a matter of waiting until the midnight visitor returned. Now he was here.

A man emerged from the mist. He wore a khaki uniform, with a peaked cap and brown boots; a revolver holster drooped from his belt. He was bigger than any of the waiting Japanese, although his features were no less Oriental.

He moved confidently, checked with no more than a slight hunching of the heavy shoulders as Kitachi stood up immediately in front of him.

'I have a safe conduct,' he said in good Japanese, taking a sheet of paper from his breast pocket. 'It is signed by General Abe.'

Kitachi took the paper. His six men spread out to either side, two of them moving behind the Chinese officer.

x

Kano remained at the captain's side, holding a small flash-light by which Kitachi scanned the paper.

When he was finished, Kitachi handed the paper to Kano, and the sergeant crumpled it into a ball and threw it into the water.

'That was signed by General Abe,' the Chinese officer said again. 'Your superior officer.'

'General Abe is not *my* superior officer,' Kitachi informed him, his voice staccato.

The Chinese officer frowned, and peered at the badge above the pocket on the right breast of Kitachi's uniform. The branch of the service to which a Japanese officer belonged was denoted by this small badge; army officers wore red, artillery officers yellow, cavalry officers green, engineer officers brown, supply units dark blue. Officers from the still-infant air force wore pale blue.

There was no badge at all on Kitachi's uniform.

The Chinese officer caught his breath, and looked round at Kitachi's men; confident in his safe conduct, he had allowed them to come too close.

Now he remembered that the kempei-tai were reputed to be a law unto themselves, even when attached to army commands. Some called them a state within a state.

'You serve Marshal Chang Tso-lin,' Kitachi said.

'That is correct,' the Chinese officer said, with a confidence he did not feel.

'And you have been to visit General Abe,' Kitachi observed. 'Tell me what you said to him, and what he said to you.'

'I cannot do that. It is a confidential matter, between the Marshal and the General.'

It was quite light now, although the mist isolated the small group of men from the rest of the world. Kitachi studied the Chinese officer, and the officer met his gaze. It was a chill morning, but the officer's face was wet with sweat: he had also heard tales of the kempei-tai's methods.

Kitachi smiled. 'It is no matter,' he said. 'Confidential matters should remain confidential.'

The Chinese officer gave a faint sigh of relief.

'Sergeant Kano,' Kitachi said.

Kano gave a quick bow. 'Proceed,' he told his men.

They knew their business; there should be no mark on their victim's body and that he should not be allowed to make a sound. The six of them closed in on the Chinese officer before he suspected their intention. Two stooped to seize his ankles and whip them from the ground. The officer gasped, but before he could cry out he had fallen over the river bank and gone head first into the water. The two soldiers retained their hold on his booted ankles, raising them high. The other four soldiers went into the shallow water and grasped his sleeves and his hair – his cap had come off and drifted away – and thus forced his head to stay under water without actually touching his flesh.

It was over very quickly. The officer was too surprised to hold his breath. When his head was pulled up after five minutes he was dead, his mouth and nostrils obscured by a mass of mucus.

They pushed him out into the stream and let his body float away, face down. Then they went to his rowing boat, and threw the oars into the water. The boat they turned upside down, and pushed after the drifting body.

'Perhaps *we* will send Marshal Chang Tso-lin an emissary, in time,' Kitachi said, and walked into the mist.

Kitachi was pleased, both with himself and with his men. He felt no remorse. Even had he not been carrying out orders, he would have considered what he had just done important, because it contributed to the coming greatness of Japan. There were those who felt, and said, that in two generations the Land of the Rising Sun had achieved greatness enough. The Emperor Mutsuhito had, in the course of a very few years, raised the inward-turned, backward, feudal state, deliberately cut off from the course of history, to the rank of a first-rate power. Manchu China had been swept contemptuously aside, as had Tsarist Russia.

As a sixteen-year-old officer cadet, Kitachi had experienced the euphoria of those heady days of endless victory, but without being allowed to take part in the triumph itself.

The Yalu river, where he now stood, had been the scene of bitter fighting, and these dark waters had been stained darker yet with blood. But he had seen none of it.

He had served in the Great War. But there had been little fighting in Asia, nothing to compare with the bloodbath that had taken place in Europe. Conduct towards the enemy, however beaten and disgraced, had been governed by strange Western notions of compassion, so confusing to the victor, so dishonourable to the defeated. Yet those had been stirring days.

In the eight and a half years since that fearful struggle, the Western Powers, once so anxious to possess the friendship and support of the Island People, had turned their backs on their erstwhile allies and their aspirations. Japan had sought to obtain from the chaos of the China of Sun-Yat-Sen and Yuan Shih-kai that breeding ground in Manchuria which she must have or perish. The Chinese would have ceded all because they had no means of resisting, but the Western Powers, led by the United States of America, had objected.

Like a large number of Japanese officers, and every member of the kempei-tai, Kitachi Tano had no doubt that the future of the Pacific, and East Asia, would one day have to be decided between the United States and Japan.

In 1918, it had been a matter for patience, because Japan did not lack friends. Her principal friend at that time was Great Britain. Japan and Britain had been allies for sixteen years. Both island people, they had more in common than might have been supposed.

But when given a choice between American friendship and Japanese in 1922, the British had opted for that of their own race, and the treaty had not been renewed. Since then, Japan had become more and more isolated, her claims to greatness rejected.

It was difficult not to suppose that differences of colour

and religion had played their part.

Equally difficult was it to suppose that Mutsuhito would have accepted such an insult to his race and his ancestors. But the Great Emperor was dead, and his successor had been an imbecile. Those who believed in the greatness of Japan, and in her obvious role as the future dominant power in East Asia, had had to grind their teeth in impotent fury, and wait for better times.

Now, surely, they had arrived. The Taisho reign of the poor, unbalanced, bewildered Emperor Yoshihito had ended only a few months before. Now a new emperor, Hirohito, sat on the imperial throne, and the empire had entered on a new era, which had been given the name Showa, or Great Prosperity. But those who knew the truth knew that such prosperity could only be obtained as all earlier prosperity had been gained, by force of arms. It would take time to educate the nation, and perhaps the Emperor himself. But there was not a great deal of time available.

Meanwhile, individual commanders, especially those known to hold liberal views such as General Abe, could not be allowed to hold secret midnight meetings with emissaries of the man who stood in the very doorway of Japanese expansion.

'Well?' demanded Colonel Tarawa.

Captain Kitachi gave a deep bow before the desk. 'I regret to inform you, honourable colonel, that Captain Tang met with an accident. As he sought to return across the river, his boat overturned. The captain was swept away. I am afraid he drowned.'

Tarawa leaned back in his chair. 'Was he injured in any way?'

'No, honourable colonel.'

Tarawa nodded. 'That was well done. I expected nothing less, Tano.'

'Will you inform the General, honourable colonel?'

Tarawa considered. 'No,' he said at last. 'It would be best to let the General wonder what has happened to the spy. You will leave today, for Tokyo.'

Kitachi gazed imperturbably at his superior. It was not the Japanese way to show surprise or curiosity.

Tarawa gave a quick smile. He wore a little moustache, which he was wont to stroke when pleased. He did so now. 'I am not removing you from General Abe's reach, Tano. You have been sent for by General Tojo, on my recommendation, of course. You will have a great future, Tano.'

'Thank you, honourable colonel.'

'Our country needs dedicated men. You are such a man. Remember this, Tano. I wish you good fortune.'

Kitachi bowed.

The train from Shimonoseki – where the ferry from Korea docked – chugged northwards up the east coast of Honshu Island, skirting the mountainous backbone of the peninsula, and stopped for the night in Osaka. Kitachi was able to visit his family. He had not seen them for a year. He made his way to the little house which nestled within sight of the great castle, the scene of many stirring battles in Japan's history, and was welcomed with much rejoicing; he was an only son.

'A summons to Tokyo,' his mother said. 'Is it promotion?'

'I do not know.'

'It will be good to have you serving in Japan,' his father said.

'If that is what they intend for me,' Kitachi agreed.

Aiwa gazed at him adoringly. She was fourteen years younger than her brother, had the same softly-rounded features and compact figure. She had always worshipped Tano. She liked him best in uniform, of course, but even sitting cross-legged on a tatami mat, wearing a kimono, she thought he was the handsomest man she had ever seen. And he lived such an adventurous life!

'Tell me about Korea,' she begged.

'There is nothing to tell. Korea is a barbarous country, inhabited by backward people.'

'Then tell me about Manchuria.'

'I have never been there.'

'But you must have heard of it.'

'Manchuria is even more barbarous than Korea,' he assured her, and then smiled. 'Perhaps I will take you there, one day.'

Aiwa clapped her hands for joy. No sister could have asked for a more loving brother. Tano was so very kind, in all things.

If his home was in Osaka, Kitachi Tano's heart had always been in Tokyo.

The approach itself was enough to stir the patriotism of any Japanese. The train wound its way from Nagoya to Shizuoka and thence along the shore of Sagami Wan, and a passenger could look up and up, to Fujiyama towering above the Hakone Mountains.

Ahead lay Tokyo Wan.

Kitachi had been in the city, learning his new profession of secret policeman, three and a half years before, when the earth had groaned, and Tokyo, together with its port of Yokohama, had disintegrated.

The horrors he witnessed that first day of September 1923 were forever etched on his memory: whole tramloads of people electrocuted by falling cables; canals filled with bodies, their heads burned out of recognition by the fire storm which had swept over them as they crouched in the shallow water for safety; the tidal wave which had smashed into the waterfront like a runaway juggernaut, the screams of women, the wailing of babies, the groans. . . .

Only three and a half years, yet the catastrophe might never have been! Tokyo had literally risen from the ashes, bigger and more beautiful than before.

Returning to Tokyo was indeed coming home. Visiting the small, dark, modern building that was the headquarters of the kempei-tai was like entering the heart of the nation.

The general was a small man, even for a Japanese. Prematurely bald, he made up for this in some measure by a bushy moustache, above which steel-rimmed spectacles hid his eyes behind a gleam of glass.

His name was Tojo Eiki.

'Colonel Tarawa reports that you are a man of both ability and discretion, Captain Kitachi,' he remarked.

Kitachi bowed. He was not going to refute his superior's opinion.

'Thus, it may be that you are the man I am looking for,' continued the commander of the kempei-tai.

Kitachi waited, with barely suppressed excitement. Having been a serving officer with the secret police for six years, recruited from the army by Tarawa himself, he knew that much of what people whispered was true. No matter who sat on the imperial throne, it was rumoured, and no matter who was prime minister, it was the kempei-tai who really ruled Japan.

Kitachi had never questioned the loyalty of the secret force to which he belonged. That loyalty was to Japan, as embodied by the Son of Heaven. But as the Son of Heaven had more than once in the past been a source of sad disappointment to those who sought greatness for their country, the kempei-tai had on occasion had to take the law into its own hands, even within Tokyo itself.

Therefore the man who sat across the desk from him, one hand flicking nervously at a pencil, was the true ruler of Japan. A man who sought to employ him.

'It will be a mission which will take both time and patience, as well as courage and determination,' Tojo said. 'It will involve you in many things, in saying and doing many things which will be abhorrent to you.'

'It will be my privilege to carry out such a duty, honourable general,' Kitachi said.

'It will involve your taking off that uniform, and becoming a civilian, at least in the eyes of the world. No one can know the truth, save Tarawa and myself. You understand this?'

Kitachi swallowed. His uniform was his proudest possession. But duty came before even pride. 'I understand, honourable general.'

'Then listen carefully. And remember that no word of what I say to you today must ever be repeated outside these walls, not even to another officer of the kempei-tai.'

'I understand, honourable general.'

Tojo studied him for a few seconds. Then he said, 'We are faced with a dilemma which must be resolved, or the nation will perish. We have too many people, and not enough food. People in the West tell us we must work harder, and produce goods to sell for food. Then they raise tariff barriers against us to make our goods too expensive to sell. Now the Americans will no longer allow our people to emigrate to California. We must have food, Captain Kitachi, or our people will die.'

'We must have Manchuria, honourable general,' Kitachi ventured. He knew all the arguments.

Tojo nodded, pleased with the reply. 'Indeed,' he said at last.

'The Chinese are nothing, honourable general,' Kitachi said eagerly. 'Chang Tso-lin is nothing.'

'He is Chinese,' Tojo countered. 'Do you not suppose that Chiang Kai-shek and his Nationalists will support him, were we to invade Manchuria?'

'They hate each other.'

'But they are both Chinese. However, you are well informed, Captain. That is good. We must, and we will, have Manchuria. But it is not the Chinese we have to concern ourselves with. It is the British, and more than the British, the Americans. Listen carefully. An invasion of Manchuria by Japan will be condemned by the League of Nations, and it will be condemned by America. These are powerful forces. We are not afraid of them, but we must be prepared to face them.'

'And defeat them, honourable general,' Kitachi said.

A shadow passed over Tojo's face. 'They are powerful forces,' he repeated. 'Our first duty must be to ensure that they cannot defeat us.'

'Is such a thing possible?' Kitachi wondered. 'Not even Kublai Khan and his Mongol hordes could defeat Japan.'

'Kublai Khan fought with bone and muscle,' Tojo said

drily. 'We have plenty of that. What we do not possess in sufficient quantities are the sinews of modern war. I am speaking of rubber, of oil. Without oil our warships cannot put to sea, nor our tanks cross a field.'

Kitachi was silent. He had never considered that simple fact.

'If we are faced with war against Britain and America,' Tojo continued, 'we must be sure we possess the material to fight with. Where is the nearest obtainable large supply of oil and rubber, Captain?'

Kitachi hesitated only a moment. 'There is oil in the Netherlands East Indies, honourable general. And rubber in British Malaya. But . . .' now he did hesitate.

Tojo's lips widened into the semblance of a smile. 'But one belongs to Holland, the other to Britain. Yet must we have their oil and rubber. And if we are going to war with Britain in any event, does it matter?'

Kitachi kept silent. The immensity of what his chief was proposing was only slowly sinking in.

'Seizing Malaya, seizing the Dutch East Indies, is a prerequisite of success,' Tojo told him. 'Failure to do so would mean certain failure. But this seizure must be accomplished with great speed and determination, before the British and Dutch, or the Americans, can mobilise their forces and certainly before their fleets can reach the Pacific. There are other factors involved, but you need not concern yourself with those. To seize Sumatra and New Guinea, Java and Malaya, it is not enough for us to launch an expedition to the south. We must also have the support of the native populations, who will rise in our support against the Dutch and British. This will also be good for our image abroad. And it is a strong possibility that, suitably encouraged, the Malays and the Indonesians, even the Chinese in South East Asia, will support us. The British and the Dutch treat them like slaves, because their skins are not white. All they need is a lead, to be shown what, under our patronage and with our support, they can achieve.'

Tojo leaned back in his chair. 'I am informed that you

speak excellent English.'

'Yes, honourable general.' Kitachi had spent two years in America, just after the Great War. 'But I do not speak Dutch.'

'That is not important. Another officer is being sent to Djarkarta.' Tojo tapped the paper on which his left hand rested. 'I have here your instructions. You will ask leave to resign from the army for personal reasons. This permission will be granted. You will then enter business with the firm mentioned here. As its representative you will visit Singapore, and set up a branch of the business there. Do not concern yourself with the details of this; your aides will arrange it. But your cover must be impeccable.

'In the course of your business you will make regular visits to Singapore. You will report on its defences and the morale of its garrison. But you will also become acquainted, and if possible friends, with the most prominent Malay and Chinese merchants and politicians. To this end you will be provided with letters of introduction from a Cantonese merchant who is in sympathy with our ideas. These letters will gain for you an entrée into Chinese society in Singapore. As regards the Malays, you will have to make your own way. You will study these men and decide which of them may be of use to us. Then you will subvert those you have chosen to our cause.' He gazed at Kitachi. 'You understand that this is an assignment which may well take some years?'

'I understand, your excellency,' Kitachi said, resignedly.

'You will be serving Japan.' Tojo opened his folder, took out a large photograph. 'Study this.'

Kitachi took the photo, frowned at the eleven young men. Five sat on a bench, the other six stood behind them. They wore matching pale-coloured jackets and white trousers, and they looked at the camera with total confidence.

'Those are Englishmen,' Tojo told him.

'I do not recognise their uniform,' Kitachi confessed.

'That is a cricket team, from Cambridge University.'

Kitachi waited. He knew what cricket was. But he did not know how such a game could interest the kempei-tai. No doubt his superior would enlighten him in due course.

'Far more than the British army, those men are our enemies, Captain. They, and men like them, are the creators and the sustainers of the British Empire. See how fearlessly they gaze at the world? That is because they believe that they were placed on earth to rule, and that nothing can ever interfere with that prerogative. They go to establishments called public schools, and from there they go to Oxford or Cambridge. Then they are sent out to rule the empire. You will meet men like them in Singapore. Study them. They are the men we must hate, the men we must bring down. You must hate, Captain Kitachi, with all of your being, even if you have to wait ten years to strike.'

Kitachi continued to study the photograph.

Tojo smiled. 'When your mission is completed, you will have the rank of colonel, Tano. I give you my word.'

PART ONE
Friends

CHAPTER 1
The Sportsman

The band played on the boatdeck, streamers drifted from the mastheads. Men, women and children of every description thronged the promenade decks. Excited chatter filled the afternoon, dispelled only by the brisk wind coming off the English Channel to give even the sheltered waters of the Solent a smattering of whitecaps.

The *Empress of India* was about to put to sea.

'We'll have them puking right and left before morning,' one cabin steward remarked to another, as they watched the passengers boarding.

'Smyth-Bronson. No, no,' the red faced man leaned across the Purser's counter. 'Spelt with a Y, man, a Y.'

'Of course, Mr Smyth-Bronson,' the officer said wearily. 'I do apologise. Number Thirty Four, B Deck, Port Side. Boy . . .' he thumped his bell, and one of the uniformed junior stewards hurried forward. 'Mr and Mrs Smyth-Bronson, Thirty Four.'

'Yes, sir, Mr Marchant.' The boy touched his cap, and escorted the Smyth-Bronsons from the queue.

'Curwen. Mr and Mrs John Curwen,' said the pink-faced man with the military moustache and the anxious wife who was next in line.

Marchant ran his pen down his list. 'Ah, Mr and Mrs Curwen. Number Forty One, B Deck, Starboard Side.'

'Starboard side? I was told the port side is best, for the voyage out,' Curwen objected.

'Well, sir, a lot of people do think that, to be sure,' Marchant agreed.

'Then why isn't our cabin on the port side?' Curwen demanded. 'I distinctly put that on my application.'

'Indeed you did, sir,' Marchant said placatingly.

'Unfortunately, there are only so many cabins on the port side, and your application was received after they had all been taken. I'm very sorry. But the starboard side will be perfectly comfortable. All the cabins on B Deck are identical, as regards furnishing and comfort.'

Curwen looked confused, and allowed himself to be led away by another steward.

The line moved a step closer.

'Are you sure you've got everything?' asked Lucy Cairns, hanging on to her son's arm.

'I think so, Mum,' Lawrence Cairns replied.

'Of course he's got everything,' his father snapped. 'If he doesn't, there's always a shop on board, you know, my dear.'

Lucy and Peter Cairns were preparing to be grief-stricken. But Peter Cairns was also aware of a distinct feeling of inferiority. There was so much wealth on board, so much pomposity and authority, would Larry be able to compete? He was only a lad. A titbit, being thrown to the wolves.

On the other hand, there could be no more confident and self-possessed young man in all the world.

Larry had reached the window. 'Cairns,' he said. 'Lawrence Cairns.'

The purser looked up, and saw a tall, sandy-haired young man, of slender build but with surprisingly broad shoulders and the powerful wrists of a racquet- or bat-wielding athlete, his face was sun-burned, suggesting cricket or tennis rather than squash. The features were perhaps a shade too neat to be described as handsome, but the wideset blue eyes were utterly fearless.

The young man wore a brand new blazer, grey flannel trousers, an Old Haileyburian tie, and a straw boater. The purser decided that the old boys' tie was also a recent purchase: this young fellow had only just left school.

'Lawrence Cairns,' he said, checking his list. 'Number Eleven, Starboard Side, D Deck.' He looked up again apprehensively, his eyes flickering over Peter and Lucy. 'I have only one passenger by that name. . . .'

'Of course,' Larry said, easily. 'My parents aren't travelling.'

'D Deck?' Lucy queried.

'Just down those stairs, madam,' Marchant said. He did not call a steward, not for an unattached male on D Deck. Larry lifted his own suitcase.

'Come along, my dear,' Peter Cairns said, taking his wife's arm before she could embarrass him. 'Let's look at Larry's glory hole.'

The Cairns family descended the broad staircase.

'C,' Larry observed. 'There must be another stairway.'

'Really,' Lucy complained, as they made their way down the next stairwell which was dark and much narrower. 'You're virtually in the hold.'

'Less movement down here,' Peter explained.

'You don't want me to be seasick, do you?' Larry inquired, smiling at her.

He was exuding a confidence he did not at all feel. He was only twenty, and although he had been separated from his parents often enough during term time, now he was actually leaving them for the other side of the world.

But Larry Cairns preferred not to think about that. He was, in the eyes of many, throwing everything away. After a sporting career such as he had had at Haileybury, captain of the First Eleven for two years, a place in the Representative Public Schools Match at Lord's, and four county championship games for Sussex last summer, a cricket blue at Cambridge had been a certainty. It had only been at the end of last summer that his father had taken him into the study and explained that there could be no blues, because there could be no Cambridge.

Peter Cairns was a reasonably successful accountant, but his income had not really been up to sending his son to public school, much less beyond. So Larry had been found a job, one which could lead to a prosperous career, but which entailed firstly a crash course in accountancy, and then banishment to the other side of the world. Would the cricket be up to much in Malaya? Larry doubted it.

'It's terribly small,' Lucy Cairns commented, peering

into the two-berth cabin. The bunks, one upper and one lower, faced a small dressing table beside which was a washbasin. 'There's no bathroom.'

'Just along the corridor,' Peter said, having checked. 'I should think you'll do very well here, Larry. And it's not a long voyage.'

Larry's father had this habit of making reassuring statements regardless of their accuracy. He must know the voyage was going to take upwards of a month.

But Larry grinned and placed his cabin suitcase on the lower bunk; his trunk was in the hold. 'Oh, I'll be comfortable,' he promised. 'I wonder who my cabin mate will be?'

'You mean you have to share?' Lucy was aghast.

'Well, the ship is full,' Larry pointed out. 'So . . .' he paused, as he heard feet in the corridor. A moment later a young man appeared in the doorway.

The Cairnses stared at the newcomer as if petrified.

'Good morning,' said the young man, smiling. 'This is my cabin, I believe. My name is Chung Kai.'

Lucy Cairns' gulp was audible, and Larry understood that he had to act fast; his mother was the kindest of women, but she had been brought up to regard people of different race and colour with deep suspicion.

'Why,' he said, smiling and holding out his hand. 'You must be my travelling companion. I'm Larry Cairns.'

Disappointingly, Chung Kai did not appear to recognise the name. But then, the Chinese didn't play cricket. Yet the young Chinese – Larry estimated them to be roughly the same age – shook his hand warmly enough. He had a rough, friendly face, and though he was hardly five foot six inches tall, he also looked fit and strong.

'Then we shall have a good voyage,' he suggested.

His English was perfect, and he was very well dressed in a three piece suit which was clearly tailor-made, a trilby, and spats over his black patent leather shoes. He carried a gold headed cane. There was a steward waiting patiently in the corridor with his cabin baggage.

6

'I look forward to it,' Larry assured him. 'If you'll excuse us, I was just going to show my parents the ship. Come along, Mum. Come along, Father.'

He virtually pushed them into the corridor, towards the stairs.

'You're not going to share a cabin with a Chinaman?' Lucy Cairns protested.

'It looks like it. And he looks perfectly decent,' Larry pointed out.

'I'm most terribly sorry,' Peter Cairns said. His tone betrayed his shame that he had not been able to afford a more expensive cabin.

'Don't worry about it,' Larry told him.

'He'll rob you when you're asleep,' Lucy moaned as they emerged on to the promenade deck.

It occurred to Larry that he had nothing so obviously affluent a young man could possibly covet.

'I'm sure he won't, Mum,' he said.

'Well, don't accept anything he offers you to eat or drink.'

'Or smoke,' his father warned. 'These Chinks are all riddled with drugs.'

'Oh, my *God!*' Lucy wailed.

Larry was quite relieved when, half an hour later, the drum sounded for non-passengers to go ashore. He promised again to write regularly and not to accept anything from his cabin-mate, lent his mother his handkerchief, and leaned on the rail with a sigh of relief as they went down the gangway.

'It is sad, to leave your country and your loved ones,' Chung Kai observed.

Larry turned his head. The Chinese apparently had no-one to see him off.

Chung Kai smiled. 'I am more fortunate than you, because I am going home.'

'Ah. To China?'

'No, no. To Singapore.'

'Singapore is your home?' Larry cried. 'Why, I'm going to Singapore.'

'What a coincidence. But how pleasant.'

'I have a job with Hammond and Teng, the import-export merchants. Have you heard of them.'

Chung Kai inclined his head. 'Everyone has heard of Hammond and Teng. They are one of the largest emporiums in the East.'

'Yes,' Larry agreed, with quiet pride.

'So we shall be rivals,' Chung Kai observed.

'Eh?'

'Possibly the only emporium in Singapore which matches Hammond and Teng is the House of Chung,' Chung Kai said.

There was much toing and froing as the gangplank was taken ashore, the mooring lines were cast off, and the tugs began to nudge the huge liner out into Southampton Water. Larry made out his mother and father, still standing on the dock and waving. Undoubtedly they would be able to see that he was next to the Chinese man, and that would upset Lucy all over again. But they were his past now. The East, and therefore people like Chung Kai, were his future. It was Larry's nature to throw himself with every ounce of energy he possessed into whatever task he was set. However disappointed he might be at the course his life was taking, he was prepared to do this now. He was determined to make a success of the career which had been so suddenly thrust at him: he had even brought along grammar and phrase books to enable him to study the Malay language during the voyage.

Then he was distracted from his thoughts. The most beautiful girl he had ever seen was standing only a few feet away!

Public schoolboys, especially those who aspire to athletic prowess, lack both opportunity and encouragement to spend much time thinking about girls. But Larry had spent the last six months in his father's office in Lewes, with cricket not only abandoned for the winter but forever as far as he was concerned. There had not been much else to do save study the opposite sex.

8

Not that he had ever done anything about it, nor met anyone to compare with the young woman who was standing so close to him, waving to people in the crowd. As the April wind was chill she was well wrapped up. Her dark brown coat had an enormous fur collar. She wore a matching brown hat and shoes, and her gloves were of kid. Wisps of deep auburn hair, worn fashionably short, fluttered in the wind. Her features were rounded, saved from total softness by the firm mouth and chin. Her eyes, he decided as she glanced at him, were green. It was difficult to decide much more than that, as her body was totally concealed by the coat. But she was tall and had slender ankles.

It was going to be a good voyage, after all.

Yet, as the ship's siren howled above their heads the girl's gaze played over him, revealing not the slightest interest, and she looked away again.

It was the man standing beside her, clearly her father, who came to the rescue.

'By Jove,' he remarked. 'Aren't you L. D. Cairns, of Haileybury and Sussex?'

Larry raised his hat. 'Yes, sir.'

'Good heavens! I saw you make forty against Lancashire at Hove last August. The way you hooked Macdonald . . . I would like to shake your hand, young man.'

Larry willingly acquiesced.

'Brian Anstey,' the man introduced himself. He was perhaps fifty, and carried a good deal of weight. But there could be no doubt of his prosperity, denoted by both his Savile Row suit and his gold watch chain as much as by his demeanour. He turned to his wife. 'Julia, my dear, I would like you to meet L. D. Cairns, the cricketer. Margaret, this young man plays for Sussex.'

Julia Anstey must have been every bit as attractive as her daughter in her youth, Larry decided. But he really had eyes only for Margaret, who allowed him a smile.

'And you're on your way to the East?' Anstey boomed. 'Bombay?'

'No, sir. Singapore. I'm with Hammond and Teng.'

'Hammond and Teng!' Anstey shouted. 'Good God! Harry Corbie is an old friend of mine.'

Larry decided this was definitely his day; Harold Corbie was Managing Director of Hammond and Teng.

'You must join us for dinner,' Anstey decided.

'That's very kind of you, sir,' Larry agreed, and remembered his manners. 'May I introduce my cabin mate, Mr Chung Kai?'

Anstey looked at Chung Kai, somewhat blankly. The ladies took a step backwards.

'You must join us for dinner, tomorrow,' Anstey repeated, and hurried them away.

The first night out, dinner was a cold buffet, and it was not necessary to dress. The ship was still in the shelter of the Solent, and the dining-room was crowded. Larry and Kai were shown to a table in a corner.

'It is good to have made friends, so quickly,' Kai observed. 'Although I do not altogether understand how it is that you are so well known . . .'

'Cricket,' Larry explained, for the first time in his life embarrassed at having to talk about the game, and his part in it.

'Cricket! Of course. They play it in Singapore. It is very popular amongst the English people. But the way he addressed you . . .'

'That's cricket again,' Larry told him. 'We only use initials.'

'I see. It is quaint.' Kai smiled. 'But I am glad for you. The presence of the Ansteys will make the voyage less tiresome for you.'

'I'm sure you were included in the invitation,' Larry protested.

'Of course I am not. Mr Anstey would hardly entertain a Chinese.'

Larry hesitated, a prawn ready to pop into his mouth. 'Would you not resent that? Supposing it were true, of course.'

Kai chewed contentedly. 'It is the way of the world.

10

One cannot change the world. It is best to accept it. Any other way is hard.'

It was not a point of view Larry could accept. 'Well, if you're not included in the invitation, then I shan't go.'

'Why not?'

'Well . . .'

'We have only just met. We are not old friends. Why should you put yourself out for me?'

Larry grinned. 'Well, as to that, sharing a cabin, by the time we get to Singapore we are going to have to be friends. Or enemies.'

'It is better to be friends,' Kai said equably. 'The Ansteys leave the ship in Bombay.'

Larry couldn't decide whether his new acquaintance was telling him that they could be more openly intimate after that or not. But in any event, he was not prepared to choose his friends on account of their race or religion.

From the start, Kai proved an absorbing companion. He had spent the preceding three years at Oxford; he was actually twenty three although he looked much younger. He had learned a great deal about the English during his time at the university. He had found them more accommodating on their own ground than in the Far East, yet he knew that they considered themselves the wisest and most powerful people on earth. Kai accepted this point of view without resentment, it seemed, although Larry very quickly realised that his strange friend's father, Chung Lo, must be a very wealthy man indeed.

'They call us the Jews of Asia,' Kai said, as they lay in their bunks the next morning and felt the ship rolling to and fro in a Channel gale; Larry had willingly allowed Kai the lower berth as the Chinese had confessed that he was not a very good sailor. 'I would say that is perfectly apt. Like the Jews, the Chinese have a head for business, a nose for discovering where there is a profit to be made and, most important, a willingness to work for that profit.'

Larry wondered if Kai was obliquely criticising him for having spent so much of his time playing cricket when,

11

presumably, had he applied himself he might have obtained a scholarship to Cambridge.

'Thus it is that so many of our people went to Singapore,' Kai went on. 'I am speaking about a hundred years ago. The famous Teng Lee, of course, the co-founder of your House, was the first Chinese ever to set foot on the island. But he was a friend of Stamford Raffles, and indeed assisted him in gaining the island for Britain. The rest of us came later. We were welcomed. The Malays are not an industrious people, and the British find the climate enervating. Now some people say there are too many of us. But Singapore is the home of my family, now. I have never even been to Canton.'

You went to Oxford instead, Larry thought. To turn yourself into a proper English gentleman. And you have succeeded. But it won't do you any good, as long as there are people like the Ansteys around.

Or my mother, he realised as he fell asleep.

Next day, as the *Empress of India* steamed out of the Channel and into the Bay of Biscay the weather was even worse. The breakfast salon was virtually empty, and so was the promenade deck. Chung Kai was as affected as anyone, and for some three days Larry was on his own. He saw nothing of the Ansteys, and the invitation to dine was not repeated.

It was an opportunity to think, something he had not had much time for over the past six months. Before then he had not had the inclination. Life had been a marvellous series of cricketing successes, with just the occasional failure just to remind him that he was human after all. The affairs of the world, even of Britain itself, had been utterly remote. He could remember swearing because the General Strike of the previous May had prevented him taking his team to an important fixture; the rights and wrongs of the situation had not interested him in the least.

Then had come his father's shattering announcement. But even that had been overlaid by the excitement of being hurled out into the world. 'A spearhead of British civilisation' was how his father had expressed it, and it was an appealing notion. He had hastily read books on Malaya and India; oddly, it hadn't occurred to him to read any on China. And, of course, he had been studying like mad. Fortunately, he had a head for figures and naturally neat writing.

And now he was actually on his way. He knew that he might be in for a very lonely time of it, which was a depressing thought, but he was not naturally given to depression, and soon recovered his spirits. However lonely he might be, he was already surrounded by interesting people, and there would be many more. It was a stimulating thought.

He wondered whether Margaret Anstey was going to be part of his new life. And what of Chung Kai? Would they finish the voyage to Singapore as friends or, as he had laughingly suggested, as enemies?

Stomachs and spirits began to recover in the warmer weather and smoother seas south of Lisbon. Larry and Kai took to playing quoits together. Although the Ansteys had still not reappeared, the night before they were due in Gibraltar a steward brought Larry a formal invitation to dine, in the corner of which someone had scribbled, 'Black tie will do.'

Larry was relieved about this; his wardrobe didn't run to evening dress.

'I am sure there is another invitation for us,' he told the steward, who merely shrugged.

'Now, you must not be foolish,' Kai admonished. 'These people wish to be your friends. And they may well prove a means of advancement. You must accept, and you must go.'

Larry was perfectly willing to be persuaded. He had thought a lot about Margaret Anstey during their week's separation. Not that he had any intention of abandoning Kai, he promised himself. But as Kai had said, the Ansteys might be able to do him a lot of good, and by

13

the same token, they might be able to do him a lot of harm.

The Ansteys were seated at the captain's table. It was a party of sixteen. Margaret Anstey and Larry were the only people under the age of forty. Yet he was greeted most warmly, introduced by Anstey as a future England cricketer, and made to feel thoroughly at home.

He was seated between Julia and Margaret Anstey, both resplendent in low-cut evening dresses. Margaret's fashionable beaded dress did not reach her knees, revealing that her legs were every bit as attractive as he had imagined they would be. Surrounded as he was not only by so much attractive femininity but also by so much wealth, he found conversation a little difficult at first – he gathered that every passenger at the table apart from himself was not only in a portside cabin to avoid the sun – working on the old precept for Eastern travellers of POSH: Port Out, Starboard Home – but in a port cabin on A Deck, where the suites were. But as he drank his second glass of wine he relaxed somewhat and began to enjoy himself.

Margaret Anstey was really an intensely pretty girl, he decided, and she seemed interested in him as well. He became sufficiently emboldened as he reached his third glass to ask her if she would like a promenade after dinner, and to his amazed delight she said she would.

Before that desirable moment could be reached, however, there were several more courses to be endured, after each of which the men changed seats to give the ladies, and themselves, a change of conversation. After dinner, the ladies went to sit in the saloon, leaving the men to their brandy and cigars. Larry found himself next to Anstey.

'Nice people, what?' demanded the businessman.

'Oh, indeed, sir. I am most grateful for your invitation,' Larry said.

'I should apologise for the other night. Mal de mer, what? Makes fools of us all. But there'll be others. Pity you're down on D Deck. No matter. We all have to start somewhere. I made my first voyage to India in Second

14

Class.' He brooded for a few moments. 'All British, of course. No damned Chinks, then. Look here, Cairns, I'll speak to the skipper, tonight. We'll find you another cabin, what?'

It took several seconds for what he was proposing to sink in.

'I am quite comfortable on D Deck, sir,' Larry protested.

'But with that damned Chink . . .'

Larry kept his temper. 'Chung Kai really is a charming fellow,' he said. 'If you'd get to know him . . .'

'I know enough goddamned Chinks,' Anstey said. 'Wouldn't trust one farther than I could throw him. I know you're in a difficult position, boy. Just remember I'm always here.'

'I will, sir,' Larry said politely, and breathed a sigh of relief as they were again separated.

Even with the liner making some fifteen knots, the wind, coming off the Atlantic behind them as they rounded Cape St Vincent, was light and balmy.

'Let's go up to the boat deck,' Margaret Anstey said, leading the way.

Larry climbed behind her, gazing at her legs and the backs of her knees, and, as the wind lifted her dress, her thighs as well – he even caught a glimpse of suspender. Her figure got better and better.

'The captain says that when we wake up tomorrow we'll see the Rock,' she said, a trifle breathlessly, moving to the rail between two of the lifeboats.

He stood beside her. 'I suppose you've done this trip often before,' he ventured.

'Oh, no. This is the first time in ten years. Since I was sent home to school. I don't really remember much about the first time.'

If she was just finished school, that would make her about eighteen, he estimated, which was perfect.

If only she weren't Anstey's daughter!

'Were you born in India?' he asked.

15

'Oh, good Lord, no. I was born in Godalming. Mumsy would never have risked having me in India. I mean to say . . .' she turned, her back against the rail, her body half against his. He could smell the wine on her breath.

'Oh, quite,' he agreed. 'I was born in Lewes.'

'And this is your first voyage east?'

'Yes.'

'Are you excited?'

'It's beginning to wear off.' He realised he was missing some choice openings. 'I mean, it *was* beginning to wear off. Until this evening.'

She gazed at him, her face just visible in the darkness. 'Yes,' she agreed.

He leaned forward. The sober half of his mind was amazed at himself, and a trifle shocked. Gentlemen just did not do this sort of thing. But the half which had imbibed four glasses of wine and two brandies kept telling him that if she hadn't wanted something she would have declined his invitation to promenade. And she had been drinking as well. And he didn't owe Anstey, or his family, one damned thing.

She was in his arms, her body tight against his, and he was kissing her mouth. Her lips were parted and he could taste as well as inhale her various scents; every one exciting. He found his hands, which had been on her shoulders, slipping down the sheen of her dress towards her buttocks and did not really know what to do next . . .

Margaret Anstey did. She took her mouth away from his. 'I think we should go back down,' she said, and then kissed him on the nose. 'Daddy says it's three weeks to Bombay.'

CHAPTER 2
The New Boy

Larry spent the night in a state of euphoria. Merely to have held a girl like Margaret Anstey in his arms, to have kissed her opened mouth, would have been sufficient. But there was all the promise of what was to come.

He was relieved that she had showed so much good breeding and good sense, and ended the evening before it had got out of hand. She was a lady, and this was a shipboard romance. Whether it would develop . . . well, he would have to wait and see.

It did not develop, not immediately. There was no invitation for dinner the next night and when, on the third, halfway across the Mediterranean, he politely invited her for an after-dinner promenade, she declined saying she had a headache. But she smiled as she said it, and he knew it was merely a matter of patience. No doubt she felt she had been forward.

Meanwhile, he went ashore with the Ansteys at Gibraltar and fed the apes. At Naples he joined them on an outing to Pompeii, where the ladies were left outside in embarrassment while the men were shown into the notorious chamber, in even more embarrassment; the ship spent three days at Port Said and the passengers were offered an excursion to Cairo and the Pyramids. Larry felt obliged to decline, because he was running very short of funds, but Anstey insisted on paying his way.

'Margaret likes you,' the older man confided.

Apparently she did. That night after dinner they promenaded together again, and again made their way to the boat deck where they could obtain a little privacy. They kissed and held hands as they talked about their schooldays and their possible futures. Larry had no doubt at all

17

that she wanted to do a lot more. She moved her body against him most suggestively, and had to be able to feel his erection against her groin, but he had no idea how to carry their relationship a logical stage further. Quite apart from being a virgin, those extra weeks beckoned, and to make a mistake, and then be trapped on the same ship, was unthinkable.

He took refuge in time, while becoming increasingly aware that Anstey was a very wealthy man indeed, and that Margaret was his only child.

He couldn't make up his mind whether or not that made her even more desirable. Certainly he found it easy to overlook Anstey's grossness in the knowledge that he was Margaret's father.

He badly needed an older male confidant for advice. But there was no one. The friendship between himself and Chung Kai remained at a superficial level. Kai recognised that the English boy had been absorbed into that society which so totally rejected him – the Chinese opted out of the trip to the Pyramids – and while he showed no resentment of this, the situation did not make for intimacy. Naturally they talked together as they breakfasted or prepared for bed, and they continued to have their morning game of quoits; Larry found Kai a continuing source of enormous interest about Singapore.

Kai told him of the history of the island, of how the name was originally spelt Singapura, and meant Lion City. The name had been chosen by the legendary prince Nila Utama, son of a Malay king and a mermaid. The prince had been wrecked on the Dragon's Teeth, the rocks which guard Singapore Harbour, and after struggling ashore had been confronted with a fearsome beast which he killed, and which the local inhabitants had told him was a lion.

'Of course, everyone knows there have never been lions in South East Asia,' Kai said disparagingly. 'Still, it makes a good story.'

Singapore had then been a nest of pirates, and had remained so for centuries, holding aloof from the inter-

18

necine wars to the north which had seen first one power and then another establish dominion in Indo-China. But then had come the Portuguese, followed by the Dutch, and the British, and eventually the French. The Dutch retained the lion's share of the islands, but the British and the French had carved up the mainland, and Britain had, through the genius of Stamford Raffles, obtained the greatest prize of all, the best and safest natural harbour in South East Asia, situated where the straights of Malacca debouch into the Java Sea, the natural gateway to all the wealth of southern China.

The British had already secured Penang, an island colony off the coast of the peninsular, and to this, after the Napoleonic Wars, was added the former Dutch settlement of Malacca. These three colonies had provided bases for penetration of the interior of Malaysia itself, which was explained as 'assisting native rulers in dealing with their rebellious subjects'.

Following the Indian Mutiny, the rule of the East India Company came to an end, and Singapore and its satellites had been renamed the Straits Settlement, but penetration of the mainland had continued, until the whole peninsula was under at least nominal British control. In 1914, British Malaya had been organised into three territories: the Straits Settlement, which was a crown colony and consisted of Singapore, Penang, Province Wellesley on the mainland opposite Penang, the Dindings and Malacca; the Federated Malay States, consisting of Perak, Selangor, Negri Selamban and Pahang; and the Unfederated Malay States, Kedah, Perlis, Kelantan and Trengganu.

The capital of all this was Kuala Lumpur in the FMS. But Singapore remained the chief port and wealthiest city.

To Larry's disappointment, Kai seldom spoke of his family, but Larry gathered that the Chinese in Singapore, like Chinese everywhere, were very closely knit in their family groups. Indeed Kai, though attending the Sunday morning service on the promenade deck like everyone else, every night took out a large framed photograph of

19

his mother and father and appeared to commune with them for some minutes. He never showed Larry the photograph, as an Englishman might have done, but Larry looked forward to meeting Chung Lo and his wife, and Kai's brothers and sisters, and said so, for all that Kai looked somewhat sceptical.

But they did not speak of women. Larry did not know if Kai was interested in the subject, but in any event, he was not prepared to discuss Margaret Anstey with any Chinese, even Kai.

Neither did Brian Anstey return to the subject of Kai. He remained as friendly as ever and, as he had remarked on the night before Gibraltar, he was well aware that his daughter found the young cricketer attractive.

'The ship spends the day in Bombay,' he told Larry, as they sat in deckchairs sipping cold beers and watching the desert slipping by in the Suez Canal. 'You must come ashore and have a meal with us. And I shall write to Corbie and give him my impressions of you.'

'You are being most awfully kind, sir,' Larry replied, not for the first time. Had it not been for Margaret, he would have found Anstey's attentions distinctly cloying. And even with Margaret in mind, he could not overcome his innate dislike of the man.

'Glad to help, dear boy, glad to help. Cambridge's loss will be Malaya's gain, eh, what?'

Larry had no reply to make to that.

The canal was left behind, and they were in the Red Sea. The weather grew extremely hot, and dressing for dinner was a curse, but everyone still did it.

'Must maintain standards,' Anstey explained.

Larry realised that the first thing he would have to do on arrival in Singapore, after receiving his first month's salary, would be to have a new dinner jacket made, the one with which he had left England was looking distinctly worn.

Margaret Anstey and her mother, on the other hand, seemed to have a different dress for every night. Margaret went in for pale colours, blues and greens and a good deal of white, which showed off her hair and colouring. She avoided the sun, wherever possible, and when ashore invariably wore a topee with a veil, although for all her caution the sun did get her hands and arms, and the pale flesh was immediately covered in a rash of freckles.

By now she was his constant after-dinner companion, and grew more pensive as they left Aden behind them and sailed east across the Arabian Sea.

'Isn't it amazing,' she remarked that evening, 'that we have been at sea for so long and still have so far to go? Pa says it is eighteen hundred miles from Aden to Bombay. Why, that's just about as far as from England to America.'

'Five days,' he agreed. 'Without sight of land. And then it's another three thousand miles, all but, to Singapore. At least by sea.'

She turned her head to look at him. There was no moon, but there were no clouds either, and the stars were making the night sky bright.

'That seems an awfully long way,' she said.

'It is.'

'Somehow . . . I thought we might be able to see something of each other after the voyage was over.'

He gazed into her eyes; neither of them had mentioned 'after the voyage' before. 'I think that would have to depend on how much we wanted to.'

She remained staring at him, but didn't speak.

He licked his lips. This mood might not repeat itself, and there were only four nights left. 'I would like to, very much, my dearest Meg. But, I'm afraid I shall have only my salary as junior accountant. It's not going to be up to financing six-thousand-mile jaunts. Even to see you.'

She gazed at him some more, then turned away and leaned both elbows on the rail, looking out across the immense darkness of the ocean.

Very cautiously, Larry put his arms round her waist, and brought her back against him.

'Dare I ask you to wait?' he whispered in her ear.

'For how long?'

21

The sharpness of her reply surprised him.

'Well, three years.'

'Three years,' she said. 'I should be twenty one.'

'Probably the right time to get married.'

She did not reply, and he slowly allowed his hands to slide upwards and cup her breasts though the material of her gown. She made no demur, but when he cautiously slipped two fingers above the bodice to feel the swell of her breast, and sent them questing into the sweat-wet valley beyond, she abruptly turned. 'We're not engaged,' she said.

He opened his mouth in surprise, and closed it again; her tone had been quite sharp.

'Would you like to be?' he asked. 'To me?'

Another silence.

'I'll speak to your father,' he said.

'No.'

He was again surprised.

Margaret rested her hand on his arm. 'You're very sweet, Larry. I have so enjoyed this voyage. Without you I'd have been bored stiff. But . . . you're very young.'

'Young? I'll be twenty-one in a couple of months.'

'You are young,' she repeated. 'Otherwise . . .' she changed her mind about what she might have said. 'Maybe we'd better leave it like that, for the time being.' She put her arms round his neck and kissed him on the mouth. 'Why don't you ask me again, in a couple of years' time?' she suggested, then released him and hurried for the ladder.

Larry remained standing by the rail for some minutes. As with everything Margaret did, her rejection of him had been so sudden and unexpected it had taken his breath away.

Her rejection of him! He was not used to being rejected. Not that he had ever proposed marriage before. But as a cricketer he had merely had to concentrate to make runs, just as when he had put his mind to it accountancy had come easily. The thought of failure, in anything, had

22

never crossed his mind. He had been forced to opt out of Cambridge, but had never doubted he would have been a success there too, just as he had no doubt that he was going to be a success at Hammond and Teng.

But none of this was good enough for Margaret Anstey. As she had said with such brutal frankness, she had needed him to keep her from being bored. She had never really cared for him.

But had he cared for her? He had wanted to make love to her, because she was a most attractive girl. The proposal of marriage had just slipped out. Yet when it had, he had realised he wanted that too. He wanted her, in every way.

And he had been rejected. Had he done something wrong, he wondered. Perhaps she had wanted him to make love to her even while she protested. In which case she wasn't a lady after all.

He discovered himself to be quite angry.

The next four days were purgatory. Naturally Margaret and her parents had to be seen and greeted every day. He declined all further dinner invitations, however, and on the day before they were due to dock in Bombay Anstey appeared on the boat deck before lunch, where Larry and Kai were as usual playing quoits. He watched patiently until the game was finished, then invited Larry for a drink in the smoking bar. He quite ignored Kai.

'Well, I should get changed,' Larry protested.

'I'd like a word,' Anstey said. 'While the ladies are absent.'

Larry went with him, accepted an ice-cold whisky and soda.

'Women are damnably strange creatures,' Anstey remarked.

'Yes, sir,' Larry agreed.

'You didn't, ah . . . misbehave with Margaret, did you?'

'I asked her to marry me.'

'Did you? Good God! And she said no?' He seemed even more surprised than Larry had been.

23

'She suggested I ask her again in two years' time, sir.'

'Well, then, that's all right, then.'

'Is it, sir?' Larry asked coldly.

'Well . . . I suppose you are a little young for marriage.'

'She pointed that out, sir.'

'Ah. Well . . . would you like me to have a word with her?'

'I wouldn't want her to be coerced, Mr Anstey.'

'Good heavens! Wouldn't think of it, my dear chap. Margaret isn't the sort of girl one can coerce, in any case. No, no. Well . . . I assume you'd rather not take up that invitation to visit us in Bombay tomorrow.'

'I think I'll stay on board ship, sir.'

'Oh, quite. I understand. But I shall still be writing to Corbie on your behalf. I think Margaret's a fool, Larry. A fool. Good day to you.'

Maybe Anstey wasn't so bad after all, Larry thought, for all his absurd prejudices. He would have made an excellent father-in-law. But, as he had said, twenty, and penniless, was a little early to be thinking of marriage. Better forget the whole damned thing.

It was not so easy to do. When Margaret formally shook hands with him at the top of the accommodation ladder in Bombay he thought he would burst with suppressed emotion, and he remained at the rail watching the launch threading its way through the native craft to the island, until it reached the dock.

'Are you not going ashore?' Kai asked. 'Bombay is a famous place. And a beautiful one.'

The launch's passengers had all disembarked. Their heavy baggage was being carted ashore, but they had disappeared into the throng.

'Why, yes,' Larry decided. Suddenly he felt like doing that. 'I should very much like to go ashore. If you will come with me.'

'Me?' Kai was surprised. 'Are you sure you wish that?'

'I won't go without you,' Larry assured him.

24

Kai grinned. 'I have been to Bombay before. I will show you the sights.'

They negotiated with one of the native boats surrounding the liner, and were put ashore at the Government Dock. Kai took Larry on a tour of Fort George, and told him how the island had originally been ceded to the English Crown as part of Catherine of Braganza's dowry on her marriage to Charles II.

'The King very rapidly gave it to the East India Company,' Kai explained. 'And for a long time it was the capital of the Company.'

'You know a lot of English history,' Larry commented.

'I am English,' Kai replied.

Larry scratched his head. But of course that was quite true.

'And I took a degree in history at Oxford,' Kai added, smiling.

From the Horniman Circle they walked across the peninsula to the park and Brabourne Stadium, the ground of the Cricket Club of India.

'Very exclusive,' Kai commented, while Larry brooded on the runs he might have scored on what he saw at once was a beautiful batting wicket, had he been allowed to continue his cricketing career.

Kai showed him Back Bay, and pointed out Government House in all its magnificent isolation on Malabar Point, then they went up to Bendi Bazaar.

'Keep a hand on your wallet,' Kai warned.

The bazaar was unlike anything Larry had experienced before, in its noise and bustle, its stench, its barking dogs, and its colour. Here one could apparently buy anything under the sun, and from the most exotic of people. Hitherto the only Indians he had seen, other than the coolies, had been wearing white duck suits and topees. In a suit, there was little difference between an Indian and a sunburned white man.

But in the market there could be no mistaking them. Many of the men wore nothing more than dhotis, while many of the women were clad in exotic and brightly coloured saris, which constantly promised to reveal more than they ever did. If Larry found the men repulsive, with their hairy bodies and clutching hands, their constant 'Very good, sahib, very good cloth. You feel this, eh, sahib? Very good,' he found the women wonderfully attractive, with their delicate features, graceful carriage and liquid dark eyes. Even the gold rings which most of them wore in their noses were not offputting. Many also wore a variety of gold bangles on each arm as well.

'An Indian woman wears all her jewellery, all the time,' Kai told him.

They had lunch in a little restaurant close to the market. Larry had not previously tasted chicken baked in a tandoori oven, and found it delightful. Kai was disparaging. 'There is no delicacy to Indian food,' he pointed out. 'Too much spice. Well, it is important, because in the heat food does not keep. Now, when you come to Singapore, we will show you how tasty food can be.'

Larry drank cold beer and felt remarkably at peace with the world. Yet Margaret Anstey remained under his skin like a constant irritation. And the irritation had been compounded by the mass of doe-eyed, sari-clad femininity which had surrounded him in the bazaar.

'India can have a powerful effect upon the senses,' Kai remarked.

'A powerfully pleasant one,' Larry suggested.

'Providing one remembers that all pleasures have eventually to be paid for, yes,' Kai agreed. 'Shall we return to the ship?'

'She doesn't sail until midnight. We have lots of time. I am sure that we have only just skimmed the surface of Bombay.'

'Of course. But perhaps you are not in the right mood.'

'Believe me, I am.'

'Because you have said goodbye to Miss Anstey?'

It was the first time Kai had brought up the subject.

Larry drank some more beer. 'I never really said hello, Kai. Miss Anstey was a mirage.'

'I have heard that some women are like this.'

'But not Chinese women?'

'Chinese women do not have the freedom of the West. I think that is a good thing.' Kai gave one of his quick smiles. 'But I am not a woman. You wish to play. Very well. Have you money?'

'A couple of pounds.'

'That is not enough. Will you permit me to lend you some?'

Larry hesitated. But if he had failed with Margaret, he certainly did not intend to fail now.

'If you have any to spare, I would be grateful. I will repay you when we reach Singapore.'

'You will repay me at your leisure.' Kai handed over twenty pounds. 'Anyone here will be glad to accept English money.'

Larry wondered what Anstey would say if he could see his would-be protégé accepting money from a Chinese? Even more he wondered at himself, not for borrowing from his friend, but for giving his virginity, as it were, into Kai's keeping. But today he was deliberately setting out to put the Ansteys and all they stood for behind him.

Kai took him down various side streets until they entered a building and went up a flight of stairs. The house was made of wood, and the hall and stairway were dark. There were a variety of odours, dominated by curry.

At the top of the stairs a man sat at a desk on the landing. He didn't speak, but regarded the two young men with a blank expression.

'We have come for tea,' Kai told him.

'English tea?'

'China tea and Indian tea.'

'Ten rupees,' the man said.

Kai gave him two English pounds, which seemed to satisfy him.

'The door is open.'

Kai opened the door and stepped inside. Larry followed him into a small vestibule. A single naked electric light bulb glowed above the counter, behind which stood a young Indian woman, picking her nose. She must have been able to hear what was said outside, because she asked without preamble, 'Which tea will you have first?'

Kai looked at Larry.

'I have no idea what we are talking about,' Larry said. If the girl was rather off-putting, he was still aware of a growing excitement.

'China tea is gambling,' Kai explained. 'Do you like to gamble?'

'I never have.'

'Then it would be unwise to start here. You would lose everything. I will pay. My friend will have Indian tea, now,' he told the girl. 'I will have China.'

'The door is open,' the girl said.

Kai nodded. 'When you are satisfied, come to me. I will wait for you.' He grinned at Larry. 'You do not wish to change your mind?'

For a moment Larry did. But, if he did, he would never be able to look at himself in the mirror again. He shook his head.

'Then I will wish you good fortune.' Kai stepped through the doorway, closed the door behind him.

'The cost is twenty rupees,' the girl said.

Presumably one didn't bargain about things like this, Larry thought. He handed over four English pounds, and she studied each one with great care. For all her vulgarity she was a pretty little thing, although she was very young. But he decided that was all to the good. And at least she had no ring in her nose.

'If the gentleman will come this way.'

Larry's head jerked. He had not heard the woman enter the vestibule. It was difficult to estimate her age, for her hair was jet black, but she was at least twice as old as the girl behind the counter, and twice as well endowed, too, in every way. In addition to the heavy breasts which the pale blue sari seemed to accentuate, she did have a ring in her nose, and several bangles on each arm. But she was smiling, which enhanced the fine bone structure of her face.

She was holding an inner door open. Larry gave the girl a quick smile and stepped into a corridor. The woman closed the door behind them.

'You have preferences?' she asked, stepping past him with a rustle of silk; one breast pushed past his arm.

'No,' he said. He had no idea what she meant.

She looked back at him. 'Some Englishmen wish to whip. Or to be whipped.'

Larry swallowed. The thought of whipping a woman was disgusting. As for being whipped himself – he had been caned a few times at school and hated it. Was it possible that there were men who actually enjoyed suffering and inflicting such pain and humiliation? And this woman, so calm and dignified? Did *she* enjoy it?

He could never do it.

'I do not wish to whip,' he said.

Her smile broadened. 'Or be whipped. You are young, and strong.' She opened the door and he stepped past her. He found himself in a surprisingly large and light chamber; there were two windows set high in the wall through which the afternoon sunlight was streaming. There was a divan bed in the centre of the floor, covered with what might have been an expensive rug, and some equally expensive-looking rugs scattered on the polished wooden floor. Against the far wall there was a washstand with basin, ewer and slop bucket.

'You need to urinate?' the woman asked.

Larry opened his mouth and then closed it again. Indeed he did need to urinate.

'Use the bucket,' the woman said.

Larry hesitated, and she gave a soft laugh.

'You have never peed in front of a woman. I will hold it for you.'

Larry licked his lips. 'I . . . ah . . .'

The woman had come closer. Now she frowned at him. 'You have been with a woman before?'

Larry knew his face was crimson. He wanted nothing more than to turn and flee. But he had paid his four pounds. And this woman would exorcise Margaret Anstey.

29

'I am honoured,' the woman said softly. 'You may call me Ayesha.'

'Is that your name? Ayesha?'

'It is the name you may call me,' she repeated, and gently unbuttoned his flies. Her touch was so soft and so knowledgeable. 'Do not harden,' she said. 'You cannot pee, if you harden.'

He didn't think there was much chance of that. He had never felt so impotent in his life.

And yet the nearness of her was overwhelming. The faint scent of coconut oil which rose from her was titilating. He found it difficult to urinate, especially with her holding him in one hand and the bucket in the other; he was over aware of the rattle, but she waited patiently until he was finished, then replaced the bucket.

'You would like me to undress you?' she asked.

'No. No, I will do that.'

She stepped away, and undressed herself. He watched to see if she would take off any of her jewellery, but she did not. The sight of the slender, dark brown body, the breasts, the wide thighs, the strong legs, adorned with gold anklets was breathtaking.

She faced him. 'Now it is your turn.'

He tore at his clothes, dropped them on the floor. She watched him with interest and, he thought, admiration.

'You are a handsome man,' she remarked.

He was fully erect. He went to her, took her in his arms. She came willingly enough, and the feel of her body was like nothing he had ever known before. To suppose that Margaret might have felt like this . . . but when he made to kiss her she turned her head aside.

'Do not kiss my mouth,' she said, and smiled at his dismay. 'Anywhere else that you choose. Kiss my breasts. Please.'

He obeyed without thinking, sinking down her body to take the brown nipples into his mouth. But he wanted all of her.

'You are very young,' she murmured again, holding his head against her.

30

He wanted to pull away in anger, but that was impossible. He stood up, and was drawn to the divan.

'There are many ways,' Ayesha said. 'Every one producing great pleasure. But you are so young. Come to me.'

She lay down on the divan, and he was inside her before he really knew what he was about. She was wet and slippery and consuming. He climaxed in seconds, while she stroked his head and shoulders.

Then he was exhausted, but also disappointed. He felt there should have been so much more. Had he been allowed to kiss her, perhaps . . . had he even been the dominant partner . . .

He lay on his back, and Ayesha got up. She went to the washstand and returned a moment later with a wet cloth with which she wiped him clean.

'Have you come to live in Bombay?' she asked.

'No. I am on my way to Singapore.'

'On the *Empress*,' she with a faint sigh, as if she would have liked to be sailing on the liner. 'But you will come to Bombay again.'

'Perhaps,' he said. Presumably, on his way home for his first long leave; he was on a four-year tour.

'Then you will come to Ayesha again,' she said. 'And I will make you very happy. Again.'

Had she made him very happy? He wasn't at all sure of that. He only wanted to get out of there as rapidly as possible.

He got up, dragged on his clothes. Ayesha also dressed, watching him. Then she accompanied him to the door, opened it for him.

'Have you no present for Ayesha?' she asked.

'I paid at the desk,' he said, ashamed of himself for his meanness.

Her mouth twisted. 'Then I will wish you good fortune,' she said.

He went along the corridor into the vestibule, the shame growing into positive self-disgust. The girl behind the counter looked up and Larry stepped through the other door, and found himself in a gambling den. Actually it

31

might have been a card room at a country club, for all the four tables were playing cards. Only in their dress, in the amount of cigarette smoke, and in the way the players thumped their cards on the table did they differ from an English bridge party.

Most of the players were Chinese, although there were a couple of white men present. They looked up without interest as Larry entered and stood by the door, trying to identify Kai. Kai glanced at him, and gave a nod. He finished the game, spoke to the men with whom he had been playing, and to an onlooker who had been sitting beside the table. Then he scooped the money in front of him into the pocket – there seemed to be quite a lot of it – got up and came across.

'Did you win?' Larry asked.

'Oh, yes.' Kai's tone indicated that he always won. 'Did you win?'

They went down the stairs. 'I don't think so,' Larry said.

'Then we must hope that you are not diseased as well,' Kai observed.

Larry hadn't considered that possibility. To his shame was now added a very real apprehension.

Kai did his best to reassure him. 'I do not think you will be,' he said. 'That is a good house. Clean and honest. Or I would not have taken you there, much less played myself. I think you will be all right.'

But Larry refused to be reassured, and inspected himself every morning as the *Empress of India* steamed across the bay and into the Straits of Malacca, with the mountains of Malaya rising to the east and those of Sumatra to the west. He knew he should be admiring the scenery, some of the finest in the world. But he was too agitated.

Larry was on deck for the passage through the Dragon's Teeth, however. He gazed at the myriad islands, the ripples of white surf which marked the deadly coral lurking just beneath the surface, and then at the island itself.

Approached from the south east it appeared rather lost against the green of the mainland of Malaysia for, although hilly, it nowhere rose above six hundred feet.

The city and the harbour clung to the southern shore, and Larry saw the teeming waterfront, from which barges and sampans were putting off even before the liner had dropped anchor. Behind the waterfront were huge warehouses, and behind them again he could make out several stately modern buildings, while on the gentle slopes behind the town were delightfully situated mansions; even at a distance their verandahs and waving palms suggested coolness.

But he was at least as interested in the roadstead itself, for in addition to several other steamers, mostly tramps, and a variety of Chinese junks, there was also a British cruiser and two destroyers, the White Ensign riding proudly from their sterns. He was suddenly aware of the might of the British Empire, in a way he had not noticed in Bombay.

Launches had come out from the shore, and officials were climbing the accommodation ladder. Customs officers briefly interviewed each passenger, and then they were free to go to those who had come to meet them.

'I will say goodbye.' Chung Kai held out his hand. 'I wish you to know that it has been a great privilege to have shared your cabin, and your thoughts, this past month. I will treasure the memory.'

'But, we're going to see each other again,' Larry protested. He did not see how they could avoid doing that; the island did not look very large.

'I shall look forward to that,' Kai agreed, unconvincingly.

'Kai, I owe you twenty pounds,' Larry reminded him; he had held on to the rest of the money Kai had given him, in case he might need it.

'Of course,' Kai said, and walked away.

Larry watched him go up to a very well-dressed Chinese gentleman who had just come on board. Kai gave a little

33

bow, and was then embraced, briefly. That must be Chung Lo.

But how odd, Larry thought, that after the very real intimacy they had achieved on the voyage, Kai had not wished to introduce his friend to his father? Perhaps, for all his dissembling, he did resent the way he had been treated by the other passengers.

'Lawrence Cairns?'

Larry turned, found a white man standing at his elbow. He was not much older than himself, although he wore a little moustache. Somewhat short, and inclined to plumpness, he was sweating profusely; his white duck suit was soaked, and he was fanning himself with his topee.

'That's me,' Larry said.

'Brent. Billy Brent.' Brent held out his hand. 'Welcome to Singapore. I say, wasn't that Chung Lo's son you were speaking to? How on earth did you come to know him?'

'We shared a cabin, as a matter of fact.'

'All the way from England? Good Lord! You'd better not mention that to the old man. He's waiting to see you.'

Brent had a motorboat bobbing at the foot of the ladder, and they threaded their way though the various bumboats until they reached one of the docks in the Teluk Ayer Basin. It was hotter than Bombay, and Larry was assailed by the heat which rose from the pavements in almost solid waves and quite took his breath away. He was wearing his new topee, for only the second time – the previous occasion had been in Bombay – but even this did not provide adequate protection from the blistering rays.

'Enervating,' Brent agreed. 'It's even worse in the monsoon. You'll get used to it, or be invalided home; it's a fifty-fifty chance.'

The head office of Hammond and Teng was on Fullerton Road, right on the waterfront. It was an imposing whitewashed six-storey building, from the roof of which flew three flags, the Union Jack and two others; from their devices, Larry guessed they were house flags. Inside, it was somewhat cooler than on the street, with huge ceiling fans constantly turning above the open-plan office. The office was full of clerks, mostly Chinese and of both sexes, Larry observed with surprise.

As they ascended the building it grew even cooler, because there was a breeze which had not been noticeable on the street, but the climb itself was exhausting and Larry was as sweat-soaked as Brent by the time they reached the top floor, having on the way been introduced to a great number of people, mainly Europeans.

Now he found himself in a large, comfortably-furnished outer office, shaking hands with a grave Chinese lady in a jade green cheong sam, with a mass of black hair piled on top of her head. She looked as if she were about to preside over a dinner party rather than bang a typewriter; her manicured nails were the longest Larry had ever seen.

'This is Mrs Lu,' Brent explained.

She was terribly thin and not pretty, but she had the aura which went with being a Managing Director's personal secretary.

'Mr Corbie is expecting you,' she said. 'He is on the telephone. Please be seated.'

Larry glanced at Brent, who indicated the leather settee along the far wall, and said, 'I'll leave you to it.'

Larry nodded, and sat down. Mrs Lu also sat down behind her desk.

'Did you have a pleasant voyage?' she asked.

'Very pleasant, thank you.'

'But you are glad to be here.' It was not a question, She was watching the various lights on her desk.

'Mr Cairns is here, Mr Corbie,' she said into a machine.

'Send him in,' the machine replied.

Larry stood up.

'The door is open,' Mrs Lu told him.

He gulped, remembering when he had last heard those words spoken in Bombay all too clearly, and wondered what Corbie would say to the news that his newest clerk had already contracted VD. Of course, nothing had gone wrong yet, but it had only been a week. . . .

He found himself in Harold Corbie's office. The present

35

ruler of Hammond and Teng was a very tall man, at least six foot three. As he was also heavily built, he seemed to fill the room. He was clean shaven and balding, his scalp bright pink in contrast to his sun-tanned face. He wore white like everyone else, but his suit was of linen; also it was not sweat-soaked; there were at least three fans in the office, all directed at him.

He did not get up, but held out his hand. 'The cricketer! Welcome.'

'Thank you, sir.' Larry felt his hand grasped firmly.

'Take a chair,' Corbie said. 'We play cricket in Singapore. Yes, indeed. I've arranged for you to meet Roly Payne this afternoon. He's captain of our club. He's tickled pink to have you on the staff.'

Larry waited. Had he been brought all this distance just to play club cricket?

'Matting wickets,' Corbie said. 'Some people can't handle them. But I'm sure you can.'

His tone indicated that if Larry couldn't, then he might as well be on the next ship back to England.

'Brent met you, did he?'

'Yes, sir.'

Corbie nodded. 'I'm putting you in his department. Invoicing, mainly.'

Larry swallowed. He had just trained like mad to be an accountant, not a clerk; of course he had a great many examinations to take before he would be qualified, but he had hoped at least to be doing some practical work while studying.

Perhaps Corbie had remembered that. 'Have to start somewhere,' he pointed out. 'Now, I've booked a room for you with Mavis Norton. Good plain food, good plain place. Mavis is a good girl. No nonsense there. You understand me?'

'Yes, sir,' Larry said, uncertainly.

'Good. It's near the cricket ground, too. You'll settle in today, start work tomorrow. On Saturday night you'll come to dinner with the memsahib. Understood?'

'Yes, sir. And thank you.'

36

'My wife likes to meet all the young fellows straight out from England. Well, nice to meet you.' Corbie pointed a finger, as Larry would have risen. 'You're very young. Think of Mavis as a mother. Do what she tells you. Understood?'

'Yes, sir.'

'And stay away from the natives. Especially the women. That way lies disaster. Understood?'

'Yes, sir,' Larry said, feeling his cheeks burn.

'Then you'll be all right.'

He looked down at the letters on his desk to indicate that the interview was at an end, and when Larry continued to stand before him, he looked up again.

'Something wrong?'

'One of the passengers on the ship was Brian Anstey, sir.'

'Was he? Good Lord!'

'He asked me to give you his regards, sir.'

'Well, well. Brian Anstey. I was at school with him. Well, well. Remember, my boy, matting has a higher bounce than grass.'

Mavis Norton was about forty years old, and had spent nearly all her adult life in Singapore; like Mrs Lu she was very thin, and traces of malaria could also be discerned in her sallow complexion. Larry gathered she had been left a widow some ten years before, and rather than return to England had opted to turn her spacious home into a boarding house for the many unattached young gentlemen who were seeking to make their way in Singapore. She had six permanent guests including Larry.

He was shown to a square room, twelve feet by twelve, which contained a bed, a dressing table, and a washstand; it was disturbingly like Ayesha's bedroom in Bombay, but neither as large nor as pleasant.

'The bathroom and toilet are on the next floor,' I'm afraid,' Mrs Norton informed him. 'Now, Mr Cairns, morning tea is served at seven sharp, followed by breakfast, in the kitchen downstairs. Supper is served at seven thirty sharp, in the dining room.'

Larry gathered that he was required to provide his own lunch.

'What you do with your time outside my house is entirely up to you,' Mrs Norton went on. 'But as this *is* my house, I would be obliged if you would obey the house rules. There are only five. One, I will permit no women in any of my rooms. Two, I will permit no alcohol in any of my rooms. Three, I will permit no smoking in any of my rooms. Four, I will permit no loud noises in any of my rooms. And five, I expect my guests to be punctual for meals.' She regarded Larry's cabin trunk, which had been delivered by the Hammond and Teng truck and was now taking up most of the floor space. 'When you've unpacked that, and I suggest you do so now, call Ahman, my gardener, and he'll help you carry it up to the loft. Good morning to you, Mr Cairns. I am sure you will be happy here.'

Larry put her in the same category as his father, given to making optimistic statements which had little to do with fact.

However, as Corbie had suggested, Mrs Norton's food was wholesome, and her establishment clean. If it reminded Larry somewhat of a prison, it was at least a temporary refuge.

'What you want to do is save like mad,' Billy Brent told him. 'Then you can get a place of your own. I've had a place of my own for six months. Costs the earth in rent, but it's worth it. It's the only way you can get the girls.'

'Getting girls' was not something Larry had in mind at the moment; he had gone off sex, terrified that an outbreak of prickly heat might be the first dread signs of gonorrhoea. But as there was no other discomfort he decided he must be wrong.

In fact, he settled down very quickly to life in Singapore. He duly went to the Corbies for dinner on his first Saturday, and was royally entertained.

'What you need is a white dinner jacket,' Ellen Corbie

told him. 'They're so much smarter and cooler. Why don't you give Mr Cairns a note to your tailor, Harold?'

This turned out rather well, as Larry discovered to his relief that tailoring in Singapore cost a fraction of the price in England, and was completed in a quarter of the time.

Then there was cricket, which he was expected to practise every afternoon. There was a match every Saturday on the Cricket Club padang, and in his very first game Larry carried Hammond and Teng to victory with a brilliant seventy not out. The opposition bowling was decidedly weak, but he was smothered in congratulations.

'You really will be the old man's blue-eyed boy now,' observed Roly Payne, the captain.

After that Larry received a permanent invitation to Saturday night dinner at the Corbies' house, a somewhat ancient building situated on rising ground to the east of the city; he learned that it had been the Hammond house in the early days of the colony and was thus one of the oldest buildings in Singapore. Built rather like a four-square fortress, although with verandahs on both floors, and high ceilings for its huge rooms to give all the air possible – together with Venetian blinds at every window to restrict the glare – it certainly needed a great deal of modernisation, in his opinion, but apparently it was the done thing for the Managing Director to occupy it. And the grounds, consisting of lawns, an orchard and a flower garden, lovingly maintained by Malay gardeners, were delightful.

'Ah, well,' Ellen Corbie said, 'we are retiring in two years' time. I imagine we can sit it out for that long.'

To his surprise, Larry found that a disturbing thought. The new man might not like cricket.

Larry had of course been employed by Hammond and Teng to work, even if he could no longer doubt that he had got the vacancy because of his cricketing ability. But work, he discovered, bore no relation to anything he had experienced in England, or had anticipated. He was, as Corbie had determined, employed in the Bills of Lading

Department to begin with, and he had imagined dreary days filling out one bill after another until he had writer's cramp.

The bills, however, were all written by the Chinese staff, mostly young men with copperplate handwriting and a great deal of industry. All that he and Billy had to do was read them and check them, and then send them round to the various consignees for signature. As the bosses, however, they appropriated for themselves the right personally to inspect the cargoes when they arrived. If they arrived on a decent-sized ship there was always the chance of a pink gin to be had with the officers.

Work commenced at eight, and they knocked off at twelve for lunch in one of the small restaurants which abounded in downtown Singapore, and in which Larry was introduced to the delights of Malay cuisine: satay, highly spiced and marinated pieces of chicken speared on thin wooden skewers and roasted in peanut sauce; pape-san, pieces of fish coated in coconut cream and broiled in banana leaves; rendang, boiled chunks of meat smothered in spices; tahu goreng, fried cubes of soy beancurd and fresh sprouts with a spicy peanut dressing; ikan bilis, miniature whitebait fried with soy, spices and peanuts; ikan assam, fried fish in tamarind curry which made the lips pucker, it was so sour; and sambal udang, or curried prawns; the whole was accompanied by some form of goreng, or rice, sometimes fried, sometimes boiled. For those, like Billy, with hardened palates, there was sambal to be added; this was a very hot pepper sauce which left Larry gasping the first time he tasted it.

He also learned to use chopsticks although, as Billy told him, and as he observed, the Malays used nothing at all, but rolled the rice into little balls together with their meat or fish and conveyed the food to their mouths with their fingers. Larry could not imagine what Mrs Norton would say were he to start doing that at her table.

Each meal was accompanied by cold beer or hot sake, and working in the afternoons was intensely difficult. Indeed the senior staff, headed by Corbie, made no effort to work at all until they had had a siesta. The juniors were expected to turn out, to sit at their desks in an alcoholic haze which had only just worn off when they called a halt at four o'clock and trooped off to practise cricket in the very brief two hours before the twilightless tropical night descended like a curtain.

Then it was into the club for a chota peg, as whisky and soda was called. At least Larry had to be sure to be home in time to dress for dinner; he gathered that Billy, being his own master, often drank well into the night. Presumably that was when he 'got the girls'. So far as Larry could see, there were very few white women in Singapore of roughly the same age as himself, and they all clearly regarded him as a very insignificant person. Undoubtedly they would take the devil of an amount of 'getting'.

But then, Billy didn't have to make runs every Saturday. Or study both accounting and Malay.

The social centre of the colony was Raffles Hotel. Everyone gathered at in the Long Bar at lunchtime on a Saturday, work having by then ceased for the weekend. The chota pegs flowed even faster on these occasions, even amongst those who would shortly be sweating it out in the middle, although the more keen players contented themselves with the weaker variety known as stengahs. Larry had his leg pulled mercilessly because he contented himself with two beers, but he could stand the chaff. They were actually a very decent crowd, he reckoned, or they could be, if they were not all so inordinately aware of bearing the White Man's Burden. This attitude manifested itself in many ways. One certainly was to prove on every occasion that a white man could drink more than any Chinese or Malay possibly could.

Another was sporting superiority, which accounted for Larry's popularity. Several of the native cricketers were quite talented, but none had had his training as a batsman, nor possessed his gift of timing. Yet they were vastly better than Billy Brent. Billy only pretended to keep

41

wicket for the company side, but his incompetence did not in any way interfere with his assumption that he, being British, was worth two of any Chinese or Malay, an assumption that permeated the British society from top to bottom.

And the bottom was where he was, Larry reflected glumly. Therefore it was necessary for him to be very careful in asserting himself. But he was determined not to just drop Kai and besides, there was the twenty pounds he owed. It took him three weeks to scrape the money together – and to be sure that he had not contracted VD. He decided against going to the House of Chung, which was situated close to the waterfront, not very far from Hammond and Teng; he had already been made very aware of the rivalry between the two houses, and of the feeling at Hammond and Teng that the House of Chung was very much an interloper.

Instead, one Sunday morning after church, about the only time of the week when the rigid social rules permitted him to do anything he chose, he obtained directions from his newsagent and strolled out to Chung Lo's house.

Mrs Norton's boarding house was situated in the suburbs of the city. Chung Lo's house was further to the north, on the lower slopes of Bukit Timah, Singapore's highest hill. The walk took Larry along the Bukit Timah Road, beside the bank of the Kallang River, then past the Botanic Gardens and the racecourse. It was all extremely pleasant; the morning was overcast, and the monsoon was due.

It was also much longer than he had anticipated, and he was decidedly hot by the time he arrived at a pair of ornate wooden gates, and pressed the bell.

'Who is it, please?' inquired a female voice over the gate telephone.

'A visitor, for Mr Chung Kai,' Larry told her.

A moment later the gates swung in. As she had not questioned him further, presumably it was his definitely English voice that had gained him admittance.

He walked up a gravel path between twin rows of royal palms, beyond which stretched lawns and flower beds. The beauty, as well as the luxury, of the place took his breath away. In the distance he could see the house, a place of verandahs and cool recesses, but long before he got there he heard cries of excited pleasure, and rounding a bend in the drive came upon a tennis court on which two people were playing with the utmost vigour.

One of the players was Kai, all white flannels and flopping dark hair. The other was a girl. She wore a white tennis dress which fell to her ankles but fluttered to the knee as she moved, and white socks and shoes. Her long black hair was secured with a ribbon at the nape of her neck, thereafter scattering as she chased the ball. She also wore a head band.

He thought he had never seen anything more entrancing.

Kai had seen him, and the game stopped. 'Larry?' he called incredulously.

'Not butting in, I hope,' Larry said.

Kai came round the net, followed by the girl. 'It is a great pleasure. Lan, this is Mr Cairns, the man I told you about. Larry, I would like you to meet my sister, Lan.'

The girl remained somewhat breathless; some of that was embarrassment. There were pink spots in her cheeks, but they added a touch of delightful colour to the pale complexion, setting off the black of her eyes.

'It is a great pleasure, Mr Cairns.'

'The pleasure is mine, Miss Chung.'

'But what brings you here?' Kai asked.

'Twenty pounds.'

Kai gazed at him for a moment, then gave a shout of laughter. 'I had forgotten. Well, as you are here, you must come up to the house for a drink.'

'I should like that,' Larry agreed, and smiled at Chung Lan. Chung Lan smiled back.

If Larry had been taken aback by the splendour of the grounds and setting of the Chung estate, with the hill

43

rising behind it and the racecourse spread out below, he was even more struck by the house. Quite apart from the Rolls Royce waiting by the front steps, here was a luxury entirely lacking in the Corbies' residence. There was a good deal of bamboo and lacquer, soft colours and softer carpets; every room was pervaded by a fragrant scent, and green-clad servants of both sexes hurried to and fro.

'Will you excuse me while I go and change?' Lan asked, and disappeared down a hallway towards the back of the building, leaving her brother and Larry in a large reception room, from which folded bamboo screens opened on to a deep verandah.

'She is going to bathe,' Chung Kai said. 'Would you like to?'

'Bathe?'

Chung Kai smiled. 'In the pool.'

'Ah,' Larry said. It had not occurred to him that a private residence would have a swimming pool. The idea was delightful, especially with Chung Lan in it. But . . . 'I don't have a bathing costume.'

'Of course. And I am afraid nothing in this house would fit you. No matter. We will watch Lan. Ting How,' he called, 'two chota pegs on the back terrace, please.'

'Oh, before we go,' Larry said, 'here's the money.'

Kai took it, and put it on an occasional table. 'I had meant it as a gift. But I realise that would have been wrong. Come.'

They went down the corridor to an inner terrace, surrounding an enclosed courtyard in the centre of which was a large pool with a springboard at one end. As Larry watched, Chung Lan emerged from a door on the far side of the courtyard. She wore a red bathing costume with a little skirt which came down almost to her knees. She ran across the wooden surround, on to the springboard, and bounced up and down several times while he watched her in total admiration, and then performed a perfect dive, legs pressed together, body entering the water with hardly a splash, black hair fanning out behind her before she surfaced.

44

'She swims very well,' Kai said.

Larry could not look away. He could not remember such grace and beauty . . . And in a bathing costume it was very obvious that she was considerably more than just a girl.

'And now, I would like you to meet my father,' Chung Kai said. 'And our house guest.'

Larry turned, reluctantly; Lan was climbing up the ladder and returning to the board for another dive.

He found himself looking at the man he had seen on board the *Empress of India* when she had docked, a somewhat portly Chinese with a small grey moustache. His hair was also greying, but he was undoubtedly Kai's father. And Lan's.

Larry shook hands.

'My son has spoken of you,' Chung Lo said. 'It is good of you to honour our house.'

'Your son was very good to me on the voyage, Mr Chung.'

'Ah. That is good. Now I would have you meet our guest.' He turned to the equally small man beside him. 'Mr Kitachi Tano is from Japan. He is a businessman, like ourselves. he is here to set up a branch of his business, in Singapore.'

CHAPTER 3
The Arrangement

Kitachi Tano gave a deep bow. 'It is a great pleasure, Mr Cairns,' he said.

Chota pegs were brought, and the four men returned into the house, to Larry's disappointment; he could have sat and watched Lan diving all morning. But he had to be polite.

'What made you choose Singapore, Mr Kitachi?'

'Singapore is the hub of the East, Mr Cairns. I am amazed that none of my countrymen has explored its possibilities before. Although . . .'

He glanced at Chung Lo.

'Mr Kitachi has been experiencing some difficulty with permits,' Chung explained.

Kitachi smiled. 'What the British have, they wish to hold. An admirable principle. That is why they are called Great, is it not, Mr Cairns?'

Larry decided he didn't like the man. His manner was impeccable, and he smiled constantly, but the smile didn't reach his eyes.

'That goes for most people,' Larry suggested. 'But I am sure you will get your permit, eventually.'

Kitachi gave Chung another glance, then bowed. 'I will put my trust in that.'

Conversation became general but, always politely, slightly disparaging to the British, at least between the two older men. Kai said little but, observant as ever, soon understood that Larry was uncomfortable.

'I have not shown you the garden,' he said. 'Would you excuse us, Father, Mr Kitachi?'

Larry would have preferred to return to the pool, where

Lan was still splashing about, but Kai took him into the gardens, which were really quite splendid.

'I must apologise for my father and his friend,' he said. 'They do not mean any harm, but of course it is not easy for them, this constant feeling of inferiority.'

'I entirely understand,' Larry said. 'And I resent it on their behalf. I'm sure it will change, one day.'

'One day,' Kai mused. 'Perhaps not soon enough for my father.'

'Has your father known Mr Kitachi long? I would have said there was some difference in their ages.'

'Oh, there is. At least twenty years. No, no, they have only recently met. Mr Kitachi arrived with letters of introduction from a mutual business acquaintance in Canton. You know what the Japanese are like, spreading everywhere. But he is apparently a very important man in Japan. I do not know the details.' He smiled. 'You cannot blame my father for seeking new business outlets, can you? It is his great dream to equal Hammond and Teng. Not that he ever will, of course,' Kai hastily added. 'Would you care to stay for lunch?'

Larry could think of nothing more pleasant, but he had already accepted a luncheon invitation from the wife of one of the senior staff. 'I can't. I'm sorry. I wish I could.'

'I am sorry too,' Kai said. 'Then what about tomorrow afternoon?'

'I'm afraid I can't then either. I have to practise cricket in the afternoons.' He grinned. 'Apparently it goes with the job.' But he could see from Kai's face that his friend was wondering if these were not merely excuses. 'I would very much like to come to see you again, though. What about next Sunday?'

Kai's face lit up. 'That would be splendid. You can play me at tennis.'

'Won't your sister miss her game?'

'She'll be relieved. She can't really give me a game. I allow her the trams and fifteen points, but I still win. Will you come?'

'I should like to very much,' Larry said.

★ ★ ★

47

Larry lay in bed that night and thought about Chung Lan. It was crazy, he knew. A teenage girl? Maybe he was sex-starved, and so relieved he hadn't contracted VD that he'd go for anything . . . But Lan *was* utterly entrancing.

And she was of a different race.

Did that matter? Surely places like Singapore were where races should mix, and surely the mixing of races was the greatest hope for the future of the world?

Hardly a point of view his mother would share, or Brian Anstey or, most important of all right now, Harold Corbie.

Besides, she was his friend's sister. That was how he would have to force himself to think of her.

And in any event, the thought that a girl like Lan, from a rich and powerful family, would be the least interested in a penniless clerk was absurd; she would laugh contemptuously at the very idea.

Disconcertingly, when he dreamed, it was of Kitachi Tano, and his so-cold smile. And Kitachi was actually staying at the Chung house, seeing Lan all day.

Definitely he did not like the fellow.

He could hardly wait for the following weekend, and it was everything he had anticipated. To his great relief, Kitachi had left to journey up to Kuala Lumpur, and it was just a family gathering. He played tennis with Kai and won, while Lan acted as line judge and ball girl. Then there was lunch with the family, which included one of Kai's elder brothers, with his wife and their two children. Apparently Kai had three elder brothers and one elder sister, all married with families; he and Lan were the only two children at home.

The Chungs wore Western-style clothes and spoke perfect English. Their table was in keeping with their house, and outshone the cuisine at Raffles. They were the most perfect hosts, and their conversation, which ranged from art to politics, and politely included sport – for the sake of their intellectually limited guest, Larry decided – was at once amusing and stimulating.

48

That they considered Singapore their home was certain. They spoke with reverence of China as the home of their ancestors. The first Chung to come to Singapore had been fleeing Manchu oppression, but they appeared to have nothing but contempt for the machinations of General Chiang Kai-shek, the new leader of the Kuomintang, the Nationalist Party which was claiming sovereignty over the whole country, and who was fighting a very long civil war to prove his point.

'He is nothing but a warlord himself,' Chung Lo remarked.

Nor did they seem to have any sympathy for the late Dr Sun Yat-Sen, Chiang's brother-in-law and political mentor, whom they described, contemptuously, as all but a communist.

Yet they were aware that they were second-class British citizens, and however much they endeavoured to conceal it, the occasional hint of resentment penetrated their easy politeness. This was even true of Kai, Larry thought, for all his friend's denial that it mattered.

It was not true of Lan, however. She was all genuine smiles and happiness.

Larry fell into a regular pattern of playing tennis with Kai every Sunday morning, and of staying to lunch afterwards. Undoubtedly his British friends knew of it – he did not try to keep it a secret – but only Billy commented. 'It's not really done, you know, old man,' he said. 'But I suppose in your case it doesn't matter.'

Larry was perfectly content to bask in Harold Corbie's approval, which was unlikely to be withdrawn as long as he made runs every Saturday afternoon, as he could hardly help doing in view of the weakness of the opposition bowling.

Life therefore settled into a very pleasant pattern over the next year. He worked hard, and on Billy's promotion was placed in charge of the Bills of Lading Department himself, which was gratifying.

He played hard, at both cricket and golf, as well as

bridge, and even tried the odd game of polo, but he was not a natural horseman and besides, it was far too expensive.

He obeyed all Mavis Norton's house rules and became one of her favourite boarders, and he drank his chota pegs at the club and at Raffles with Billy and his friends.

He was unfailingly polite to Mrs Lu, which he gathered was as important to advancement as remaining in Harold Corbie's good books.

He sat up for an hour each night studying either Malay or accounting, and wrote home every week.

He smiled at various young ladies who, in the course of time, started to smile at him. But he never asked any of them out, even on New Year's Eve, when every white woman in the colony needed a man to escort her to the ball. He understood that he was considered distinctly odd, and didn't care.

To his surprise, after he had been in Singapore just over two months he received a letter from Margaret Anstey. It was a chatty letter, schoolgirlishly affectionate, and recollected the voyage with some pleasure, but made no reference to their after-dinner spooning on the boatdeck. He decided she was merely bored, and brooded for some time before replying. When he did, it was in the same vein.

Only his inability to repay Kai's hospitality jarred. He did approach the secretary of the Club to ask if it might be possible to introduce a Chinese acquaintance for a game of tennis, and was met more with bewilderment than hostility; the answer was still negative. 'It simply wouldn't do, old man. It simply wouldn't do.'

Even that rebuff ceased to rankle in time, because it was unimportant, in that Kai would never even have considered it. The Club itself became unimportant, a necessary social requirement. Larry's life revolved around his Sundays, in the peace and relaxation of the Chung household, and in watching Lan growing from a slightly awkward girl into a lovely young woman.

★ ★ ★

It had never been Larry's intention to do more than look at Lan, and enjoy her company. There were too many imponderables in the way of attempting a relationship on any other level. If after a year he felt he was now accepted by the Chungs, and considered slightly different from the average white person in view of his sympathy and understanding, he remained very aware of the differences between European and Chinese, in many things, not just in colour. Even between Kai and himself, while they were genuine friends, there were areas on which they never touched in conversation, simply because of a mutual acceptance that neither would be able to understand the other's point of view.

The ramifications of explaining to the Chungs that he was falling in love with their daughter were too immense to contemplate.

The idea of explaining to Harold Corbie that he wanted to marry a Chinese girl was simply unthinkable. And as for his parents . . .

Yet he knew that he *was* falling in love with Lan, and that he would like nothing better than to be able to marry her. But understanding the impossibility of the situation, it was a passion he was prepared to keep secret, in the hope that conditions might change, or that he might be sufficiently promoted to choose a wife in defiance of society. As if any man could so subdue a nightly dream.

Kitachi Tano had become quite a regular visitor at the Chung house. He had finally got his permits, and had opened his office in downtown Singapore. His arrival in the business community caused no more than some adverse comment, while his desire to photograph every possible sight in the colony caused some amusement.

'Goddamned Japs,' Billy Brent grumbled. 'Pushing in everywhere!'

'He can hardly pose a threat to Hammond and Teng,' Larry pointed out.

'It's the principal of the damned thing. This is a British colony, not some confounded Asian League of Nations.'

51

Kitachi's desire to share in the prosperity that was Singapore was certainly not resented by Chung Lo. In fact it seemed to Larry that the two men were growing more and more friendly every time the Japanese came to the island.

Equally, every time Kitachi was there, the anti-British resentment was more obvious.

This was irritating, but not half so irritating as Kitachi's obvious interest in Lan. The thought that he might have her in mind as a wife . . . but she was half his age! And he was a damned Jap, as Billy had said. Larry's dislike for Kitachi grew.

But as there was no evidence of Kitachi's intentions, Larry kept his feelings to himself, until the day Kai slipped on the stairs and broke his ankle. He was taken to hospital, and Larry naturally went to see him.

'I shall be here for several days,' Kai said, grimacing with pain. 'But there is no need for you to miss your Sunday game. Lan will be happy to play with you, if you can stand it. And I know my parents would be most disappointed if you did not go to lunch.'

The monsoon was due, and Sunday was a sultry and cloudy day. Lan and Larry had not completed a set – she had not won a game although she attacked every ball with great *élan* and much laughter – when it started to rain, and within seconds had developed into a tropical downpour.

They instinctively ran from the court to the shelter of the little pavilion which overlooked it, which was no more than a shed for storing nets and balls and racquets. They were still some distance from the house, and in the teeming rain, which brought visibility down to less than twenty yards, as isolated as if they had been alone in the middle of a jungle.

Lan towelled her hair and shoulders vigorously; she was wet with both sweat and rain. 'I think the weather has saved me from a thrashing,' she remarked.

Larry watched the flailing black strands; her face was invisible. 'This rain always amazes me,' he said. 'We have nothing like it at home.'

Lan's face emerged from beneath the towel, pink with exertion. 'There is no monsoon in England. Kai has told me. Yet he has also said it is one of the wettest places on earth. I do not understand this.'

'It's because, instead of a couple of months of really heavy rain, in England we have a kind of constant drizzle which sometimes goes on all the year round.'

She gave a mock shiver; despite the rain falling only a few feet away, it was perfectly warm – there was no wind. 'That sounds terrible.'

'It can get pretty boring. But it's still the loveliest country on earth.'

Lan laid down her towel. 'Is it? I would love to see it.'

'I would love to take you there,' Larry said, without thinking.

'And I would love to go with you,' she said.

They gazed at each other. Lan was seventeen now, and this morning was oddly *en déshabillé*, her hair an untidy black mess and her tennis dress damp; one sock had slipped down into its shoe. Yet she was more appealing than ever, because of the intimacy of her appearance; Larry knew there could not have been many men who had seen her like this.

He also knew what was going to happen. What had to happen, or he could not stand the thought of coming here again. But after it happened, would he ever be able to come here again?

'Would you?' he asked, and moved towards her.

She was in his arms, her face turned up for his kiss, her body moving against his. His hands closed on her shoulders and then slipped down to her buttocks, without hesitation. She was already on tiptoe to reach him; now he held the mounds of firm flesh to raise her entirely from the earth, and she moaned with pleasure.

They ran out of breath. He allowed his hands to slide up her body again to her armpits, and lifted her away from him to sit her on the table which occupied the centre of the hut. Her tennis dress rode up and her legs were

53

exposed, but she didn't seem to mind. Instead she opened her legs for him to come between and hold her again.

'I love you,' she said. 'Oh, how I love you, Larry.'

He felt like exploding with happiness. To think that he had been afraid of her contempt!

'I loved you from the moment I first saw you,' he told her.

'Yes. I knew it.'

'Did you?'

She laughed. 'Don't worry. I have told no-one. I have been content to wait.'

'Oh, my darling.' They kissed again, and he allowed his hands to roam, knowing that he could do this with Lan without fear of rejection. He stroked her back and shoulders before coming round in front to find her breasts.

She took her mouth away from his, and unfastened her buttons; the dress buttoned up the front. To his surprise she wore nothing underneath save for a pair of knickers. Her breasts were small, but perfectly shaped with pointed little nipples. He bent his head to kiss them, and she wriggled with pleasure. He had never supposed a girl could be so unrestrainedly erotic, could not believe his fortune when she unbuttoned his flannels in turn to put her hand inside. Her fingers were so soft, and so certain. She drew him out, and before he had quite understood what was happening, she had slipped her knickers down to her ankles and moved her own body forward so that she was only half sitting on the table, and he was inside her, holding her tight against him, and surging back and forth with the purest pleasure.

She continued to cling to him after he had climaxed, her body still moving for several seconds. Then she gave a little gasp and fell backwards, across the table, her body arching.

Larry looked down, at the mound of black hair, the smooth thighs . . . and the trickling blood. 'Oh, God!' he muttered. 'Oh, God!'

But hadn't he known she would be a virgin?

Lan sat up again. 'Have I hurt you?' She gazed at his dwindling penis.

'No,' he said. 'But I have hurt you.'

'You have made me happy. You will not hurt me the next time.' She began to kiss him again, while all manner of thoughts went tumbling through his mind.

'I know,' she said. 'We cannot marry. Just let me be your lover.'

Once again she had taken him entirely by surprise.

'But Lan, I do intend to marry you. I want to.'

She shook her head. 'It will ruin your career. I understand about these things.'

'If we were to wait a few years, then I'd be in a position to marry whoever I like. I'm sure of it.'

She shrugged. 'Then we will wait a few years. It is not important, as long as we are lovers.'

He felt quite humble. To have so adorable a creature so totally determined to be his!

'Oh, Lan,' he said, holding her tight against him. 'Oh, Lan. We shall be lovers. But . . .'

'I know,' she said seriously. 'It will be difficult. Kai will be here next week. Can you go out at night?'

'Well, yes. But surely . . .'

'Oh, I am not allowed out at night, except with a relative. But I can get out, after I am supposed to be in bed. We could meet at the racecourse.'

Larry hesitated. He had not anticipated anything quite so clandestine. But there was no alternative. He could not take her back to Mrs Norton's, and it would be the sheerest folly for him to attempt to come here at night. The racecourse was at least close to her house. But the risk . . .

'Suppose you were found out?'

She gave another delightful shrug. 'Father would whip me. But do not be afraid; I will not betray you.'

'Oh, Lan . . . should I not speak with him?'

'No,' she said. 'Or everyone will know, and it will be the end of your career. They would send you away. I do not wish you to be sent away, Larry. I wish you to stay, and make love to me. Now, Larry . . .'

To his amazement, he was again ready.

'Oh, how I love you,' he breathed into her ear as she came against him.

It was impossible that any man had ever been so happy in the entire course of history. It was also a situation that was impossible to keep secret, however determined Larry was to do so. But his life was so ordered by the society in which he lived that the slightest variation from the norm was bound to be noticed. Thus, as he and Lan had agreed that their secret meetings were to be on Tuesday nights, he found it necessary to excuse himself from the Tuesday bridge school. This caused, at first, merely a lot of grumbling, as a fourth had to be found.

Leaving Mrs Norton's after supper was not difficult; she supposed he was going out to play bridge. But by the next week it had become apparent to everyone that Larry Cairns had completely abandoned Tuesday bridge, and was still going out on Tuesday evenings, and staying out quite late.

Mrs Norton was not amused, but as Larry had never broken any of her house rules she was prepared to accept the situation. Male reaction was almost entirely composed of envy.

'You sly dog,' Billy commented. 'Here were people regarding you as the biggest bore on the face of the earth and all the time you were setting yourself up. Come on, now; tell me all. Is she Chinese or Malay?'

'She is my business,' Larry told him.

'All right, old man, keep your shirt on. Just watch you don't get clapped. Ninety per cent of these local girls are.'

Filthy-minded clot, Larry thought. But then, someone as gross as Billy Brent would not even suspect a woman like Lan even existed.

Dissembling to the Chungs was far more difficult. The following Sunday Kai, although home again, had his ankle in a cast and was unable to play tennis, but he insisted that Larry and Lan do so, while he watched.

To be their usual ebullient laughing selves, while looking at the hut where it had all begun, and while both remembering the frantic moments in the racecourse pavilion on Tuesday night – they had climbed up the railings on to the first rows of seats as the grass had been too wet – required a good deal of effort. But apparently they succeeded.

Lunch was no less difficult, as they gazed at each other across the table. But again, no-one seemed to suspect for a moment that anything had changed. As the weeks went by their deceit became second nature, while their love for each other grew. If Larry still found it difficult to believe that any woman could be so uninhibited in her sexuality, he could not deny the evidence of his own senses. He could only understand that any European who had not experienced oriental lovemaking was a sadly limited fellow. Lan sat on him, had him sit on her, knelt before him, straddled him, sucked him and fondled him, as the mood took her, and expected him to do the same to her.

Life became an erotic paradise. Even fears that Lan might become pregnant soon dissipated; he did not ask her if she took any precautions but it seemed likely that she did. Or he was sterile. He did not care if he was. All he wanted was, one day, to make his love public and take Lan for his wife. It was a decision he was determined to take as soon as possible.

But he had not reckoned with events quite outside his control.

He had been in Singapore just over two years when the American stock market crashed in October 1929. The impact of this catastrophe was immediate and savage. World commodity prices fell sharply, and with them the profits of such firms as Hammond and Teng. Local staff were cut back, and the Europeans were warned that there could be no salary increases for the foreseeable future.

Presumably the House of Chung was also suffering, but there was no evidence of it on Bukit Timah.

That Christmas, Harold Corbie retired. He had been due to do so anyway, but now there could be no doubt that he was glad to get out. He had a chat with each of the white staff before leaving. 'Keep making runs, and you'll do well,' he told Larry. 'Rumours get to me, you sly young devil. Just be careful.'

Larry never knew whether or not he had ever received Anstey's letter of commendation, or indeed whether Anstey had even written it.

The new Managing Director was Ronald Lees, who had been manager of the Hong Kong Branch. New brooms as a rule like to sweep clean, and Lees was in addition on his mettle as the man put in to cope with a crisis which had now assumed worldwide implications.

He was a heavily built man with a military moustache and jet black hair which he brushed straight back in an apparent attempt to resemble Douglas Fairbanks. His appearance in Singapore sent a cold shiver through the staff, and indeed he immediately did some cleaning out, even of Europeans who he felt were not pulling their weight.

Billy Brent was one of these. He came to see Larry, and sat on his bed, the picture of utter dejection. 'Six years I've been with this firm,' he said. 'And I'm out. Just like that. It's criminal.'

'What will you do?' Larry asked.

Billy sighed. 'Can't stay here. No prospects. I've been offered a passage back to England. There's generosity, eh? But I suppose I'll have to take it. Maybe we'll be on the same boat.'

Larry made no reply to that. He had that very day been promoted to take Billy's place in the accounts department.

In fact Lees, if not a cricket fan like Corbie, was extremely nice to Larry. This could have been because of Corbie's recommendation, or it could have been because he had arrived with a wife and unmarried daughter in tow. But

Joan Lees, somewhat tall and angular, was not the sort of girl to send a man wild with passion, even had Larry been in the mood to feel passionate about anyone except Lan.

There was, however, another reason, of which Larry remained blissfully unaware until one afternoon in the early summer of 1930, about six months after Lees' arrival, he was summoned to the Managing Director's office.

'Sit down, Larry, sit down,' Lees invited. 'Cigarette? But you don't smoke, do you? Very wise. I wanted to invite you to dinner next Saturday night.'

'That's very kind of you, sir. Thanks very much.'

'Well, the pleasure is mine. But actually it's to meet an old friend of yours.'

'Indeed, sir?' Larry couldn't imagine who it might be.

'She's actually a school chum of my daughter's. Margaret Anstey. She's coming to stay with us for a while.'

Larry was only mildly interested. Remembering Margaret Anstey and his attempt to romance her was like looking through the wrong end of a telescope at another world. Had he really once been such a nervous, naive nitwit?

They had continued to correspond, in a desultory fashion, over the intervening years, and had exchanged Christmas cards, but there had never been any suggestion that she intended to visit Singapore. And although he knew that when he took his first long leave the following year the ship would certainly call at Bombay, he had no intention of going to seek her out. His thoughts were entirely of how to say goodbye to Lan for four months, even if it might be possible to have her come with him, and return from England with their love a *fait accompli*. He could not imagine Margaret Anstey having the slightest effect on him now.

But he was surprised. Not only had Margaret filled out a good deal and lost the slight tendency to scrawniness that he remembered, but she seemed to have become even more *soignée* than before. Beautifully dressed in a halter-necked but bare-backed pale blue evening gown with

59

silver kid shoes, she was by far the most attractive of the several women at dinner. She also seemed delighted to see him again.

'Lawrence Cairns!' she cried, holding both his hands and presenting her cheek for a kiss. 'How well you look!'

'As do you, Margaret,' he said.

'It's *so* good to see you again. When I remember that voyage . . .' she paused, archly.

'Oh, do tell,' begged Joan Lees.

'We did a lot of sightseeing together,' Margaret said primly. 'It was such fun. I hope you're going to take me sightseeing in Singapore, Larry.'

'Well – ' Larry said.

'Of course he is,' Ronald Lees said, joining them. 'Do you know what I think you should do, Larry? Take a week's leave starting tomorrow, and give Margaret and Joan a guided tour. You must know the island pretty well by now.'

'Well – ' Larry said again, totally surprised.

Lees grinned at him. 'That's an order. You can use the company car. You do drive, don't you?'

There could be no argument with that, even if Larry wished he had not learned to drive. But it was apparently essential for every young white man in Singapore to hold a driving licence, even if he had no hope of owning a car for several years, as another proof of superiority over the natives.

And when he thought of it, it sounded a very pleasant way of spending a week, in preference to being in the office. Nor did he suppose it would interfere with the private part of his life at all; after church the following day he explained that he had a prior engagement, and that their grand tour would start on Monday. Nor did he have any intention of allowing it to stretch on into the evenings, at least on Tuesdays.

Over the next week he took the girls into downtown Singapore, let them stroll through Orchard Street and Elizabeth Walk, and *ooh* and *aah* at the zoo in the Botanical Gardens; he took them for a boat ride on the Singapore River and showed them the Sri Mariamman Hindu Temple; he bathed with them on the east coast beaches, privately amused at the careful modesty with which they hid behind the car to change into their costumes, the way they avoided touching him when in the water. He was certainly unable to overlook the fact that Margaret Anstey was now a very shapely young woman indeed, or to prevent himself, as he lay in bed that night, wondering what she might be like to make love to, could she ever shed her inhibitions and be like Lan, an idea he immediately rejected.

There was also a boat trip out to the islands, but he steadfastly ignored any hints that they might like to see something of Singapore night life. They seemed pleased enough by it all, and were lavish in their praises of him. Well, he thought, if it's what Lees wants . . .

There was another dinner party at the Lees's house the following Saturday.

'Now, what are we going to do with my second week?' Margaret asked.

Larry had had no idea she was staying another week.

'What would you like to do?'

'I would like to do some exploring just with you. As we did on the voyage.' She gazed at him. 'Wouldn't you like that?'

'Well, I'm sure that would be very nice,' Larry said cautiously. 'But what about Joan?'

'Oh, we can ditch her, surely.'

'She happens to be the daughter of my employer.'

'I'll sort that out.'

'There is also the small matter of work. I do have to do some from time to time.'

'I'll get you another week off. I will. Really and truly. Uncle Ronald is my godfather. Didn't you know that?'

'As a matter of fact, I didn't,' Larry said thoughtfully.

'Don't you want to take me out on my own?'

'Well . . .'

'You're not still angry with me, are you? About the ship, I mean.'

'Oh, of course not.'

'Yes, you are. I could tell it from your letters. They were awfully stiff.'

'I'm afraid I'm not a very good letter writer. I didn't mean them to be stiff.'

'Pa says I was very foolish to ask you to wait.'

'Oh . . . er, well, I was very forward. And as you said at the time, I was very young.'

'But you have waited,' she said softly.

He began to feel uneasy.

'I'm still only twenty-two,' he said.

'And I'm twenty. We're all growing up, aren't we? I know, Larry, let's sneak away tomorrow, right after church. I get so bored with these continual entertainments.'

'I can't.'

'Why not?'

'Well . . .' he didn't suppose it would go down very well for him to confess that he preferred to play tennis with a Chinese than take Margaret Anstey out, even if Lan's name never came up at all. 'There's not much to do on Sunday mornings.'

'I'm sure we'd think of something. Oh, come on. Be a sport.' Her eyelids fluttered. 'Or don't you like me any more?'

Definitely she was in the mood for another wild flirtation, which would undoubtedly end with him being slapped down as he had been on board the boat. Therefore he should slap her down now, he realised, good and proper.

But he caught sight of Ronald Lees, winking at him from across the table. Lees definitely wanted her entertained, and if it was only going to be for another week . . .

'Where would you like to go?' he asked.

'The beach,' she replied, without hesitation.

He telephoned Kai next morning, to say that he wouldn't

62

be able to make their tennis game. Kai naturally did not seem the least upset, but it was not of course possible to send any sort of message to Lan. Larry could only hope she would understand as well; in any event, he would explain the situation on Tuesday night.

Anyway, Sundays were no longer as important as Tuesdays.

After church he returned to the Lees's house with the family, and was presented with the keys of the Armstrong-Siddeley.

'Do bring her back in one piece,' Joan remarked, the first indication that she was not altogether pleased with the way things were going.

'Jealous bitch,' Margaret remarked as they drove out of the gate.

'I hadn't realised that you were rivals for my affections,' Larry commented.

'Don't get swollen-headed about it. But eligible males are thin on the ground in this part of the world.'

'The same could be said of eligible females.' He concentrated on the road. Driving the Armstrong-Siddeley always terrified him – in case some scatter-brained Chinese or Malay should drive into him.

'Oh, quite,' Margaret agreed. 'That's why we should stick together.'

His uneasiness grew. Had she come to Singapore looking for more than a flirtation? But having turned him down once, surely she wanted nothing more from him?

It took only half an hour to arrive at her 'favourite' beach, which was one of the most secluded.

'Give me a shout when you've changed,' he said, and walked away from the car.

'Larry,' she said. 'There's no need. We're both adults.'

He turned without thinking, and saw that she had removed her dress and was wearing only a brassière and knickers, although with stockings and a suspender belt. And of course, high heels.

His jaw sagged. She made a very compelling picture.

She smiled, nervously; she was acting a part. 'I once

63

thought you had something going for me.' Hesitantly she reached behind her to unclip the brassière.

'Meg,' he protested. 'That was two years ago.'

'We agreed to wait two years,' she said, staring at him. She was not apparently prepared to go any further with her striptease until she was sure of him. Here was none of the spontaneity of Chung Lan, but rather a studied, and very anxious, coquetry.

My God, he thought; I've been trapped! But he felt powerless to do anything other than gaze at the most shapely female body being slowly unwrapped for his inspection.

'Have you thought of me often?' Margaret asked, unclipping her stockings and self-consciously taking them off. Her cheeks were pink, and she was breathing rather quickly. This was obviously not something she did every day, or had ever done before, in fact.

He gazed at the high full breasts, the tight ribcage, flat belly, and quite magnificently long legs. She was the most beautiful woman he had ever seen – she was only the third he had ever seen undressed. She had the breasts of Ayesha without the heaviness, and her legs were perfection; he realised that Lan, although the most adorable of creatures, had no figure at all by Western standards.

Yet it was Lan he loved.

'It was difficult to tell, from your letters,' Margaret said. If she had been contemplating nude bathing, she had changed her mind. She turned her back on him, and in a quick movement slid down her knickers, stepped out of them, and into her bathing costume, which was hastily pulled up to her shoulders; he caught no more than a glimpse of white buttocks which certainly matched the rest of her. 'I suppose you were too busy playing cricket to think of me. Aren't you coming swimming?'

'Oh . . . yes,' he said.

To his relief, she didn't wait for him, but walked down the beach and into the water; she had to be aware that her striptease had not been all that successful. Hastily he changed into his costume and followed her. Seeing her naked had aroused him, but a hasty plunge into the cool water cured that.

She tucked her hair into a bathing cap and secured the strap under her chin. 'I think Singapore is a wonderful place,' she remarked.

'I've enjoyed it here.'

She splashed over, and took his hand.

'Larry, I know you're still angry with me.'

'Well, I do wish you'd believe that I'm not.'

She stopped wading; the water was to their thighs. 'What do I have to do to convince you that I'm no longer a fool.'

He gulped. He had never had a plainer invitation.

He gave a nervous smile. 'You'll have me thinking you came to Singapore just for this.'

'I did. The two years are up, and I've decided to say yes.' She put her arms round his neck and kissed him on the mouth, her body tight against his.

He couldn't resist her, short of throwing her away from him. Besides, he didn't want to. It was a damning thought, but this was a woman he had always wanted to hold in his arms. And now that he knew what could happen when two people made love . . .

'Oh Larry,' she breathed into his ear. 'I have dreamed of you, so often.'

He simply didn't know what to do. She wanted to kiss some more, so he went along with that. But at least she didn't strip again. They swam together, and then returned up the beach to the car. Here she wanted to kiss again, and do some fondling as well. Resisting her was impossible. But when he tried to ease the straps of her costume from her shoulders, she took her face away and held his hand.

'Don't make me, Larry,' she begged. 'Not . . . not until we're married.'

If she had got hold of the wrong end of the stick, she had at least saved him from making a terrible mistake.

But it was a situation which had to be put right, with no delay.

★ ★ ★

65

He asked for an interview with Lees next morning, and was granted one immediately; his request had apparently been expected.

'Sit down, dear boy, sit down,' Lees said. 'Now, then, let's get down to cases. You're young, very young. But there's no doubt you have a great future with the company. Oh, yes, indeed. So I'm prepared to make a very special exception in your case. I am not only going to up your salary, but I am going to give your marriage my blessing.'

Larry sat with hunched shoulders. Throughout the night, while his resolution had hardened, the extent of his own stupidity had become more apparent. And he had no one to blame but himself. He had walked into the trap as meekly as any lamb. 'I have come to resign, sir,' he said.

'You've come to . . .' Lees' heavy brows drew together. 'Because of you and Margaret?'

'Well, yes, sir.'

'My dear fellow, I've just explained that there is no need for that. No need at all. Were you some fly-by-night, well then, things might be different. But you're Larry Cairns.'

Larry sighed. 'Do you know what happened, sir?'

Lees looked embarrassed. 'Well, Margaret has no secrets from Joan. They were at school together, you know. So you had your bit of jig-jig. That's all right, as long as you marry her quickly enough.'

Larry drew a long breath. 'I did not have sexual intercourse with Miss Anstey, sir.'

'There's no need to be coy with me, Cairns,'

'I did not, sir. If she says I did, then she's a liar.'

'She certainly seemed to think you'd made love.'

'Well . . .'

'You'd better tell me the truth.'

'Well, we kissed, and cuddled . . .'

'In bathing suits, or less, on a lonely beach? I wasn't born yesterday, Larry. I can see you're embarrassed by the whole thing. And frankly, it wasn't what I would have expected of a gentleman. But I know how these things can get out of hand and, as I said, it's a very simple matter to put right.'

Larry took another long breath. 'I can't marry Miss Anstey, sir.'

Less frowned again. 'Can't?'

'I do not love her, sir.'

'Oh, come now, boy. You had it off with her, didn't you? All right, maybe you didn't. But you sure as hell made love to her.'

'It was what she wanted.'

'Larry, you are starting to sound like a cad. And I know you're not a cad. You'd better tell me what's on your mind.'

Larry sighed. 'I am already engaged to be married, sir.'

'Engaged? You can't be engaged without my say-so. Who to?'

'Miss Chung Lan, sir.'

Lees stared at him for several seconds, then gave a shout of laughter. 'Chung Lo's daughter! By God, so she's the bit you've been keeping hidden away. It's the talk of the company. Damn me, but you're a sly fellow. Does Chung Lo know about this?'

'Well . . . no, sir. We've been waiting . . .'

'Oh, quite. So it's not really an engagement at all.'

'It is, in my eyes, sir.'

'Because you've been having it off with her as well. Bloody hell, you young fellows have all the luck.' Lees leaned forward, his elbows on the desk. 'It seems to me the time has come for you and me to have some very plain chat, Larry. You're a bright, likeable chap, who seems really to have fallen on his feet. Or should I say prick? But you're only twenty-two. You know you're not yet a third of the way through your life, unless you're damned unlucky? You certainly have forty-three years with the company before you retire. Now, it seems to me that you want to think very carefully about how you're going to spend those forty-three years. You can do 'the honourable thing', as you seem to consider it, always remembering that the honourable thing as regards Miss Chung will be the dishonourable thing as regards Miss Anstey. But if you do let Margaret down, you're going to be out of this company. I don't recommend you take your Chinee beauty back to England. She wouldn't be accepted. And jobs are damned hard to come by right now. So maybe you think you'll stay here and work for Chung Lo. Well, he might give you a job. But you'd be working for a Chink. And you'd be a second class citizen for the rest of your life. You'd be black-balled from the Club. Good God, man, you'd be a write off.'

But I'd be an honest man, Larry thought. Even so, his heart was sinking. He knew he didn't have the guts to face all of that.

'Now let's consider the alternative,' Lees went on, leaning back. 'Right now you're about the most promising future executive we have. You play hard . . .' he grinned, '. . . maybe harder than we reckoned. But you also work damned hard. Now you have a chance to marry well. The very top, as far as the East is concerned. I may as well tell you now that Brian Anstey is a share-holder in Hammond and Teng, and a big one. You marry his daughter, who also happens to be my goddaughter, and the only way ahead of you is up. Dammit I'll bet you a hundred quid that you'll be sitting in this chair inside twenty years. Think about that, boy.'

Larry stared at the floor. How proud his parents would be.

And how horrified they would be at the other.

Lees leaned forward again.

'Listen to me, boy. Marriage isn't the end of the world, not by a long chalk. You can still keep your Chinee bit. You're not going to tell me she's really expecting marriage, is she?'

Larry raised his head. Chung Lan had made it perfectly plain that she didn't expect marriage.

Lees grinned at him. 'So there's your answer. Run them both. Why not? It'll be our secret. Just yours and mine.'

The temptation was enormous. Especially as it was the

only answer. Every word Lees had uttered with such brutal frankness had been true. To opt out of marriage to Margaret would merely ruin him; it would take him no closer to marrying Lan. In fact, if he then went along to Chung Lo and told him he had been his daughter's lover for a year, he wasn't at all sure that he *would* be well received, and given a job.

But there was a more insidious power at work. Of course, he had not intended to make love to Margaret. He realised he had been most shamelessly vamped, by a girl who very clearly had decided it was time to marry, and who, after looking over all the eligible bachelors in Bombay, had remembered the young man who had appeared so madly in love with her on the voyage out from England, or had been reminded of him by her father and her wretched godfather. But he had held her almost naked in his arms, and it was an experience he wanted to repeat, again and again. Margaret might have none of the spontaneous eroticism of Lan, but she was a most beautiful girl, and if she seemed determined to be a virgin when she married, he could hardly criticise her for that as she wanted to marry him, while the fact that she had been prepared to strip for him promised that there might be some hidden fires under that cool exterior.

To be married to her . . .

The fact was that, without meaning to be, he was definitely a cad. He had no course left to him but to attempt to make both women happy, if that were possible.

It was equally tempting for him to put off telling Lan for as long as possible; he had assumed that his engagement to Margaret would have to go through the formalities of letters to the Ansteys and a good deal more. But he was wrong. Ronald Lees announced with great glee that he had been placed *in loco parentis* and his permission would be sufficient; obviously the Ansteys had been entirely aware of Margaret's intentions in visiting Singapore. The Lees also announced their intention of having an engagement party the following Saturday. The following Monday

69

it would be in all the newspapers. Lan had to be told immediately.

But there was one saving point. Margaret announced her intention of returning home to Bombay as soon as the engagement had been announced. The wedding would of course take place in Bombay, and when they talked about it over luncheon, Larry being now very much a part of the family, they estimated this could not be prepared until November. November was four months away!

On Tuesday night Lan was waiting as usual by the grandstand. Larry had only got away with difficulty. Margaret was proving very demanding, now that it was official, and yesterday, after buying the ring, she had insisted on being taken dancing in the evening.

'Our own private celebration,' she called it.

When he had told her he had a long-standing engagement on Tuesday night which he could not break she had looked quite upset for a few minutes, before accepting the situation.

It seemed an age since he had last held Lan in his arms, so much had happened in that week. And being forced to make love by Margaret's rules, which really banished him from all that wonderland below the neck, had left him feeling unwholesomely randy.

But first Lan had to be told.

She came to him, silently, as she always did, and put up her face to be kissed. Then, without further ado, she spread the blanket she had brought on the grass, and sat down.

He knelt beside her. He had never been so nervous in his life.

'I have something to tell you,' he said.

There was no moon, but the night was bright; in the shade of the grandstand, however, Lan's face was in shadow. She had been unbuttoning her blouse; now she stopped.

'You are going away,' she said.

'Not for several months, and then only briefly. But when I come back, I will be married.'

70

He listened, for some sound, even an intake of breath. But could hear nothing.

After a moment she said, 'To Miss Anstey.'

He had forgotten how small a society Singapore was.

'Yes,' he said.

'She is very lovely. I saw you with her in the Padang, last week.'

Larry held her hands. 'I did not mean it to happen. But I proposed to her once before, long before I met you, and she asked me to wait. Now she has come . . . to claim me, I suppose. I wanted to refuse her. But I have been told that if I do so I will be sacked and sent away from Singapore. While if I marry her, I will be very successful. Her father is a powerful man. From my point of view, her godfather is even more powerful.'

'She is very lovely,' Lan said again.

'But I love you, Lan.'

'You will learn to love this woman. She will be the mother of your children. And as you say, she will be good for your career. I am nothing. I can do nothing but bring harm to you.'

'Oh, Lan!' He took her into his arms, hugged her close. 'You are the most wonderful thing that has ever happened to me.'

For the first time in their relationship, her body was flaccid in his arms. When he released her, she refastened her blouse, and began folding the blanket.

'Lan . . .' he held her hands again. 'I know I am behaving terribly. I want you to understand that I have no choice. To be sent away from here would be to lose you. I could not bear that.'

'I understand that you have no choice, Larry. But you will forgive me if I wish only to go to bed, tonight.'

'My darling, it is you who must forgive me. Lan, will you meet me next Tuesday?'

She hesitated. 'Your fiancée will not like that.'

'My fiancée will not know of it.'

Another hesitation. 'You must allow me time to think of it. I will send you a message.'

71

She was on her feet, but he still held her hand. 'Lan . . .
for God's sake say that you forgive me.'

'I forgive you, Larry.'

'And that you love me.'

'I will always love you, Larry. Only you.'

Gently she freed her hand, tucked the blanket under
her arm, and disappeared into the night.

Larry remained kneeling, with bowed head, for several
minutes. He was the most wretched of men.

Lan reached the gap in her father's fence without quite
knowing how she had got there; she had paid little attention to the actual business of walking home.

Her brain was clouded with so many things. One part
of it wanted to scream and shout in anguish. But that was
how a white woman would behave, and she had no desire
to behave like a white woman.

Another part wanted to curl up in a dark corner and
die. Suicide was an honourable end to an intolerable situation. The Christian priests would not think so, but she
had never been able to bring herself to believe fully in the
priests and what they had to say, partly because she knew
her parents did not truly believe either. Becoming Christian had been an act of policy, in order to be accepted
into the British community, rather than an act of faith.
Father still burned a joss stick every night in his bedroom.

But suicide was so final. She had so enjoyed her life up
till now. If this past year had been the most enjoyable of
all her years, they had all been worth living. Should she
not believe that somewhere in the future they would be
worth living again. Even if she could never marry, could
never be anything now, never do anything, save
remember?

But would she remember with love, or hate? Both, she
decided. She had loved Larry Cairns with all her heart,
and she would always love him. Or at least she would
always be unable to love anyone else, because of him. But
she would always hate him, too, for what he had done to
her. No matter that she had always known this was how

it would end. To know something, in the cold calculations of her mind, could not compare with the dreams arising from the heart, the dreams he himself had inspired, that one day it might be possible for him to marry her, to live with her openly . . . that was the hateful thing. Had she never dreamed, she would not now feel as if every devil in hell was tormenting her.

She stopped in confusion, bathed in light. In her preoccupation she had walked up to the very front of the house instead of circling the garden to enter by the window she had left open behind the swimming pool. Worse, as she had returned at least two hours earlier than usual, the family had not gone to bed. Her father and mother and Kai were all seated on the front verandah, staring at her.

She drew a long breath. But if this night was to be the nadir of her life, then so be it. She walked up the steps.

'Lan?' Chung Tzu's tone was amazed. 'What are you doing?'

'Where have you been?' demanded Chung Lo. 'You went to bed, an hour ago.'

Lan reached the top of the steps. 'I have been out,' she said.

'Out?' Chung Tzu's normally high voice rose an octave.

'Out of the grounds?' Chung Lo inquired. His voice was dropping, ominously.

Chung Lan stood before them, her head drooping.

'She has been with a man.' Chung Tzu's voice dropped to an incredulous whisper. 'Our daughter, like a thief in the night consorting with a man.'

'Is this true?' Chung Lo asked.

Lan raised her head. 'Yes.'

'Which man? What kind of a man is it that will not come boldly to my door and ask for your hand?'

Lan said nothing.

'Speak, girl.'

'I cannot, Father.'

'Cannot?'

'I have sworn that I will not reveal his name.'

73

'Larry Cairns,' Kai muttered.

Chung Lo's head turned, sharply. 'Cairns?'

'It can be none other.' Kai pointed at his sister; even in the lamplight her cheeks could be seen to be glowing.

'Cairns,' Chung Lo growled, and stood up. 'You have dishonoured yourself, you have dishonoured your family, you have dishonoured me, with an Englishman?'

Chung Lan hung her head.

'You are a slut! A wanton! A whore!'

She felt rather than saw his approach, knew he was going to hit her, could do nothing but tense herself for the blow. Yet its force, on the side of her head, took her by surprise. She lost her balance and staggered, reached for the railing and clung to it, was hit twice more. Tears burst from her eyes, but she wouldn't cry out, or beg him to stop.

'You will hurt her!' Tzu protested.

'I should kill her,' Chung Lo panted.

'This is not China. You would be arrested. And hanged.'

Chung Lo stepped away from his daughter. Lan continued to cling to the railing, tasting blood from her cut lips seeping through her teeth.

'Leave my house,' Chung Lo said. 'Leave it, and do not come back. I renounce you. I will never speak your name again.'

Chung Lan raised her head in horror. She had anticipated a beating, if caught, but not to be thrown out.

She looked at her mother, and saw nothing but determined anger. She might be the youngest in the family; she might have been the darling of them all – but the family honour, the family name, stretching back into history and in the present time stretching to either side to encompass not only her brothers and sister and their children in Singapore, but untold uncles and aunts and nephews and nieces and cousins in Canton whom she had never met, was far more important than any individual. Were she not punished, savagely, then the House of Chung would be forever held in contempt.

She looked at her brother. As the two youngest they had always been closest. But Kai's face was even more closed than her mother's. Above everything else, she had dishonoured him, and with his friend.

Chung Lan turned and stumbled down the steps into the darkness.

'Larry Cairns!' Kai spat. 'I thought he was my friend!'

'Put him from your mind,' Chung Tzu said. 'They would hang you for murder.'

She began to weep.

PART TWO
Enemies

CHAPTER 4
The Husband

The engagement party for Margaret Anstey and Lawrence Cairns, though given at short notice, was the event of the summer in Singapore. Every white person of any consequence, including the Governor, was there, and people even came down from Kuala Lumpur. Only the unavoidable absence of the Ansteys and Larry's parents was regrettable, but they had all sent their blessings by telegram, and looked forward to the wedding in Bombay later on in the year.

Ronald Lees, thoroughly enjoying his role of surrogate father to Margaret, beamed on the whole proceedings, and everyone agreed that Larry Cairns was a lucky devil. He was also clearly a most eligible bachelor, and his athletic handsomeness was a match for his fiancée's beauty. Margaret Anstey, it was also said, must be quite the loveliest girl east of Suez.

She was also the most triumphant. She had come to Singapore to collect a husband, and had done so with the minimum of time and fuss.

'Happy?' Margaret asked him as they waltzed together.

'Very,' he told her, smiling down into her eyes. 'Confused' would be a better word, he thought. When he remembered last Sunday on the beach, his whole being was set tingling at the thought that so much beauty had been yielded into his keeping. But then he remembered that he had once thought that about Chung Lan.

Since that day Margaret had been very proper. They had been out dancing together every night, and when he had taken her home she had kissed him most passionately, had allowed his hand to rest on her breast, but he had understood that nothing further would be permitted until

79

after the wedding. Not that he had wanted to make love to her; every time he thought about it, a vision swam before him of Chung Lan in tears.

He told himself that these were early days and that everything would settle down soon enough. Chung Lan would become reconciled to her role as his mistress – a role she had herself suggested, he reminded himself – and he would become reconciled to his role as Margaret's husband . . .

And all would be helped by Margaret's coming absence, for she was booked to travel back to Bombay on the following Tuesday, which meant he would be able to see Lan again on Tuesday night.

And then, with a beautiful wife and a beautiful mistress, he could settle down to being the happiest and most fortunate man in the world. Providing he made no mistakes in the interim . . .

Margaret was frowning at him. 'I don't think we should ever have secrets from each other, do you, Larry?' she asked, rather sharply.

The music stopped, but instead of returning to her seat she moved towards the verandah, still holding his hand. Their elders smiled indulgently as the couple disappeared into the evening.

'Of course we shouldn't,' Larry lied.

'Then tell me what is on your mind.'

'What makes you think anything is on my mind?' he sparred.

'Because every so often you get a very pensive, faraway look.'

'Maybe I just can't believe my good fortune.'

She turned, leaning on the verandah rail, searching his face with her gaze. The garden was decorated with lanterns and it was perfectly bright; the night was filled with the subtle scent of jasmine. 'Can't you?'

'When I look at you, I can't.' At last he was telling her the truth.

She smiled, and ran her fingers down his cheek. 'Dear Larry. Sometimes I can't believe mine, either.' He wondered whether she was thinking of him, or merely of having been born Margaret Anstey. 'Have you quite forgiven me?'

'For what?'

'Well, for putting you off for two years. And then for sort of . . . well, shanghaiing you, I suppose some people would say,' she said thoughtfully.

'Perhaps I needed shanghaiing.'

'Most men do,' she agreed. 'Larry, I am going to make you the happiest man on earth. I do promise you that.'

'No matter what my faults? You haven't discovered any of those yet.'

'Well, I have a few too. No matter what your faults.'

'Promise?'

'Promise,' she said fervently.

He nearly told her about Lan there and then, but decided against it. If she were ever to be told about Lan it would have to be after they were married.

Naturally she wanted his company all the next day, so again he had to telephone Kai and postpone their tennis game for another week. Kai was unavailable, but the servant who answered the phone promised to deliver the message.

They spent the last two days of Margaret's stay house-hunting, and chose a delightful little bungalow on the rising ground behind and to the east of the city, not very far from the Managing Director's residence. It had only recently come on the market and needed a good deal done to it, but Margaret was content to leave that to Larry, supervised by Ronald Lees. Lees, who seemed as happy about the whole thing as if it were Joan who was getting married, also told Larry what he proposed to give them for a wedding present: he was turning over the company car for a Daimler, and therefore offered the Armstrong Siddeley to Larry.

'It's only five years old,' he said. 'Perfect condition. And . . .' he winked, 'rather appropriate, eh, in all the circumstances?'

81

Larry was delighted, and he drove it when he and the Lees family escorted Margaret to the liner – the *Empress of Japan* – which was to take her back across the Indian Ocean.

'November!' they all said.

'And you'll write every week,' Margaret told Larry.

'I'll write every day,' he promised.

They had a farewell drink and then boarded the launch for the journey back to the dock. Margaret stood on deck waving them out of sight.

'Such a darling girl,' Elizabeth Lees said.

Joan wept crocodile tears into her handkerchief.

'You must be a very proud man,' Ronald Lees told Larry.

'I am, sir,' he assured him. And also a most relieved one. He had four months to put himself in order.

He had to begin with a total reconciliation with Lan. Although he had had no message from her, he was at the racecourse a quarter of an hour before their usual meeting time at ten o'clock. But she never came, and at midnight he went back to Mavis Norton's, very disturbed.

On the other hand, careful consideration in the light of day convinced him that she was just piqued. He would have to work on her, make her believe that he still loved her more than anyone else – as perhaps he did. Certainly it would be a mistake to lose his head and go rushing off to see her and perhaps give the whole game away. He would see her, on Sunday when he played tennis with Kai, and he would find an opportunity to be alone with her long enough to reassure her.

But on Sunday, when he rang the bell of the Chung residence and announced that he had come for his game of tennis with Mr Kai, he was told by the servant that Mr Kai was not at home.

'Then let me speak with Miss Lan,' he said. 'She will give me a game.

'Miss Lan is not at home either, sir,' the servant informed him.

Something had happened! Now he simply had to throw caution to the wind.

'I must speak with Mr Kai,' he said. 'It is most urgent. Will you ask him to telephone me as soon as he comes in?'

Not that he had any doubt that Kai was at home all the time. Had Lan, in her anger and misery, confessed to her brother? That might well have happened.

But Kai was such a reasonable fellow, so tolerant of the ways of the world . . . But then again, no man was really tolerant where the virtue of his sister was in question. Oh, damn, he thought. Damn, damn, damn.

Kai did not telephone, and Lan was not at the racecourse the following Tuesday, either.

And now there were rumours of crisis in the Chung household. Miss Lan had either run away from home or been sent away; no one seemed certain. But she had definitely left Singapore.

Lees sent for Larry.

'Anything to do with you?' he inquired.

'It must be,' Larry said miserably. 'I had to tell her about Margaret.'

'I mean, you haven't spirited her away, have you?'

'Good Lord, no, sir. But I'm afraid her family must know something about it. Kai won't speak to me.'

'Well, I think it's all turned out for the best. You have probably had the most fortunate escape in the history of illicit sex. For Christ's sake, stop looking so miserable! So you had your wicked way with the girl a few times. It makes me sick with envy every time I think about it. Now you're engaged, and she's gone. Who could ask for anything better? And in her place you're going to have Meg Anstey. And you can have your wicked way with her for the rest of your life. I say again, it fair makes me sick to think about it. Forgive my vulgarity, but you are the luckiest man alive.'

I will forgive your vulgarity, Larry thought. Only because you can't help it, you overstuffed bastard. But he didn't say it. A small voice was suggesting that the blighter might even be right.

But oh, Lan, Lan. How he hoped she would find happiness.

And he would miss Kai, probably the only true friend he had in the world.

Lees might have been prescient.

'I also think it's a damned good thing that your friendship with that Chink has ended too. I would take care it doesn't start up again.'

'Small chance of that,' Larry said. 'But we were friends, sir. And it is my fault it has ended.'

'It's still a damned good thing. Friendship, my hat. The Chungs have their own axe to grind. And it has nothing to do with friendship for any white man.'

'With respect, sir,' Larry snapped. 'Chung Kai has never asked me a single question about business affairs.'

'Maybe he hasn't. Let me tell you something very confidential. Chung Lo has a friend, a Jap named Kitachi. Did you know that?'

'I have met Mr Kitachi, sir. In Chung Lo's house.'

'Have you now? Then maybe you'd better have a word with Superintendent Delaney. He's in charge of the local Special Branch, you know. Colonel Billson has told me, in the strictest confidence, that they suspect Kitachi may not be a genuine businessman at all, but rather an agent for the Imperial Japanese Government.'

Larry frowned at him. 'A spy?'

'Call it what you like.'

'But, what would he be doing in Singapore?'

'You may well ask. It happens to be one of the most important naval bases in the world.'

Kitachi, a spy? He had never liked the fellow, Larry knew. But that had been mainly because of Lan. And yet, all that anti-British talk . . .

'You may also ask,' Lees went on, 'just where a friendship like Chung Lo's with this Kitachi fellow might spring from. For God's sake, the Chinks and the Japs are actually fighting each other in Shantung. They may pretend it's just skirmishing between hot-headed border guards, but only a fool would believe that.'

'But I don't see what Kitachi is hoping to accomplish here in Singapore,' Larry said.

Lees sighed. 'Supposing there were to be a war between Britain and Japan, don't you think the Japanese would like to have detailed plans of Singapore?'

'A war? But how can there be a war? I mean, what about the League of Nations? Anyway, Japan and Britain have always been friends.'

'Times change. So do friendships. Anyway, who wants to be friends with a lot of yellow-skinned bastards? Oh, the Japs are out for something. Of course they know we'd smash them hollow. Our fleet is twice as strong as theirs, for a start. So they're trying to subvert our Chinese and Malay work force. That's as plain as a pikestaff.'

Larry wondered if he'd nearly said 'slaves' instead of 'work force'.

'But, if our people are so sure of all of this, why don't they just arrest Kitachi and deport him?' he asked.

'On what grounds? He's broken no law, yet. Anyway, what would it accomplish? The Japs would know we were on to them, and they would just send someone else, and we'd have to winkle him out all over again. No, no, the powers that be are perfectly happy with the situation. They can keep their eye on him, and on his associates here in Singapore. And if there was ever any trouble, bingo, we'd have them all in the lock-up together. But every little helps. Yes, I think it would be an excellent idea for you to have a chat with Delaney.'

'I will, of course, sir,' Larry agreed. 'But I will make it perfectly clear that Chung Kai is not anti-British, nor would he ever take part in any subversive activities. He doesn't even like Kitachi.'

'Tell all that to Delaney,' Lees advised.

Larry did as his boss wished, and felt better afterwards. If he had somehow become involved with a spy ring, then perhaps he had had a lucky escape. That Kai and most

85

certainly Lan were only innocent bystanders was neither here nor there, in the circumstances.

But he didn't really believe any of it. It was incredible to suppose that little Japan had any designs upon the British Empire. But then it was quite incredible, in this late summer of 1930, with Don Bradman making a century every time he went in to bat – how Larry wished he could be there to watch the Australian wonder – that anyone was preparing to fight a war at all. Wars were things of the past. The carnage of the Great War and the formation of the League of Nations had surely made that certain.

Anyway, now he could justifiably turn his back on the whole family. He knew he would always feel responsible for Lan's quarrel with her parents; on the other hand, they would undoubtedly be reconciled, for she was their youngest daughter. November was rushing at him, and there was a great deal to be done.

He made no effort to see Kai again, or to trace Lan's movements. The past was the past, and he had his future to think about.

'Twenty dollars,' Kitachi Tano said, and paid over the money. 'Take me to see her.'

The woman counted the notes, put them in her pocket, and opened the inner door.

Kitachi had smoked opium himself, occasionally; he had never doubted its destructive powers. Now his nostrils twitched as he followed the woman down the inner corridor. This was a brothel. But a brothel where the sweet dreams of the poppy made every woman a goddess, every man a demi-god, at least in his imagination.

'There is an extra charge after half an hour,' the woman said.

'There will be no extra charge for me,' Kitachi told her. 'I have come to take this girl away.'

The woman frowned.

'And if you wish to call your people,' Kitachi told her, 'I suggest you look out of your windows first. My men entirely surround this building. If you cause trouble, we will burn it down.' He smiled at her. 'With you inside it.'

The woman goggled at him. He spoke so softly, and was so well-dressed. Yet she could not doubt that he meant what he said.

'Now go,' Kitachi told her.

The woman scuttled along the corridor, and Kitachi opened the door.

'You have come to see me?' Chung Lan asked.

She reclined on a bare mattress on an iron bed, naked, hair loose, body flaccid; a half-smoked pipe drooped from her fingers. There was no other furniture in the room save for a latrine bucket.

Kitachi stood above her, looking down on all the beauty he had ever wanted to see, beauty he would possess, he knew, because he had wanted it for so long. But not in this disgusting place.

'Put your clothes on,' he told her. 'And come with me.'

She sat up, recognising the voice even through the opium haze, instinctively reaching for a sheet which wasn't there.

'Do you not wish to come with me?' Kitachi asked.

Chung Lan drew up her knees.

'Do you not hate your parents, for throwing you out?' Kitachi asked her.

Chung Lan stared at him.

'Do you not hate Chung Kai, for not siding with you?' Kitachi asked.

Chung Lan licked her lips.

'And do you not hate Cairns for abandoning you?'

Chung Lan inhaled, her nostrils dilating.

Kitachi took her hand. 'Put on your clothes, and come with me, Chung Lan. I will teach you how to hate.' He grinned at her. 'If it can be experienced successfully it is the most satisfying of emotions.'

'I would like to visit China,' Chung Kai told his father.

Chung Lo peered at him over the tops of his rimless glasses, then looked round at the busy office, the clacking

87

typewriters, the hurrying girls, the sweating young men, who made up his staff, and beyond to the piles of bags and bales and boxes stacked against the far walls. Unlike the bosses of Hammond and Teng, Chung Lo worked in the middle of his main warehouse, surrounded with the odours of tea and sugar and rum and raw rubber awaiting shipment.

He had been aware, over the past month, that his younger son was unhappy. And he knew the cause, of course. They had received information that Chung Lan had gone down to the port after leaving the house that Tuesday night, and found herself lodgings in a brothel. But when they had sent to the brothel to get her out, she had disappeared, and the woman who had kept the place refused to say where she had gone, save that she had left Singapore. How she had accomplished that Chung Lo did not care to think.

He was also aware that Kai and Lan had been very close; Kai had not really been the same since his sister had left. But now he was being ridiculous. As for raising a personal matter in the office . . .

'You will not find her,' he said. 'Do you know how many people there are in China?'

'I am not going to look for Lan,' Kai said. 'I know she is gone, forever. I wish to go and see China for myself.'

'Why?'

'It is my country, is it not?'

'Of course it is not. Singapore is your country.'

'Singapore is not a country, Father.'

'Well, then: Malaya.'

'The Federated States are not a country, either. They are part of an empire. Are you saying I have no country?'

'Well, then, Britain is your country. You have a British passport.'

'Can you really sit there and make a statement like that to me, Father?'

Chung Lo sighed. He had often thought that he should have had his youngest son trained as a lawyer.

'But China? China is an expression.'

'It is going through a difficult time. But it will become great again. I wish to see for myself. Mr Kitachi tells us that China will never be strong again by itself, that only through friendship with Japan can it regain its unity. He also says that only through friendship with Japan can we here in Singapore ever gain equality with the British. But there is fighting going on in north China now. Japanese are killing Chinese. I do not see how he can reconcile these things. I do not see how *you* can reconcile these things, Father.'

'The people being killed are bandits fighting for any warlord who will pay them. They are the people who are keeping China down.'

'Perhaps you are right. But I wish to go and see for myself.' He leaned on Chung Lo's desk. 'You can spare me from the office, for a little while. I will come back to you, a wiser man. I may even know what is the best course for us to follow. But I must go and see for myself. I cannot just accept what Mr Kitachi says, what the news-papers say.'

Chung Lo sighed again. My family, he thought, is threatening to disintegrate.

Chung Kai understood his thoughts. 'You have my brothers, and my sister,' he said. 'They will always be here.'

'But you will come back,' Chung Lo said.

'I have said that.'

'Mind that you do,' Chung Lo told him. 'Or your mother will be upset.'

Ronald Lees was of course going to Bombay with his wife and daughter for the wedding. The entire world might be sinking deeper into the clutches of the Depression, as it was being called, but that was no reason for the Managing Director of the Far East's biggest and oldest trading concern – at least since the demise of the East India Company itself – to lower his standards. Ronald Lees booked a suite on A Deck of the *Empress of India*.

Larry was installed in a cabin on B Deck, Starboard Side, by courtesy of Hammond and Teng.

Roly Payne came along to act as best man. A confirmed bachelor at thirty eight, Roly was occasionally looked at with suspicion by the establishment, but his sexual conduct seemed to be impeccable, since it was non-existent. Almost every unattached white female in Singapore had been taken out at least once by Roly Payne, and not one of them had ever received more than a kiss on the cheek.

'The fact is,' Lees commented, 'the only breasts Roly has ever been interested in are off a chicken and well cooked. And touch wood, the only balls he's ever been interested in are ones that can be batted, hit or thrown.'

Roly was always a lot of fun, however, and as Larry was his best and favourite opening batsman, they had seen a lot of each other over the three years since Larry's arrival in Singapore.

'You aren't going to give up cricket?' he asked anxiously, as they paraded the promenade deck.

'Good Lord, no. Why should I?'

'Well, some fellows do. The memsahibs get at them. They're inclined to find cricket boring.'

'Well, I promise you I shall continue playing as long as you want me.'

'Oh, no fear of that. Even if you do lose form.'

'Lose form?'

'Well, lots of fellows do, after marriage. Something to do with concentration.'

Larry stared at him.

'Fact,' Roly said, flushing. 'I suppose it's . . . well, having it regularly.'

'And that affects a chap's concentration?'

'That's what they say.'

'It may affect *some* chaps' concentration. But it won't affect mine.'

'That's the spirit,' Roly said.

So here I am, Larry thought, standing on the bridge, by special invitation, together with the rest of the marriage party, to watch the *Empress of India* entering Bombay Harbour.

I am about to marry the most beautiful girl east of Suez. I have a career in front of me which seems to have limitless scope. I am a much-envied man.

I must be the most fortunate man on earth, as everyone agrees. Therefore I must also be the happiest man on earth, as everyone supposes.

However, I am also the biggest cad on earth. But only a handful of people know that, and perhaps I can set that right, by making a success of my marriage as well as my job.

And that means making Margaret as happy as she's promised to make me.

The Ansteys were on the dock to greet the Singapore contingent. Margaret was positively shy as she kissed Larry, but her eyes were radiant.

'It has been such a long four months,' she said. 'And you didn't write every day, after all.'

'Every other day,' he reminded her.

'Larry, dear boy, you look fitter than ever,' Brian Anstey declared. 'Can it really be three years? Never mind, it's all behind you now.' He grasped Larry's arm to pull him aside and whisper, 'Told you she'd come round, didn't I? Women need patience. That's the only rule. Patience. You remember that.'

Julia Anstey was waiting to embrace him. 'What a pity your family can't be here,' she said.

'Well, Bombay is rather a long way from Lewes . . .' An expensively long way. But he was due for long leave the following year, and they would be able to meet their new daughter-in-law then.

With the Ansteys was a young man named Rawlings, who was one of Brian Anstey's under managers, and was apparently in charge of the 'stag' side of things. Into his care Larry and Roly were delivered, and indeed Larry saw very little of the Ansteys or the Lees for the next couple of days, as he was whisked to and fro. Rawlings organised an enormous stag party at which naked nautch girls not only danced but sat on the laps of the guests and indulged in a good deal of sexual horseplay.

Larry gazed at the swinging midnight hair, the undulating brown flesh and the gold bangles and nose rings, inhaled the scent of coconut oil, and found himself remembering Ayesha and wondering if she was still in business. But that part of his life was linked to Kai and the must-be-forgotten past.

Because of the heat, the wedding was held at six o'clock in the evening. And instead of morning suits the men wore white dinner jackets, very crisp and cool.

Larry, Roly and Rawlings were at the church early, and chatted with the bishop and the rector while the pews behind them filled up with people Larry had never seen before and presumed he would never see again. The Lees sat on the right hand side, and the ushers shifted more and more people from the left until the congregation was evenly balanced.

The bridal party was only ten minutes late. By then the cathedral was a glow of candlelight, in which the tones of the organ, as it played Mendelssohn's Wedding March, sounded most romantic. Larry saw Julia, wearing an enormous picture hat, hurry up the aisle to take her seat, and looked over his shoulder for the appearance of his bride. Margaret rested her hand on her father's arm, and was followed closely by Joan Lees, her maid of honour, and then by several bridesmaids. Her veil was thrown back to reveal her face, a necessary ruling in an evening marriage, Larry had been told; in the old days it had not been unknown for parents to switch a plain daughter for a handsome one at the last minute to get her off their hands, confident that in the gloom the ceremony would be completed before the deception could be discerned.

But this was undoubtedly Margaret, smiling, confident, even arrogant as she moved smoothly forward. Her responses to the questions were given in a clear, low voice, while she gazed up at him, and when he drew off her glove to slip the ring on her finger her hand was dry and steady.

Larry, however, had never been so nervous in his life. He felt that he had taken a step into space, and where he would land he had no idea.

But for the moment there was only Margaret: Margaret laughing as the register was signed; Margaret smiling, her fingers tight on his arm, as they walked down the aisle; Margaret pouting contentedly as they stood in the courtyard of the cathedral waiting for the flashbulbs to explode; Margaret nestling against him as they sat in the Rolls which was driving them back to the Ansteys' home; Margaret bubbling beside him as they greeted a seemingly endless procession of guests; Margaret circulating briskly, dragging him behind her, introducing him to this or that treasured friend; Margaret seated beside him at the head table as Roly read out the telegrams; Margaret applauding vigorously as he replied to the speeches; and Margaret blowing him a kiss as she was escorted upstairs to change into her going-away outfit.

Without her at his side he felt oddly lonely. But he was also being hurried away, by a crowd of young men he didn't know – Roly had quite disappeared into the throng – to get changed as well.

Actually they weren't going very far, owing to the lateness of the hour. A discreet hotel had been chosen for their first night, and they would leave for Simla on the early morning train. Only one or two people knew the name of the hotel, officially.

He emerged on to the balcony, and a moment later Margaret was beside him, wearing a knee length electric blue dress with a fringe and with a matching head band. She looked exquisite; she had allowed her hair to grow even more, and it now reached her shoulders. It was such magnificent hair it had surely been a crime ever to cut it at all.

The guests applauded, and Margaret laughed and tossed her bouquet in the American fashion. Then they were

93

hurrying through the crowd, laughing and shouting greetings, being slapped on the back, hugged and kissed, until they reached the safety of the Rolls. This drove off immediately, to the accompaniment of a clatter of tin cans and empty bottles. Two blocks away the Indian driver apologetically stopped the car and got out to release the debris, which had attracted a large crowd of small boys and half-starved dogs.

'Oh, Larry,' Margaret said, turning into his arms. 'I do love you.'

It was difficult to know where to begin, and when. There was so much beautiful flesh, and so little skimpy dress. But there was also the driver, who got in, again most apologetically, before Larry had had time to kiss her more than once or twice; in a second, Margaret was sitting straight and stretching her skirt down to her knees.

The hotel was not very far from the Ansteys' house, although they drove some distance out of their way before doubling back, just in case anyone had had the idea of following them. Then they were greeted by a very well briefed and smiling Anglo-Indian hotelier, who personally escorted them up to the bridal suite, where there was a bottle of champagne waiting, with the compliments of the management.

This the manager opened with some effort, and a lot of noise, while their bags were brought in by the porters.

'May I wish you all the happiness in the world, Mr and Mrs Cairns,' the manager said, and ushered his people to the door.

'You'll call us at seven?' Larry reminded him. Their train left at eight.

'At seven sharp,' the manager agreed with a sly grin, and the door was closed.

Larry turned the key in the lock, and turned back to Margaret, who had lifted both their glasses.

'To all the happiness in the world,' she said.

He took the glass from her hand, kissed it, and drank. Then he set it on the table, and she did likewise, gazing at him as she so liked to do.

He took her hands and brought her to him for a long, slow, intimate kiss. You are mine, he thought, after three years.

Had Chung Lan ever been his, so totally? But now was not the time to think of Chung Lan.

He slipped the straps of her dress from her shoulders; she wore nothing under it.

'You are very beautiful,' he said. 'And I love you.'

'I belong to you,' she replied.

She herself released the waistband. Now she shrugged, and the dress slipped past her hips and gathered around her ankles. She wore no stockings either. And still she stared at him, willing him to possess her. Or willing herself to possess him?

He took her in his arms again, crushed her against him while he kissed her mouth quite savagely. Then he stepped away from her and began to undress himself. The final act of surrender had to come from her.

She waited until he was stripped to his own drawers, before she pushed her knickers past her thighs. Thus they matched each other exactly in their nakedness. But his was far more intense. It was the beach all over again, only now she would not resist him.

He brought her against him again, kissed her mouth, and let his hands wander, over her shoulders, down the deep curve of her back to hold her buttocks, then back up in front to find her breasts. She shivered, and seemed to be holding her breath; she kept her hands on his shoulders although she had to be feeling him against her.

He half carried, half pushed her to the bed, and she fell on her back. He realised that she would know no other way of love-making, but that was sufficient for the first night. He lay beside her, and sent his fingers coursing down to those auburn curls and beyond. Her eyes, tight shut, shot open in alarm.

'It will make it easier,' he promised, already searching her secret valley with the utmost gentleness.

'No,' she begged. 'Please, Larry . . .'

He so wanted to play with her, as Lan had liked him

to do. He knew she would enjoy it, love it, want more and more . . . but she was clearly very nervous: every muscle in her body was tensed.

He lay on top of her. She was also dry. He was as careful as he could be, but she gasped with pain, and her nails bit into his shoulders as he surged to and fro. Only after he had climaxed was there any ease of movement.

'I didn't mean to hurt you,' he told her. 'Please forgive me.'

She smiled, bravely. 'I know you didn't mean to hurt me, darling. It was just one of those things. But now it's done.'

He wasn't quite sure what she meant.

They slept, deeply, in each others' arms, her head on his shoulder, her hair scattered across the pillow. But only briefly. Both were awake well before seven, listening to the many cockcrows, the church bells. When he put his arms round her she nestled closer.

'Did I hurt you?' he whispered into her hair.

'Only a little. Did I satisfy you?'

'Of course you did. But I must satisfy you.'

She raised herself on her elbow and looked down at him, her face serious. 'I am perfectly satisfied.'

'My darling girl, you have had nothing but pain.'

Her face was that of a very young girl. 'Ma told me to expect that.'

'And nothing more?'

'Of course not. Making love is a man's privilege. A woman must be patient, and bear it, and hope for happiness.'

'My dearest Meg, your father must have been a most neglectful lover. And he would have robbed himself of a great deal of happiness.'

She stared at him for several seconds, then lay down again and hid her face in his shoulder.

'Like now,' he said. 'Have you never masturbated?'

'Mastur . . .' She sat up again, her face crimson. 'Of course not.'

'But everyone does, at some time or other.'

'Of course they don't. That's disgusting.'

'Meg . . .'

'I must go to the bathroom,' she said, and leapt out of bed.

He sat up to watch her, and listen to her, for these were the intimacies of marriage which were so important. When she re-emerged, and found him looking at her, she hesitated, and half turned away.

'Meg!' he commanded.

She hesitated again, then picked up her underclothes. 'We must hurry, or we'll miss the train.'

What had Brian Anstey said, and of this very woman? Patience. Women need patience.

Larry got out of bed and began to dress.

From Bombay to the hill station at Simla is some nine hundred miles, as the crow flies. It seemed much longer as the train chugged.

Yet the journey was absolutely fascinating, and brought home to both Larry and Margaret just how little they knew of the vast country which formed such a large part of the British Empire.

The railway first of all clung to the coast almost up to the head of the Gulf of Khambhat, crossing as it did so innumerable small creeks and rivers, before they rumbled across the Narbada into the town of Bharuch. By then it was late afternoon, and they stopped for the first night in Baroda, where they had booked a room at one of the local hotels.

They were still very much on the coastal plain, and it was very hot, hotter than Bombay because of the complete absence of wind. Nor was the hotel up to the best standards. Fortunately, Margaret had lived in the East long enough not to be alarmed at finding a cockroach in the bed, or to be put off by an unfailing diet of curry.

He felt that his best course was to apologise for that morning. But she laughed when he attempted to do so. 'I said I'd forgive all your faults, didn't I, Larry, my dearest.

I do know about men's lusts, believe me, and about the things they do.' She pinkened again. 'Mumsy did tell me. But now you're married, you'll never be that lonely again.'

She was bubbling with good humour and love, determined to forget her earlier embarrassment. Larry was beginning to understand that she had had a most sheltered upbringing, at least in Eastern terms. Her concept of lovemaking consisted of kisses and caresses, above the waist. That she had actually to allow him inside her was clearly a cross she had been prepared to bear.

He knew he had to educate her to the knowledge that there was so much more to physical love than that, that out of such profane intimacy could grow a sacred love greater than any she had imagined. The question was, when, and how. It seemed to him that Simla, the end of their travels and the true beginning of their life together, would be the right moment.

For the time being, her determination that, despite the heat and the bugs and barking of dogs outside their window, as well as a growing uncertainty as to whether they were going to be able to have a bath in the morning, he should each night obtain his pleasure, as she saw it, had to be satisfaction enough.

They did obtain a bath, and next morning resumed their journey, the railway now swinging inland and climbing quite sharply. This was exhilarating, even if there were times when they wondered if the puffing, gasping engine was going to make it.

That night they stopped at Ghangar, which was blessedly cool. On the fourth night they were at Ghangapur, and on the fifth afternoon they rolled into Delhi.

As they were due to leave at dawn the next day for the last leg of their journey, it was a matter of frantic sightseeing during the remaining hours of daylight. Fortunately, as they had arrived at the main New Delhi Railway Station, the exquisite Ajmer Gate was just around the corner, and they had time to take in the Red Fort, immortalised during the Mutiny, before being whisked off to their very good hotel.

'This really is the trip of a lifetime,' Margaret confessed. 'Especially for a honeymoon.'

She was blissfully happy. So happy that he thought he could trust her with anything. And it really was not in his nature to be deceitful. He was still not quite twenty four, and not yet aware that there were some secrets which just had to be kept.

Next morning the train wheezed and gasped up into the foothills of the Himalayas, to a height of seven thousand feet, and Simla. Here at last it was cool even in the day, once one was out of the sun, and the nights were cold enough for blankets.

The air was invigorating, although the slightest exercise made the heart pump, and the views were magnificently rugged and dramatic.

'I've never been this high up before,' Margaret confessed.

'Neither have I,' Larry agreed.

'It's like being in heaven, with you.' She glanced at him, still shy at moments like this.

They had just returned from a walk, and were pleasantly tired. But not too tired, and there were still two hours until dinner.

Hand in hand they went up to their bedroom, past bowing waiters who wore white jackets with brass buttons over white dhotis, and bare feet. Everyone in the hotel naturally knew they were honeymooning, and loved them for it.

'Do you think they know what we're going to do now?' Margaret asked, as Larry locked the door.

'Well, of course they do.'

She sat on the bed. 'Isn't it strange. All my life I've been looking at people, and not really seeing them. I mean I've seen their faces and watched them smile or frown, and I've listened to them talking or laughing . . . but they were all celluloid, weren't they? Not real. Because people are only real when they are making love. I don't mean the preliminaries. But the real thing . . .' she paused, staring at him with that intense expression and little pink spots in her cheeks.

He sat beside her to unbutton her blouse. 'I like the real thing, as you call it.'

It must be the altitude, he thought, but even after five days of making love to this woman, I want to do so more than ever. To do more to her than ever before.

He wanted to do so much more than just lie on her belly. As he had learned from Lan, to masturbate a beautiful woman is far more exciting than merely to enter her, because one can see the pleasure one is giving. And surely now the moment had arrived for her really to learn to live.

She anticipated his routine now, lay back with her eyes closed to be caressed. 'The "real thing",' she murmured. 'What I was going to say was, now I look at everybody I meet, even the Indians, and I think to myself, what is he like when doing it? Or she?' She gave an embarrassed little shiver.

Gently Larry stroked her breasts, which she obviously both expected and liked, then cautiously, even casually, allowed his hand to slip down towards her groin. Would she allow it? His fingers touched the silk of her pubes.

'You've never been with an Indian, have you, Larry?' Her eyes were still closed.

'Ah . . . well . . .' He parted her thighs, very gently, slipped his hand between.

'Larry?' Her voice rose an octave. 'Larry!' She twisted, violently, legs flailing, and threw him off balance, so that he fell out of bed, receiving a kick in the groin as he did so.

'For God's sake . . .'

She sat up, cheeks crimson. 'What on earth were you doing? I've asked you not to touch me there, with your hand. That's horrible.'

'My darling Meg,' he said as patiently as he could, getting up. 'It is not in the least horrible. I was going to make love to you, the way people should. I was going to

100

give you pleasure. Meg . . . if you'd just believe me, I could make you the happiest woman in the world.'

She drew up her knees. 'I don't believe you. Where do you learn all of these things?'

'Well . . . from books, I suppose.'

'Books! Filthy books! I don't believe that either. I believe you *have* been with an Indian.'

She paused, slightly panting, aghast at the temerity of what she had suggested.

But Larry was now angry; to his surprise, it was a spontaneous emotion. 'All right,' he retorted. 'Since you're so sure of it, I *have* been with an Indian!'

'You . . .' she moved further up the bed. 'But that's horrible. You . . .' she gave his penis a hasty glance and looked away again. 'You've been inside an Indian? And then . . . oh, my God!'

'And then inside you? I have bathed since, you know. About a thousand times. Meg, you really are being un-utterably childish.'

'All Indians are diseased. Mumsy says so.'

'Just as Mumsy has always lain on her back with her eyes closed and accepted whatever enormities your father decided to perpetrate, I suppose?'

'Daddy would never have dared . . . well . . . to *touch* her!'

'Because he's as hidebound as your mother, I daresay. God protect us from women like Mumsy. I suppose she thinks all Chinese are diseased too.'

'Chinese? You haven't been with a Chinese!' She scrambled out of bed and stood against the wall, on the far side of the bed.

'Yes, I've been with a Chinese. I've been with the most beautiful girl in the world. Until a couple of months ago she was my mistress. And I stupidly threw her over to marry you. I need my head examined.'

'A couple of months ago? When I was in Singapore, with you?'

'Yes. When you were in Singapore.'

101

'Oh, my God!' she shouted again. 'You . . . you bastard!'

'You're right,' Larry agreed savagely. 'I was a bastard. To Chung Lan. But it's all over and done with. I did the "right" thing and married one of my own. Now stop acting like a fool and come here.'

'Don't touch me,' Margaret wailed. 'Just don't come near me. Don't touch me, ever, as long as you live. Don't touch me!'

CHAPTER 5
A glimpse of the Sun

'Come in, Larry, come in! Welcome home!' Ronald Lees
was all smiles behind his big desk on the top floor of the
Hammond and Teng building; Larry had already had to
endure a congratulatory kiss from Mrs Lu. 'You look as
if you need a holiday, to recover from your holiday. At it
morning, noon and night, eh? Lucky devil. How's the
memsahib?'

'The memsahib is fine, sir,' Larry said carefully.

'Splendid, splendid. Does she like the house?'

'I am sure she will. We've only just moved in.'

'Oh, quite, quite. Well, now you're back, I have some
news for you. Not very good, I'm afraid.'

Larry waited; there was nothing his boss could tell him
which could be considered bad news in his circumstances.
Even the information that he was about to be fired would
come as a welcome relief.

'The fact is, things are getting worse rather than better,'
Lees said sombrely. 'There's talk that some of the bigger
European banks are in trouble. I don't mean any of the
good British ones, of course, but still . . . in all the circumstances, the Board don't feel they can continue the
present practice of all-expenses-paid long leaves every
fourth year. It so happens that you are the first to be
affected.'

'Yes, sir.' A huge feeling of relief spread through his
body.

'You may describe the decision as a breach of contract,'
Lees said, but in a tone of voice which conveyed that it
wouldn't be very wise. 'And of course you are entitled to
the leave. I don't suppose you have the money . . .'

'No, sir. I'm setting up house.'

'Quite. I could of course make it a loan . . .'

'Thank you, sir, but no. I'd rather not begin married life with that millstone round my neck.'

'Very wise, too. But, won't Margaret be upset?'

'I think she'll accept the situation, sir.'

'Oh, quite. She's a marvellous girl. You're the luckiest chap in the world, you know, Larry.'

Larry gritted his teeth. The next person who reminded him of that, even if it was Lees himself, was going to get a punch on the nose!

'Well, then, would you like to take the leave here?' Lees grinned. 'Prolong the honeymoon for a few months, eh?'

'You're being very kind, sir. But I'd rather get back to work.'

'Do you know, I had a notion that would be your attitude. I wish to God all the rest of my staff looked at it that way. All right, Larry. You want to get back to work, so I'm going to put you to work. Lawton is retiring next spring.'

Larry frowned at him, scarce daring to believe what he was being told.

'But he's not of retirement age.'

'No, he's not. But the fact is, he's not well. Some kind of stomach trouble. Between you and me, Doc Wright thinks it could be cancer. Anyway, he's being invalided out and sent home. I want you to take over the Main Accounts Department.'

Larry swallowed.

'When do you take your final exams?'

'Not for another three months, sir.'

'Well, you'll have to study hard. The head of Main Accounts has got to be at least Certified. I know you're very young for the position. And it'll mean putting you up over the heads of several more senior staff. But you're the man for the job, Larry. Now, Elizabeth and I are giving a dinner party tomorrow night, for Meg and yourself, to celebrate your return. And your promotion, of course. I'll make the announcement then. Congratulations, my boy.'

Congratulations indeed, Larry thought as he drove up the hill to his house.

So, he was going to move steadily up through the firm, to sit in Lees' chair – he did not doubt that now – because he was Margaret Anstey's husband. He possessed a golden key, but one which he could no longer turn.

He was reminded of Wilde's famous story, *The Picture of Dorian Gray*. To the world he must indeed appear the most fortunate fellow alive, handsome, talented, married to a beautiful wife, the boss's favourite. The world could not strip away that veneer and reveal the mess that lay beneath, the seething guilt and the surging desire, the perpetual realisation that he had not only treated Chung Lan most cruelly, but had then lacked the courage even to take a firm line with his wife.

His wife! he thought bitterly.

Joan Lees's runabout was parked at the foot of the steps. That was predictable. Larry wondered if Margaret had done any confiding.

Mansur the butler waited at the top of the steps, with a tray and an iced chota peg. 'Welcome home, sahib,' he said.

'Thank you, Mansur.'

'The memsahibs are in the drawing room, sahib.'

Larry nodded, exchanged his topee for the whisky, and went into the house.

'Larry, darling!' Margaret kissed him on the cheek. 'You're late.'

'First day back. There was a lot to do. Hello, Joan.'

'Larry!' Joan kissed him on the mouth. 'Welcome home. You're coming to dinner tomorrow night.'

'So I have just been informed.'

'Then you can tell us all about Simla. Meggy has just been whetting my appetite. Now I must run along and leave you two newlyweds to play house. Bye.'

She kissed them both again and hurried down the steps, waved on her way by Mansur. Margaret went as far as

105

the door, then returned, picked up her gin sling, and went on to the verandah, looking down at the city and the harbour, basking in the glow of the setting sun.

Larry followed her. 'Well?' he asked.

She didn't turn her head. 'Well, what?'

'What did you two old chums talk about?'

'Nothing that's any concern of yours, if that's what's bothering you.'

Larry sat in the swinging hammock. 'So we keep our skeletons in the closet. Do you like the house?'

'I think it's charming.' Still she stared at the harbour. 'I've made one or two . . . adjustments.'

'Oh, yes?'

'Pa always had a room of his own. I think you should have one too. There's an adjoining door.'

'Which you will keep locked.'

'No one need know that.'

'And don't you suppose the maids will know that my bed has been slept in every night?'

'As mine will have been slept in, Larry. They won't know who went to whom.'

'Meg, don't you think this farce has gone on long enough?'

Now she did turn, resting her thighs on the verandah rail. 'This "farce", as you call it, will go on for as long as I choose.' She spoke in a low, angry voice.

'And suppose I do the sueing for divorce?'

'On what grounds?'

'Well, I could try the withholding of conjugal rights.'

She tossed her head. 'You do that, and I'll ruin you. You know I can do that.'

They glared at each other, and he thought: what an incredible conversation to be having, in perfectly polite, well-modulated tones – they couldn't shout because the servants might hear.

But then, he had been living in an incredible world for the past four weeks. He wasn't even sure how it had happened. One moment they had been the most ardent of lovers, and the next she seemed to hate him.

106

At first he had been inclined to treat her anger, her outrage, as a joke. but when, the next day, she remained as cold as before, he had suggested divorce. 'I'm afraid we can't just have the marriage annulled,' he explained. 'It's been consummated. As a matter of fact, I'm not even sure we have grounds for divorce, but I'm sure they can be organised.'

'You want to divorce me?' she had demanded.

'No, I don't. I want you to be my wife. I want to make love to you. But if you don't want that . . .'

'I am certainly not going to divorce you,' she had declared. 'No one is going to make a laughing stock out of me.'

'Then come to bed.'

'I'll sleep on the sofa, thank you. and if you touch me, I'll have you charged with rape.'

'You don't think that will make you a laughing stock? Anyway, a wife can't charge her husband with rape.'

'Then you mean to rape me?'

'Oh, my God, what a conversation! No, I do not mean to rape you. I'm going to pray that you'll wake up one morning in a sensible mood. Until then, *I* will sleep on the sofa; *you* can have the bed.'

'Thank you.' She had gone into the bathroom to change into her nightgown; it was the first time since her marriage that she had worn one.

That had been three weeks ago. Three weeks of the sheerest hell. But how many more weeks, how many more years of this elaborate play acting lay ahead of him? Throughout their honeymoon, throughout the train journey back down to Bombay, when they had met her parents again, and throughout the voyage back to Singapore, when in company she had been a smiling, charming, even loving wife. But in private, she refused to let him touch her. Of course she had to get over that hump. But would they ever be the same again? Could they, now?

He had been tempted, more than once, to take her by force. But he was not that sort of person. He had never needed to be, until this moment. He had never, in fact, raised his fist even to a man, since his very earliest school-days. The thought of forcing Margaret was abhorrent to him.

But so was the thought of continuing this useless existence. Yet she *could* ruin him, as she had said, merely by withdrawing her support as his wife. It wasn't Larry Cairns who was being thrust up into the managership of the Main Accounts Department way before his time: it was Margaret Anstey's husband.

But might not even that be preferable to living such a sham? Then he could go looking for Chung Lan . . . and become a penniless wanderer. There were enough of those to be seen in the East, though they were more often brought down by drink than by a woman. He had no desire to become one of them. Chung Lan was lost forever. If he ever did see her again she would probably stick a knife in him.

'Yes,' he said wearily, and finished his drink. 'Well, I have some news for you. There's to be no long leave next year.'

'Why not?'

'No money.'

'That's incredible.'

'It's a fact of life even you are going to have to get used to, my darling.'

'Pa . . .'

'I am not going cap in hand to your father, Meg. And neither are you.'

She glared at him.

'Anyway,' he said. 'I don't suppose you'd want to go on long leave with me. We'd have to share a cabin on the boat, and my parents' spare room only has a double bed.' He got up. 'I'll go and have a shower before dinner.'

'I did want to go away next year,' Margaret said in a low voice. 'I think I'm pregnant.'

She had not, it seemed, even told Joan. She did so the following night, at the Lees's dinner party, which caused

108

an extra half dozen bottles of champagne to be opened for this additional celebration.

'Well,' Larry said as they drove home. 'Don't you think this might make a difference, to us?'

'I don't know,' she replied.

He understood this well enough. She was more confused than he. He was sure she found him desirable, even if he had never been absolutely sure she loved him. He was the most eligible young man she had been able to find, and so he had been selected as her husband. He had resented that from the beginning, but had swallowed his resentment in his awareness of her beauty and her value. Now she was the one doing the resenting.

He also understood something of her feelings, brought up as she had been. Not only had she never been introduced to 'that sort of thing', even by her mother in conversation, but she had also been educated to feel that there was something vaguely unclean about anyone with 'coloured' skin, that to be white necessarily meant good health and spotless linen.

The important thing was that she approximated 'colour' and deviant sexual practices.

But as she had said so candidly, divorce was out of the question, certainly while they were still virtually honeymooning. Also, he had no doubt that before their wedding she had told everyone that he was the most wonderful man in the world, and equally that she had sat in on private meetings between her father and Ronald Lees in which they had mutually decided to push him as hard as they could. To go back on that now would have everyone whispering that the real failure was hers. They would laugh at her.

Now she was pregnant, divorce was again impossible, for a considerable time. His heart went out to her, strangely. It was the one thing she must have feared. But surely it was the one thing that could bring them back together.

Mansur opened the front door to them. They went upstairs together, and he held her hand. 'I am so awfully proud of you, dear Meg,' he said. 'We are going to have a beautiful baby.'

'I hate you,' she whispered. 'I hate you! Why don't you go and find yourself an Indian?'

'Sit down, Tano, sit down.' General Tojo was all smiles. 'Tell me about Singapore.'

Kitachi bowed, and sank into the chair before the desk. 'There is little to report, honourable general. Sometimes I despair.'

'You, Tano?'

Kitachi sighed. 'There is so little anger down there, honourable general. I wonder if I am not wasting my time.'

'You have made many contacts.'

'That is true. I know a great many people, Chinese as well as Malay, who hate the British, who dream only of expelling them. But they do nothing but dream. To act is beyond them, even in personal matters.

'Let me give you an example. I know a man named Chung. His family trades out of Singapore, and has been there for three generations. He hates the British, because while he is as wealthy as anyone in the colony, he is not allowed into any of their clubs. Now he has additional cause. An English lout, one of those young men you told me to mark and hate, seduced and debauched this man Chung's daughter, and then abandoned her. Can you believe such dishonourable conduct?'

'What did this man Chung do?' Tojo asked.

'Nothing. Oh, he expelled his daughter from his house. No doubt she deserved that. But as regards the Englishman, nothing. There is nothing that can be done, he said. When I pointed out that this Englishman had treated him and his family as slaves, he agreed with me, but still insisted that there was nothing he could do without breaking the law. The law! I asked him what would happen had a Chinese man treated an English girl in that fashion? Would any law protect him? He was angry, but I could not budge him.'

'Nevertheless,' Tojo said. 'As you say, he is angry. And he will remain angry, with the British. A father whose daughter has been debauched does not forget. He may well be useful, before too long.'

Kitachi sat straight.

Tojo smiled. 'We have decided to act.'

Kitachi waited, his heart pounding.

'When Premier Hamaguchi was so sadly shot last May,' Tojo said, still smiling – Kitachi knew that the kempei-tai had almost certainly been involved in the Prime Minister's assassination, 'we had hoped for a more forward-looking ministry to be formed. But this fellow Wakatsuki is even worse than Hamaguchi. He says such things as that we cannot afford to maintain so large an army in the present economic climate; we cannot afford to press the Chinese in the present political climate; we cannot afford to thumb our noses at Britain and America and withdraw from the naval agreements, as Yamamoto would have us do, in any climate. He is totally passive.

'Well, we cannot simply assassinate another Prime Minister in hardly more than a year. Besides, some other nonentity might replace him. So we have decided to force the issue, in Manchuria. I will not tell you exactly how it is to be done. That must be a very closely-guarded secret. Suffice it to say that it will cause things to happen. It is very necessary for you to be on your guard, to be prepared to act.'

'You are speaking of war, honourable general?'

'It is certainly possible. In fact, I will go further than that. It is extremely probable.'

'With China?'

'That is almost certain.'

'And with Britain and America?'

'I have said, it is extremely probable.'

'Can you tell me when, honourable general?'

'No. Our plans are still in the course of preparation. But it will be within the year, I can tell you that. You must be prepared.'

111

'I will be prepared, honourable general. Am I to remain in Singapore?'

'Yes. When Great Britain declares war on us, as a civilian you will probably be interned. Thus you must set yourself up a system of communicating with your friends even from prison.'

'That will not be difficult.'

'By then, too, you must have prepared them to act. You must convince them that now is their chance to get rid of the British, but that they can only accomplish this with our aid.'

'I will do that, honourable general,' Kitachi said, eyes gleaming. Was this not the moment for which every Japanese soldier had been waiting, for more than ten years?

When he first saw Peking, Chung Kai at last felt his journey had been worthwhile.

He had gone by ship from Singapore to Canton, and stared in wonder at the muddy banks of the Pearl River, at the distant mountains which loomed on every side and made those of Malaya and even Sumatra seem like pimples.

But Canton had not impressed him as much as he had hoped. The people, his countrymen, were aggressive and certainly close to being Communists. They accepted Kuo-Min-Tang rule, but spoke of Chiang Kai-shek as a man to be feared rather than respected, hated rather than loved.

And the best architecture in the city was European. Perhaps it was French rather than British, but nonetheless it was distasteful to him.

Chung Kai wondered if he really hated the British.

Or just one man?

He did not think the latter. If he was appalled at the way Larry Cairns had accepted his friendship and the hospitality of his parents, and used them to seduce poor Lan, he had no doubt that any Englishman would have done the same. When he had been at Oxford his fellow students had boasted of their conquests, had seemed to consider any young woman perfectly fair game, without the slightest thought of dishonour, or of marriage.

No, the fault was his, for liking Larry Cairns, for supposing he might be different, for introducing an Englishman into his home. It was not a mistake he would make again.

But what if he never had a home again? He could no longer so regard Singapore. Even the beautiful house on the hill was distasteful to him now. He did not quarrel with his father's treatment of Lan. That was how it had to be, for the sake of the family name. But without her joyous laughter, her infectious energy, he no longer wished to live there.

Yet Singapore was the source of his father's wealth, and therefore of his own wealth as well. It was only because of Singapore that he could afford to travel the length and breadth of China in complete comfort, while the grip of the Depression was tightening throughout the world.

According to Kitachi Tano, it should be possible one day, perhaps in his lifetime, to throw the British out of Singapore, and thus make it again an acceptable place to live. Kai thought that would be an admirable deed, but he did not believe for a moment it would ever happen. Only one colonial people in all history had ever succeeded in throwing the British out, and the Americans had been British themselves. Besides, that had been a long time ago, when the British had been less certain of their God-given right to empire.

But if he was not going to live in Singapore, and he had no desire to emigrate to the United States and become just another faceless Chinese, that left only China, the land of his ancestors.

But certainly he could not make a home in Canton.

The House of Chung traded with many cities and many people in China, and Kai was equipped with letters of introduction to anyone Chung Lo had considered might be of use to him. These men, in Canton, entertained him, and spoke of nothing important. He was glad to leave.

From Canton he took ship again, round the coast to

Shanghai. To do this he sailed past the British colony of Hong Kong, but he had no desire to visit it. He had come on this journey to escape British colonialism.

The junk made its way between the islands into the mouth of the Yangtse, the mother of rivers, which rose in far-off Tibet and here debouched its tremendous torrent into the sea. It was a river of moods, which could not be predicted by those on the coast, for its floods and its droughts were entirely dictated by what was happening in the Tien Shan. But Kai's first sight of the coast was of the massive sea wall built to keep out both sea and flood water when the river was angry.

At Wu-Sun he disembarked, and caught a train into Shanghai itself, some miles up the Whang-Po tributary. To do this he had to pass by the International Concession, at which station the train stopped. He looked across the wire fence at the neat little houses in their neat little gardens, at the racecourse, at what was obviously a club, at automobiles hurrying along the well-maintained roads. There was apparently no escaping Western colonialism; this enclave of it was parked right on the Chinese mainland.

But the guards on the platform, there to make sure that no undesirable – that is to say, no Chinese – disembarked, were little brown men who wore the green uniforms of Japanese soldiers. He wondered what they would say or do if he insisted on leaving the train, and produced his British passport to prove his right to do so?

Shanghai itself had the reputation of being one of the largest cities in the world. Kai had been to the largest city in the world, London, and could well believe that this teeming metropolis was not much smaller, in terms of population. It was also, by repute, the trading centre of the Chinese nation, and this too he found easy to believe as he made his way through the crowded streets. But here all resemblance to London ceased. No dogs had barked at his heels and sniffed his trouser legs in Central London; the sidewalks in London had not been crowded with stalls selling everything from suits to contraceptives; no woman

114

had ever come up to him on Piccadilly, holding a twelve-year-old girl by her hand, and offered to sell her daughter; he had never seen the accountants and managers of Woolworth's doing their sums on the street with the aid of an abacus.

It was another world, and an unhappy one. Shanghai had been the centre of Chinese Communism. As the son of a long line of successful capitalists, Kai had no use for the Communist system. But as he had never seen it at work, he had no great antipathy towards it, either. But some people did, and at their head was Marshal Chiang Kai-shek. In the beginning he had been allied with the Communists, through the influence of Dr Sun Yat-Sen. But after Dr Sun's death the Marshal had fallen out with the Communist leaders, and determined to stamp them out of existence.

His first blow had fallen here in Shanghai, when his soldiers had invaded the city, forced its surrender, and then ruthlessly shot anyone with the slightest Communist affiliations. The Communists had been crushed; the survivors had fled south to the mountains where they waged a kind of continual guerilla war against the Kuo-Min-Tang forces. But in the city the hatred smouldered on.

Kai was glad to catch the train back down to the port.

He took a sampan upriver to Chin-Kiang, a slow journey against the current, but always interesting. The river, far more than the still-young railroad – there were no motor roads at all – was the highway of the country. Its course was dotted with cities only less great than Shanghai itself: Chungking, Hankow, Nanking – this last chosen by Chiang Kai-shek as the new capital of China. All of these needed the waterway of their trade, and thus the river had become a busy street on which sampans, junks under sail, steam-driven boats, and even some quite large ships, made their way constantly up and down.

But even here were the evidences of colonialism: British and American river gunboats, shallow-draft but heavily-armed war vessels, designed specifically for the task of patrolling Chinese rivers. Kai doubted they were actually for the protection of the Chinese.

Opposite Chin-Kiang began the Grand Canal, a waterway hardly less remarkable than the Yangtse itself for the fact that not only was it man-made, but it had been man-made some two thousand years ago when London, Kai reflected with some satisfaction, had been a river crossing for men who painted themselves blue.

The canal had been allowed to deteriorate over the centuries, but was still used by small craft making their way north to the Pei-Ho and thence to Peking, and although he had been warned against it on account of the time it would take and the discomfort it would involve, Kai was determined to use this means of reaching his goal: he would be living history.

The journey did indeed take a fortnight, and was both difficult and dangerous. A few years earlier, Kai was told, it would have been impossible, because then there was a clear delineation between that part of the country controlled by the Kuo-Min-Tang, south of the Yangtse, and that controlled by various warlords of whom the most powerful had been Marshal Chang Tso-lin, who claimed all the country north of the Great River as far as the Great Wall itself and even beyond, the huge land known as Manchuria. This area, considerably larger than France and Germany added together, included the old capital city of Peking.

Chang no longer ruled this vast territory; he had been assassinated back in 1928, when his train was blown up. It interested Kai to discover that no-one seemed to have any doubts that the bomb had been planted by the Japanese, who had found Marshal Chang – whose claimed territory in Manchuria abutted the Japanese colony of Korea – something of a nuisance.

Chang Tso-lin had been succeeded by his son, Chang Hsueh-liang, to whom Kai had a letter of introduction. The young Marshal, as he was known, imported Havana cigars through the House of Chung in Singapore. As to

116

whether Chang Hseuh-liang was any more amenable to Japanese infiltration was open to question, but he had succeeded in keeping himself alive. He had also had the sense to cease opposing Chiang Kai-shek, and now to some extent acknowledged the rule of Nanking. Thus passage up the canal was less dangerous, but the crew of the sampan on which Kai was travelling were nonetheless armed and prepared to defend themselves. There was much famine in this part of China, which had been fought over for so long, and thus a good deal of banditry.

On one thing everyone he met on his journey was agreed, the more so as he travelled north: they hated and feared the Japanese. He wondered what his father, so friendly with Kitachi Tano, would say to that.

The voyage took him through reed-filled lakes, beneath towering mountains, then across the Hwang-Ho, the Yellow River, scarcely smaller than the Yangtse. At last Kai arrived in Tientsin, the port for Peking, and once again had to admire the classical European architecture of the French cathedral in preference to the multi-roofed pagodas which sprang up either side.

He spent only one night in Tientsin before crossing the Pei-Ho to the railway station, to begin the very last leg of his journey, to Peking itself.

The railway ran from Tangku on the coast in a virtually straight line to Tientsin; then it performed a gentle curve which took it across the Pei-Ho a few miles north of its confluence with Han-Ho, and over the plain to the junction at Feng-tai. There Kai changed trains for the short run north to the terminus station at Hachiapo.

To reach here the train skirted the famous old Imperial Park, beneath the trees of which flocks of sheep were grazing. The countryside was quite lovely, in some contrast to the starkness further south. But Kai was already thinking only of the purple walls of Peking, and felt tears spring to his eyes as he saw them rising out of the plain.

It took him some time to understand why. His family came from the south. He had no actual affinity with this

117

huge and famous city, save that of history. But that was the affinity he sought.

Seated in his rickshaw, with another behind carrying his bags, he passed through the Yun-ting-men and up the Grand Avenue to the Chinese City, gazing at the Tien Tan, the Altar of Heaven on his right, the Altar to the Inventor of Agriculture on his left.

The Tsien-Men admitted him through the inner wall into the Tartar City, where he was driven past the Foreign Legations, all rebuilt since their destruction in the Boxer Rebellion only just over thirty years ago, but now hardly of importance in view of the rise of Nanking. His hotel was in this part of the city. He had no sooner been shown to his room than he was out again, to wander into the Imperial City, once the Forbidden City, and gaze at the famous buildings and temples in which the Manchu Ch'ing Dynasty had lived and ruled for three hundred years. The Ch'ing, dominated by the never-to-be-forgotten Dowager Empress Tzu Hsi, had been ruling China when he had been born. Now they were swept away, their secrets exposed to the prying multitude.

Here he could gaze at the Ornamental Water on which the Manchus had disported themselves, walk across the exquisitely carved bridges to the islands which had once been reserved for the Dowager Empress and her ladies, and look at the huge stone model of a Mississippi paddle steamer which that improvident old lady had caused to be erected for her pleasure – consuming in doing so, it was said, the entire year's budget for the Chinese navy.

More awe-inspiring than any of these relics of the recent past was the Altar to Heaven. He stood at the foot of the famous Dragon Staircase, so exquisitely painted as to suggest that the monster which filled it from top to bottom was actually moving, and gazed up at the three-tiered pagoda above. Here, in Kai's own lifetime, every 21 December by the Western calendar, the Emperor had sacrificed to Heaven to ensure a prosperous year. All gone!

But here, too, he could call upon Marshal Chang Hsueh-liang.

★ ★ ★

118

The Marshal was a dapper little man, surprisingly young – he was thirty-three – who, like his famous father, sported a drooping moustache and a remarkable uniform, the jacket of which seemed to possess more red tabs and red stripes at collars and cuffs than khaki cloth, and the left breast of which was covered in medal ribbons, most, Kai suspected, representing decorations created by the Changs themselves.

But he was courteous and smiling, and very knowledge-able, not only about China, but about world affairs. And like the majority of the people he ruled, he was concerned about the looming menace just to his east.

'I envy you, Chung Kai,' he remarked, 'living in a part of the world which is not only well removed from Japan, but lies beneath the embracing protection of the British. We could do with some of that protection up here, believe me.'

The world grew even more confusing, Kai thought. Which is best, to live in precarious freedom, threatened by an aggressive neighbour, or in contented inferiority, protected by a powerful overlord? But Chang Hsueh-liang had never sampled the second alternative.

'Now, you must tell me what you wish to do, where you wish to go,' Chang said jovially.

'Well, your excellency, I would count myself a poor traveller if I came this far and did not visit the Great Wall.'

'Ha-ha. Everyone wishes to visit the Great Wall. Me, I sometimes feel like pulling it down, as it neatly bisects my dominions. However, you shall visit the Great Wall. And then you must go on, into Manchuria, and visit Mukden.'

'Is it very beautiful?' Kai asked. He had not had any previous intention of going so far north.

'It is a great city,' Chang told him. 'The capital of my province of Manchuria. A visit there will also make you understand some of our problems. For instance, while Manchuria belongs to me, my illustrious father leased the right to build, and maintain and guard the railroad from

119

Mukden to Korea to the Japanese. This was admittedly in return for Japanese assistance in gaining his dominions, but it is nonetheless intolerable, is it not? Here we have armed Japanese soldiers riding the train and patrolling the stations, in the middle of my territory.'

'With respect, your excellency, there are armed Japanese soldiers patrolling the International Concession at Shanghai,' Kai ventured.

'What Chiang Kai-shek permits and what I permit are not necessarily the same things,' Chang pointed out. 'I permit this present situation only because it is called for in an agreement signed before I took office. I will be frank with you; as I have said, my father needed Japanese support to gain power, and they demanded a *quid pro quo*. This would be acceptable. But when they sought more and more, and my father realised that they had to be opposed, they had him murdered. And yet they continue to claim the rights he gave them. The Japanese government, of course, denies any knowledge of the explosion which blew up my father's train, and I am unable to obtain proof of their complicity. Thus I must sit out the terms of the agreement. It will be abrogated as soon as it can legally be done. However, I am sure you did not come all this way to talk politics. I have another reason for you to visit Mukden. The man I am going to ask to escort you to the Great Wall will be on his way back to Mukden, and would greatly enjoy entertaining you in his home. He is a close personal friend of mine, and also deals with the House of Chung. You will meet him at dinner, in my house, tonight.'

It obviously pleased the Marshal to describe the old Imperial Palace, in which he now lived, as his house. Equally it intrigued Kai, who had read his history, to think that this man's father, Chang Tso-lin, had been a common bandit who had seized this prize of prizes after the death of Yuan Shih-kai in 1916 and the consequent disintegration of all authority in North China.

Now the Marshal, his ladies, his aides and his guests,

dined off golden plates and goblets and used ivory food-sticks, while liveried footmen waited at their elbows, and invaluable hangings concealed the walls.

Kai was seated next to the Marshal, who had obviously taken a considerable liking to him, while on his other side was his future host, Wu Chen the Mukden merchant.

Chang, wearing tonight an amazing pale blue tunic over dark blue trousers, and was liberally bespattered with both medals and gold braid, was, as usual, expansively boastful.

'I was with my father when we rode into Peking in 1923. It was one of the most remarkable experiences of my life. You must remember that since the death of President Yuan, North China had been in a state of total anarchy. There were bandits everywhere. My father commanded the only disciplined troops for hundreds of miles.

'Peking was in the most anarchic state of all. There is nothing quite so breathtaking as a great city which has collapsed into human ruin, while its buildings are still intact.

'It was necessary to shoot quite a few people to restore order and the rule of law. But the truly emotional moment was entering this Forbidden City. Here were we, fighting men, soldiers, nothing more, suddenly masters of every secret of the Manchus. We were amazed. We were greeted by more than a hundred eunuchs, on their knees, begging for mercy.'

'What did you do with them?' Kai asked.

Chang gave a shout of laughter. 'Oh, we spared their lives. My father pensioned them off. Some of them are still alive. But there was more to come. We explored this palace like men entering the heart of another world. It is a labyrinth of inner courts and private apartments. The things we found! But do you know what was the most remarkable? At the end of one long corridor we entered a secluded court, off which opened two rooms. And in these rooms, shrieking their heads off as they saw us rough riders from the steppes entering their sanctuary, were two old ladies. They were imperial aunts or cousins who, like all imperial relatives, were entitled to perpetual board and lodging in the Imperial Palace. But these two ladies, unlike all the others, had neither fled nor been turned out following the Revolution in 1911. Amazingly, no-one apparently knew they were there, save their eunuchs. No-one had ever explored down this corridor. Thus they had lived for twelve years, as they had lived since birth – since of course they had never been permitted to marry – doing their sewing, their painting, walking in their little garden, brought food and drink in secrecy by their faithful eunuchs, until we arrived.'

'What happened to them?'

'They were pensioned off as well. They did not wish to leave. They wailed and screamed and tore their hair. They even begged us to shoot them. They had never lived anywhere but the palace, you see. They had never even seen outside the palace walls. They were terrified. But we found them a home, and I believe they are still alive.'

'That is the stuff of which novels are made, your excellency,' ventured Wu Su, Wu Chen's pretty daughter.

'Ha-ha,' Chang roared. 'I like a little more action in my novels. Now, if we had raped the poor old dears . . .'

Wu Su smiled politely and fluttered her fan.

Chung Kai was fascinated, not so much by the stories which were interesting enough, but by the woman with whom he was going to be spending the next few weeks, travelling. Mukden suddenly seemed a much more attractive prospect.

Wu Su was unlike any Chinese woman Kai had previously met, or had ever expected to meet. He was amazed to be told that she was twenty-four years old, only three years younger than himself, and that she was still unmarried.

Certainly she did not appear to have any physical defects. She wore a western-style evening dress – all the ladies did, as the men who were not in uniform wore dinner jackets – so he could tell that she had a good body even if he could not judge her legs; even more daringly, her black hair was worn short and just covered her ears.

Her face did not suffer from being exposed. She had somewhat bold features, suggesting there was Manchu in her ancestry. She made her mouth wider than it was with lipstick, and had added make-up to her eyes and cheeks.

But it was less her physical appearance than her manner which was arresting. For she had just returned from three years at college in the United States, spoke English perfectly and was perfectly willing to converse on equal terms with men, even the Marshal.

Anyone less like Lan could hardly be imagined. But anyone more exciting, when compared with the Chinese girls with whom he had grown up in Singapore – and one of whom his father expected him to marry – could also not be imagined.

Wu Su paid no more than polite attention to the guest of honour at Marshall Chang's dinner party. Afterwards there was western-style dancing, at which the younger officers and their wives – including the Changs – disported themselves, while their elders sat against the walls and no doubt deplored the habits of modern youth. Kai asked Su to dance, and they did a quick-step which earned applause.

'You must do a lot of dancing in Singapore,' she remarked.

'I did a lot of dancing at Oxford,' he countered.

He had not told her that little secret before, and she was impressed. They spent the rest of the evening comparing English and American universities, and she looked forward to continuing their discussion when they set off for home.

Kai was looking forward to discussing more than that. He felt as if this journey, undertaken in a mood of black despair, a sort of Chinese Pilgrim's Progress which would hopefully take him to a better land, had at last fulfilled itself. He did not suppose for a moment that Manchuria was a better land. But for the first time in his life he had

123

met a woman he could conceivably love, and with her at his side, even Singapore might be acceptable.

The railway ran from Peking to Mukden; Mukden was second only to Peking as the rail centre of North China. But the line ran steadily to the north-east, away from the Wall. Wu Chen quite happily agreed to take the young visitor from the south to see the Wall first, before catching the train.

They travelled by motor-car, a cavalcade of three, over an uneven road, stopping for the night at a Chinese inn. They made a jolly and intimate party, Wu and his wife, Su, Kai, and two officers sent by Marshal Chang. The officers wore resplendent uniforms and paid a great deal of attention to Su, but Kai was prepared to be as patient on this venture as he had been in his entire approach to life. The soldiers were certainly not on Su's intellectual level.

They went by way of the Nankow Pass, a narrow defile through craggy rocks surmounted by a temple to the God of Literature. The pass was blocked by a huge gateway, the centrepiece of which was a Buddhist arch, covered in exquisite carvings.

'They are scenes from Indian mythology,' Su explained. 'Some of them are quite indecent.' But she would not decipher them for him.

Not even the presence of Su at his side, in a skirt and a jumper and dark glasses, could distract Kai from the immensity of the Great Wall. He stood on the battlements and looked down at the rolling country beyond, and imagined that day some three hundred years previously, when Nurhachi had led his Manchu bannermen out of the steppes to complete the ruination of the Ming Dynasty.

What had those hardy horsemen felt as they had come face to face with this symbol of the eternity of Chinese power? They certainly had not let it stop them. But then, it had failed to stop so many marauders from the steppes in previous years.

It is not walls which repel an enemy, he thought; it is men who have hearts, and hopes, and determination.

The soldiers returned to Peking, while the Wu party went directly to the railway station. It was past mid-September now, and cooling. Soon the autumnal winds would be blowing, and would be followed by snow.

'Once we are home, we will stay there until the spring,' Wu Chen told Kai. 'When is the time for snow in Singapore?'

'There is never snow in Singapore, at any time of the year,' Kai replied.

Wu Chen looked at him in amazement, and Su clicked her tongue in annoyance at his embarrassment. Her father was a shrewd businessman but singularly ill-informed about anywhere south of Tientsin.

'In fact, I have only seen snow on a few occasions in my life,' Kai said. 'During my stay in England.'

'Then you have never truly seen snow,' Su pointed out.

'I would very much like to do so, but, I'm afraid I cannot possibly spend the entire winter here. Now, you have never been as far south as the Equator. I would very much like to show you Singapore.'

It was the first time he had ventured so much, and he found himself holding his breath.

Su had been looking out of the window. Now she turned her head towards him. 'Why, that sounds a delightful prospect. When could I come?'

Her directness took him by surprise. 'Well, you could return with me. I am going straight home from Mukden.'

She gazed at him. 'I shall have to think about that,' she said.

At least she had not immediately rejected the idea as unthinkable. She was a woman of the world, quite capable of travelling alone, or in the company of a man, without compromising herself, and no doubt without yielding herself either.

He found it a curiously exciting thought.

125

That afternoon they crossed the border into Manchuria proper.

'This is a country worth exploring,' Wu Chen told Kai. 'Quite close to where we are now is the burial ground of the Ch'ing Emperors. It is a most evocative place, where the tombs are guarded by gigantic stone animals.'

'Many of the tombs have been entered and looted,' Su said. 'It is very sad. But saddest of all, the Dowager Empress is buried there. Marshal Chang's father had the tomb opened, and discovered that grave robbers had got there before him. Do you know, they had criminally assaulted the corpse!' Her lip curled in disgust. 'How can men be so horrible?'

Towards dusk, they were drinking tea when the train suddenly ground to a halt. Several cups were spilt, and Mrs Wu exclaimed in disgust.

Wu Chen was also very angry, and opened the door to find the conductor and demand an explanation; in the corridor he found himself in the midst of a mass of people, shouting and complaining.

Kai rolled down the window and looked out. There was no sign of a station, or of any habitation at all, just the undulating Manchurian plain; there weren't even many trees.

But there was a group of horsemen jostling around the engine, and these were undoubtedly responsible for the sudden stoppage.

'Do you have bandits in Manchuria?' he asked Su, rather pleased to discover that he wasn't actually afraid, only excited.

'There are bandits everywhere,' Su told him. 'But they do not usually attack the railway line, certainly not this close to Mukden; we can only be about ten miles from the city. Besides, there are guards on this train.'

Kai looked out of the window again, and discovered she was right. To the horsemen there had been added a good dozen Chinese soldiers, who had climbed down from the carriage in which they had been riding, immediately behind the engine, and were engaging the horsemen in animated conversation.

Perhaps banditry in China is by negotiation, he thought, and sat beside Su.

'Do not be afraid,' he told her.

'I am not the least afraid,' she assured him.

Wu Chen appeared in the doorway, looking distinctly hot and bothered after pushing through the crowd. 'I cannot believe it.'

'What has happened?' asked his wife.

'There is fighting in Mukden, between our people and the Japanese. There was a bomb explosion yesterday, which destroyed part of the railway guarded by the Japanese. They are saying it is an act of war and are attempting to seize the town.'

Mrs Wu gave a cry of alarm.

'Can they do that?' Kai asked. He certainly hadn't come up here to become involved in a war.

'Well, there are a lot of Japanese soldiers encamped outside the town. They have been adding to them over this year. Far more than is needed to guard a railway.'

'What are we going to do?' Su asked.

'The train driver wishes to reverse his engine and return to Peking. The Marshal will have to be told what is happening.'

'The Marshal already knows what is happening, Papa,' Su told him. 'He will have been telegraphed.'

'If the Japanese have not destroyed the telegraph,' Wu Chen said gloomily.

'My home, my home,' moaned Mrs Wu. 'It will be looted by the Japanese.'

Kai looked out of the window again. It seemed that most of the passengers had disembarked, and were standing beside the track, arguing about what they should do. The evening was filled with high-pitched conversation, and there was a great deal of gesticulation.

'We must decide what we are going to do,' Su said again.

'I think we must go back to Peking,' her father said.

'Those horsemen say the Japanese are shooting civilians as well as soldiers. They will shoot us,' he glanced at his daughter, 'at the very least.'

My God, Kai thought; I *am* involved in a war. We all are.

He looked at Su, who looked back. Her face was expressionless.

Then they heard a noise. It was not a noise Kai had ever heard before, a distant sort of crrummp.

Wu Chen had certainly heard it before, however. 'Those are bombs,' he snapped.

One of the people standing beside the track gave a shout of alarm, and pointed.

Kai leaned out of the window again, and saw three biplanes flying towards them. They seemed to be travelling quite slowly, and they began to drop lower as he watched; they had sighted the train. He could make out their markings, a red sun exploding out of a white background.

He discovered Su was pressed against him at the window. 'Those are Japanese,' she said.

Dropping bombs? Even as Kai watched, little egg-like objects dropped from beneath the planes' fuselages, spiralling downwards to land beside the track, some sixty feet in front of the train. There were more explosions, and pieces of iron and wood mingled with the earth hurled skywards.

The watchers screamed, and Kai put his arm round Su's waist; she did not demur.

Another of the planes had flown behind the train, and now it too dropped its bombs. Again the earth shook.

'We are trapped,' Wu Chen said, joining them at the window. 'Oh, the scoundrels. We will have to walk back to Peking.'

Kai watched the planes. After dropping their bombs, so that the train was, as Wu Chen had said, unable to move either backwards or forwards, they had turned away as if leaving, and come together in formation. But now they were banking again, still in formation, and flying back towards the train, lower than ever, in line abreast.

The horsemen waiting around the engine galloped away as fast as they could.

One or two of the Chinese soldiers raised their rifles and fired at the approaching aircraft. But the aircraft had machine guns.

Kai watched, horrified as the planes opened fire. The people standing below gave a moan of apprehension, which rose to a gigantic wail of terror.

Kai tightened his grip on Su and threw her and himself heavily to the floor of the compartment. He kept on rolling, over and over Wu Su, to the door.

He got to his knees and dragged her through; she was still gasping from the fall. Suddenly, he saw Wu Chen falling back from the window as if pushed, his waistcoat an exploding mess of blood. The bullets cut across the floor where they had lain a moment before, tearing into the leather of the upholstered seats, and tearing too into Mrs Wu, as she sat there staring at them, alive one moment, dead the next.

Wu Su screamed.

CHAPTER 6
The Fury

Singapore was brilliant with Christmas lights and decorations as Chung Lo stood on the dock to greet his youngest son, who landed from the Hong Kong ferry. They embraced. Kai, having been supposed lost in the turmoil of northern China, had managed to send a wire from Hong Kong. There had been great rejoicing in the Chung household. Now there would be more.

Kai released his father, and turned to Su. She had held back, because she was the stranger here, the orphan brought in from the storm.

She had dressed herself carefully, in a quiet frock and a cloche, for this first meeting with Kai's family. She might have been what she was by instinct and education, an American woman. Her eyes were opaque. Externally, she had been less shocked than Kai by what had happened. Internally, he knew, she was a molten mass of confused emotions.

'Welcome to Singapore, my child,' Chung Lo said. 'Welcome to my home, daughter. You will replace the daughter I once had, and have now lost.'

Chung Su hesitated, looked at Kai, and then allowed herself to be embraced in turn. A tear trickled out of her eye and down her cheek. She did not often weep.

There were newspaper reporters waiting. Chung Lo had told everyone who would listen that his son was after all alive, and would be returning with his bride.

Questions were hurled at them, flash bulbs exploded. Kai answered as best he could, all the while urging Su towards the gangway and the safety of the launch. Chung Lo fussed around them like a protective hen.

They reached the dock, and the waiting automobile.

Chung Lo's chauffeur touched his peaked cap, and held the door for the three people to enter the cavernous interior of the Rolls-Royce.

Su looked around her with wide eyes. For all Kai's promises, she had not anticipated that Singapore would be so clearly prosperous, so modern and clean, so bustling, so . . . unafraid. Just as she had not anticipated that the Chungs could be so wealthy. She had never ridden in a Rolls before.

'There is something I must tell you.' Chung Lo said. 'Kitachi Tano is staying with us.'

Kai's head jerked.

'He is my friend,' Chung Lo reminded him.

'Father, do you not understand what the Japanese are doing?'

'They were set upon. They must defend themselves.'

'Who has told you this? Kitachi?'

'It is certainly what he believes happened. It is in the newspapers.'

'Even if it were true, does that permit them to kill innocent women and children, take over an entire country?'

'I am not a politician,' Chung Lo said.

'Who is this man, Kitachi?' Su asked.

Kai hesitated before replying. The murder of her parents was now three months in the past, and she had not stopped hating.

'He is a friend of mine,' Chung Lo said again. 'An old friend.'

'He is Japanese?'

'Yes, but he is not a soldier. He is deeply concerned about what is happening. You must understand this. But as I have said, he believes it was the Chinese who planted that first bomb.'

'That is not true,' Su said.

'He thinks it is. He thinks that explains why the Chinese have not gone to war, why they have pulled their soldiers out of Manchuria. Because they understand their guilt.'

'They have not fought for Manchuria because they were

131

forbidden to do so,' Kai told his father. 'Marshal Chang Hsueh-liang sent to Marshal Chiang Kai-shek for aid in defeating the Japanese, and was told there could be none. Marshal Chiang Kai-shek is fully occupied with fighting the Communists in the south. He told Marshal Chang Hsueh-liang to withdraw his men and let the Japanese have Manchuria. He is sending a delegation to the League of Nations to denounce the Japanese aggression.'

Kai could still remember the bitterness dripping from Chang's lips as he had read the fateful orders.

'The League of Nations,' he had said contemptuously. 'Will they aid me? Will they avenge your parents, Wu Su?'

The car was turning into the drive. Chung Tzu waited on the verandah, bathed in the lights of the lantern. With her was Kitachi Tano.

Chung Tzu wept as she embraced her son, and again as she took her new daughter-in-law in her arms.

'You will be married, here,' she said.

'We were married in Hong Kong, Mother,' Kai explained.

'But you must be married again, in the cathedral, with all our family there,' she insisted. She peered at Su. 'You are a Christian?'

'Yes, Mother, I am a Christian,' Su said. But she was looking at Kitachi.

Kitachi bowed to Kai. 'Your return, safe and sound, greatly relieves my heart, Chung Kai. What is happening in Manchuria is not your quarrel. Your future is here.'

'Is not my future Chinese?' Kai asked him.

'Singapore Chinese. It is here.' He bowed to Su. 'Please accept my humble condolences upon the death of your parents.'

He had been fully briefed by the Chungs.

Chung Su's face was cold. 'Your Japanese soldiers murdered my parents. Will you denounce them?'

Kitachi's face stiffened. 'I cannot, Mrs Chung. They were carrying out orders.'

Kai frowned. The Japanese government had claimed

from the first day that their army in Manchuria had acted without orders. Indeed, they were unable now to order them to cease fighting and return to their cantonments.

Su's face was colder still. 'Then you too are a murderer,' she told Kitachi.

Chung Lo walked in the garden with Kai after dinner.

'I hope your wife will not prove disruptive,' he said.

'She hates all Japanese. Thus, at this moment, she hates Kitachi Tano.'

'You must persuade her he is not as the soldiers who killed her parents.'

'I will endeavour to do so, Father. If you will persuade *me* that he is not.'

Chung Lo stopped walking and frowned at him. 'How can you say that?'

'Because we know nothing of this man.'

'He came to us with a letter from Wong Tung. Wong Tung and I have done business together for years. I would trust him more than anyone. And did he not entertain you in Canton?'

'Wong Tung did entertain me in Canton, Father. Therefore I have met him, where you have only corresponded with him. I met a great many people in China. It is a huge, confused country. In the south there are many Communists, who hate Chiang Kai-shek more than they hate anyone.'

'Wong Tung is not a Communist.'

'Agreed. Not openly, at any rate. But he hates Chiang Kai-shek as much as any Communist. To people in the far south, who have never seen the Japanese, who do not understand their ambitions, they seem like useful allies in attaining their ends. Wong Tung is certainly one who thinks like that.'

'Who is to say he is not right? I hear little good of Chiang Kai-shek.'

'There have been others who have sought Japanese aid to advance themselves, to get rid of their enemies. One such was Marshal Chang Tso-lin. The Japanese helped him become ruler of the north. But when he sought to oppose them they had him murdered. Now his son, Chang Hsueh-liang, is their enemy, but he cannot oppose them without help. He has learned his lesson too late. One should pray that Wong Tung and his friends do not also have to learn a severe lesson.'

'The Japanese are the hope of Asia,' Chung Lo declared. 'Do you suppose Britain will go to war in defence of China?'

'Hardly, since China has not gone to war in defence of itself.'

'Suppose the League of Nations condemns Japan as the aggressor? Kitachi thinks it is possible this will happen.'

'I should think he is absolutely right, as they are the aggressors.'

Chung Lo ignored the point Kai made. 'Then is it not likely that Britain will go to war on behalf of the League?'

'That will have to be seen.'

'If the British go to war,' Chung Lo said, speaking very earnestly, 'Kitachi says we must be prepared to throw off their yoke, and declare our independence.'

Kai stared at his father in dismay. 'You are speaking treason.'

'I am speaking to my son, in confidence. Should there be such a war, the Japanese will need Malayan rubber and tin, and Indonesian oil. They are prepared to seize these things. Kitachi has told me this. He has also told me that if we assist them, they will guarantee our independence.'

'Kitachi has said all this?'

'In confidence. You will not betray this confidence.'

'Has he said what will happen to us when Japan is defeated?'

'Japan will not be defeated. Britain will not fight for long, at so great a distance from her homeland. Kitachi has told me there are Japanese agents even in India, ready to raise them in rebellion. The British will have their hands full. And do you not think there are many people in the world, in the League of Nations, who will be happy to see an independent Malaya, an independent Indonesia? Are you not one of them?'

Kai realised that he had never thought in terms of an independent Malaya, only an independent Singapore.

'Did not your British friend destroy my daughter? Your sister?' Chung Lo hissed.

Chung Kai preferred not to think about Larry right now.

'And what if America supports Britain?' he asked.

'Kitachi says that will not happen. America will not fight for the British Empire.'

That, at least, could be true, Kai thought. But his head was still spinning with the import of what he had been told.

'Kitachi wishes us to prepare ourselves for the outbreak of war. He does not wish us to take any risks, begin any political movements. When war is declared, he merely wishes us to oppose it, without being subversive. He wishes us to convince all the Chinese in Singapore to do this. He is already sure of the Malays. And then, when the Japanese fleet appears off Singapore, and the British are driven out, you and I and your brothers will be given positions of authority in the community.'

Kai snorted. 'And has Kitachi also told you that in the opinions of most experts Singapore is impregnable? You have seen the guns covering the sea. Any warship approaching the island would be blown out of the water.'

'Kitachi says it will fall. I do not understand military matters, I wish to know if you are with me in this, or if you will betray our aspirations.'

'I will never betray your aspirations, or yourself, Father,' Chung Kai said. It would never be necessary, because no Japanese fleet would ever appear off Singapore. Of that he was quite certain.

'Then you must persuade your wife to think likewise. Do not tell her anything of our conversation. It is unnecessary and it would disturb her. But convince her that what is happening in Manchuria is no longer any concern of hers. We all grieve for the death of her mother

135

and father, the loss of her home. But we have given her another home, here, where she will be happy and give me strong grandsons. Singapore is her country now, and her future. You must persuade her of these things.'

'I will certainly try, Father,' Kai agreed. Because in that, at least, they were in agreement. For Su to continue brooding on what had happened outside Mukden, and hating, would be to destroy herself. He could not stand the thought of that.

Chung Su sat at her dressing table and carefully removed her make-up with various cleansers.

Kai loved to watch her, for she had undressed, and was naked. Her skin was the most fascinating thing about her, for it was very white, not pinkish-white like a Caucasian, but pure white, and yet not dead, but rather glowing with an indefinable sheen. In the strongest contrast her nipples were dark brown and her pubes silky black; that mat apart she had little body hair.

As he suspected and hoped the first time he saw her, she had wide thighs and sturdy legs; if her breasts were small they were full and high. She was made to be a mother.

And a woman like Su would be the mother of fine strong sons, who would also have minds of their own.

He had discovered all of these things during the trauma of their escape from Manchuria, their flight from China, when they had necessarily been thrown into great intimacy.

They had lain in the corridor of the train for half an hour, huddled against each other, while the Japanese planes strafed until they ran out of ammunition. After her initial scream Su had lain still, drawing strength from his body, from his own determination to survive.

When the planes had gone, and they had ventured outside, they had been aghast. The people beside the train had run for shelter, but there was no shelter on the open plain. Now there were nothing but crumpled masses, and trailing blood, and the stench of death and fear.

It had not been possible to bury so many, with the survivors in a state of terror that Japanese soldiers would follow the planes. Chung Kai and Wu Su had buried Su's father and mother, themselves, scratching shallow graves using the bayonets of two of the dead soldiers. Then they had walked back to Peking.

Kai had armed himself with a rifle and bandolier as well as the bayonet he had used to dig the grave, and had felt rather an heroic figure, even if he had no idea how to use the weapons. But Su had been proud of him, and had picked up a rifle and cartridge belt as well.

It had taken them two days to regain Peking, and it would have taken longer had they not encountered another train, loaded with soldiers, feeling its way towards the Japanese position. That had been before peremptory orders had come from Chiang Kai-shek not to go to war, but to pull out of Manchuria and await events. Chang Hsueh-liang's soldiers, no less than the marshal himself, had felt betrayed by that.

By the time they encountered the soldiers, Kai and Wu Su had learned to rely on one another. There had been no food for those two days, and only a little dirty water from a muddy stream. yet they had known they would survive, and each had watched while the other slept.

In Peking there had been food, and water to bathe in as well as to drink. Chang Hsueh-liang had been solicitous; Wu Chen had been a good friend.

'You will have an apartment, here in my house,' he had told Su.

Su had looked at Kai. 'I would like to leave China,' she said.

Chang Hsueh-liang had given them his blessing. Their clothes had been left on the train; their suitcases had in any event been torn apart by machine-gun bullets. Chang had new clothes made for them, and had given them sufficient money to get home: it would be repaid by the House of Chung. He had asked no questions as to their relationship.

That had been already established in their minds, even

if Kai had never asked her, and had never touched her sexually. He would not, until they were married. And then was not the time to speak of marriage. He had only known Su a week, and her parents had just been most horribly murdered.

He had spoken of it in Hong Kong, still not knowing what she thought of him. He was a port in a storm, and he was sheltering her from the storm that was Manchuria. He had felt he was taking advantage of her, but had not been able to stop himself. He said, 'When you are able to stop grieving, I would like to marry you. I know what I am doing is incorrect, but there is no one but you whom I can ask.'

She had raised her head to look at him. 'I would like to marry you,' she said. 'Can it be done now?'

From that moment he had known great joy. Although he reflected that a man should not know joy after having watched people killed so that he might attain his ends, he could also reflect that the immutable laws of yin-yang – that the reverse side of every good is evil – equally establishes that the reverse side of every evil is good. He and Su were good. He had felt, from the beginning, that here was a woman he could love; now he did love.

And he felt she loved him too.

'You walked with your father a long time,' she said.

'We had much to say to each other, after so long.'

'Of my rudeness?'

'Of how much he likes you. And wishes to love you. Do you like them?'

'They are your father and mother. They are my father and mother, now.'

Kai undressed and washed himself, then sat in the armchair. It was a large armchair, his favourite. As he watched her, he became ready for her. It was not difficult, watching her.

'My father wishes you to be happy. He begs you to forget the past and look to the future. He knows no one can entirely do this, but he begs you to try. My father

138

and mother have known only happiness, here in Singapore, save in the matter of my sister. I wish you to understand this.'

She finished with her cleansers, went into the bathroom to wash herself. When she returned she came to him. She moved without coquetry, but with much grace.

'I understand this. Tell me about your sister. Is she dead?'

'I do not know. Neither do my parents. She disgraced our name, and had to leave.'

Su shivered. 'She must be very lonely.'

'Would you have had us do otherwise?'

She shook her head. She climbed on to his lap, placing one knee on each side of his thighs, holding his shoulders until she was in position, then slowly lowering herself on to him. It was the way they both liked best, for it seemed that he was entering her forever. She sighed, as she encased him, and leaned forward to rest her head against his cheek.

'I will never disgrace your house, Kai. I swear this on the memory of my mother and father.'

'Congratulations,' Ronald Lees said to Larry. 'What does it feel like to be a CPA?'

'It's a relief not to have all that studying to do any more,' Larry confessed.

'Well, now no one can say you're not worth the job. Not that you weren't worth the job even without the qualification. Yes, indeed. Meg must be pleased.'

'I'm sure she is.'

Lees frowned at his protégé. 'All well there, I hope?'

'Well, of course.'

'Marion well?'

'She suffers from prickly heat.'

'Don't we all. Well . . .' Lees fidgeted with the pens on his desk. 'No thought of a little brother for her?'

'Not at the moment.'

'You don't want to leave it too long.'

Definitely, Larry thought, the boss has been hearing

139

rumours. As he was quite certain Margaret had kept to her resolve not to confide in Joan, or any of her other friends, it was probably by way of the servants' grapevine. The servants were not by any means as unimaginative as Margaret seemed to think they were. It wasn't enough that both beds were always slept in; they could tell when there had been sex in either, and there never had been.

'I'm sure the little fellow will come along in due course,' he said equably. Years of mock marriage had made him a very convincing liar.

'Oh, quite. Tell me, what do you think of your friend Chung Kai's adventures?'

'I've been reading about them in the papers. They sound horrendous.'

'Well, he seems to have done all right out of it, judging by the photograph of that wife of his.'

'What do you think is going to happen?' Larry remembered sitting down with Inspector Delaney to tell him everything he knew about Kitachi Tano.

'About Manchuria? Damn all.'

'But, we can't just let one nation take chunks of another. Can we?'

Lees grinned. 'We spent a couple of hundred years doing just that, my boy, and prospering.'

'We had to beat other people to do it.'

'So let the Japs beat the hell out of the Chinks, if they can. It's all a long way away.'

'You told me once that the day might come when we'd have to fight the Japanese.'

'It might very well. But it isn't going to come over Manchuria, you can bet your bottom dollar on that. Bring Meg up to dinner tonight, and we'll celebrate your certificate.'

'Thank you, sir.'

Ronald Lees, Larry thought, lived from one celebration to the next.

Before he went home, he wrote Kai a note, congratulating him both on his marriage and on his safe return.

Predictably, he did not get a reply.

* * *

140

Ronald Lees was proved absolutely correct in his prognostication. Marshal Chiang Kai-shek duly denounced the Japanese invasion of Manchuria to the League of Nations, and the League appointed a commission to investigate the truth of the situation. Gratifyingly for the British, the commission was headed by an Englishman, the Earl of Lytton.

While this investigation was continuing, the Japanese declared the independence of Manchuria, which they renamed Manchukuo, and established as ruler the last surviving Manchu Emperor, Pu-Yi, who as a little boy had been forced to abdicate the Throne of Heaven in 1911.

They also landed seventy thousand men in the vicinity of Shanghai and defeated the Chinese 19th Route Army in a pitched battle, forcing the Chinese to call off the economic boycott of Japanese goods which had been instituted following the 'Mukden Incident'.

In all of these things they were scrupulous to avoid in any way harming any Europeans or Americans, or their property, but when, predictably, the Lytton Report, presented to the League on 2 October 1932, condemned their actions as naked aggression and suggested that the creation of Manchukuo had been undertaken without the whole-hearted consent of the Manchurians, the Japanese showed their contempt for the Western powers by continuing their advance into Jehol, immediately north of Peking, and by March of the following year their troops were south of the Great Wall.

In fact, the immediate success of the Mukden coup had caused the fall of the ministry of Premier Wakatsuki, He had been replaced by another civilian, Ki Inukai, who in turn was assassinated in May of 1932, after which the army unashamedly took control of the country. Thus, after the publication of the Commission's report, followed by the League's recommendation that it be accepted and that Japan withdraw immediately from Manchuria to allow the setting up of an independent country under Chinese suzerainty, Japan announced her withdrawal from the League, at the same time denouncing the naval treaties which had limited her navy to two thirds the size of the British and American fleets.

To most people, even those in Singapore, what was happening in north-east China seemed very remote; as the economic blizzard grew colder there was too much to be thought about closer to home. Yet there was a ripple of alarm before it became obvious that the League had no intention of backing any of its resolutions with force. The United States Secretary of State, Henry Stimson, contented himself with suggesting that the Japanese occupation of Manchuria not be recognised, and this was agreed.

Such a resolution made little difference to the Japanese.

Kitachi returned to Tokyo for consultation with General Tojo a sorely puzzled man.

'I had everything prepared, honourable general,' he complained. 'And now, nothing. What am I to do?'

'Be patient, Tano. You are promoted to Colonel.'

Kitachi bowed. 'Then am I allowed to resume my place in the kempei-tai, honourable general?'

'You have never given up your place in the kempei-tai, Tano. But I do not wish to have you back in uniform just yet. There are great events in the making, and Singapore is still of much importance to us. I wish you to continue in your present role for the moment.'

'I do not know that I can maintain my position *vis-à-vis* the Chinese and Malays for much longer without something developing, honourable general.'

'Of course you will do so, Tano. Have we not proved the greatness of Japan? Have we not defied the world and forced it to bow to our will? Are we not therefore more desirable as friends than ever, by the downtrodden peoples of South East Asia? Remind your friends of this, and remind them, too, that when we choose to move further afield, then will we also triumph. It is up to them to triumph with us, or perish.'

Kitachi bowed.

★ ★ ★

142

It was on Christmas Eve the following year, 1934, that Ronald Lees called Larry into his office.

'Looking forward to long leave?' he inquired.

'Well, sir . . .'

'Of course you are. And you need it. You've been out here seven years now. Too long. It'll do Meg good too. She's not looking her best.'

'Yes, sir,' Larry said. Both he and Margaret had been aware that the crisis of long leave was looming, but they had not yet discussed it although he knew she wanted to spend some of it with her parents in Bombay.

'And I want you at your best this coming year,' Lees continued.

Larry waited. He knew his employer's weakness for keeping people on tenterhooks.

'How old are you, Larry?'

'Twenty seven, sir.'

'Hm. Young. But still our best man. When you come back from England, I'd like you to take the Hong Kong office.'

'Sir?' Larry sat up straight.

'I've recommended Burns for early retirement. Well, between you and me, I've sacked him. The thing is, Larry, as you well know, this stagnation is not going to cure itself. We all had great hopes of Roosevelt, and I think some of his ideas are sound, but he's having to hurry slowly because of the amount of opposition he's meeting in the States. And until their economy takes off, the world economy isn't going to take off again, either.

'But that doesn't mean we can't help ourselves. We're starting to show good profits again here in Singapore. Hong Kong is not. Burns claims it's because all trading up there is upset by this niggling unofficial war that's going on, plus Chiank Kai-shek's private war with the Communists. He says he cannot conduct any proper negotiations with the people in Shanghai because the Japs have virtually put an embargo on the Chinks dealing with anyone but themselves. There may be some truth in that, but you're not going to tell me that a young, ambitious, talented manager wouldn't be able to go out and get business. That's what I want you to do, Larry. You have Canton and Shanghai, two of China's biggest ports, virtually on your doorstep. I want you to put Hammond and Teng back on the map in Hong Kong and on the China coast, and back in the black. Will you take the job?'

Larry hesitated. He couldn't imagine what Margaret would say to leaving the home she had made for herself here, or the cosy social life, the bridge afternoons and the tennis matches and the cocktail parties, which she had set up.

'I may say,' Lees went on, 'that I have spoken with Brian Anstey, in confidence, of course, and he is entirely in agreement with my choice. I may also remind you that the manager of the Hong Kong branch is generally regarded as a future Managing Director of the company, provided he makes a success of it. Did you know I am due to retire in 1944? How old will you be in 1944?'

Ten years' time. 'I'll be thirty seven.'

'You could be sitting in this chair at thirty seven, Larry. You'd be *tuan bezar* – the Chief of Commerce – of Hammond and Teng. Think of that.'

Larry did think of that. Presumably Meg would enjoy thinking of it too, And if she didn't, well . . . his rising in the company while remaining in a state of constant humiliation at home was part of their bargain.

Yet he still felt some protest was in order. 'It'll upset a lot of people, sir,' he said. 'I mean, what about Roly? He's years senior to me, and he's a good man . . .'

'Larry, some men are management material, others aren't. Roly isn't. It's as simple as that. Now, do you want the job or not?'

Indeed he did want the job because, he was realising, it was the biggest chance of his life, in every direction, if he handled it right.

'I should be very happy to accept, sir,' he said. 'Providing it is understood that I cannot improve the Hong Kong figures without taking some pretty radical steps. I mean, things aren't going to get better just by patience.'

'I never thought they would. That's why I've chosen you to put things right. You have *carte blanche*. Just give me advance warning if you intend to fire anyone. But keep the appointment under your hat for the moment. I'll announce it on New Year's Eve.'

Even in the euphoria of the quite staggering appointment, Larry's mind had flickered ahead to how it could be made to work. The only way it *could* be made to work, if he had the guts to do it, would be the most radical, perhaps unethical – especially in present circumstances – approach to business any employee of the firm had ever tried.

And he had only his hunch, and Delaney's suspicions, on which to go. He might be proved utterly wrong, in which case disaster would be total. But he knew he was going to try it. He might be a mouse in his own household, but he had his eyes firmly set on the Managing Director's chair. Because not only was that the only reason for accepting his private humiliation, it was also, so far as he could see, the only way of ever reversing his situation. No one could fire a Managing Director except the Board of Directors; in ten years' time neither Brian Anstey nor Ronald Lees would have any say in company affairs.

As for patriotism, if in four years Delaney had never found enough cause to act, then it was time he used his information for his own profit.

He left the office and drove to the Nipponese Trading Company on Robinson Street. There was some demur when he requested an interview with Mr Kitachi, but when he sent his name up he was admitted quickly enough.

'Mr Cairns.' Kitachi Tano stood behind his desk and bowed before shaking hands. 'This is a great pleasure. Please sit down. You will take whisky?'

Larry looked at his watch. It was quarter past twelve. 'Yes, thank you.'

Kitachi smiled as he opened the bottom drawer of his desk. 'You English, always drinking by the clock.'

'It's better than being drunk,' Larry pointed out.

145

'Indeed.' Kitachi half filled two tumblers. He did not offer ice or water. 'Do you know that you are the very first member of the staff of Hammond and Teng to sit in this office? I am greatly honoured.'

'I have come to ask a favour,' Larry said.

'My dear Mr Cairns, anything I have is yours.'

'I am being sent up to Shanghai on business,' Larry said. 'And I am informed that your people are making it rather difficult to obtain access into the city at the moment.'

Kitachi bowed. 'There are many problems up there.'

'I'm sure there are. But I thought that if you would give me a letter of introduction to the Japanese commanding officer, asking him to give me all the assistance in his power, it might help.'

Kitachi raised his eyebrows. 'I, Mr Cairns? What influence could I expect to have with a Japanese general?'

'Come now, Mr Kitachi, Mr Chung has told me that you are really quite an important man in Japan. You are certainly the only Japanese to have established himself in Singapore. I am sure your name must carry some weight.'

Kitachi allowed himself a modest smile. 'It is gratifying to hear your thoughts, Mr Cairns. But, even supposing you are right in your assumption, are you not asking me to perform a most remarkable favour? My house is endeavouring to create business for itself. It is natural for me to look to Shanghai as an outlet. Why should I encourage so great a house as Hammond and Teng to share my market?'

Larry smiled back. 'Simply because, if you do not, you may find yourself expelled from Singapore.'

Kitachi frowned at him.

'I have a friend named Delaney,' Larry went on. 'I am sure you know the name. Perhaps you have met him. He is a police officer, and he is in command of what we British call the Special Branch, here in Singapore. Suppose I were to tell you that he has a large file on you and your activities? If he has not yet arrested you and charged you with subversion, and then closed your business and expelled

146

you, it is because he feels that it is quite useful to have you here, known to him, so that he can keep an eye on you, instead of having to find your probable successor.'

Kitachi gazed at him. 'You know these things?'

'I have said, Inspector Delaney is my friend.'

'And you are telling me these things? You are betraying a confidence.'

Larry shrugged. 'Mr Delaney has a job to do. So have I. I wish to make a success of my job.'

Kitachi studied him for a few minutes longer. Then he said, 'And if I give you this letter of introduction, I will be allowed to remain in Singapore?'

'You have my word.' Larry held up his finger. 'Providing you are discreet.'

'Indeed. The commanding general in Shanghai is General Abe.'

'Do you know him?'

'We have a slight acquaintance. He used to command in Korea. I will give you your letter, Mr Cairns. And I thank you for your warning.' He smiled at Larry. 'It is good to know that there are Englishmen who put profit before . . . shall I say, authority? Perhaps it will be possible for us to do business again together, at some time in the future.'

Larry grinned. 'Who knows, Mr Kitachi. Who knows.'

Larry decided not even to tell Meg about his new appointment. Of course he had no intention of telling anyone about his interview with Kitachi. It was not something he would ever be proud of; he was well aware that Kitachi had really meant that he was putting profit before patriotism. But Hammond and Teng, and therefore Larry personally, would be laughing all the way to the bank, no matter how contemptible Kitachi might consider him. Yet Margaret's possible reaction to the news that she was leaving her home, even temporarily, was potentially explosive; he found himself feeling quite nervous as they dressed for the dinner dance at the club.

For all that had happened, or rather, not happened,

147

over the past four years, he still dreamed of a reconciliation with Margaret. Often he felt savage resentment towards her and the way she had made his life a sham, but there were also occasions when he wanted her with a yearning which was almost desperate. She grew more lovely with every year, as her face took on a little maturity; if only her mind would do the same.

They spent more time together nowadays, since the birth of Marion. They both adored the little girl, and wanted to spend as much time with her as possible. But there was no softening in Margaret's attitude towards the sexual side of their marriage.

He wondered if Brian and Julia Anstey's marriage had been similarly barren, which would explain why they had also had only one daughter.

He realised, studying the other married couples around them, that his situation might not be as uncommon as he had first supposed. Nearly all his friends and acquaintances kept a 'bit' on the side, and supposed he did too. If he didn't, it was purely because he knew that to do so would not only be to surrender to Margaret's repeated insults, but would also reinforce her position and make that eventual reconciliation impossible to achieve. Presumably the others had reached some sort of accommodation with their wives. Well, presumably he had reached some sort of accommodation with Margaret, but it was a negative one.

He also felt that she was fortified in her position by her friends, most of whom were older than herself. If she did not confide in them she could certainly study them as much as he did, and no doubt draw the same conclusion, that she was not in any way unique. To get her away from them and their opinions, to throw her entirely on him for company, at least until she made new friends, seemed to be his best chance of remaking their relationship.

They kissed Marion goodnight, and were as usual waved away from the house by Mansur.

Mansur! Larry thought. He would certainly wish to

take Mansur to Hong Kong. He wondered what the butler would think of that idea.

They drove in silence. There wouldn't have been much chance to speak anyway, because downtown Singapore was one enormous cauldron of sound, with firecrackers exploding, people shouting, dogs barking, car and motorbike engines roaring, cyclists weaving to and fro before and behind them. But they always did drive in silence.

'These people certainly seem to know how to enjoy themselves,' Larry shouted.

'It's New Year's Eve,' she shouted back, staring straight ahead.

Margaret was surrounded by men eager to mark her card, immediately they arrived at the club. In her high-necked dark green crêpe dress, which had skilful draperies across the bodice and at the waist, and her usual silver *lamé* accessories, she was the most striking woman in the room. She was wearing her hair longer, nowadays, and its auburn waves were utterly lovely.

Larry found himself next to Joan Lees. Politely he marked her card twice for waltzes; she waltzed very well.

She frowned at it. 'You realise you've marked the midnight waltz.'

'Oh, have I? Well, if you'd rather have it with someone else . . .'

'My dear Larry, there is no one else in all Singapore I would rather dance the midnight waltz with! But what about your wife?'

'Ah . . . I should imagine she's already been asked.'

'Well, she shouldn't have been.' Joan clasped his hand and led him across the room. 'May your husband have a look in, Meggy?'

Margaret raised her eyebrows. 'If he hurries.'

Joan took the card away from her. 'There,' she said. 'It's free.'

'Oh,' Larry said. 'Well, then . . .'

'I'll just scratch you out from mine,' Joan said, 'and put you down here.' She looked from one to the other.

149

'If you don't dance together, I shall start to believe all these rumours.'

'All what rumours?' Margaret challenged.

'All the rumours I know can't possibly be true,' Joan said, and swept away.

Margaret was left staring at Larry.

He shrugged. 'The old boy was on about it too. Seems we'll just have to mend our ways.'

She tossed her head and turned away, to find her partner for the first dance.

They did not encounter each other until at eleven o'clock there was a drum roll, and the MC announced that Mr Ronald Lees had something to say.

Lees took the podium and smiled at them. 'Just a quick word, ladies and gentleman,' he shouted. 'Some of you may know that Jimmy Burns has decided to retire from our Hong Kong office. We shall be sorry to see him go. Jimmy was always one of our best and brightest. But of course his departure means that we have to find a new manager for Victoria. Well, I can tell you now, that our board of directors have chosen the very best man they could find for the job, Larry Cairns.' He paused to let that sink in, and there was a moment of surprised silence before someone started to clap.

Lees raised his hands for quiet. 'I know cricket in Singapore will be the poorer, but cricket in Hong Kong will be the richer, eh? Ladies and gentlemen, I give you our youngest ever branch manager, Larry Cairns! And Margaret, of course.'

There were cheers and kisses and handshakes, and the man who had marked Margaret's card for the next dance gallantly offered to stand down in favour of her husband.

'I'm sure that won't be necessary,' Margaret protested.

'But I insist.'

She found herself in Larry's arms, with the band playing a slow fox trot.

'I suppose you knew all about it,' she remarked, looking over his left shoulder. She was speaking quietly, but he could tell that she was seething with anger at having been

150

left out of the secret; she regarded his advancement as being entirely at her discretion.

'I was told just before Christmas.'

'And decided I wouldn't be interested.'

'Ronald wanted it kept a secret. And he's the boss.'

'And suppose I don't want to go?'

'Now Meg . . .'

She was as he had feared, very clearly going to make a big issue out of it.

'Why should I uproot myself to go to a dump like Hong Kong? I like it here.'

But at last she could be challenged, directly. 'You are being absurd, as usual. Hong Kong is not a dump. It is a very lovely place. It is also the opportunity of a lifetime, as Ronald has pointed out. My appointment was recommended by your father, and I have accepted it. If you start pushing oars in now, and behaving like a spoilt little girl, you are going to look like a fool. And you don't want that, do you?'

She stopped dancing to stare at him. He had never spoken to her like that before.

'You bastard,' she said.

'I do hope you're going to behave yourself, darling,' he said, keeping his voice down. 'You said that rather loudly.'

'I'll speak as loudly as I damned well please,' she shouted.

Heads turned, people stopped dancing, and then the music stopped as well.

Lees had been dancing with his daughter. Now they came hurrying across.

'What on earth's the matter?' Lees asked in a stage whisper.

'Margaret is unhappy about moving to Hong Kong,' Larry said. He was enjoying himself for the first time in years, because she had put herself so utterly out of court.

'Now, really, Meg,' Lees protested.

'Oh, why don't you go to hell!' Margaret snapped at

151

him. She had also realised her predicament, but didn't know how to extricate herself from it.

'Meggy . . .' Joan attempted.

'Shut up, all of you. It's all a conspiracy. A bloody conspiracy,' she shouted, and ran from the room.

Everyone looked at everyone else.

'She must have had too much to drink,' Joan suggested.

'I think you should go after her, Larry,' Lees suggested. 'Fetch her back.'

'Well . . . I don't know if I can do that,' Larry said, but he went anyway.

He ran down the steps of the club and heard the grating of gears. There went a year off the life of the Armstrong-Siddeley. But he'd be selling it anyway when they left Singapore. He ran across the car park and reached her just as she got the car straight.

'I'll drive,' he said.

'Bugger off,' she told him.

He held on to the door. 'If you don't let me in, I'll hit you!'

Once again she was taken by surprise. He seized his opportunity to wrench the door open. 'Slide over.'

She hesitated, then obeyed. It took her some time as her skirt became entangled in the handbrake. He got in while she was struggling to free herself, and their thighs touched.

He was aware of being more aroused than for a long time.

Margaret tucked her skirt round her legs, and Larry closed the door. 'They want you to go back.'

'I am not going back.'

'Maybe it'd be an idea not to. Is there anywhere you'd like to go? There's a do on at Raffles.'

'Do you think I want to rub shoulders with a lot of wogs? I want to go home. I may as well enjoy it while I can.'

'You're not going to lose your home. We'll rent it out while we're in Hong Kong. We will be coming back here, you know.' He glanced at her. 'When I'm Managing

152

Director.' She didn't respond, and he concentrated on the road; the streets seemed busier than ever. 'You'll love Hong Kong. You really will. And it's a much better climate, too. Better for Marion. Maybe she'll get over her prickly heat.'

Still Margaret said nothing. They emerged from the traffic and raced up the hill and into the front drive.

Mansur immediately appeared, clearly mystified; he would not have expected them back before dawn in normal circumstances.

'Would you like some more champagne?' Larry asked, as they went up the stairs.

'Why not? What else is there to do?'

Mansur was already hurrying to the refrigerator. He returned with two glasses.

Larry raised his. 'Well, here's to Hong Kong.'

'Fuck Hong Kong,' she told him. She drained her glass and then hurled it against the wall. 'We have no more use for those now, do we?'

Larry caught Mansur's shocked glance, and Margaret went up the stairs.

'You'd better clean that up, Mansur,' Larry told the butler, and followed.

She was already in her bedroom and the door was locked. Patiently Larry went to his own room. It was dawning on him that he had, subconsciously, made up his mind that he was going to have her tonight, and end this whole charade one way or the other.

But the connecting door was also locked.

He knocked, politely. 'Meg! Open up.'

'Go to hell,' she said. 'No, go to Hong Kong.'

'Meg,' he said, as reasonably as he could, 'you and I have got to have a little chat. Right now.'

'So you can rape me?'

'It could come to that.'

'If you want me so badly, why don't you break down the door?'

He stared at the panelling, feeling a tremendous urge to do just that.

153

Wouldn't that give the servants, the gossips, a field day? But if they were leaving Singapore anyway . . .

'Or why don't you just go out and pick up a whore?' Margaret inquired. 'All you want is to ram yourself into someone, don't you? You'll have a better time with a whore. So go and get yourself a whore.'

Larry's fists clenched. They were strong fists, supported by powerful wrists and shoulders; years of wielding a cricket bat had seen to that. He could easily break down the door, and she would be unable to resist.

But later she would taunt him. And on the evidence of this evening, she still hated him.

He turned away from the door and went downstairs. Mansur had just finished locating the last sliver of broken glass.

'Mansur,' Larry said. 'Which is the best whorehouse in Singapore?'

Mansur looked startled; whether at the request, or because he would have expected his employer to know the answer already, Larry couldn't decide.

'Come along, Mansur.'

'Well, Mr Lawrence, they say the Blue Room is the best.'

'Right. Don't expect me back before dawn.'

'But I am thinking it is the Bamboo Curtain that you are wanting, Mr Lawrence.'

Larry, already at the front door, checked. He had, of course, heard of both establishments, but had never gone into details about them. 'Why do you say that?'

'Because I am hearing that at the Bamboo Curtain a man can do what he wants, Mr Lawrence. It is a good place for . . .' he hesitated.

'Letting off steam,' Larry suggested.

'I am only hearing these things, Mr Lawrence. I have not been there.'

'Thanks anyway.' Larry closed the door behind him, went down the stairs and got into the car. Once before Margaret had driven him to a whore. And then he hadn't known enough to enjoy it. This time he intended to. He

154

felt more sexually aroused than at any time in his life before.

And if he got the clap, then he'd go home and rape his wife and give it to her too, wouldn't he!

He gunned the engine, sent the Armstrong-Siddeley roaring out of the drive. He didn't want to have the time for his resolution to slip away, the time to allow exhaustion to creep into his mind and send him meekly home to bed. That had happened too often in the past.

It was very nearly midnight, and Singapore throbbed. It occurred to him that he could park the car and enter any one of the blaring nightclubs and find a partner at a fraction of the price he was going to have to pay at either the Blue Room or the Bamboo Curtain, and far more certainly get the clap.

He turned away from the lights and the noise, down a quiet street that led towards the suburbs. A couple more lefts and rights and he pulled into the kerb and switched off the ignition, pocketed the keys.

The house was dark and quiet. Just before midnight on New Year's Eve was time off for Singapore's prostitutes; their business would begin in the small hours.

He rang the bell, and was admitted by a Malay maid wearing an apron over her uniform. 'Good evening, sahib.'

'Yes,' he said.

'You wish a drink?'

'Why not?'

She bowed, and opened a door for him. He stepped into a discreet little bar. The barman was Malay; the three girls seated on the stools drinking coloured water were Chinese. Their long skirts were slit to the thigh, their bodices high and prim.

'Welcome,' one said. 'Champagne for the gentleman.'

The barman placed a bottle on the table, and Larry gathered that he had bought it, regardless of the cost.

'Why don't you join me?' he invited, and they giggled. One pressed a bell.

He drank some of the champagne; it wasn't Bollinger, but it wasn't all that bad.

A woman stood at his elbow. 'Good evening, Mr Cairns.'

He looked up at her. She was Chinese, considerably older than any of the girls, but similarly dressed, save that her black hair was caught up in a chignon, and her jewellery looked as if it might be real.

'Welcome to my house,' she said.

He raised his glass, and offered her one.

'Perhaps later. Do you like any of my girls?'

'I was told I could have whatever I liked here.'

Her eyes flickered. 'Within reason. What would you like?'

'The best girl you have, for whatever I wish.'

'That sounds like Little Orchid. Would you like Little Orchid?'

He looked at the girls. 'Which one is she?'

'She is not on display.'

'You expect me to take a girl, without seeing her first?'

The woman smiled. 'You will not regret it. If you do, I will refund your money. If you enjoy her . . . she is very expensive. But for you, Mr Cairns, that will not matter.'

'You're right,' he agreed. 'It will not matter.' He took out his wallet. 'How much?'

'With the champagne, sixty dollars.'

He took out the notes, gave them to her.

'You can bring the champagne, if you like,' she told him.

He thought he might as well; this Little Orchid might well demand a drink. He took the bottle by the neck, hooked his fingers around two glasses, and followed the woman through an inner doorway into a long, brightly-lit corridor.

'It is just coming to midnight,' the woman remarked, without looking round.

'Yes.' he agreed. He was not going to humour her obvious curiosity.

She led him to the very end of the corridor, knocked on the door, then opened it. 'I have brought a gentleman to see you,' she said. 'Mr Lawrence Cairns, of Hammond and Teng.'

Larry stepped past her, and gazed at Chung Lan.

There was no doubt that it was Chung Lan, although in four years she had changed; her face had hardened as her body had filled out. But it *was* Chung Lan, still with the exquisitely carved features, the slightly scattered black hair. She wore a green silk dressing gown embroidered with dragons, but he did not doubt that beneath it her body was just as he remembered it.

He almost stopped breathing.

'Yes,' the woman said. 'She is very beautiful. But there is yet more beauty to be known with her. Mr Cairns has paid for everything,' she told Chung Lan.

Chung Lan had been seated in a chair, reading a book. Now she placed the book on the table beside her, stood up and bowed.

'Enjoy her,' the woman recommended, and closed the door behind her.

Chung Lan gazed at Larry, and he gazed back.

'I wondered how long it would be before you came to me,' she said. 'I had not expected you tonight.'

'*You* are Little Orchid?' he asked. He felt physically sick.

She shrugged, and in the same movement allowed the dressing gown to slip from her shoulders. 'It suits my name. In Chinese, Little Orchid is Lan Kuei. Did you not know that?'

He had never troubled to learn Chinese, had never troubled to ask her what her Chinese name meant in English.

He gazed at breasts which had grown since last he had touched them, at thighs which had rounded, at legs which were no less beautiful.

And her eyes the last time he had seen them, they had

been filled with tears. He did not think they were capable of weeping now. Instead, they glittered.

He sat down in the chair she had just vacated, the champagne bottle drooping from his fingers. Lan Kuei took the bottle and the glasses, and filled one each. She sipped her own, gave him his.

'How long have you been here?' he asked.

'Only four months. But I am already famous, as Lan Kuei.'

'I have not been there, you understand, sahib,' Mansur had said.

By God, if he thought Mansur had been in this room, he would throttle the little man.

Or Kitachi? By God, Kitachi . . .

But could he throttle all the other men who must have been here in four months, whose pleasure had made her famous?

'Do your parents know of it? Kai?'

'No,' she said. 'Are you going to tell them?'

'We are no longer friends.'

'Drink your champagne,' she suggested.

He put the glass on the table. Leaned forward. 'Lan . . . what happened?'

She shrugged. 'My father threw me out. I fled Singapore. I went to China, then to Saigon. I had to live. I learned how to live well. When I had nothing more to learn, I decided to return here. Singapore is my home.'

'To . . . this?'

She laughed, and for a moment was again the girl with whom he had fallen in love. 'This? I think this is the life I was intended for, by fate. No one can go against fate.'

She left the bed and knelt before him, undid his trouser buttons. Once before she had done that, the first time they ever made love.

And he desired her as much now as he had then.

He held her head and lifted her face. And remembered Ayesha. 'May I kiss you?'

She gazed at him for some seconds. 'You may kiss me,

Larry,' she said, and gave another laugh. 'My Lai said you had paid for everything.'

He wanted to slap her. But he wanted to kiss her more. He touched her lips with his own, and she opened her mouth to him, sucked him inside, while her hands delved into his pants.

Then she took her mouth away. 'I am glad you have come to me, Larry. Why do you not undress?'

He wished he could think clearly. There was so much to be said, so much to be done. At this moment more than any other, his life had definitely reached a watershed. There had been a time when he thought that only with Lan could he ever find happiness. And now she expected him to make love to her, as a whore!

Lan Kuei smiled, and reclined on the pillows facing him, one leg up, the other stretched to one side, totally exposing herself.

For the first time he noticed the bed, which was large, with a gold-coloured spread; the room was decorated in gold, with slashes of crimson. The washstand was crimson and gold, as were the basin and pitcher and ewer.

No doubt she had a crimson and gold toilet through the adjoining door.

She had seen where he had looked. 'You may use it,' she said.

He did need to, and accepted her invitation. As he expected, the toilet was crimson and gold. He left the door open.

'You are looking well,' she remarked. 'But then, you always look well, my Larry. You are a very healthy person. It is the cricket.'

He came back into the bedroom, closing the door behind him.

'But you are upset,' she said, glancing at him. 'Come here and let me help you undress.'

He stood beside the bed. 'Lan . . .'

'We will talk after, when you are recovering,' she said. She knelt on the mattress, eased off his jacket, and unbuttoned his shirt. 'What would you like? You have paid for everything.' She raised her head to look at him. 'You can even beat me, if you like.'

Would he ever forget Ayesha? Would she let him?

'What would *you* like?' he asked.

She turned to face him, and smiled at him. 'It is not often I am asked that. You might not like what I desire.'

'I would like it.'

She gazed at him for several seconds, in that grave way she had, not the least like Margaret's intense stare, but like an inner communing.

'You are not really in the mood,' she remarked. 'Would you like to tell me why you quarrelled with your wife?'

'How do you know I quarrelled with my wife?'

She laughed. 'You, a man like you, would not have come here on a night like this if you had not, Larry.'

'My wife and I have one long quarrel,' he said.

'Then you should divorce her, and find another.'

'Yes,' he agreed. Then suddenly, all the frustration of the past four years overwhelmed him. He had truly loved her, and had treated her despicably. He had exchanged all her affection and devotion for a loveless marriage, and the guarantee of worldly success, a success which, at this very moment, he truly believed he no longer wanted. 'Lan . . . I should never have let you go. I love you. I have only ever loved you. Lan, come away with me. Please.'

She frowned at him in what appeared to be genuine bewilderment.

'Come where?'

'Anywhere. Anywhere you choose.'

'I am very expensive.'

'I don't mean as a whore. As my wife. I'll divorce Margaret.'

Her mouth puckered. 'It would ruin your career.'

'To hell with my career!'

'Well, then, it would ruin mine.'

He stared at her. 'You call *this* a career?'

'My Lai is a very rich woman,' she said seriously. 'I

160

will be even richer, because I am more beautiful, and I have more brains.'

'Lan . . . for God's sake, this isn't something to joke about. I love you. I want you. Just tell me what you want and I'll give it to you! But come and live with me.'

'What I want,' Lan Kuei said, 'is for you to come and see me from time to time. There was a time when I hated you, when I wished you were dead. But I have grown out of that. Since you, I have known a lot of men. They are all the same. You are not the first who has asked me to marry him. You will not be the last. But why should I marry any man? I am doing what I enjoy best, I am being well paid for it, and I call no man my master. Why should I change that?'

He could not believe his ears. 'But Lan . . . you are committing suicide. All that lies in front of you is disease, and poverty, and . . .'

'I am twenty-one, Larry,' she said. 'My Lai is fifty-two. She is not diseased. And she is *very* rich.'

'But . . . I am not any man, Lan. I am Larry. We loved each other. We do love each other.' He was on his knees, begging.

Her mouth twisted. 'I did love you once, Larry. I am sure of it. But you taught me what a stupid emotion that is. Love is a weakness. You taught me that the important things are money and strength. I will not love again. Now Larry, as you have paid for everything, you must tell me what you wish to do. Anything you wish.'

Larry stepped away from the bed and rebuttoned his shirt and pants, straightened his jacket.

Lan Kuei frowned at him. 'What are you doing?'

'Going home.'

'But, you have paid for everything. You have paid a lot of money. There is no possibility of a refund.'

'Keep the money,' he told her. 'Use it as the start of your nest egg.'

161

CHAPTER 7
The Success Story

Larry got into the Armstrong-Siddeley and drove east to the beach where he had proposed to Margaret, parked the car, stripped, and plunged into the lukewarm water.

He didn't go out very far, as he had no desire to encounter a shark. He just wanted to cool off, sober up, get his brain working.

He was realising for the first time what a mess he was making of things, that life wasn't just a matter of keeping a straight bat and letting the runs come, knowing that they always would. The runs had certainly come for him, so far. Manager of the Accounts Department at twenty three, Manager of the Hong Kong branch at twenty seven . . . translate those successes into cricket terms, and he'd be Captain of England!

And there was a whole lot more to come.

But sitting back and accepting what life had to offer wasn't enough. He had recognised that with regard to his career, but he had never applied that essential reasoning to his private life. Hence his own misery, and the misery he spread around himself.

Was Lan miserable? She had not shown any sign of it. Maybe she truly did want to do no more than make love to a variety of men, and be well paid for it.

But she must, in her heart, have wanted more to be married to him. And she must know, too, that however well My Lai had prospered, the odds were against her doing the same. Surely it was only pride that had prevented her from accepting his offer.

But thank God for her pride! He would have ruined his life, and a whole lot of other lives besides. Running off with Lan Kuei, Singapore's most notorious prostitute, would be the disaster of the century. It could lead only to oblivion.

They would never even be able to make love without the memory of all the other men who had been able to afford her.

For a few minutes, he had wanted to turn the clock back, be once more the lovesick boy of several years ago, with the carefree, loving Chung Lan of those days. But he knew he could never see her again. He must forget her, drive her from his mind. He must make his marriage work. Perhaps the shadow of Lan lying across his mind all these years had prevented him wanting to fall truly in love with Meg, or even wanting to be happy in their marriage. All else, taking what being her husband had to offer, persuading himself that it must come right in the end, had been sheer self-delusion. He had been waiting, however subconsciously, for Lan to reappear.

Well, now she had, in the most salutary fashion.

It was his marriage or nothing, now. And fate had offered him one last winning card; Margaret had put herself into a position where she could not win. She could no longer even threaten. She could only accept defeat.

He fell asleep behind the wheel of his car, to be awakened by the first rays of the sun. He felt stiff, but the swim had cleared his head and there was no trace of a hangover.

He drove home, parked the car, unlocked the front door; Mansur had long since gone to bed.

He went up to his room, shaved and had a shower. Then he tried the connecting door to Margaret's bedroom, discovered it was now unlocked. He went into the room, softly closing the door.

The blinds were drawn, although the sun was now high and traces of light were seeping round the edges of the windows. He let the blinds go; they rose with a rattle and instantly the room was flooded with light.

Margaret gave a startled exclamation and sat up.

'What time is it? What . . .' She stared at her husband. 'You've nothing on!'

163

She retreated against the bedhead, pulling the sheet with her to cover her breasts.

'Neither have you,' he pointed out.

'Get out of my room,' she snapped.

'*Our* room,' he reminded her, and sat on the bed.

'You were out all night,' she said. 'You're drunk.'

'I've been for a swim. It was delightful. And very sobering.'

She was glaring at him, attempting to control him as she had done so easily at the beginning. But her gaze dropped as his hand stretched out to grasp the sheet.

She took a deep breath.

'You can scream if you like,' he told her. 'You'll wake Marion. And the servants. And probably the neighbours. But none of them will come charging to your rescue. Not today.'

She held on to the sheet for a few more seconds, but Larry was too strong for her, and she let go. She leaned back against the bedhead, drawing up her legs protectively.

'You've been with a whore.'

'On your recommendation.'

'You're filthy. You are . . .'

'Your husband.'

She hissed. 'It will be rape.'

'No, it won't.'

He grasped her ankles and dragged her down the bed so that she lay on the pillows. Margaret kicked violently, but Larry threw himself across her thighs and held her down by the wrists.

'I'll fight you,' she warned.

'Do that,' he grinned. 'I've always wanted to wrestle with a naked woman.'

Tears suddenly appeared in her eyes, as if she knew she was defeated. But it could just be a second line of defence; Larry was not going to let her get away with it.

He lay on her and kissed her mouth. She kept her lips shut for a few seconds, then without warning she bit him.

'Damn you!'

'You only want to humiliate me!' she spat defiantly.

'No,' he said levelly. 'I don't want a humiliated wife. Or a hurt one. I want a happy wife – one who enjoys making love with her husband.'

Her breathing quickened.

'I hate you!'

'No, you don't,' he said. 'You just don't want to believe that I love you and want you. God knows why, after the way you've kept us apart all this time, but I do.'

He bent to kiss her again, and warily let go of her wrists. Margaret still lay lay rigid beneath him.

Then so suddenly that Larry was taken by surprise, they were both a tangle of writhing limbs, panting and gasping, rolling around in the frantic throes of love. My God, the thought flashed through Larry's mind, even with Lan it was never like this! In a few explosive minutes, it was over, and they were lying in a mess of sweat soaked sheets.

The pillows had ended up on the floor.

For a minute, as he got his breath back, Larry felt suddenly nervous and apprehensive, as though Meg were a stranger. What would she say or do now?

Then he realised that to expect her to make the first move was asking too much of her. He leaned over and brushed the wet hair from her face. Then he realised that the auburn strands were wet not with sweat but with tears.

'Oh, Larry. I've been awfully stupid, haven't I?'

'Yes,' he said lovingly, kissing her tears away. 'Very. But I love you anyway.'

There was a soft knock on the door, and Maline came in, as she did every morning. 'Breakfast, Maline,' Larry shouted. 'For two in here.'

She gave her mistress a startled glance, then bowed. 'Yes, sir, Mr Lawrence.' Then she scuttled away.

'It'll be all over Singapore by lunchtime,' Margaret giggled.

'We should put a notice in the *Straits Times*.'

'Larry . . . was I terrible, last night?'

165

'You caused a stir.'

'My God! How can I ever face any of those people again?'

'You won't have to,' he reminded her. 'Not for a long time. We're going to Hong Kong, remember?'

Like Singapore, when approached from the sea by the West Lamma Channel, Hong Kong seemed part of the general topography of China. It was only when the ship came abeam of Victoria peak, nearly two thousand feet high, that the harbour opened out and Hong Kong could be seen to be an island.

Then the bustling city of Victoria came in sight, and on the port side of the ship, the hardly less bustling suburb of Kowloon in the New Territories; the two halves of the colony were connected by a constant flow of ferries, but already there was talk of a tunnel beneath the harbour.

'It seems crazy to talk about such an investment,' Margaret commented. 'Don't we have to give the whole thing back to the Chinese, sometime?'

'Not until 1997,' Larry reassured her. 'That's more than sixty years away.'

He held Marion up to the rail for a better view. At four and a half she was a pretty child with a mind of her own. Having been fractious and difficult as a baby, she somehow sensed the new contentment between her parents, and was now sweet tempered and affectionate. Larry and Margaret adored her.

Mansur and Maline, the only two of their Singapore servants they had brought with them, were even more appreciative of the new conditions under which they lived. Gone were the tension and the innuendo, the muttered insults which had made up so large a part of the Cairns' previous domestic life. Now the master and mistress seemed to be honeymooning again.

A good deal had become apparent to Larry since that tumultuous morning six months ago, six months in which they had had the happiest holiday of their lives. During their long leave in England, Margaret had become deeply

166

fond of Peter and Lucy Cairns, and they had certainly adored her. And Larry and Margaret had renewed their own love time and again. Lan might never have been.

The most important thing, he had realised, was that Margaret had never ceased loving him. It had been a struggle between her rigid upbringing and his conjugal requirements, and she had felt it necessary to make a protest. He had obviously made matters worse by being too candid; there were limits beyond which even honesty was a mistake. Then in her outrage she had dug herself into a hole, and just as had happened on New Year's Eve, she had had no idea how to dig herself out again.

Thus she had been waiting for him to make another approach, while resisting him with total determination. It was her own father who had said that women were difficult creatures to understand, and he had been absolutely right. Margaret had actually wanted him to be firm with her, all those years . . . while determined to fight him to the last, to remain angry to the last.

So, had he wasted four years? He doubted it. To force her would have destroyed their marriage. He had had to wait, without being aware of it, until he had begun truly to prosper, and until she had herself made a mistake and been left vulnerable. Then the surrender had been easy; having made a fool of herself, she needed his strength on which to lean.

And Lan Kuei? A catalyst, undoubtedly, but now someone to be forgotten, finally and forever.

Now there was only happiness ahead. He put his arm round his wife's shoulder as the ship nosed towards the docks, and she leaned her head on his shoulder and smiled.

Operating on the principle that there can only ever be one king, Jimmy Burns had already left Hong Kong before Larry arrived. Thus the Cairns entourage was met by Burns's deputy, Peter Firth.

Firth was a pleasant fellow with dark hair and a military moustache. He was also several years older than Larry and, while he had clearly been briefed, his attitude none-theless, said: well, if you're such a damned prodigy, show me.

Larry could see some problems ahead, but his immediate concern was getting Margaret settled.

The Hammond house was old, though not as old as the one in Singapore. It had been built by Michael Harring-ton, the nineteenth century adventurer who married Alicia Hammond and eventually become head of the firm, way back in the 1860s.

Built on the lower slopes of Mount Victoria, four-square and uncompromising, surrounded by verandahs and a terrace of gardens, it had spectacular views. Inside, it had been to a certain extent modernised once or twice, and the rooms were at least large, high-ceilinged and airy, but the plumbing was antiquated, and some sections of the floor were unsafe because of the activities of wood ants, while the furniture was definitely tatty.

'Oh, no,' Margaret said. 'Oh, no, no, no, no, no.'

Firth looked at Larry, who shrugged.

'We'll take a suite in an hotel in Victoria. And you'd better have the builders meet us up here tomorrow morning.'

Firth scratched his head. 'You do realise, Mr Cairns, that things are . . . well, a little tight at the moment.'

'I'll take full responsibility,' Larry said pleasantly.

'Very good, sir,' Firth agreed, clearly delighted to have his new manager begin with a stand-up row with head office.

An hotel was found, and several rooms taken.

'Larry,' Margaret said, 'there isn't going to be trouble, is there?'

'No,' Larry said. 'Because I'm Larry Cairns and you're Margaret Anstey. Remember?'

He was content to make the very most of his position, and sent Ronald Lees a telegram that night: HOUSE UNLIVEABLE MARGARET NOT AMUSED STOP COMPLETE RENOVATION NECESSARY STOP KINDLY AUTHORISE OTHERWISE UNABLE

GUARANTEE IMPROVEMENT IN TRADE FIG-
URES STOP REGARDS CAIRNS.

The authority came through the following afternoon,
by which time Larry and Margaret, and a much chastened
Firth, had already met at the house with the recommended
builders and outlined a plan which was going to cost
several thousand pounds.

'And while we're at it,' Larry said, remembering Chung
Lo's mansion, 'we'll have a swimming pool.'

'A swimming pool!' Margaret clapped her hands. 'That
would be simply marvellous.'

'With a springboard,' Larry added.

When Larry moved into his new office, he was regarded
with ill-disguised curiosity by the staff. Some were resent-
ful at having such a young managing director and clearly
imagined he had got the job through his marriage rather
than his own ability. Others appeared more eager to be
helpful. Among the latter was his secretary, Janet Ogilvy,
a nice sensible girl with huge horned-rimmed spectacles,
and the largest bust Larry had ever seen. She was the butt
of many jokes behind her back but Larry liked her and
immediately thought of her as a good sort.

He called a meeting of the senior staff on his first afternoon, after having inspected the books.

'This branch is not pulling its weight,' he told them. 'I
have no doubt a lot of this was to do with the attitude of
my predecessor, which is why I was sent to replace him.'

There was an almost audible gasp.

'The fact is,' he went on, tapping the accounts, which
still lay on his desk, 'that a good half of these accounts
were secured by Michael Harrington, more than fifty years
ago. The amount of new business generated by this office
over the past twenty-five years is a disgrace. Business is
our business. We must create it. It is not enough to have
an old and famous name, and wait for people to come to
us. From now on, we will go to them. Where necessary,
we'll undercut our competitors. We know their rates.
Where Smith and Smith say they will deliver goods to

169

Shanghai at seven and a quarter per cent, we are going to promise to deliver at seven per cent, and we are going to *deliver* at seven.'

'With respect, Mr Cairns,' Firth said, 'Smith and Smith aren't delivering goods to Shanghai at all, any more. Nobody is. It's just too dangerous. The place is like a powderkeg. No one can tell when it's going to erupt in our faces.'

'We are going to resume shipping goods into Shanghai,' Larry told him.

'Who to, Mr Cairns?' asked Bunbury, the chief account-ant. 'We don't actually have any customers there any more.'

'We're going to go up there and get them,' Larry told him.

Bunbury gulped. 'You're going to send a sales force up to Shanghai?'

Larry grinned at him. 'No. I'm going up to Shanghai myself.'

Clearly they thought he was mad. But he had no doubt he could do it, or if not, call a lot of bluffs.

Margaret wasn't so sure.

'Isn't it really very dangerous?' she asked.

'Not in the slightest,' Larry told her. 'I have a few aces tucked up my sleeve.'

'But what do I do while you're away?'

'Relax, I'm not going away for a while. And anyway, you'll have the builders to keep an eye on.'

They found themselves immediately in the the middle of a social whirl. The arrival of a new manager at Ham-mond and Teng would in any event have caused a stir, but for him to be young and handsome and accompanied by a beautiful wife who was also one of the Far East's élite brought them a stack of invitations in the first forty-eight hours.

In addition, Larry was still L. D. Cairns, the cricketer, and British society in Hong Kong was even more keen on cricket than in Singapore. Larry was amused to find a

170

large crowd turning up to watch him practise, and an even larger crowd for his first match, in which he gratified everyone, including himself, by scoring a century.

The favourite sport in Hong Kong, however, was sailing. Larry had done some in Singapore – Roly Payne had kept a twenty-footer in which they had often sailed out to the reefs to fish – but now for the first time he considered taking it seriously; cruising amongst the myriad islands which surrounded Victoria was the most pleasant way of spending a Sunday afternoon, and it was a sport in which both Margaret and Marion could share. As was his nature, he threw himself into his new hobby without reservation. Soon he was attending navigation classes, and before he had been in Hong Kong six months he had bought himself a yacht of his own.

But his mind was mainly set on making a success of his new appointment. Having conquered Margaret he could see nothing to stop him conquering even mainland China, especially with Kitachi Tano's precious letter in his pocket. As soon as he was satisfied that the Hong Kong office was reorganised to his requirements, and that the renovation of the house was proceeding well, he set off on his sales tour.

He took his time, however, and felt out the ground by first visiting Canton, taking a trading steamer up the Pearl River. He supposed he should have been far more excited than he was about this, his first visit to China. But all he saw was a desperately poor countryside and people, and a city which had known better days. Besides, his mind was filled with what he wished to accomplish.

He went to the House of Wong Tung, who had been trading with Singapore for a century. Ironically a good deal of Wong's business had in recent years been diverted to the House of Chung, but he still had old ties with Hammond and Teng, and he was clearly delighted to receive a visit from the manager of the Hong Kong office; such a thing had never happened before.

Larry was entertained to a twelve-course dinner with several other Cantonese merchants of standing; no women were present, although he understood that they were available after the meal should he so choose. He did not suppose he would choose, being far more interested in the conversation around the table. Not for the first time he kicked himself for not having learned Mandarin. Nearly all the men spoke sufficient English to talk to him, but they were inclined to carry on conversation between themselves in Chinese, from which he was excluded.

But he appreciated what he learned. Canton was taking on a new lease of life. It had been very depressed until the previous year, because of the presence of a large Communist enclave immediately to the north. The Communists had traditionally drawn their strength from the south, and had expected to continue shipping arms and supplies through the Pearl River. This had displeased Marshal Chiang Kai-shek, with the result that punitive duties had been levied on the city.

But only a couple of years previously, the Marshal had decided to deal with the Communists once and for all. He had launched an all-out offensive on their towns in the mountains. Many people thought he had been mistaken in this, and that the real threat to China was the Japanese army occupying Manchuria and Jehol and making threatening gestures in Shantung and outside Shanghai. But the move had succeeded in shifting the Communists. Those of them who had survived the Marshal's attack had packed up their belongings and, with their women and children, their dogs and chickens and goats and cattle, had set off into the mountains.

There they had disappeared. No one knew what had happened to them. But the last winter had been unusually severe, and it was not supposed that many of them had survived.

'It is a sad story,' Wong Tung confessed. 'There cannot have been less than a hundred thousand of them. All perished. Some of them were people of talent. I knew one of their leaders, a fellow called Mao Tse-tung. He used to be a librarian right here in Canton. All gone.'

'China has many such tragedies in her history,' observed the man sitting beside him, whose name was Tang Li.

'It is still sad,' Wong Tung commented.

'But now your Marshal will be able to deal with the Japanese,' Larry suggested.

'That will mean war,' Wong Tung said. 'War is bad for business.'

'But you have come here to do business, Mr Cairns,' Tang Li suggested.

'I have indeed. I am disturbed at the way Hammond and Teng's business with Canton has declined.'

Wong and Tang exchanged glances.

'I understand,' Larry said. 'You perhaps prefer to do business with the House of Chung, because you speak the same language. But there is only one language for businessmen. It is an international language. It is figures, profits and losses. I am here to talk in those terms.'

Once again the two Chinese exchanged glances. It was totally foreign to their way of business, their way of life, to be so straightforward, even so aggressive.

But Larry knew no other way. 'Has the House of Chung ever sent a representative to speak with you in person?'

'Indeed,' Wong Tung said. 'Four years ago Chung Lo's son, Chung Kai, came to Canton in the course of a journey through China. We had dinner in this very room.'

'Ah,' Larry said. Damnation! He hadn't expected that. The Chungs seemed set to haunt him wherever he went.

'Chung Lo charges six and a half per cent for goods delivered in Canton,' Tang Li said. 'There is no-one cheaper in the world.'

'Hammond and Teng will be cheaper,' Larry told him. 'We will deliver your goods at six and a quarter per cent. Providing,' he raised his finger, 'that we have your exclusive business.'

Tang Li looked at Wong Tung, who looked back.

At last Wong Tung said, 'We will meet again tomorrow, Mr Cairns.'

★ ★ ★

173

Larry returned to Hong Kong with several very large orders in his briefcase.

Firth was aghast. 'Six and a quarter per cent, Mr Cairns? I'm not sure we'll even clear our expenses.'

'Yes, we will. And anyway, this is only a foot in the door. The real profit is going to come out of Shanghai.'

'You still intend to go up there?'

'I'm leaving next week.'

Margaret was delighted. 'Oh, Larry, Uncle Ronald is going to be thrilled!' She took him for an inspection of the house, where the renovation work was going on well and the foundations for the pool had already been dug.

She was pleased with the progress, but she was also apprehensive, about many things.

'Did you miss me, in Canton?'

'Of course. When I had the time.'

'Oh, Larry! I suppose you went with a Chinese girl.'

'Several.'

'You brute.' She sighed, and held his hand. 'You don't really have to go to Shanghai, do you?'

'Really,' he said. 'Canton was the bread and butter. Shanghai is the jam.'

He could not help being elated because, after so long, everything in his life was coming together, and he was making it all happen himself. It was a heady feeling to know that beneath the somewhat ineffectual exterior he knew he presented to many people there was a framework of steel.

He went up to Shanghai by one of the coasting steamers, which had a Chinese crew but a British captain and chief engineer.

'It's a rum business,' commented Captain Macfarlane. 'But then, I've lived in the East forty years, man and boy, and I still don't understand the people. How Chiang Kai-shek can allow a foreign power like Japan to take over chunks of his country, and move troops to and fro and back again, and even fight pitched battles with his own people, and still insist that there is no war between China and Japan, defeats me.'

'Maybe it's because the Chinese have lived with some sort of foreign occupation for so long they'd feel odd without it,' Larry suggested.

'It's a point. But the Japs, they give me the shivers. The way they look at you . . . you can almost feel their thoughts: one day, you big white bugger, you are going to crawl to me.'

Larry thought of Kitachi, and reckoned the captain could be right. But he had surely put Kitachi in his place.

'That day is probably a few hundred years off, Captain, no matter how much they dream. I wouldn't lose any sleep over it.'

But he saw what the captain meant as the little steamer entered the Yangtse. The left bank was completely occupied by a vast army camp, above which waved the Rising Sun of Japan. And this was Chinese soil!

He had telegraphed ahead, and was met on the dock at Wu-San by Hammond and Teng's local agent, an Englishman named Freddie Cox. An old China hand, Cox was in his mid thirties, red-faced and decidedly taken aback by the youth of the new Hong Kong manager.

'Glad to meet you, Mr Cairns,' he said. 'I wish I could say business is booming, but it's not.'

They rode in the train to the International Concession. The train carried Japanese soldiers as guards, and they passed a good number of them undergoing training exercises in the countryside.

'Amazing,' Larry commented. 'Don't the Chinese object?'

'Not since that battle a couple of years ago. The Chinese have neither the equipment nor the know-how to oppose these chaps. Only the courage, and that won't keep out a bullet.'

'Well, it's their concern, not ours,' Larry told him. 'Ours is business. What's happened to all of these fellows?'

He gave Cox the typewritten list of erstwhile Hammond

and Teng customers in Shanghai, and while the agent scanned it, continued to look out of the window as the train approached the International Concession. Here everything was as he had expected; flags of different nationalities, amongst them the Union Jack, flew above various buildings, and there were other uniforms to be seen. But for every French grey or British or American khaki there were at least ten Japanese greens.

Cox returned the paper. 'I'm afraid that's quite accurate, Mr Cairns.'

'Tell me why?'

'Well, simply, the Japanese now have a stranglehold on the city. That means on the mouth of the Yangtse. And that in turn means that the other big cities up the river, Nanking and Hankow, for example, are also caught in the net. The Japs are virtually forcing the locals to buy Japanese products, and are putting all manner of hindrances in the way of anyone else muscling in. There is also a certain amount of intimidation of Chinese merchants here on the coast.'

'Is there any open antagonism to us?'

'Oh, no. It's all done velly poritely, so velly solly. Makes one damned angry, but there's not a lot we can do about it. If old Ting Ho in Shanghai wants to buy whisky, and is approached by a Japanese agent, and says "but I have always bought Haig and Haig from Hammond and Teng", the Jap agent asks him to count heads in the Concession, especially heads carrying rifles, and old Ting thinks again and imports it from Tokyo. Nowadays, of course, it's next to impossible to get in to see Ting, because the Japs won't let anyone into the Chinese city without a pass signed by their commander, and that's worth its weight in gold. I can tell you, Mr Cairns, that I'm not alone in wishing that the British government would revert to the good old gunboat diplomacy we used to practise fifty years ago, send in a couple of heavy cruisers, and tell the Japs to pull out or be blown up.'

'I suspect there are too many people in London who are afraid the Japs might say, two can play at that game.

Anyway, I have every intention of having a word with Ting Ho myself, tomorrow.'

Cox pulled his nose. 'You'll have to apply for a permit. Even you, Mr Cairns.'

Larry grinned at him. 'You just telephone the Japanese commander and tell him that the Manager of Hammond and Teng, Hong Kong, would like to see him urgently.'

General Abe was a precise little man with somewhat tight features, but a very smart uniform. He stood up to greet Larry, and gave a brief bow.

'I am honoured, Mr Cairns,' he said in good English.

'So am I, General.'

'Will you be seated?'

Larry sat down in front of the desk, and the General sat behind it.

'My secretary informed me that you have an important reason for wishing to see me, Mr Cairns.'

'Important to me and my company, General. I would like you to issue me with a pass to enter Shanghai to see Mr Ting Ho and others. I would also like you to issue my agent, Mr Cox, with a pass so that he can go and come from Shanghai as he chooses.'

General Abe placed his elbows on his blotting paper, and brought his fingers together in front of his face. 'I would very much like to do that, Mr Cairns, but you will understand I am acting under certain restrictions, imposed by my government, on trade in and out of Shanghai. It hurts me to have to refuse a man as distinguished as yourself, but . . .'

'I have a letter here which may be of interest to you,' Larry said, and laid Kitachi's letter on the desk.

The General frowned, and picked it up. His frown deepened as he read.

'I understand that Mr Kitachi is known to you, General,' Larry said. 'He seemed to think that his recommendation might be of some help.'

Abe continued to gaze at the letter for some moments.

177

Then he raised his head. 'Yes,' he said. 'Mr Kitachi is known to me. Is he a friend of yours?'

'Well, you could say that.'

'I see. Of course, it will be a great pleasure for me to honour Mr Kitachi's request. May I ask what business he is in, in Singapore?'

'The same as me. Import and export.'

'Then you should be rivals for trade.'

'Well, we are, of course. But we also understand that we can help each other, in certain directions.'

'I see,' Abe said again. 'I will write out a pass allowing you to enter Shanghai as you wish.'

'Thank you. And one for Mr Cox?'

'Of course. Are you staying with Mr Cox?'

'Yes.'

'Then I will send the passes over this afternoon.'

'Thank you,' Larry said again. 'You are being most kind. May I have that letter back?'

Abe handed it over, and Larry folded it and placed it inside his wallet.

'I'll say goodbye.'

Abe stood up and bowed. 'Goodbye, Mr Cairns.' He hesitated, then added, 'May I be so rude as to ask you a question?'

'Anything you like.'

'Have you ever heard of the kempei-tai, Mr Cairns?'

Larry frowned. 'Yes. I think I have. It's your sort of equivalent of our Special Branch.'

Abe gave a quick smile. 'Not exactly the equivalent. It is a very specialised organisation, the kempei-tai. Were you aware that your friend Mr Kitachi is an important member of this organisation?'

Larry stared at him, open-mouthed.

Abe smiled again. 'It is something to bear in mind, Mr Cairns. This man Kitachi once murdered an acquaintance of mine. I am sure it is not the only illegal death he has on his conscience.' The General shrugged. 'I should not be telling you this. But there was nothing I could do about it at the time. I think these are all things for you to

178

remember, Mr Cairns, in future dealings with your "friend".'

'Yes,' Larry said. 'Yes, indeed. I will remember what you have said, General Abe. And thank you again.'

'I do not understand this,' Chung Lo remarked. 'Wong Tung has dealt with the House of Chung for twenty years. Now he has withdrawn nearly all of his orders. I do not understand it at all.'

'He is dealing, I would suspect, with Hammond and Teng,' Kitachi Tano said.

The two men, and Kai, were seated on the front verandah of Chung Lo's house.

'With Hammond and Teng? But why should he change from us? We have never failed him. And we have offered him the best rate on the coast.'

'No longer,' Kitachi pointed out. 'Hammond and Teng are undercutting you. They are also expanding on the China coast. They have now secured an entry into Shanghai, and are dealing with several merchants there.'

Chung Lo frowned at him. 'How do you know these things, Tano?'

Kitachi tapped his nose. 'I have an informant inside Hammond and Teng.'

Chung Lo's frown deepened. 'Is that ethical?'

'The English themselves have a saying: all is fair in love and war,' Kitachi pointed out. 'Business is a form of war between rivals. I believe in knowing what my competitors are doing.'

'And have you therefore an informant inside the House of Chung?'

Kitachi smiled. 'We are not competitors; we are friends, allies, are we not?'

Chung Lo stroked his chin.

Kai hated to hear his father and Kitachi talk like this, after his experience in Manchuria. 'Larry Cairns,' he said, suddenly.

'What is that?' asked his father.

'This sudden undercutting, this surge of activity from

the Hong Kong branch, has only occurred since Cairns went there as manager.'

'Why, do you know, you could be right,' Kitachi remarked. 'I had not thought of that. This young fellow is a hard and ruthless competitor. A hard and ruthless man,' he added. He was amused at the Chungs' total ignorance at what was going on, their ignorance of his ability to destroy them whenever he chose. He wondered if the Chungs knew about Lan Kuei? He did not see how they could avoid doing so, in so small a society. But, although he had sponsored her return to Singapore, and was also a frequent customer of hers, he was not yet ready to raise the subject. She remained, as she had been from the beginning, an investment for the future.

As was Lawrence Cairns, he thought with a private smile. He had enlisted an Englishman, by placing him in his debt. General Tojo would be pleased. And he had also increased the rivalry between the Chungs and Cairns.

All in all, he thought, his affairs were going very well.

Margaret Cairns swam slowly up and down her pool. It was her favourite occupation, as she had never had a pool of her very own before. Now she owned the largest pool in Hong Kong. What a brilliant idea it had been of Larry's, even if it had been horrendously expensive.

Marion splashed at the shallow end. In the early spring of 1937 she would be six. She was beginning to look very like Larry, and Margaret was happy that she should. With every month, every day of her marriage, she was realising how much she both loved and admired her husband.

She had liked him from the first, when he had been a somewhat awkward public-school boy, veneered with that thin layer of self confidence so often displayed by the successful athlete.

Even then she had been looking at men as possible husbands. This too was a part of her upbringing, but one in which there were so many strange contradictions. On the other hand Mumsy had always said that an unmarried woman was only half a woman – she regarded 'spinster' as the most unfortunate word in the language.

But on the other hand Mumsy, while she so vehemently believed in marriage and motherhood, had never had the slightest understanding of what it was all about. Mumsy's concept of marriage was of being mistress of a house; the more successful a marriage one made, the bigger and better house one would have, the more servants, the more expensive furniture and carpets and pictures. Within this framework one would give parties, and go to parties, and make friends . . . even, in the course of time, if one was lucky, with one's husband.

That there was another side to marriage, the side from which, indeed, came the child who completed the picture, was one of those unfortunate facts of life, like having to 'wash one's hands' – Mumsy never used anything other than this non-committal phrase – or go to the doctor. A wife's purpose in life was to train her husband, as rapidly as possible, that 'that sort of thing' was really unnecessary once one had had a child, and that it was a far better thing for them to live comfortably together as friends rather than have all the mess and beastliness, of going to bed together.

Poor, poor Mumsy.

Margaret had not yet ceased to marvel at how lucky she had been. In the beginning she had behaved exactly as Mumsy had taught her, with the addition of some suggestions from Joan Lees. Joan it was who had put her up to that ghastly, never-to-be-forgotten strip tease on the beach. What a conniving little so-and-so she had been brought up to be!

Larry Cairns had, however, been her very own idea. Daddy had been all for it; Mumsy had thought him rather shallow, and really not old enough or sufficiently well-off to make a satisfactory husband. But Daddy and Uncle Ronald had at least solved the well-off bit, and she was rather glad Larry was only two years older than she.

In the beginning she hadn't known what was happening. Mumsy had told her that on their honeymoon Daddy had had some rather unfortunate ideas, but she had soon put a stop to that. When Margaret had pressed her for details, she had refused. She had even refused details about the most orthodox of sexual behaviour. 'My dear,' she said, 'just lie on your back with your eyes closed until he is finished. I always did.'

'And always smile,' she had added.

Then there was Mumsy's prejudice against people of 'colour'. With all that she now knew, Margaret had no doubt at all that her father had found the sex he lacked at home outside his marriage. That almost certainly meant an Indian or a half-caste. But equally certain, he had never told Mumsy about it!

She had never thought of her father in that way before her marriage. Yet when Larry had told her of his own Chinese mistress, she had hated him for it. That had been unforgiveable, but equally it was unforgivable of him to tell her. Mumsy would have said it was because he was so young, if they had ever discussed it. They never had because Mumsy had also held that there was only one thing worse than not being married at all, and that was a failed marriage. Marriage was not something to be undertaken in a spirit of romance or great hope. It was a job, in which, if one kept one's head and kept working, one would eventually arrive at the position of managing director. To quit because one found out unpleasant things about one's partner in business was both futile and self defeating; it would involve starting all over again, and in a worse position than before.

Poor, poor Mumsy.

And yet, without Mumsy, she might well have made all of those mistakes. Her instincts had been to rush from that hotel bedroom in Simla and jump on a train all the way back to Bombay. Only the thought of how great a failure that would be had prevented her. She had Mumsy to thank for that, just as she had Mumsy to thank for the grim determination with which she had stuck to her guns. and had confided in no one, not even Joan.

And Mumsy had been right about so many other aspects

of a marriage as well. Where she had been so disastrously wrong was in not at least sampling sexual pleasure. Then she would have found out that it was possible to have all of the things she thought essential, and be happy as well.

Poor, poor, Mumsy.

There was nothing she could do about Mumsy now. She could only relish her own happiness, her own success. She could lie back in the pool, and look up at her lovely house, and think about the cocktail party she was having on Saturday evening, and decide what to wear to church on Sunday, and to lunch at the Ogilvys afterwards – she and Janet had become fast friends – and listen to Marion splashing happily. The scent of various exotic dishes wafted from the kitchen where Mansur was busy, and mingled pleasantly with the fragrance of the garden. Margaret could feel a tremendous glow of health and strength through all her limbs, and she reflected that, as she was only twenty-eight years old, this happiness, this contentment, would stretch in front of her for as long as she could imagine.

She could also look forward to Larry's return from the office, at twelve thirty. He did not go back again until three, and lunch was always finished by two . . .

She noticed Mansur standing at the edge of the pool, looking anxious.

'Is something the matter, Mansur?'

'Oh, no, madam. But there is a visitor.'

'Oh, yes?' Margaret dropped her legs and waded to the side; she picked up her robe and wrapped it around herself as she came out of the water.

'A man, madam.'

'I see. Well, you had better show him down here, and bring down some drinks. Tom Collins would be nice.'

'Yes, madam.' Mansur still looked uncertain, but he went up the steps to the inner verandah, while Margaret – pleasantly anticipating this unexpected company – brushed her wet hair and made sure she was adequately covered, then looked up as Mansur reappeared with the visitor, who smiled at her, and bowed.

183

'Mrs Cairns. I have not before had the pleasure. I am a friend of your husband. My name is Kitachi Tano.'

CHAPTER 8
The Warning

Margaret had no idea Larry had any Japanese friends, although presumably he must meet them often enough on his visits to Shanghai.

'Do come in,' she said. 'I'm afraid my husband is at the office.'

Kitachi bowed again, and descended the steps. 'If you do not mind, I would like to wait for him here.'

'Oh. Please do. Will you have a drink?'

'That would be very kind of you, Mrs Cairns.'

'Do you take gin?'

'Gin?' Kitachi appeared to consider. 'Of course, if it is what you are drinking, Mrs Cairns.'

Margaret had never encountered such excessive politeness before, except from a servant, and it slightly unnerved her. 'Mansur . . .'

'Yes, madam. Two Tom Collins.' Mansur hurried off.

Kitachi had reached the foot of the steps. 'Such an elegant mansion. And is this your daughter? Such a lovely child.'

Marion goggled at him.

'Thank you,' Margaret said.

'But of course she takes after her mother.'

Margaret was now feeling distinctly uneasy. The wet bathrobe was clinging to her like a second skin. She might as well take it off.

She walked round the pool to the table and chairs set beneath the beach umbrella, and sat down, crossing her legs.

Kitachi followed. 'Mr Cairns is a most fortunate man,' he remarked.

'He works very hard,' Margaret said lamely, and then wondered if she would be misinterpreted.

'This I know. I have a great respect for him. Do you like living in Hong Kong?'

'Oh, very much. Do you?'

'Alas, I am only here on a visit. My ship leaves again tomorrow.'

'Oh, what a shame,' Margaret said, with great relief.

Mansur arrived with the drinks, and Kitachi continued to make polite conversation, all of it complimentary, about the colony, about Singapore, about how much he liked the British . . . while Margaret prayed that Larry would come home early.

He did, just as they had started their second Tom Collins; Marion had by then been removed by Nanny to be dressed for lunch.

'Mr Kitachi!' Larry exclaimed in surprise, and, Margaret thought, some dismay. 'What brings you to Hong Kong?'

'I am travelling from Singapore to Nagasaki, and my ship called here. So I thought I would take the opportunity to visit. I trust I have not offended you?'

'Why, my dear fellow, of course not.' Larry glanced at Margaret. 'I think perhaps we should invite Mr Kitachi to stay for lunch.'

'Of course. I'll just go and have a word with Mansur.'

She hurried for the house, glad of the chance to put some clothes on. All the time he had been talking, Kitachi had been looking at her, from her face to her breasts to her legs and then back again.

She shivered.

'I was telling your charming wife what a beautiful place you have here,' Kitachi remarked.

'It is rather nice,' Larry agreed. 'The site was chosen a long time ago, by the first manager of Hammond and Teng, years before Hong Kong was anything like it is today.'

'This I know,' Kitachi said.

186

Larry waited. He did not for a moment assume this was either an accidental or a social call. Well, he had supped with the devil, now he must see how long a spoon he had. But Kitachi would have no idea how much he knew. That information he had passed on, in the strictest confidence, to Delaney in Singapore; otherwise he had told not a soul.

'It is good to see that you and your firm are prospering,' Kitachi observed.

'With your assistance, for which I thank you,' Larry prompted.

'It was my pleasure. Was General Abe co-operative?'

'Oh, indeed, as soon as he saw your name.'

Kitachi smiled. 'That is good. Ah, China! What a tangled mess it is in, to be sure.'

'You are thinking about this Chiang Kai-shek business.'

'Can you believe it? Here we have a man who claims to be the master of his country, kidnapped by one of his closest associates. I know this fellow Marshal Chang Hsueh-liang. A treacherous man.'

'Isn't he the warlord opposing your people in Manchuria?'

'Bah, he has accepted that situation. He dreams of some counter-stroke, certainly. But to kidnap his superior, and carry him off to a meeting with the Communists . . . do you know, we had supposed all those vermin to have perished in the mountains.'

'I thought most of them had,' Larry said.

'Oh, a great number did. Out of a hundred thousand who set off, it is said, only ten thousand reached Szechwan. But these are the hard core, vicious men. And now they have all met round a table. One wonders what they have decided. It can be nothing good.'

Larry grinned at him. 'They may well have decided to end their differences and pool their resources to oppose further Japanese encroachments.'

'That is perfectly possible,' Kitachi agreed, with apparent ingenuousness.

'And they can probably do it,' Larry told him. 'I am

very impressed with the way China is developing. You know the railroad from Canton to Hankow is now opened?'

'Yes,' Kitachi said.

'So Hankow, and Nanking, can no longer be cut off by closing the mouth of the Yangtse. Goods can easily be sent up the Pearl River to Canton, then overland by railroad.'

'We are aware of these things,' Kitachi said.

'So don't you think it's time you called it a day? You're getting a very bad press worldwide. It would do your image a great deal of good were you to recall your garrison from Shanghai, and pull back north of the Great Wall. I am sure that some reasonable formula could then be worked out for Manchuria. I beg your pardon, I meant Manchukuo.'

Kitachi gazed at him. 'It is no longer possible for us to, as you put it, call it a day.'

Larry frowned. 'You'll have to explain that.'

'Very simply, our people would not stand for it. I have come to see you in that regard.'

So, at last he was coming to the point. Larry waited.

'You will agree I did you a great favour, three years ago.'

Larry became aware of tension in the air. 'Yes, you did.'

'Now it is possible for you to do me a favour in return.'

'If I can.'

'It may be necessary, at some time in the near future, the very near future, for my government to take more positive steps with regard to China.'

'What sort of steps?'

'Who can say? Who knows how things will develop?'

'But you're sure they are going to develop?'

'Things always develop,' Kitachi said carefully. 'Should they do so, it will be necessary for Japan to look to her own interests, and this my people will certainly do. It would be interesting for us to know what would be the reaction of the British to a positive development in China.'

'You mean a full-scale war?'

Kitachi did not lower his gaze. 'I mean, a positive development.'

'Well, I would say that is something your ambassador in London should be investigating.'

'Oh, he is,' Kitachi said. 'But ambassadors, and the foreign ministers to whom they apply, speak in such riddles. It is very difficult to get the truth out of them. In any event, they are largely controlled by the opinions of the men on the spot.'

'I am not in politics, Kitachi.'

'Perhaps not. But you are Lawrence Cairns. You are a very successful man, and you are known, in British circles at the very least, the length and breadth of East Asia. In Singapore you dined with the Governor and the Colonial Secretary often enough. I cannot suppose you do less here, in a more senior position.'

Larry gazed at him. 'You know a lot about my affairs.'

Kitachi smiled. 'It is my business to do so.'

'So what do you want of me?'

Kitachi leaned forward, and spoke with great earnestness. 'I have been encouraged, by you, to believe that you are a businessman. I think that is splendid. It is business which makes the world go round. You may believe me when I say that we Japanese are all for business. We also remember that the British are not only the best businessmen in the world; they are also our oldest occidental friends. That we have drifted apart may be put down to the Americans, who have reasons of their own for wishing us to be apart.

'But the Americans need not concern us now. It is Japan and Great Britain we are speaking about. We are well aware that we have had, as you have said, a bad press over our moves on the mainland. But I am sure you can appreciate that these moves were necessary for our existence as a nation. Should it be necessary to make further moves they will be dictated by the same basic necessity. No nation can be expected to perish. Great Britain has undertaken expansionist policies time and again in the past three hundred years to deal with that very problem. Our people have always faced similar dilemmas.

'Thus I would put this to you, Mr Cairns. We have established that you and I understand each other, that we can do business together. Very well, let us continue to do so. It is very important to Japan to be sure that, should events in China develop along the lines we anticipate, Great Britain will refrain from condemning us. We ask nothing more than that.'

He leaned back in his chair.

Larry glanced up to where Margaret had reappeared on the verandah, now wearing a dress. However, she had obviously decided against coming down to join them; she had realised that they were having a very serious discussion.

Perhaps the most serious discussion of his life.

'You seem to think I have some say in government policy, Mr Kitachi,' he remarked.

Kitachi smiled. 'You are Lawrence Cairns,' he said again. 'Your opinions will certainly be respected by those in authority here, and in Singapore. Those opinions will certainly find their way back to London. That is all we ask of you. Have we not already shown our generosity to those we consider our friends? I am sure a glance at the books of Hammond and Teng over the past couple of years would confirm that.'

'You are using what we in England call the royal "we",' Larry told him. 'Are you speaking for your government, or for the kempei-tai?'

Kitachi's smile faded, and for a moment his breath made a peculiar hissing sound through his nostrils.

Then the smile returned. 'I had forgotten how well informed you are, Mr Cairns.'

'As you have reminded me, it pays to be well informed, in business. But you have not answered my question.'

'Shall I say, that whenever the kempei-tai speaks, it does so with the voice of the government.'

'And you would like me to put forward my opinion that should an all-out war break out between China and Japan, it would be in the interests of Great Britain to preserve a benevolent neutrality, especially benevolent towards Japan.'

'Your command of English is so much better than mine,' Kitachi said, admiringly. 'You put things so succinctly.'

'Thank you. Unfortunately, that is *not* my opinion. Nor would it do much good if it were, because it is not the opinion of most of my countrymen, certainly not those in administrative positions in the Far East. They, and I, are already of the opinion that your encroachments on China represent an intolerable aggression, a crime against international law and against humanity, which will one day have to be answered for.'

Kitachi frowned.

Larry continued, 'You were kind enough to do me a favour three years ago, which I much appreciated, although your favour to me was in return for some very useful information I was able to give you. Now I think I should give you some more useful information, or at least advice. You should return immediately to your ship and remain there until she sails. Because this afternoon I am going to have a talk with the Colonial Secretary, as you suggest, and when I have told him everything you have said, and everything I know about you, he might well wish to have you arrested.

'Having returned to Nagasaki, I should remain there, if I were you, and not return to Singapore, because I intend to report this conversation also to Inspector Delaney. I suggest, too, that you close your business down. Both of us know that it is only a front for your activities. Well, those activities must now come to an end, Mr Kitachi. I strongly recommend that you take my advice.'

Kitachi's frown had cleared. Now his face was as bland as ever. He looked into his glass, which was empty, then put it down and stood up.

'It appears that for the last few years I have been under a misapprehension. I had assumed that we were conducting a trade, in which I gave you what you wanted, in return for something I might want, at a later date. I see now that you were under the impression that you had blackmailed my assistance from me, with your talk of special branches and possible arrest. Now you are using the same tactics again.

'In these circumstances, I will take your advice, Mr Cairns. But I am disappointed in you. I had thought you were a man who sympathised with our point of view, our necessities. I think you deliberately misled me.'

'I am not misleading you now, Kitachi.'

'I am sure you are not. Nonetheless, I feel betrayed. I am sure you will understand this, Mr Cairns. Thus may I, in turn, offer you a piece of advice?'

'If you wish.' Larry remained seated.

'I have no doubt,' Kitachi said, 'that for all your brave opinions, which may well be held by your friends in government here in the East, it will serve Great Britain best to remain at peace with Japan, no matter what the future may hold. However, should events develop to the stage where war between Japan and Great Britain becomes unavoidable, then I would most strongly recommend that before that sad occurrence, you remove yourself, and your wife and your daughter, far away from Hong Kong. Or Singapore,' he added. 'We of the kempei-tai have very long memories. And we remember longest those who betray us. Good day to you, honourable Mr Cairns.'

He bowed, then turned and went up the steps.

Margaret was waiting at the top. Kitachi bowed to her also. 'Sadly, Mrs Cairns, I find that I am unable, after all, to accept your kind invitation to lunch. I do beg of you to forgive me.'

His gaze again drifted from her face to her breasts, to her hips and then down her legs. Then he bowed again, and went through the house. Mansur was waiting by the front door.

Margaret gazed at Larry. 'What on earth . . .'

'I'm sorry. The little bastard was offensive. He had the nerve to threaten me.'

'The way he looked at me . . . he was stripping me naked with his eyes.'

Larry put his arm round her shoulders. 'As I said, he is an offensive little bastard. We won't be seeing him again, I promise you. Let's have lunch.'

That afternoon, Larry telephoned and asked for an immediate appointment with the Colonial Secretary, and recounted his conversation in full.

The Colonial Secretary stroked his moustache. 'You say you have known for some time that this man Kitachi is a member of the Japanese secret service?'

'Well, from what I understand, the kempei-tai is not actually a secret service as we understand it,' Larry said. 'More like a secret police.'

'More like the Gestapo in Germany,' the Colonial Secretary agreed. 'A very unpleasant organisation.'

'I couldn't agree with you more.'

'Yet you never reported this fact to the police here, or to my office.'

'I saw no reason to. Until today, Kitachi has operated entirely out of Singapore. I have reported, fully, to the Singapore police.'

'Hm. Well, we shall certainly keep our eyes open for the gentleman should he endeavour to return.'

'And you will, I hope, inform London of his activities.'

'Oh, I will. But I would not like you to go away with any false optimism, Cairns. There is not the least possibility of HM Government overtly taking the Chinese side in any escalation of their quarrel with Japan.'

'You seriously mean those idiots in Whitehall would sit back and let Japan take over China?'

'Those idiots in Whitehall, who happen to be my employers, are almost certainly aware of various facts of which you are in happy ignorance, Cairns.'

'You're not going to tell me they're afraid of Japan.'

'Were there only Japan and Great Britain on the surface of this earth, the answer would be no, we are not afraid of Japan. Unfortunately, the situation is not so simple.

193

Whitehall has to be aware that we have potential antagonists in Europe in Germany, and, since the Abyssinian debâcle last year, in Italy.'

'Oh, come now, what about the French alliance? Don't they have the most powerful army in the world? What about the Maginot Line?'

'It is encouraging to think that the French army is the most powerful in the world. As to whether it *is* . . . the Maginot Line will probably save France from invasion, but that does not alter the situation from our point of view. We are responsible for affairs at sea. Were there to be another European war, our navy would not only have to cope with Germany and perhaps Italy, but also protect our empire.'

'Are you suggesting the Navy's not up to it? For God's sake, Germany doesn't *have* a first line navy. As for Japan, they're only allowed two thirds of our strength.'

'That was the agreement of the Naval Conferences. But the Japanese opted out of those limitations several years ago. I think you should put the following facts into perspective. We happen to have a fleet of twelve battleships and three battlecruisers. That sounds good, doesn't it? But, of these fifteen ships, ten – the Queen Elizabeth Class and the Royal Sovereign Class – are more than twenty years old; they were all laid down during the Great War. The same goes for the battlecruisers, *Renown* and *Repulse*. Only three of our capital ships, *Nelson*, *Rodney* and *Hood*, are what can be called modern vessels, and *Hood* was launched in 1918. Even *Nelson* and *Rodney* are both more than ten years old. Certainly we have a new class on the drawing board. The keels of *King George V*, *Prince of Wales* and *Anson* have been laid. But the earliest any of them can come into service is 1939. The very earliest.

'Now let's take the French. They claim eight battleships. But the newest of them is twenty-four years old; they were all laid down *before* the Great War. Now, they have six new ones on the stocks. One of them, *Dunkerque*, is about to be completed. *Strasbourg* could be ready in a couple of years. But the rest are a long way off. So we have a possible joint potential of one modern and three relatively modern capital ships.

'And what have we got against us? The Germans actually have four old battleships. We won't talk about their three so-called pocket battleships, because they are really only heavy cruisers. But they also have two being built, bigger and more powerful than anything we have in mind. The Italians also have four old battleships in service. But they are also building four brand new Littorio Class ships, again as big and powerful as anything we have on the stocks, of which two are due for completion as soon as any of our George V Class. So you'll agree there isn't too much margin for error in the North Sea.

'Now, what have the Japs got? They have eight battleships in commission, every one newer than any of our old ones; several of them are only fractionally older than *Nelson* and *Rodney*. They also have four battlecruisers. Moreover, they have designed, and one at least is about to be laid down, four absolute monsters. We're talking about over sixty thousand tons' displacement, and carrying eighteen-inch guns. That makes even our George V Class look like river gunboats. One of these could be ready in three years, perhaps two, if they hurry. If you add those figures together, the French and ourselves have twenty old capital ships, three middle-aged, and four, possibly five modern but not excessively large ships coming off the stocks within the next three years. If we lump the Japanese together with the Germans and the Italians, and we must do so because even if they are not allied they are all our potential enemies, we are faced with eight old capital ships, twelve middle-aged, and eight due off the stocks within the next three years, of which four at least are going to outgun and outrange anything we shall have by then. Also, by the nature of the beasts, the aggressors have choice of where and when hostilities will commence. Should it ever come to shooting, we are going to be very thinly-stretched everywhere, but in the Far East most of all. After all, I'm sure you'll agree that defending Great Britain has to come first.'

195

Larry gulped. He had never had such a baldly succinct account of the true naval position put to him before. Like everyone else, he had hitherto blandly assumed that because she had always possessed the most powerful navy in the world Britain always would.

'But what about the Americans?'

'What about the Americans? Their policy is neutrality at all costs. They have said so, and they have proved their point. They claim to regard China as being of special interest to them, but they didn't go to war when Japan invaded Manchuria, did they? They protested, as did we. I don't see them doing much more than that even if a full scale war does break out between China and Japan.'

'Not even if we went in first?'

'Why should they pitch in to help us? No, I'm afraid that, until the European business is sorted out – and that could take some time – we are going to have to suffer the Japanese, and so are the Chinese.'

Larry went home in a thoughtful frame of mind.

'Now that is very strange,' Chung Lo remarked. 'Here is a letter from Kitachi Tano informing me that he is closing down his company here and will not be returning. Just like that.'

Kai took the envelope and studied it. 'This has been opened.'

'Opened? How can it have been opened?'

Kai showed his father the telltale marks.

'But who would have done such a thing?' Chung Lo wondered.

'Only the Government has the power to tamper with the mails,' Kai told him.

'I do not understand.'

'Father, it is clear that your friend Kitachi has been discovered to be anti-British. He is, in fact, an agent for the Japanese government, and you are well aware of that. What else did he put in that letter?'

'It is no concern of yours.'

'Father, if he has said anything incriminating, you, the

entire family, the House of Chung, could be in serious trouble.'

Chung Lo gazed at him, then looked down at the letter again. 'He has written nothing incriminating.'

'He must have made some reference to your various conversations.'

'He merely says that he hopes I will not forget the things of which we have spoken, and looks forward to the day when we may again work shoulder to shoulder.'

'He is a foolish man,' Kai snapped.

'That is hardly incriminating.'

'It will have been noted by the police who read that letter. Let us hope and pray there is never any need for them to use it.'

'I have failed, honourable General,' Kitachi Tano said. He sat before General Tojo's desk with bowed head. 'I contemplated seppuku on the voyage here from Hong Kong, but I deemed it my duty to report to you first. Now, if you will give me permission to withdraw . . .'

'Why do you think you have failed?' Tojo asked.

'You gave me a mission and a post, honourable General. I have not accomplished my mission, and I have been ignominiously expelled from my post. Is that not failure?'

'You were faced with circumstances I did not envisage. Your only real mistake was in trusting this Englishman. The English are all the same, not to be trusted. But if you have learned so good a lesson at so little cost, then you are a fortunate man. As for Singapore, I have no doubt that you have sown well there. And there is nothing more for you to do there now. Events are already beginning to take their shape, a shape which will be excellent for us.'

Kitachi gazed at him, eyes glowing.

'When next you go to Singapore, Tano,' Tojo said, 'it will be in uniform, and you will go as a conqueror.' He smiled. 'For the time being, you may resume wearing that uniform, Colonel Kitachi.'

Kitachi bowed.

★ ★ ★

197

In July 1937, the long-smouldering conflict between Japan and China burst into open flame.

On 7 July, Japanese troops on night manoeuvres at Lukouchiao, not far north of Peking, clashed with Chinese. This time, as the Japanese command had suspected would happen following the rapprochement between Chiang Kai-shek, Mao Tse-tung and Chang Hsueh-liang, the Chinese did not withdraw with protests. They stood their ground and fought.

This did not prevent them being defeated. Marshal Chang had to retreat even from Peking, which the Japanese entered three weeks later, using it as a base from which to launch a campaign which by the end of the year had conquered huge areas of northern China.

The following month fighting began outside Shanghai once more. This time the Chinese were prepared, and the Japanese there found themselves surrounded by a vastly superior force. For a few weeks the world waited for the unique spectacle of a Japanese army being forced to surrender, but the Japanese held on, reinforcements were poured in from Japan, and at last the Chinese were forced to retreat. Shanghai, which had been savagely bombed from the start of the war, was occupied on 8 November, and the Yangtse lay at Japan's mercy.

And the rest of the world did nothing more than protest.

The Japanese offensive continued, and it was clear that they meant firstly to conquer the entire Chinese coastland, and then to use the great rivers, the Yangtse and the Hwang-Ho, to penetrate into the interior of the country.

Canton would be invaded next.

Larry and Margaret stood on the front verandah of their house and watched the rows of bombers flying just to the east, taking great care not to overfly British territory, but circling Hong Kong before sweeping up the Pearl River.

'Is there nothing we can do?' Margaret asked sadly.

'Not a bloody thing,' Larry told her.

Then refugees started arriving at the New Territories borders, with the most harrowing tales of Japanese atrocities. These were dismissed as propaganda at first, although some of the injuries were real enough. But just before Christmas news arrived of the sack of Nanking. The Chinese government had already retired to Hankow, and the city was virtually undefended. The Japanese soldiery were turned loose on the people, and reports of the orgy of murder, rape and destruction, attested by photographic evidence, shocked the world.

'To think that we entertained that man Kitachi in our house,' Margaret said.

Larry wrote to both Brian Anstey and Ronald Lees and asked their advice as to whether Margaret and Marion should move to a safer place than Hong Kong, which was the British colony nearest to the fighting. Both men wrote back pooh-poohing his fears. 'The Japs have more sense than to trouble Hong Kong,' Ronald Lees wrote. 'They are showing that with every day. They don't want to have to take us on as well as the Chinks.'

Clearly Lees had never really studied the situation.

Brian Anstey was more resonable. 'I understand your concern, on both moral and physical grounds, that Meg and Marion should be so close to such an unpleasant war. However, I doubt they are in any real danger, and it may be essential that our loved ones do see the horrors of war at first hand, as it were, to prepare them for the real thing when it comes, as it may well do in Europe within a few years.

'More important, I think it is very necessary that those of us in positions of responsibility reveal not the slightest suggestion that we are in any way frightened of the Japanese. For you to send Margaret away would give a very unwelcome indication of fear for the future, and this in turn would have a very bad effect upon business, which is in any event suffering. I do not anticipate any worsening of the situation for a long time to come. Japan is fully committed to China, and it seems clear that as they advance into the interior of that huge country or, to put it the other way, as the Chinese are forced back into their hinterland, the Japanese are going to find the going far rougher than at present.

'I would strongly recommend that you proceed with the plans you have outlined to us. When Marion is ten or eleven, you will of course send her home to school, and it would be natural for Meg to accompany her and see her settled in. I think we could review the situation then.'

Since Marion was still only six, Larry hoped his father-in-law was right.

As for business, that was at rock bottom. Neither Wong Tung nor Ting Ho had been heard of for some time.

So Larry made his own decision. He would accept the prevailing opinion that nothing untoward was likely to happen for another year at least. In 1939 he was due for long leave again. He would then take Marion to his parents to start school, although she would only be eight years old. And he would persuade Margaret to stay with her until the situation in the East clarified itself.

Chung Kai was horrified by what he read of the Japanese onslaught. Chung Su was less so. 'It is how they have always behaved,' she reminded him.

Her family had lived in northern China for generations, and her grandparents had been in Port Arthur when it fell to a Japanese onslaught in 1894. Her grandfather had been decapitated and her grandmother had been repeatedly raped across his dead body.

'It is because they do not believe someone who has been defeated has any rights. To do them justice, they do not believe that they have any rights either, once they have been defeated. That is why they often commit suicide rather than surrender. It is still a barbarous moral code.'

'What am I to do?' Chung Lo asked. It was typical that he should ask Chung Kai this question, instead of one of his elder sons. Chung Kai had a toughness, and an experience of the world, that his brothers lacked. It was to Chung Kai that Chung Lo had turned when they heard the rumour that Lan was back in Singapore, living as a prostitute. Then it had been necessary to assemble the entire family. Chung Cheong had wanted to have his sister arrested and deported.

Chung Kai had pointed out that one could not be deported from one's own country.

Chung San had then wanted to go and burn the Bamboo Curtain down.

'You would be gaoled for arson,' Chung Kai had told him.

He had volunteered to go and visit Lan, and ask her to leave. He had done so, and Lan had treated him with contempt.

'I like it here,' she had said. 'And I am making a lot of money. I am not going to leave. But since you are here, Kai . . . have you never wished to screw your own sister? It is only sixty dollars.'

Then Kai had felt like burning down the Bamboo Curtain himself, but instead he had left.

'She is no longer my sister, or your daughter,' he had told Chung Lo. 'She has changed.'

'Because of that English scoundrel,' Chung Lo growled.

'Yes. But looking over our shoulders is a waste of time, Father.'

'Then what are we going to do?'

'We are going to ignore her, forget her. All of us. She does not exist.'

Chung Lo had understood that was indeed the only sensible solution; it had increased his realisation that Kai was the most level-headed of his children.

Now he said, 'But Kitachi Tano was our friend. More, he was our hope of gaining our independence from Britain.'

'He was never your friend, Father,' Chung Kai said severely. 'As for gaining independence from Britain, it was only in order to exchange being a British colony for being a Japanese one.'

'What am I to do?' Chung Lo asked again. He was an old man now, and he hated the thought of upheaval.

'I think you should go to the police, and tell them

everything that was ever said between Kitachi and yourself,' Kai recommended.

The old man shook his head. 'I cannot do that. That would be to betray a confidence, and a friend.'

Chung Kai sighed. 'But he is *not* your friend, Father.'

'His people are at war, and war is terrible. We have no proof that Kitachi Tano was involved in any of these atrocities. I gave him my friendship, and he will retain my friendship until I have proof that he is my enemy. I will not betray him to the police.'

Kai sighed, and went to play with the little boys. He was beginning to wonder just what his father had agreed with Kitachi.

'Tano, my brother!' Aiwa bowed before embracing Kitachi. He was so handsome, in his uniform, so distinguished in his new, senior rank.

Not for the first time, she wondered why he had never married. He was forty now. Surely a man should be married by forty.

But then, she was twenty-six, and she was unmarried as well. She knew her reason well enough: she had never met a man the equal of her brother.

But he should be married, for the sake of their dwindling family. She walked with him to the shrine, and he lit a candle to place there in memory of their parents.

'It grieves me,' he said, 'to think of you living here alone, while I am away. You should have a husband.'

'I am content to keep house for you, my brother, until you find yourself a wife.'

'I have no desire for a wife.' He changed from his uniform into a kimono, and they sat down opposite each other to drink tea served by the girl.

'Then I shall be content,' Aiwa said.

They gazed at each other, unspoken, almost unthinkable thoughts drifting across their minds. Their parents were dead. They had no brothers and sisters. Because of Tano's work, they did not even have many friends.

Within these walls there were only themselves.

Aiwa shivered. 'I am so afraid, when you go to war. Before, I was afraid because of what you were doing. Now . . . I read the newspapers and I listen to the wireless . . . is it as terrible as they say?'

'It is terrible,' Tano agreed. 'But less so for me. I am not a front line soldier. I follow behind our troops, to deal with those of the enemy left behind.'

'But that must be terrible too,' Aiwa said. 'If what I read and hear is true.'

'Yes,' Tano said. 'It is often terrible. Modern war spares no one. It cannot afford to. I cannot afford to spare anyone, when I interrogate them. They are enemies of our people, of our ancestors and our descendants.'

Aiwa shivered again. She could not imagine what it must be like to be a helpless, defeated Chinese, about to be interrogated by Tano. He could look so stern, and yet, while looking stern, he could also look so transfigured with the spirit of bushido, the code of the warrior, which spelt out that when a man fought it must be to victory or to death. There was no possibility of compromise, and there was only contempt for those who sought to surrender.

'I wonder you are not afraid,' she said.

'Me? Afraid? I have told you, there is no danger in what I do.'

'I meant, I wonder you are not afraid of what you do.'

He studied her for several seconds. Afraid of what I do, he thought. His little sister was nearer the truth than she supposed.

He looked past her at the samurai sword, standing in the corner. It had always been his dream to use that sword in battle. But he had never been allowed into battle. Yet he had used the sword.

His men had been surprised, during the sack of Nanking, when he had told them he would personally execute the Chinese colonel; but after all, an officer should be executed by an officer of equal rank, rather than a common soldier.

Already wounded, the prisoner had advanced towards

the Japanese, hands held high, perhaps expecting to be nursed and sent to a prison camp. But the orders were that no prisoners were to be taken in Nanking; it was to be so sacked and devastated as to be a warning to the rest of China.

Tano had never been so nervous in his life. The Chinese had knelt, head bowed, and he had stood beside him, legs spread, fingers wrapped around the great two-handed grip. His men had watched him eagerly, certain of his prowess. Only he had doubted. Suppose he missed, and cut the man on the shoulder? Or suppose he did not sever the neck with a single blow? He waited so long the Chinese colonel raised his head in anguish.

In the end, there was nothing to be afraid of. Tano had swung the great sword truly and accurately, with all his strength. The head had flown away from the body, which had remained kneeling there for perhaps a second, blood spouting from the severed arteries, before collapsing.

He had felt a curious tingling spreading through his body. He had never killed before. Now he wanted to kill again. But these were not things he could expect his sister to understand.

So he asked, 'Are you afraid of the meat you cook for my supper?'

'It is already dead. And it is a necessary part of our existence.'

'The people I question are to all intents and purposes already dead, and they are a necessary part of the existence of our army, and therefore of our nation.'

'Do you hate these people?'

Kitachi considered. 'No,' he said at last. 'I do not hate them. I feel contempt for them.'

'I am glad you do not hate them,' Aiwa said.

Kitachi's eyes gleamed. 'There are people amongst our enemies whom I hate,' he said. 'But I have never yet had the pleasure of interrogating one of them. That day will come.'

And Aiwa shivered a third time.

★　★　★

The war intensified as the year ended. Inevitably there were mistakes. Japanese planes bombed and sank the United States gunboat *Panay* on the Upper Yangtse, with considerable loss of life. The event sent a thrill of alarm through the capitals of the world, but the United States was determined to maintain its policy of strict neutrality, and the Japanese apologised for the incident and paid an indemnity.

In the following year their armies pushed on to Hankow, and it seemed only a matter of time before all of China was theirs.

But in 1938, events in China suddenly seemed unimportant. For now it was Europe that came to the boil, as Hitler's Germany forcibly achieved the *anschluss*, the unification of Germany and Austria, in the face of world condemnation. By the end of the year Germany had also forced the annexation of the Sudetenland from Czechoslovakia, an event in which the British and French governments, as bent on maintaining the peace as America, could only acquiesce.

Yet these evidences of the Nazi intention to obtain hegemony in Europe also sent shock waves around the world, and in Hong Kong the Governor held a meeting of the more senior members of the British community.

'No one can possibly tell,' he said, 'what is going to happen in the next couple of years. Mr Chamberlain has said that he believes we have achieved a lasting agreement with Herr Hitler which will ensure the peace of Europe for the foreseeable future. We must all hope and pray that he is right.

'However, I have to tell you, in the strictest confidence, that the Colonial Office has advised me, as it has advised all its officials, that we must be prepared for the Prime Minister to be proven wrong.

'Now, you may well ask yourself what effect a war on the other side of the globe will have on us here in Hong Kong. The short answer is: if the conflict is confined to say, Britain and France against Germany and Italy, very little, although we may well anticipate that German raiders, whether surface or submarine, will appear in these waters.

'However, it is known to HM Government that there have been several meetings between the Japanese Foreign Minister and Herr Ribbentrop, and in the event of a war between Britain and Germany it is not beyond the bounds of possibility that hostilities will take on a wider significance. I would prefer to say nothing more than that at the moment.

'Steps are already being taken to increase the defences of those colonies which are considered vulnerable to alien pressure. The garrison of Hong Kong is to be raised from one to three battalions in the near future.'

He paused to give a brief cough, well aware of the thoughts filling the minds of the men in front of him: three battalions, perhaps two thousand men, to defend Hong Kong against a Japanese army?

'However, it is felt that it would do no harm, and might even do a great deal of good, were we also to raise a volunteer force from amongst the British community here. I may say,' he hurried on, as there was a rustle of comment, 'that such a step is in the very best traditions of British history. When Bonaparte was encamped outside Boulogne, it was a poor patriot who did not don uniform. And it was the readiness of the Territorial Army to defend Britain which enabled our entire regular army to be sent to France in 1914.

'I would like to feel, and to be able to report to Whitehall, that my appeal has met with a positive response here in Hong Kong. We have much to defend, in this distant outpost of empire. It is not merely our wives and loved ones, the businesses we have created, the homes we have built. We have also created a little bit of England in this alien land. We have perhaps taught the native populations a better way of life, certainly a more acceptable way of justice. It remains to us to continue to show the way. Thank you.'

★　★　★

206

'A volunteer?' Margaret inquired, trying not to laugh. 'A volunteer what?'

'A volunteer soldier,' Larry said with dignity.

'But you've never soldiered in your life. I bet you weren't even in the OTC at school.'

'Well, I wasn't,' Larry confessed. 'It was a choice between OTC and cricket, and I opted for cricket. But now I'm opting for the Volunteers. And it may interest you to know that I have already been made sergeant.'

'Sergeant? But you haven't even had a parade yet. How did you get to be sergeant already?'

'I do happen to be Manager of Hammond and Teng,' Larry reminded her.

The Volunteers were issued with khaki shirts and shorts, khaki stockings and brown shoes, and a khaki forage cap. They were also issued with Sam Browne belts from which hung a lethal-looking bayonet in a leather scabbard – lethal if one could get within four feet of an enemy. Rifles were as yet in short supply and had to be shared, one to each platoon.

The sergeant's stripes were issued separately, and Margaret had to stitch them on to Larry's sleeves. As she was no great seamstress she did it crookedly, and ended up sending them to a Chinese woman in Victoria to be sewn on straight.

'You look very smart,' she commented as he set off for his parade. 'At least you have the legs to wear shorts.'

'You can thank cricket for that,' he reminded her.

'What a shame the rest of them didn't play cricket,' she observed.

For Larry, the Volunteer parades and field days came to replace cricket and even sailing in the early days of 1939. It was all great fun, and he showed a natural aptitude for leading men, which seemed to be taken for granted since he was manager of one of the colony's leading firms. By March he had been promoted to lieutenant; the stripes disappeared and Mansur found himself cleaning a pair of 'pips', or tiny silver stars, one for each shoulder.

'If this goes on you'll be a general in four years,' Margaret commented.

But then it was time to put away such boyish toys as rifles and bayonets, and go away on long leave.

This was a repetition of 1935, save that everything was grimmer. They stopped in Singapore, naturally, and Larry, although officially on leave, had to have a long chat with Ronald Lees.

'Of course everyone understands that with the entire China coast closed business out of Hong Kong is going to go through one hell of a slump,' Lees assured him. 'I don't suppose there is any chance of doing some with the Japs?'

'I doubt it. Anyway, with respect, Ronnie, I would rather not. To do business with those thugs would rather tend to condone what they're doing in China.'

'Mm. I suppose you're right. On the other hand, informed opinion seems to think that they're going to remain in occupation of the Chinese coastland for some time. If that is so, we're going to have to do business with them eventually. I would think about that if I were you.'

Larry did, and didn't like the prospect at all. It would be rather like eating his words to Kitachi.

But Lees had a great deal more on his mind than Hong Kong.

'We have all kinds of trouble breeding here,' he grumbled. 'Do you know, there's now a Communist Party in Singapore? Stirring up all manner of trouble, riots against British imperialism, strikes for higher wages, you name it. There have even been pitched battles between strikers and the police on the rubber plantations on the mainland. Why they don't move in and lock the lot up I can't imagine.'

'Free society, old man,' Larry reminded him. 'That's what it's all about.'

That the British Government was alive to the tensions

and possible dangers in the Far East was evidenced when he and Margaret, after inspecting their bungalow to make sure it was in good order – it was rented to an English couple named Sharples; he was a doctor at the Queen Alexandra Hospital – took a stroll down to the harbour. Massive fortifications were in the process of being built, as well as facilities for what was obviously going to be a sizeable garrison.

'Singapore is going to be an impregnable naval base, just like Gibraltar,' Roly Payne told them. Singapore, like Hong Kong, had raised a corps of Volunteers, and Roly was a captain. 'Just the sort of thing to make the Japs think twice about ever chancing their arm.'

Larry had another long chat with Brian Anstey in Bombay.

'I retire next year,' Anstey told him. 'And frankly, I'm quite happy to be getting out. India is an unhappy country right now. All this agitation, that bloody Gandhi fellow . . . are you planning to leave Margaret and Marion in England?'

'I haven't mentioned it to Meg yet. But I have that in mind. Marion is going to stay, of course.'

'Yes. I think you're probably right this time. Well . . .' he gave a bright smile. 'We'll be able to look after them when we come home. Hate to think of you on your own in Hong Kong, old man . . .'

'I'll manage,' Larry promised him.

Larry mentioned the idea to Margaret as the ship made its way up the Red Sea, and found her unresponsive.

'Just forget it,' she said. 'I am not leaving you on your own, anywhere.'

He couldn't resist a quip. 'Because you'll worry about me, or about me shacking up with a Chinese?'

'We wasted the first four years of our marriage,' she said, perfectly seriously. 'I don't intend to waste another moment of it.'

'But we'll leave Marion.'

209

Margaret surveyed her daughter, who was sitting in a deckchair reading a comic and sipping iced orange juice. 'She's only eight. That's far too young. I had planned to wait until our next long leave.'

'But that's not for four years,' he protested.

'Are you really expecting some kind of world war to break out in four years? I should think all these tensions will have been sorted out, by then.'

He didn't return to the subject. He only hoped she was right.

England was a shock, however. 1939 was the wettest summer for years.

Larry tried to see some first-class cricket. Having missed the Test Match at Lord's, this year between England and the West Indies, he made a special journey up to Manchester for the second international, and spent most of the three days huddled in a mackintosh while it either blew a gale or poured with rain.

But worse than the weather, there was a feeling of desperation. While Larry and Margaret were still at sea, Hitler had scornfully ignored the terms of the Munich Agreement and absorbed the rest of Czechoslovakia. Now there was no doubt in anyone's mind that there was going to be a war, however horrible and unpleasant it would be: the Government had even given unconditional guarantees against German aggression to countries such as Poland and Rumania, with whom Britain had absolutely nothing in common, and who were themselves under virtually fascist dictatorships.

People were queueing up to obtain gas masks, and the Territorials – 'volunteers,' Larry reminded Margaret – were drilling in the parks.

'You know what,' Margaret said. 'Hong Kong feels a lot safer. As well as warmer and drier. Marion is definitely coming back with us.'

Peter and Lucy agreed with them.

'Wish we could come back with you too,' Peter told Larry in private.

'Well, why don't you? You're retired. Sell, or rent the

house, and come on out. You'll love it out there. And it'll do Mummy's asthma no end of good.'

'Do you know, I'm entirely tempted. Give me a chance to talk it over with your mother.'

But within a week it became necessary to make a very quick decision indeed. First came the news of Hitler's non-aggression pact with Russia, and then, on 1 September, Germany invaded Poland.

CHAPTER 9
The War

The British ultimatum requiring Germany to withdraw from Poland, and the consequent declaration of war on Sunday 3 September, left everyone feeling somewhat breathless but also less apprehensive. The prospect of such an immense plunge into the dark had been hanging over the nation for so long that most people felt relieved that the decision had at last been taken. People were surprised to find that war did not immediately mean a sky black with enemy bombers obliterating all of Britain's major cities. There was an air raid warning within minutes of Mr Chamberlain's speech, but this turned out to be a false alarm.

Yet that the war would intensify, and bombers appear over Britain, no one doubted. Larry had booked return passages to Hong Kong for 10 September, and it seemed to both Margaret and himself that it was a good idea to leave Europe behind them; he had to get back in any case: Ronald Lees sent a telegram, putting an end to any thoughts of Larry joining up. He was still only thirty-two, very fit, and had had some military training with the Volunteers, but Margaret was naturally dead against it. In any case Lees's cable read: we need you here.

The only question was whether or not to leave Marion behind, but the opinion of Larry's parents coincided with their own: that anywhere in the world had to be safer than England.

They received a considerable shock when news arrived of the torpedoing of the *SS Athenia* off the west coast of Ireland on the very day war was declared, with considerable loss of life. But Larry reasoned that she had been bound west, and the Atlantic had always been the U-boats' hunting ground. They were bound for Gibraltar and the Mediterranean, and Italy had declared her neutrality.

Peter and Lucy Cairns decided against accompanying them.

'We may be needed here,' said Peter who, still vigorous at fifty-seven, had every intention of offering his services.

So Meg and Larry bade England farewell. After a nervous passage through the Bay of Biscay and along the Portuguese coast, when they were required to wear their lifejackets at all times and sleep on deck in deckchairs, they arrived at the safety of Gibraltar and the sunlit waters of the Mediterranean.

Now the war seemed very far away, although there were more warships in evidence than usual, since no one quite trusted Mussolini. But the rest of the voyage was uneventful, and with no news of any importance coming out of Europe save for the disappearance of Poland from the map, the sense of unreality grew.

In Bombay, the Ansteys were quite confident.

'It's all working out to our advantage,' Brian Anstey told Larry. 'Chamberlain knows what he's doing. The campaigning season is over now, and by next spring we'll be at full strength, and the French, too. We'll see what Mr Hitler does then.'

'What attitude are the Japs taking?' Larry asked.

'Oh, they want no part in our fight, and have said so. They have their hands full with the Chinese. If you ask me, our most serious problem out here is going to be these bloody Indians. Naturally now we have our hands full in Europe they're clamouring harder than ever for at least dominion status. Gandhi and Nehru should be locked up.'

Soon they were.

In Singapore, business was going on as usual, and there was a feeling of total confidence.

'According to everything I hear,' Ronald Lees said, 'Hitler can't afford a defeat, or his generals will throw him over. He'll certainly be defeated when we get going

213

next year, so the war will probably be over by next Christmas.'

Larry went to see Delaney.

'Well,' the policeman said. 'We do have a file, quite a large one, on people, both Chinese and Malay, who had contacts with Kitachi – he's a colonel, now, by the way – and who certainly talked subversion. But that was a few years ago, and frankly, we are spending more time keeping an eye on the Communists nowadays. I've had to lock up a few of their leaders.' He grinned. 'That's the great advantage of actually being at war; you can do things you can't do in peacetime. But, seriously, since you warned Kitachi off, the Japanese influence here has all rather fizzled, so far as we can make out. Don't worry, we have our eyes on everyone who had any contact with Kitachi, just in case they start to make trouble. You know your old friends the Chungs are on that list.'

'I thought they might be. I'm still sure Chung Kai wouldn't have been involved.'

'Well, I'll agree we have nothing concrete on him. His father and elder brothers certainly were involved. Did you know that old Chung Lo is seriously ill?'

'No, I didn't. I'm sorry to hear it. Tell me, do you keep an eye on the red light district?'

'Of course we do.'

'Is there still a girl named Lan Kuei operating there?'

Delaney grinned. 'Little Orchid is our biggest madam. If you wanted to snuggle up to that one, Larry, even you would have to book weeks in advance. And even then, there's no guarantee she'd accept you. She takes her pick.'

Well, I'll be damned, Larry thought. So she had made it, after all.

Delaney was studying him. 'I assume you know who she really is?'

'Yes,' Larry said. 'Do the Chungs know?'

'I don't see how they can avoid knowing; Singapore is a very small community. But they take no notice of her, pretend she doesn't exist, at least in public.'

'That sounds fairly typical.'

★ ★ ★

Larry called a taxi and drove out to the Chung estate. To his surprise he was admitted without demur and, ascending the steps to the verandah, found himself facing an exceptionally pretty and chic Chinese woman, in her early thirties, he estimated. She wore Western-style clothes and her hair was cut short, while the somewhat bold features denoted a north Chinese background.

'I am Chung Su,' she said. 'Welcome, Mr Cairns. I'm afraid my husband is out; he's at the warehouse.'

'I actually called to ask about Mr Chung Lo.'

She sighed. 'He is not well. I'm afraid he is forbidden visitors. But it is very good of you to call. Will you take tea?' She rang a little silver bell.

'That's very kind of you.' Larry sat in a wicker chair, and thought to himself: Kai is a lucky fellow; but then, he deserves it.

Then he wondered what Chung Su thought of having a prostitute for a sister-in-law, and wondered if she knew his part in that?

Two little boys ran screaming down the drive, shooting at each other with toy pistols containing very loud caps.

'They are very noisy,' Chung Su conceded.

'They look almost like twins.'

'They are twins, Mr Cairns. I often think I owe the world an apology for inflicting such monsters on it.' But she smiled fondly as she spoke.

'Forgive me,' Larry ventured, 'but you have an American accent. Have you ever been there?'

'I was educated there.'

'Ah. And you met Kai there?'

'No, I met my husband in Manchuria. He saved my life after my parents had been murdered by the Japanese.'

'Of course.' He snapped his fingers. 'I remember reading about it.'

Tea was served. Larry couldn't remember if it was the same servant as a dozen years ago.

'My husband has spoken to me of you,' Chung Su said.

Larry waited.

'I think he is sorry for much that happened,' Chung Su said.

'So am I,' Larry said.

So she does know about Lan, he thought. And about Lan Kuei.

'But what is done, is done,' Chung Su said. 'It is difficult to reclaim the past.'

So he has not yet forgiven me, Larry thought. He finished his tea. 'I must go. Please give your husband my regards, and tell him I am sorry about his father.'

'I will do so, Mr Cairns. And thank you for calling.'

At the top of the steps Larry turned back for a moment. 'Do you still hate the Japanese, Mrs Chung?' he asked.

'Oh, yes, Mr Cairns. I will always hate the Japanese.'

He nodded, and hurried down the steps, reassured that Kai, however much he might loathe his former friend, would never work for Kitachi.

For all the powerful fortifications and the presence of an Australian brigade supposed to be on its way to the Middle East, the drilling of the Volunteers, and the air-raid warning drills, life in Singapore did not seem to have changed a great deal.

The Lees had a cocktail party for the Cairns, as did the Sharples, who took great pleasure in showing Larry and Margaret over their house to reassure them that it was being kept in perfect order.

Molly Sharples, small and intense, was one of those women for whom everything had to be just so. Her husband, twice her size, reminded Larry of a friendly bear.

'He's a sweetie, actually,' Joan Lees confessed. 'I'm going to work for him.'

'You?' Margaret was astounded; Joan had never done a day's work in her life.

'I've signed up as an auxiliary nurse. Can you imagine?' Joan giggled. 'Bedpans and bedbaths.'

'Good Lord!' Margaret was even more astounded. 'But you won't have to . . . well . . . look after men, will you?'

'Of course,' Joan said. 'That's what I told you. Bedpans

and bedbaths. But only our own people; they'll have Chinese nurses for the others.'

'Hm,' Margaret commented, thoughtfully. 'I suppose one should do one's bit . . .'

Hong Kong also appeared very much as they had left it.

'Things seem to have quietened down on the mainland,' Firth told Larry. 'I would say the Japanese are just starting to realise what they've taken on. I suppose they expected the Chinese to cave in once they lost the coast. But they seem to be as prepared to fight as ever.'

Larry considered the accounts. Trade with Canton and Shanghai had just about finished. Presumably he could no longer use Kitachi's letter of introduction to get into the country and drum up business. Ronald Lees had been entirely reassuring in Singapore. 'We recognise the circumstances are exceptional, Larry,' he had said. 'And we know you did your damndest. For those couple of years, before the shooting started in earnest, Hong Kong was doing more business than any of our other branches. Now, we'll just have to wait for the shooting to stop. Hell, they've been at it two years. They'll both be exhausted in another six months.'

But this didn't happen, for by the time Larry and Margaret had been back six months the entire situation had changed. Hitler was master of Europe; Britain was a beleaguered island; Italy was now an enemy, and the future looked very grim.

'There's a rumour that the Japs are demanding bases in French Indo-China from the Vichy Government,' Brigadier Maltby, the new commander of the Hong Kong Garrison, told his officers, who included in their ranks the captains and major of the Volunteer Corps. Now well over two hundred strong, and at last armed with not only a rifle apiece but with several machine gun sections, the Volunteers felt able to give a good account of themselves if they ever had to start shooting.

The whole garrison had been strengthened, and

altogether Maltby commanded some twelve thousand men.

'It is very unlikely that Vichy will deny that request, as the Japs will certainly be able to put pressure on them through Germany. Now, it is entirely possible, even probable, that the Japs want those bases to advance into China from the south, and cut the Burma Road which, as I am sure you know, is the sole supply route for Chiang Kai-shek's armies in the interior. However, it also means that they will have air bases, and presumably troop garrisons, very close to Malaya. I can tell you, they're not very happy about it down there.'

'At least they're not paying any attention to us, sir,' someone said.

'Perhaps not, but the whole situation is tending to escalate, and I don't want any slackening of our precautions.'

The rest of 1940 was very tense indeed. The Japanese duly got their bases in French Indo-China, and then demanded that the British close the Burma Road. In their beleaguered circumstances, the British Government, now led by Winston Churchill, could do nothing but agree, to the humiliation of their representatives in the Far East.

Things looked so bad that when Larry took Margaret and Marion down to Singapore for the Board Meeting and Christmas, he again discussed with Lees the possibility of sending them home.

'I wouldn't, old man,' Lees said.

'Don't tell me, people would think I'm scared.'

'Well, they would. I mean, Joan and Lizzie are still here.' He brooded for several seconds.

'But there are other factors which are more important,' Lees went on. 'For example, getting anyone home to the UK isn't just a matter of booking a passage, any more. You have to have priority. Then, even when you've got priority and a berth, it's a damned dangerous operation. There are Axis submarines even in the Indian Ocean.

'Thirdly, what makes you think England is a safe place to be? Quite apart from the Blitz, there can be no doubt that Hitler means to invade next spring. I can tell you that Brian and Julia Anstey have put off their retirement, simply because they don't want to go home right now. No, no, Margaret and Marion are safer here in Singapore. This fortress is impregnable. And the Japs know it.'

'We happen to be living in Hong Kong,' Larry pointed out.

'The Japs aren't interested in Hong Kong. But I tell you what you do, old boy. Should they declare war on us, for any reason, you have my permission to send Meg and Marion down here to us. Hell, you have my permission to close the Hong Kong office and bring all your staff down as well. You wouldn't be doing any good up there and we could use you here. That sound all right to you?'

It had to, as there seemed no alternative.

But then everything changed again. Churchill announced the re-opening of the Burma Road, which caused some alarm amongst the locals, though the Japanese hardly reacted at all. Their failure to force the Chinese to surrender had had repercussions at home, and the government was again in civilian hands; thus they were now engaged in a lengthy diplomatic dispute with the United States, who were becoming more and more concerned about the situation in the Pacific. When the news was received that a large proportion of the American fleet, including several battleships and three aircraft carriers, was being ordered to concentrate at the naval base of Pearl Harbor in the Hawaiian Islands, everyone felt greatly relieved.

'I'm sure you will agree with me,' Lees wrote, 'that it is as plain a warning as can be given to Mr Tojo and his friends without actually opening fire. The Yanks are prepared to stop him if he goes too far.'

In addition to the reassurance of America's support, by now Britain was no longer quite so beleaguered. True, defeat followed victory in the desert with alarming rapidity, and the British were also thrown out of Greece but, most importantly to those at the end of the lifelines maintained by the Royal Navy, in May the giant German battleship *Bismarck*, turned loose in the Atlantic to cause as much havoc as possible, was sunk by the Royal Navy. Britannia still ruled the waves. It was the best tonic anyone had received since the war began.

Brian and Julia Anstey, who had postponed their retirement by a year, now returned home.

Two months later the threat of invasion receded with the German attack on Russia, and the gaining of Russia as an ally was in itself heartening.

'I don't understand it at all,' Chung Kai confessed to Su. 'I had always supposed the British were entirely against Communism, yet here they are allying themselves with the Russians.'

'The British are pragmatists,' Su pointed out. 'They would ally themselves with the devil to defeat Hitler.'

'That is just what they have done,' Kai agreed.

He was in a sombre mood, having just buried his father. Nor could he feel any pride in having been unanimously chosen, by his brothers, to succeed as President of the House of Chung.

He might be the youngest, but he was clearly the most forceful and the most talented, and he had been Chung Lo's own choice. But it was a sad time to be taking charge of the House, even if business, with so much rubber and rice to be shipped, and so many goods required in the colony, was brisker than ever.

How could a man know where to turn?

He had gained access to his father's secret papers, and discovered that Chung Lo had indeed come to certain agreements with Kitachi Tano, to the effect that should war break out between Japan and Britain, the House of Chung would pursue a policy of non-co-operation with the authorities, as would, apparently, a great many others. Moreover the House of Chung would stand ready to play a prominent part in the acceptance by the colony of Japanese rule. This rule, according to Kitachi, would last only until Britain was utterly defeated and stripped of her empire, at least in the Far East, when Malaya would

220

be granted independence within the Greater East Asia Prosperity Sphere, which would of course be under the hegemony of Japan.

Kai hastily burned the incriminating papers, without even telling Su. But he did not suppose he had accomplished much, if there were incriminating papers in the hands of other Singapore Chinese, and if, as seemed probable, the police knew of it anyway.

He saw each of his brothers in turn. They had never seen the papers, nor had they discussed them in detail with their father, but they had been warned of what they might have to do, and seemed perfectly happy to do it.

But that had all been a long time ago, Chung Cheong said reassuringly.

'It's catching up with us now,' Kai said despondently.

Even more on his mind was the question of Lan.

The family continued to pretend she did not exist. Their friends also pretended she did not exist, and no-one ever inquired after her. If one encountered her in town, shopping, one carefully looked the other way. But at least she had the good taste not to importune, and kept out of trouble.

No doubt, Kai thought bitterly, she felt she had scored a sufficient triumph by just being what she was.

But now he was head of the family, and the responsibility was his. He was sure that Lan's presence in Singapore had contributed to his father's decline. She was a totally irresponsible, amoral, vicious creature. Yet she had once been his favourite sister.

He could not even discuss the situation with Su; it simply was not something one did discuss with one's wife, because it was even more of an insult to her than to any other member of the family. Su was aware of the situation, of course; she met it as did everyone else, by pretending it did not exist. To discuss it with her would be to bring it out in the open between them, and he did not know what her reaction would be. He loved her too much to risk it.

And on top of all that there was the matter of the

221

Communists. As both a capitalist and an employer, Kai had turned his face resolutely against the Singapore Communist Party. He had been all the more embarrassed because it was mainly composed of Chinese. The House of Chung had always been a sufficiently paternalistic employer for him to have no trouble with his own people, but inevitably he had become involved with the dock strike and other labour disturbances which had swept the colony. There again, he had set himself inflexibly to oppose those who wished to disrupt Singapore's booming economy, at the cost of a good deal of personal vilification, and even some threats.

Now suddenly it was government policy to be friendly to the Communists. Their leaders had been released from gaol, and for their part the Communists had agreed to support the war effort. But it was all simply because Britain and Russia had, so strangely, found themselves fighting on the same side. It made no sense in the long term.

Once he had been a happy man, Kai thought. Now he was surrounded by all the ingredients of happiness: wealth, a beautiful wife, two fine sons . . . and the burdens seemed to grow heavier with every year.

For all the sense of impending disaster, the danger of war in the Far East seemed to recede steadily throughout 1941. The new government in Japan, under Prince Konoye Fumimaro, seemed determined to mend its fences with the West, or at least with the United States.

'Because they're in dead trouble, economically,' Lees declared.

Whatever the reason, Konoye decreed a reduction in the campaigns in China, and engaged in high-level discussions with the Americans, who were bringing a great deal of pressure to bear, such as freezing Japanese assets in the United States, in their determination to end the fighting in Asia.

That there was still a strong pro-war party in Japan was evident, and in July the Prime Minister found it necessary to make General Tojo Minister of War to placate the army. This news was disturbing, since it was well known that Tojo had once been head of the kempei-tai, but it was followed by no great change in Japanese policy, and even the resignation of Konoye in October, and his replacement as prime minister by Tojo himself, appeared to be only a storm in a teacup.

Even Larry was feeling more secure than for a long time as the year drew to a close, but just before the family was due to make their annual descent on Singapore, Marion began to complain of violent stomach pains. She was rushed to hospital with acute appendicitis.

An emergency operation was successfully performed, but she would have to remain in hospital for a fortnight, and then take it very easy for another couple of weeks after that. Travelling to Singapore was out.

'I'll wire Ronald that it's not on this year,' Larry decided.

'But you must go to the board meeting,' Margaret insisted.

Larry supposed he should; in any case, the other branch managers never took their wives and families.

'But I'm not staying for Christmas.'

'Well, of course you're not, not without me.'

Nowadays, he had to apply to the army for leave whenever he wanted to go anywhere, but this was granted without demur.

'I really think the crisis is over,' said the major who signed his warrant. 'Having Roosevelt hold up his hand has made the Japs do some thinking.'

This, Larry found, was also the opinion in Singapore, where he arrived on 2 December. Singapore was *en fête*, because immediately after the Hong Kong ferry had disembarked its passengers, two British capital ships, the battleship *Prince of Wales* and the battlecruiser *Repulse*, steamed into the harbour.

Larry and Lees stood together at the window of the office and looked out at the great ships, the immaculate pearl-grey hulls and superstructure, the massive fourteen-

223

and fifteen-inch guns, the huge white ensigns floating from the sterns.

'Really makes you proud to be British,' Lees said. 'It's a shame Meg and Marion can't see them. But maybe they'll go on up to Hong Kong in a few days.'

'What exactly are they doing here?' Larry asked.

'Just showing the flag. Reminding the Japs that we have teeth. God, it's good to be alive! Now, you'll stay with us, of course.'

'But not for Christmas,' Larry reminded him. 'I'm booked to go back on the eleventh.'

Lees winked. 'We can do a lot in nine days, apart from talking shop.'

'I'm so sorry about Marion,' Joan Lees told him, not for the first time. 'And that Meggy can't be here. But it's nice to have you all to myself for a while.'

They were sitting on the verandah with their drinks. Sunset in Singapore was the best time of day, perhaps anywhere in the world, and was the more impressive this Saturday evening because the warships were still anchored off shore. The city was humming with sailors on shore leave. Lan Kuei, Larry reflected, could be having a busy time tonight, if she chose.

'So, are we going to go dancing?' Joan asked.

He glanced at her. Her expression was one of hopeful defiance. Poor Joan; life *had* rather passed her by. He could still remember that amazing night when he had regained Margaret, when Joan had said there was no-one in the world she would rather dance with. But surely she couldn't be thinking of doing more than flirt with her best friend's husband?

'It'll be like a rugby scrum down there,' he told her.

'All the more fun.'

'Then why not?'

Larry decided to hire a car and drive it himself rather than borrow Ronald's Rolls.

They started at the top, with the dinner dance at the Raffles Hotel, danced some smoochy numbers cheek to cheek; Jean wore a flame red dress, cut in a deep décolletage which did nothing for her rather flat figure. But she rested her cheek against his and sighed suggestively.

From Raffles they went on to a nightclub where there were several naval officers with English girls in tow, some of whom Joan knew. So they got together to make up a party, which Joan encouraged, just after midnight, to go on to one of the local clubs by the waterfront. Larry was a little doubtful about this, but reflected that there were six well-built young men to look after the girls, and that Joan was having the time of her life.

They found the place humming with shore-leave sailors and their Malay or Chinese companions. There was a risqué floorshow, in which a Chinese girl stripped to her underwear with a series of bumps and grinds, and then, apparently by accident, lost her brassière. The lights were immediately doused and she fled with loud giggles, but the sailors hooted and banged on the tables for her to come back.

'I think we'd better move on,' said the lieutenant-commander who was the senior of the officers. 'We don't want to get caught up in a Shore Police raid.'

The party then broke up, each couple no doubt having their own idea of how the remainder of the night should be spent.

'Let's go to the beach,' Joan said. 'Please, Larry.'

He drove over to the east coast, where they could watch the moon streaming across the water. It was three o'clock in the morning, and the beach was deserted.

'I'm going in,' she said. 'Coming?'

He made no reply, and a moment later she was out of the car, kicking off her high heeled sandals, and allowing her dress to slide past her hips. In the tropical heat she wore only knickers, and these immediately followed the dress.

How the clock went whirring back, and back, and back to the evening when Margaret had done the very same thing. But then the clock came forward, to when Larry

225

had sat here alone, waiting for the rising sun, and had decided to make his marriage work.

'Aren't you coming?' Joan asked again, and walked down the beach to the water.

He stripped and followed, uncertain of what she wanted, or even of what he wanted. He didn't want to cheat on Margaret – he never would – and certainly not with Joan. But he had no wish to upset her, either. She waited for him in the shallows, up to her waist in the warm water. When he came up to her she put both arms round his neck and kissed him, her body tight on his; if her breasts were small she had surprisingly good legs.

When they ran out of breath, he said, 'I proposed to Meg on this beach.'

She gazed at him – she was almost as tall – then released him and slid away; he had an erection and she must have felt it. She swam out a little way, and then swam back.

'I put her up to that,' she said.

'To what?'

'Oh, she came here to marry you. But when you were so slow on the uptake, I put her up to stripping off. I didn't think you'd be able to resist her. And you weren't.'

'And now you reckon I won't be able to resist you, is that it?'

She put her legs down and stood up. 'But you can.'

He held her hands. 'Not you, Joan. I just don't want anyone but Meg.'

She freed herself and walked up the beach; the moonlight was as bright as day. He followed her.

'I always thought there was something not quite right between you two,' she said. 'But Meg would never tell me.'

'There was quite a lot not quite right, in the beginning. But we've sorted it all out.'

'Bully for you.' She threw her clothes in the back of the car and got in, although water was still dripping from her hair and body.

'Ahmed is going to complain when he gets his car back,' Larry pointed out.

'Fuck Ahmed,' she said, almost in tears.

He spread his shirt on the seat and got in beside her. 'And you recommend we drive home in the altogether.'

'Are you planning to have an accident?'

He wasn't at all sure what situation he was going to encounter when they got home, but he drove carefully; from the beach it wasn't necessary to go into town to regain the Lees' house.

But Joan had realised the enormity of what she had attempted, and was now experiencing the humiliation of utter failure. The moment the car stopped she was out and running up the steps; fortunately the servants were fast asleep.

Joan didn't appear until lunch the next day, and was then very stiff and standoffish. Her parents were entertaining the captain of the *Prince of Wales*, Tom Leach, to lunch, with a couple of his officers, and she decided to flirt with them, to Larry's great relief.

The talk was very interesting.

'Admiral Phillips has just come back from Manila,' Leach told them, 'where he's been conferring with the Yankee brass. The idea is that if there's any trouble out here our two navies will co-operate. This is very confidential, of course, but it has to be the best thing that has happened since sliced bread, as the Americans say; it virtually means that the Americans and ourselves are in whatever happens together.'

'But are you expecting something to happen?' Larry asked. 'I thought things were going rather well, in the negotiations.'

'Actually, they aren't,' Leach said. 'They've reached a stalemate. And making Tojo prime minister, although it didn't mean an immediate change in policy, was their way of letting us know that the pro-war party has got the upper hand again. Which is why we're here. If the Japanese do decide to start shooting, we're on the spot. But the mere fact that they know we're here, and that there are eight American battleships in Pearl Harbor, is going to make them think twice. We've got them across a barrel, and they know it. They've only got their own procrastination to blame. When you think how defenceless places like Hong Kong were only a couple of years ago . . .'

Larry was not the least reassured by that. 'Thank God I'm going back on Wednesday,' he told Lees that night. 'And the moment Marion is well enough to travel, I'm going to do as you suggested and send her here to you with Meg.'

'Well, if you feel it necessary . . .'

'I wish to God I'd done it a month ago. I had no idea things were approaching such a critical stage.'

'Well, neither did I,' Lees confessed. 'But I do feel you are being a little alarmist. Even if the Japs do decide to terminate the negotiations, there'll be months of sabre-rattling, and ultimatums, and heaven knows what else. You'll have time.'

'The Japanese,' Larry reminded him, 'have never sent an ultimatum in the past.'

Nor did they now. Larry and Ronald had just returned from a lengthy lunch, the following afternoon, Monday 8 December in Singapore – it was still Sunday 7 in Hawaii, east of the International Date Line – when there was a great deal of hubbub from the harbour, and Roly Payne burst into the office.

'The balloon's gone up,' he shouted. 'The Japs have attacked Pearl Harbor – '

'You must be joking!'

'– without even a declaration of war, or an ultimatum, or anything!'

'The bastards,' Lees growled. 'Where are you off to?'

Larry was already running down the stairs. 'The Cable and Wireless Office. I'm getting Meg and Marion out of Hong Kong right this minute, even if I have to charter.'

'Steady on.' Lees ran behind him. 'They haven't attacked us yet.'

'But we'll be at war with them soon enough,' Larry answered over his shoulder.

He felt sick. He should have been there, with them, rather than gallivanting about on the beach with Joan Lees.

Singapore was sheer pandemonium. Larry found himself in the middle of a shrieking, seething crowd. He fought his way through, but the Cable and Wireless Office was also packed, the operators besieged by people screaming instructions in an attempt to get hold of relatives.

Relentlessly Larry pushed his way into the throng and at last reached an operator.

'Hong Kong,' he said. 'A message to Mrs Lawrence Cairns, care of Hammond and Teng.'

'I am sorry, sir,' said the Chinese clerk. 'There is no communication possible with Hong Kong.'

'No communication? What do you mean? Why the devil not?'

'I do not know the reason, sir. I only know that all communication has been ordered cut.'

'For God's sake . . .' Larry fought his way back out into the street, and encountered the lieutenant-commander he had met with Joan, fighting his way back to the dockside.

'What a fucking awful show,' the officer said. 'We'll have to teach those buggers a thing or two.'

'You putting to sea?' Larry asked.

'I've no idea. But I would say so. That's what we came here to do, lick the Japs if they got uppity.'

'Christ, I wish I were coming with you,' Larry said.

He got back to the office at five, and ran up the stairs. Lees stood at his window, watching the ships. 'They're just sitting there,' he fumed. 'They should be at sea!'

'Presumably they're waiting for information. Ronald, I can't get hold of Meg.'

'Can't get hold of her?'

'That what I said. What the hell am I going to do?'

'Keep calm, for Christ's sake. Obviously everyone is in a hell of a flap.'

Roly Payne came in, his face as white as a sheet. 'It

just came over on the wireless,' he said. 'We've declared war on Japan.'

'Had to happen,' Lees said.

'Yes. There was another item of news,' Roly said miserably, looking at Larry.

'What?'

'Hong Kong is under attack from Japanese forces on the mainland.'

'Oh, my God,' Larry shouted. 'I should be there!'

'Now, Larry, simmer down,' Lees ordered. 'Hong Kong is well defended. How many men does Maltby have?'

'Perhaps twelve thousand.'

'Um. Well, they may have to evacuate Kowloon, but I'm sure they'll hold the island. Meg and Marion will be all right, Larry. They're civilians.'

'I have to *do* something,' Larry said. 'God, I should be there with the Volunteers for a start. And I should be with my wife and child. For God's sake, Marion is due out of hospital tomorrow!'

Lees put his arm round his shoulders.

'Larry, there is nothing you, I, or anyone can do right now. We just have to sit it out. Look at those ships. They have steam up. They're on their way. Just a couple of salvoes from those big guns will scatter the Jap army. Hong King is going to be all right.'

The door opened and Mrs Lu rushed in. Larry had never seen her looking anything but immaculate. This afternoon somehow her hair had come down, her dress looked as if it had been slept in, her face was pale, and she was panting.

'Mr Lees,' she cried. 'Have you heard the news?'

'Of course I've heard the news,' Lees snapped.

'About Malaysia?'

They stared at her.

'What about Malaysia?' Roly asked.

'The Japanese have landed in the north. We're being invaded.'

* * *

Margaret had risen early, as she usually did, and had her pre-breakfast swim. It was early December, but it had still not become the least chilly; that seldom happened until well into the New Year.

Monday was a shopping day, and she intended to combine it with a visit to the hospital to see Marion. Marion was coming along splendidly, and was due out tomorrow, as planned. Margaret was pleased about that.

She smoked a cigarette, an occasional habit, and wondered what Larry was doing now. She had no doubt that he would be in great demand – he always was, especially on his own. He would be squiring Joan. Poor Joan. How she would love to have a Larry of her own.

She didn't feel the least jealous of what they might be doing. Larry was hers; she no longer doubted that.

She went up to her room to shower and change, had just started to dress when she heard a sudden outburst of noise. It began with the scream of an air raid siren. Since the outbreak of the war with Germany they had had several air raid alarm drills, and at the scream of the siren everyone not on duty was supposed to make their way immediately to their allotted shelter; hers, fortunately, was in the garden.

But as an auxiliary nurse, she should be on duty. Then, at least, she would be at the hospital and able to make sure Marion was all right.

Then she heard the sound of aeroplane engines, and almost immediately the boom of explosions from the harbour. Then there came other, deeper explosions from Kowloon on the mainland.

There was also a great deal of confused noise drifting up from Victoria.

Mansur ran into her bedroom without knocking, something he had never done before. She gazed at him with her mouth open, aware that she was wearing only bra and panties, but he didn't seem to notice.

'We are attacked, madam. We are attacked.'

'Attacked?' She ran to the window, and saw the smoke rising. 'But . . .'

231

'It is the Japanese, madam, the Japanese.'

He had quite lost his normal calm.

Downstairs, she heard the maids screaming.

Then a bomb fell quite close to the house and the building shook; she heard the sound of breaking glass.

Think, damn you, she told herself. But she could only think, *if only Larry were here!*

'All right, Mansur,' she said, pleased with herself for speaking calmly. 'I want all the shutters closed, and food taken down into the cellar. Just as if there were a typhoon coming, right? Hurry, now.'

She virtually pushed him out of the door, closed it, ran to the bedside telephone. The was a series of clicks and crackles and she heard voices, but no one took any notice of her.

'Hello!' she shouted. 'Hello! Answer me, damnit.'

It was five minutes before one of the operators said, 'There are no lines.'

'Listen,' Margaret said, keeping her temper with difficulty. 'This is Mrs Lawrence Cairns. I wish to speak with Miss Janet Ogilvy. The number is six-four-three. Kindly put me through.' Janet would hardly have gone to the office yet, and she would certainly know what was happening.

'There are no lines,' the girl said again, and the key went dead.

Margaret glared at it in impotent fury for several seconds. But she had to do something. There really *was* an emergency.

She went to the wardrobe and took out her khaki uniform: heavy drill skirt, tunic, stockings and heavy low-heeled brown shoes; there was a khaki shirt to go under the tunic and a khaki tie, as well as a khaki forage cap. There was even a pair of khaki drawers, but she was damned if she was going to wear those; nobody was going to look under her skirt. The ensemble did not look the least like a nurse's uniform, but it was the one decided upon for the auxiliaries.

Anyway, she only intended to wear it until she could

get Marion out of hospital and back to the safety of the house.

She ran down to the garage, started the car, drove down the hill. The raid was over and the planes had gone, but several fires had started, and the entire city was shrouded in black smoke. There were still planes over Kowloon; on the mainland the explosions had merged into a general cacophony, and the noise was much louder.

She raced down the hill, passing crowds of people streaming out. They shouted at her but she ignored them until she ran into a roadblock in the suburbs.

'No one is allowed to go into the city centre, madam,' said the Chinese policeman.

'But I have to report for duty,' Margaret explained.

He looked at her uniform. 'Well, I suppose you must go. But leave the car.'

'Leave it? Why on earth . . .'

'It may explode and cause a fire.'

She supposed that made sense. She pulled it into the side of the road and pocketed the keys.

'Mind how you go, madam,' the policeman said. 'It is very dangerous.'

Margaret knew there were fires burning, and she expected to see some damage, but what she did see appalled her.

The bombs had been dropped indiscriminately; the Japanese had decided to regard all of Victoria as a military target. She had hardly entered the city when she came upon a bomb crater, and several shattered bodies oozing blood and brains.

She had never seen a dead body before, and felt physically sick. She began to run, panting, her nostrils assailed by the most frightful odours.

She was buffeted by screaming people, some running to and fro, others staring at the wreckage of their homes and shops and almost literally tearing their hair. Some knelt by dead bodies at the roadside, weeping.

She ran past people who had been burned or maimed, who called out to her for help because she was wearing

233

uniform. But her training had taken place in clean and sanitary, and above all, quiet surroundings. There was nothing she could do to help them. Clouds of smoke swept across the road driven by a sudden wind, to leave her gasping. Her forage cap came off, but when she looked back for it, it was in a pool of muddy water stained with blood, so she left it.

Then the planes were back again, whining overhead, and all around her came the crump-crump of bombs, interspersed with the shorter barks of the anti-aircraft guns replying. She threw herself into a doorway and crouched there with half a dozen Chinese children.

The anti-aircraft guns did not seem to hit any of the Japanese planes, although these were flying very low. But the Japanese bombs couldn't miss Victoria. The building in which Margaret was crouching shook, and dust and debris crashed into the street. The children screamed and ran from the doorway. She shouted at them to come back, but they vanished into a cloud of smoke and dust. She had no idea what became of them.

Her only companion was a mongrel bitch, who licked her hand and whimpered.

When the planes went away a few minutes later, she resumed her journey. Now she ignored everything she saw, and when she tripped over a dead body and landed on her hands and knees, tearing her stockings, she merely picked herself up and hurried on.

There was a huge crater in the lawn, although no one could doubt the building was a hospital; it was marked with a red cross on the roof. And the lawn was even more crowded than the streets, a large number of people having decided that they would be safe here; fortunately they seemed to have arrived after the bomb had burst.

At least the building itself was undamaged. Orderlies and nurses were rushing to and fro in the entrance hall, wheeling patients down to the cellars, shouting and yelling at each other. Margaret ran for the stairs leading to the private wing, and encountered a doctor. 'Mrs Cairns,' he said. 'Well done. I want you in Ward E.'

'But I've come for my daughter,' she told him.

'Your daughter will be quite safe,' he said. 'All the private patients have been moved down to the cellars. You are on duty, as of now. I want you in Ward E.'

She hesitated and considered telling him to bugger off; but she had volunteered for this stupid business, and she was in uniform. She decided to go along with him until she could speak with Dr Matthews, her own doctor, and get him to straighten things out.

She ran up the stairs to Ward E, and found herself with several other auxiliary nurses and a couple of Chinese professionals – and four wounded men.

They had just arrived, having been brought across from the mainland. They lay on stretchers, their uniforms grimy and bloodstained. Two of them were white, Canadians she presumed, since they made up a large part of the garrison, but the other two were Indians.

'Come along, girls,' Sister said, bustling into the ward. 'Let's get them undressed and into bed before they wake up.'

Margaret realised they had been sedated, but were not quite unconscious; they were writhing and groaning.

'Cairns, Evans, Lawrence, Smith, take the first stretcher,' Sister said.

The four women gazed at the Indian in dismay. Their training had been performed on dummies or on each other. They had never actually seen a war casualty before. The Indian had been hit in the chest; a field dressing had been put on but the entire upper half of his body was wet with blood. His eyes flopped open and then shut again, and his left hand also opened and closed, repeatedly.

'Shouldn't he be bathed, Sister?' asked Jennie Lawrence, wrinkling her nose.

'That is what you're going to do,' Sister said patiently. 'A bed bath. But get his clothes off first. Quickly, now.'

Margaret made a grab for his boots; that seemed safest.

She unlaced them and pulled them off, and the man groaned.

'Cairns,' Sister said, standing above her, 'he is a human being.'

'Sorry, Sister,' Margaret gasped, and began unwinding his puttees.

Jennie Lawrence had released the man's shorts, and they now came sliding down his legs, followed by his underpants. Margaret had to pull them over his feet, and discovered they were soaked with urine and faeces as well as sweat.

I am going to be sick, she thought. My God, I am going to be sick.

Sister was standing at her shoulder. 'Always happens when a man is hit,' she said. 'Or a woman. You'll get used to it.'

Never, Margaret thought. Never. Oh, Larry, where are you?

She did get used to it, very quickly. There was simply so much of it. The little garrison fought desperately, but was overwhelmed by the numbers of Japanese, an entire infantry division supported by artillery and aircraft, thrown against it. More and more wounded were brought back across the harbour, and within two days Brigadier Maltby had been forced to withdraw his men to Hong Kong Island itself; Kowloon was in Japanese hands.

By then, the true horror of the situation was clear to everyone. The Japanese, rather than risk a conventional confrontation with the combined fleets being assembled against them, had decided on a pre-emptive strike – as indeed they had begun both their previous wars, against China in 1894 and Russia in 1904.

Their attack on Pearl Harbor had been devastatingly successful. Five of the eight battleships in the base had been sunk, and the other three badly damaged, in addition to scores of other craft and 188 planes. The only saving grace was that the three aircraft carriers had been absent

on an exercise, but it left the Americans virtually defenceless in the Pacific.

And it had left the British with their two capital ships
in Singapore. But on the evening of 10 December, the
day Kowloon was abandoned, news came in which totally
devastated the British community: *Prince of Wales* and
Repulse had been attacked by Japanese aircraft off the east
coast of Malaya, and both sunk.

On top of all this came news of Japanese landings in the
Philippines and Malaysia, and that Singapore had been
bombed.

Larry! Margaret thought. He was in danger!

She had managed to get some time off to take Marion
home. The girl had been frightened by the bombing, but
had recovered well. She was unhappy about being left at
home alone, but Margaret pointed out that no bombs had
fallen near the house, and that she was safest there;
Mansur would look after her. She wished she could stay
there too, and be looked after by Mansur.

Margaret's life became centred around the hospital.
Apart from working sixteen hours a day, she ate and slept
there. Once every other day she was allowed to go up to
the house to bathe and change, and check on Marion,
who was resting as much as could be expected, gazing at
the devastation in the city below.

'How can men be so wicked, madam?' Mansur
wondered.

For the bombers were back, and the Japanese artillery
had advanced into Kowloon itself to shell across the harbour. Then only three days after the garrison had evacuated Kowloon, the Japanese got across also and established
a lodgement on the island itself.

Life became a nightmare. Now there was no time off
at all, and with bombs bursting all the time, and the
garrison fighting to the very last man in every position,
the numbers of wounded grew until they were lying on
the floors and in the corridors. Those who died were

dumped unceremoniously in the yard; there was no time to bury them.

The nurses worked up to their elbows in blood and filth, amid shrieking despair, as sedatives and antiseptics ran out, and the dying men screamed and howled their agony.

Naked bodies, inflamed genitals, white, brown or yellow, became commonplace. But then so did exposed intestines, gaping, gasping lungs, splintered bones, oozing blood and faeces.

Without Janet Ogilvy, Margaret thought, she would have gone mad. Janet had been late getting in to report, but she had arrived on the first night, and the two friends had been able to work shoulder to shoulder.

Wiping sweat from her glasses, huge bust heaving with every breath, irrepressibly good humoured and optimistic, Janet was a tower of strength. But even her smile faded as hour succeeded weary hour, light followed dark, and the groans and screams never ceased. The miasma of death and the stench of burning wood and flesh hung over everything, and the nurses kept going by snatching a hasty bite here and a rushed cup of tea there, steadily growing more filthy and exhausted.

And Margaret worried incessantly about Marion, up there on the hill.

They lost all track of time, until Sister came into the ward which now contained some thirty people, twenty four casualties and six nurses – it had been designed for six beds – brandishing a bottle of champagne. They stared at her, uncomprehending.

My God, we've made peace, Margaret thought wildly. But there was still firing, from very close at hand, as the Japanese fought their way into the suburbs.

'It's Christmas Eve,' Sister said. 'Didn't you know that? It's Christmas Eve.'

They laughed hysterically, and a Canadian soldier, who had been shot in the leg but still had the use of both arms, popped the cork. Even the Indians were happy to take a swig from the bottle. The havildar who was the senior

NCO present drank immediately before Margaret; the neck was still wet with the touch of his lips. She took a swig without hesitating.

Only three weeks ago she would have died rather than done such a thing. But had there ever been an 'only three weeks ago'? Or had this nightmare gone on forever?

The champagne and the knowledge that it was all but Christmas briefly restored their spirits. Then they realised that they had been living this hellish life for over a fortnight, that they were doomed, and that there would be no time for celebrations. Margaret had hardly had time to worry about Larry; no further news had come out of Malaya, but at least everyone knew that the peninsula, and particularly Singapore, was adequately defended. She was more concerned with Marion, sitting up at the house with Mansur, so near, and yet as distant as if she were a thousand miles away.

And tomorrow was Christmas.

At midnight Margaret was off duty and sleeping in a corner, when the staff officer appeared. Janet shook her awake, and they scrambled to their feet to see Major Crombie, with whom they had often played bridge in happier times.

He cleared his throat, nervously.

'I am instructed to deliver this message to all personnel. It is from His Excellency.'

He cleared his throat again, and read from the paper he held in his hand.

'Having been informed by Brigadier Maltby that the enemy forces are in the city, and that they have captured our main reservoir; having been informed that the number of men still capable of fighting has been reduced to an unacceptably low level; having been informed by the chief of police that his men can no longer maintain order, and by the chief fire officer that his people can no longer cope with the fires, I have reluctantly come to the conclusion that we have no alternative but to lay down our arms.'

Another cough. 'We were given the duty of holding this

remote outpost of our great Empire for as long as humanly possible in order that the vast forces and resources which the British people command could be adequately mobilised. We have done our duty, and I wish you all to know that our sacrifice has been recognised by the Prime Minister, Mr Winston Churchill, with whom I have been in contact, and who has given me permission to surrender at discretion.'

Crombie raised his head. 'I wish you all to know how proud I, and indeed every member of the British Commonwealth of Nations, is of every one of you. I do not know how soon the Union Jack will again fly over Hong Kong. That it will do so is undoubted. Until that glorious moment, may I wish you all Godspeed and good fortune. Thank you.'

Crombie folded the paper and placed it in his pocket. Then he saluted, turned on his heel, and marched out.

For a moment no one spoke. Then Sister said, 'Listen!'

The sound of firing was slowly dying.

'Can we go home, Sister?' Janet asked.

'Certainly not.'

'Just for a bath and a change of clothes,' Margaret begged.

'You must remain on duty, at least until Japanese doctors and nursing staff take over the hospital,' Sister said. 'I suppose that's what they'll do . . .' her voice trailed away. Everyone in Hong Kong had heard tales of Japanese atrocities in China. But that had been in China. This was a part of the British Empire, and they were British – well, most of them.

'I think,' Sister said, 'that we should make an effort to look our best. You will go to the bathroom in pairs. Wash your faces, comb your hair. If you have any lipstick or rouge, wear it. We must show the enemy that if we have been defeated, we have not been beaten.'

Margaret went down with Janet.

'What will happen to us?' Margaret wanted to know.

'Well . . . I suppose nothing. It's over,' Janet said. 'I suppose they'll want to requisition rooms in our houses.'

Japanese? Little brown men in her house, Margaret thought. Suppose Kitachi came here. My God!

'Well, we can't do anything about that,' Janet said cheerfully. 'God, I wish I knew where Mummy and Daddy were.'

'You'll soon be with them again,' Margaret said. Which is more than I will be with Larry, she thought. But maybe there would be some way to let him know that she was all right.

And she would certainly be reunited with Marion. Perhaps in only a couple of hours.

But the thought of the Japanese in her house . . .

The almost uncanny silence was broken suddenly by a noise none of them had ever heard before, a noise they would all remember to their dying days.

It was a tremendous shriek, uttered from ten thousand throats, a paean of victory which reminded Margaret of an enormous pack of dogs sighting a hunk of raw meat.

Sister stood in front of them. 'The Japanese will be excited, naturally, at having won,' she told them calmly. 'Now, we must at all times be calm, and reserved, but also polite. The Japanese are very keen on politeness. You will stand to attention when addressed, and you will address any officer as sir. Understood?'

The nurses nodded.

One of the Chinese regulars, Nurse Ching, stood beside Margaret. 'I am so afraid, Mrs Cairns,' she whispered.

'There is nothing to be afraid of,' Margaret told her.

'Not for you,' Nurse Ching said. 'You are British. But I am Chinese.'

'There's nothing . . .' Margaret began again, and then checked. Because suddenly she was afraid herself. The noise was coming closer, a cacophony of whoops and gunshots. And now screams.

She looked at Sister. Sister was a tower of strength, standing by the door in her white uniform, which somehow looked starched and pristine even though it had been worn for days on end and was stained with blood. Her cap was set squarely on her curly fair hair, and her face set in a pleasant but determined expression; like her chunky body it bespoke resolution.

Boots sounded in the corridor. Margaret took a long breath and stood to attention.

The door crashed in, with such force that even Sister took a step backwards. Margaret saw a little man, wearing a sweat- and blood-stained green uniform, leggings and brown ankle boots. He wore a green steel helmet, and a cartridge belt slung over his shoulder.

He carried a rifle with a fixed bayonet, and the bayonet was stained with blood.

Behind him came another twenty-odd men, similarly dressed and armed.

They stared for a moment at the nurses and prisoners, who stared back. Then the Indian havildar pushed himself up in bed and saluted.

The first Japanese soldier gave a shriek of blood-lusted frenzy, ran across the ward, and plunged his bayonet into the havildar's chest.

PART THREE
Partners

CHAPTER 10
The Defeat

Colonel Kitachi Tano contemplated the fires rising above Victoria as his boat nosed into the dock, the sailors standing smartly to attention. There seemed to be even more fires on the island than there were behind him, in Kowloon.

Kitachi was aware of a feeling of exultation. This was correct, at such a moment. Soldiers of the Emperor were expected to exult in victory: those on the dock were still occasionally giving shouts of 'Banzai', the victory cry of the Japanese.

To them, veterans all of several years' campaigning in China, the assault on Hong Kong was just another battle, yet another victory. Only the fact that the skins of the defenders were white had invested this battle with interest; they had not really fought as hard as the Chinese. They had been taken by surprise, and they lacked experience.

But for Kitachi it was the most important day of his life. He had been seconded to spearhead the assault on the British possessions in East Asia, fourteen years ago, and this initial penetration represented the first fruits of his efforts. He would be the first to admit that he had played no part in the downfall of Hong Kong. But equally he did not doubt that Singapore would also fall, and there he had most certainly played a part.

And in Hong Kong, there was a personal matter to be settled.

There had been times in the past few years when Kitachi had doubted this day would ever come.

The imponderables of assuming hegemony over all of East Asia, by force, had seemed to grow with every year.

In 1931, when the 'Mukden Incident' had been revealed to an unsuspecting world, the signs had been propitious. The West was reeling under the impact of its self-inflicted financial wounds; it had also been disunited and pacifist. Yet it had still come as a surprise to him, and to most other Japanese serving officers, that not a single rifle had been raised to defend China. Even more surprising had been the Chinese decision to accept the *fait accompli*.

Then it had been doubted that the West would ever fight, the more so as the situation in Europe had slowly changed during the thirties, with the return to the pre–1914 situation of two armed camps, glaring at each other from behind a steadily growing stockpile of weapons.

Again, surely, the moment had been propitious. Yet the various governments which had succeeded each other with bewildering rapidity in Tokyo had hesitated for six years before making a decisive move into China. The army had done their best to force the matter. In 1936, at the very moment when that dishonourable scoundrel Cairns had been blackmailing him, a group of army cadets had assassinated the prime minister and every senior member of the government they had been able to find, and then had committed seppuku on the balcony of the parliament building after demanding that the nation fulfil its destiny.

The young assassins had become national heroes, and there could be no doubt that their self sacrifice had played a successful part in forcing the government to launch the campaign against China a year later.

Kitachi could remember as if it were yesterday how proud he had been at that moment, even while he had been seething with anger at his contemptuous dismissal by Larry Cairns.

But the war had been undertaken two years too late. It had come just as Chiang Kai-shek and Mao Tse-tung had mended their fences under the skilful manipulation of Chang Hsueh-liang; in 1937, the Chinese had been prepared to fight and they had a lot of territory to sacrifice. Equally, the West had begun its recovery, and if Britain had still been in a state of disarray following her own humiliation over Abyssinia, the Americans had been flexing their muscles. Japan's leaders had hesitated, and hesitated even more when half of the US fleet had been sent to Hawaii.

Kitachi had been in despair. He knew that the nation's shipyards were working day and night to produce battleships and aircraft carriers the like of which the world had never seen before. But such great monsters of destruction needed time. And until they were ready, it seemed, there was no way the Japanese navy could take on the Americans, or even risk a confrontation.

He had not been aware of the secret consultations in the War Office and the Admiralty, of the great plan which had slowly been evolved by Admiral Yamamoto Isoroku to create a Greater East Asia Prosperity Sphere, within which the Japanese people could live and indeed prosper without fear of the outside world. That plan could yet succeed, if the United States' battleships could be destroyed at one stroke. No one doubted that the United States would be outraged, and would then build more warships and go to war. But would they ever have sufficient warships to carry the war to Japan, once Japan's new fleet was ready? Now, at the end of 1941, Japan's navy was the strongest in the world, especially in the most vital of new capital ships: aircraft carriers. In addition, *Yamato*, the greatest warship ever built, was on her sea trials, and her sister ship, *Mushashi*, was soon to follow.

Thus, after all the waiting and the disappointments, it had happened, and succeeded beyond anyone's wildest dreams. And Colonel Kitachi could step ashore in Hong Kong as a conqueror.

He glanced at Captain Kano. His first step on rejoining the kempei-tai had been to regain contact with his trustworthy aide, and have him once more at his side.

Kano smiled; he knew Kitachi's secrets. 'It is a great day, honourable captain. A great day for Japan. And a great day for you.'

★ ★ ★

The fires had been brought under control in the immediate vicinity of the docks, and here the exhausted, filthy, dejected survivors of the British-Canadian-Indian defence force were being assembled, driven by the rifle butts of their conquerors. They hung their heads, and shambled; most were in the peculiar British tropical uniform of shorts and stockings; their stockings had slipped down to their ankles and they looked pitiful.

Captain Ishimutsi, commander of the kempei-tai on the ground, bowed. 'Welcome, honourable colonel. Do you wish to interrogate any of these men?'

'Perhaps later. I wish to inspect the town.' It was not Kitachi's way, it was not the Japanese way, to reveal impatience. Larry Cairns would be here, somewhere. His only fear was that he might have been killed.

Ishimutsi led Kitachi and Captain Kano up from the docks into Wan Chai, where Japanese soldiers were rampaging through the shops, looting and shooting indiscriminately.

'The men are elated,' Ishimutsi remarked.

'And undisciplined,' Kitachi commented.

He heard a scream, and saw a Chinese woman being bundled to the floor of her shop by four soldiers, who tore at her clothing like angry ants.

They walked on, through drifting smoke and devastation; bomb craters gaped on either side, and the stench of death was everywhere.

'The dead bodies must be cleaned up, or there will be disease,' Kitachi observed.

'The prisoners will be set to it as soon as they have all been identified,' Ishimutsi said.

'There is one man in particular I wish to interrogate,' Kitachi said casually. 'His name is Lawrence Cairns. He was manager of the firm of Hammond and Teng.'

At that moment they stopped in front of the Hammond and Teng office building, which was still burning.

'He would probably have been serving in the Volunteers,' Kitachi said.

'I will have a roll call made of the prisoners,' Ishimutsi said.

Kitachi walked on, gestured at the Red Cross. 'You will also check the hospital for this man.'

'If he was in the hospital, honourable captain, then he is dead.'

Kitachi glanced at him enquiringly.

'The men were excited, and it seemed best,' Ishimutsi explained. 'Wounded prisoners are a great nuisance.'

Kitachi frowned. While he agreed with Ishimutsi in theory, he would be very angry if Cairns had been carelessly bayoneted to death.

'I must see these people,' he said.

Ishimutsi nodded. 'It stinks in there,' he warned.

Kitachi snorted, and went into the hospital grounds. He stopped to look at the women, who had been herded together on the lawn in front of the administrative building. There seemed to be equal numbers of white and Chinese. Nearly all of them were in various stages of undress, some were naked, their white skins glowing in the sunlight; most had their hands tied behind their backs. They huddled against each other, and did not look at the Japanese officers; some wept.

'We let the men have them for a while,' Ishimutsi explained.

Kitachi nodded. He would have done the same. To humiliate the enemy's women was an essential part of the victory. He felt the urge himself. But there were more important things to do first.

Larry Cairns was not recognisably among the dead in the charnel house that was the hospital. Nor could he be found amongst the prisoners.

'One of them will tell us where he is,' Ishimutsi suggested.

'I know someone who will tell us sooner,' Kitachi told him.

He summoned a staff car and, with Kano and four soldiers, drove up the mountain. Here the air was at last sweet, and there were no bomb craters. The house waited, peacefully looking out at the shattered harbour, the sunken ships, the billowing smoke, its trees nodding in the gentle breeze. Close by, the Botanic Gardens were also relatively untouched. Kitachi realised that Hong Kong was really a very beautiful place; he had not been in the mood to appreciate it when he had last been here, in 1937.

Soon it would be beautiful again.

Kano looked round at the verandahs, the garden, the swimming pool. 'These people lived well,' he remarked.

The car stopped before the wide front steps, and the soldiers leapt out, rifles at the ready.

Mansur stood at the head of the stairs.

'Do not shoot him,' Kitachi ordered, and went up the steps. 'Where is your master?'

'Mr Cairns is not here, sir. He is in Singapore.'

Kitachi felt a pang of angry disappointment. 'Then where is your mistress?'

'Mrs Cairns has not been here for some days, sir. She has been at the hospital, helping to tend the wounded.'

She had been in that crowd? That tall, elegant, sophisticated, red-haired bitch had been thrown to the ground with her hands tied behind her back, stripped, and raped?

He didn't know whether to smile or weep.

'Find her,' he told Kano. 'She will be with those women at the hospital. Mrs Lawrence Cairns. Bring her up here.'

Kano bowed, and got back into the car. Kitachi watched him drive down the hill, then went into the house. 'I will have a whisky,' he told Mansur.

'Yes, sir.' Mansur knew these men were the conquerors. He remembered Kitachi's face, and knew too that there was a crisis approaching. He could not help either the master or the mistress by being beaten up or shot himself.

Kitachi left his men on the verandah to explore, and sat down in a comfortable chair, his booted feet on another set of chintz cushions. He heard muted noises, and turned his head. Several Chinese maids peered at him through a curtained doorway; when they realised they had been seen they hastily scurried away.

He thought he would give them to his men, after. He intended to stamp this family out of existence.

He heard another sound, and raised his head to look at the staircase to the upper floor. A girl stood there. He did not suppose she was much over ten years old, but she was tall and strongly built, like her parents. She had grown a lot since last he had seen her four years ago.

Mansur re-entered the room with a tray and a glass, and halted, his face a picture of dismay. No doubt, Kitachi thought, he had told her to keep hidden.

'Please, sir,' the girl said. 'Have you news of my mother? Is she all right?'

Kitachi smiled. The war had not yet touched this pretty little flower. And he could do nothing important until her mother was brought to him. And the urge still lurked in his belly.

'Come here, little girl,' he said.

'Cairns,' said the English-speaking Japanese officer. 'Margaret Cairns. Step out.'

Margaret attempted to shrink into the ground. She had hardly moved for several hours, for all that she was in pain, her mouth parched and her muscles cramped, while she had lost all feeling in her wrists and hands. Her mind was in almost catatonic state.

She supposed it had happened when she had watched the blood spurting from the havildar's chest. She had seen a great deal of blood during the preceding fortnight, but nothing like that.

And even that had not been horrible, compared with what happened afterwards.

Every man in the ward had been murdered in a matter of minutes; most had been too surprised even to shout.

Sister had been the first to react, had seized a Japanese bayonet with her bare hands in an effort to save a life, and lost her own. Margaret would never forget to her dying day the expression of total disbelief on Sister's face as the bayonet had pierced her white uniform and the

251

blood had spurted there too. Sister had gasped in amazement in that last fleeting moment.

Sister had been a heroine. She had also made the right decision. The rest of them had lacked her courage, and had suffered for their cowardice.

Janet Ogilvy had screamed and run for the door. The soldiers had not bayoneted her; instead, they had laughed, and tossed her from man to man, each toss stripping off an item of clothing. Janet had fallen to the floor, men kneeling on her and around her. Their high-pitched laughter had been perhaps worst of all. They had been delighted; they had never seen a woman with breasts quite so large. They wanted to play with them.

Jennie Lawrence had screamed and screamed and screamed as she had been stretched across a dying body to have her uniform torn away. Each scream had sounded like the death cry of a valkyrie. They echoed still, in the minds of all the women, though Jennie was now a sobbing wreck.

Margaret had remembered only that Sister had told them to be dignified. Besides, she had not believed that anything would happen to her. She was Margaret Cairns. Even more, in moments of stress, she was Margaret Anstey. The only catastrophes she had ever endured had been of her own making. She had stood against the wall, and for perhaps five minutes had been ignored. Thus she had watched what was happening to Janet and Jennie and the two Chinese girls. Then the men had noticed her.

They had stared at her for some seconds, then they had reached for her. She had not attempted to resist them, and yet they had kicked her and beaten her and tied her hands behind her back, while they had ripped away her clothes. It was then that the catatonic state really set in. Her brain had closed to what they were doing to her, because it was not acceptable to her that such a thing should happen. She had known only that she was on the floor, and that there were men, and odours, and noise.

She had thought she would vomit, but she had not. She

had thought she would faint, but she had not. She had wanted to die, but she had not.

The sunlight, playing on her body as she and the others were herded outside, had been almost like a soothing balm. She cared nothing for the whimpering, moaning, distraught mass around her, brushing her, leaning on her, speaking to her. They no longer existed, not even Janet, who lay beside her, constantly sobbing. She wished only to be left alone.

The Japanese officer had signalled his men, and they came marching into the herd, throwing wailing women to left and right as they sought her. They knew for whom they were looking. One seized her hair and dragged her face up.

The officer gave a command.

Margaret was pulled to her feet and pushed towards the waiting staff car. The men had only torn away her skirt and knickers; her stockings had fallen down to her ankles. Her blood- and sweat-stained jacket came down to her thighs and afforded some covering.

The car door was opened, and she was thrust into the back seat.

The officer got in beside her, and the car drove up the hill. They are taking me home, she thought. They are taking me home. Surely I have been saved.

She knew she should feel guilty at having abandoned Janet and Jennie, but the thought of her own home, of a bath and a change of clothing, of being able to look and feel like a human being again . . .

The car stopped and she was pushed out. The officer had not spoken a word. Her heart gave a great lurch as she saw the Japanese soldiers lounging on the verandah. *Marion!*

Margaret took great gasps of fresh air, and suffered herself to be pushed indoors. She gasped again as she saw Kitachi standing at the top of the stairs. Instinctively she strained on the ropes binding her wrists. Those other men, even the captain who had brought her up the hill, were faceless. But not Kitachi.

253

In addition to her semi-nudity, she was suddenly aware of her filth, of the mess her hair must be in, of the tear stains on her face and the bruises on her body.

The officer pushed her at the steps, and she went up them.

'Mrs Cairns,' Kitachi said. 'You do not look as good as when last we met. And you are stupid; you did not take my advice, and leave while you could.'

Margaret heard a whimper. She looked past Kitachi to see Marion, lying on the settee, her clothes torn, and weeping uncontrollably.

'You bastard!' Margaret screamed, and leapt at Kitachi. Her movement took him by surprise, and her teeth scoured his face before Kano seized her shoulders and dragged her back.

She panted, and thought, can that really have been me? Margaret Anstey Cairns? Whatever would Mumsy say? Or even Joan?

Larry would have cheered!

She watched Kitachi raise his hand and stroke his cheek, then stare at his finger, which was covered in blood. Now, she thought, I am going to die.

But I cannot die, and leave Marion alive!

Kitachi gave an order in Japanese. The soldiers seized Margaret and bundled her to the verandah rail. Her tunic and shirt were pulled from her shoulders. Her wrists were released and her arms extended above her head and tied to the rafter, so that she dangled, her thighs banging the rail. Naked, she hung in the morning sunlight. Incongruously, the only thing she still wore was her tie.

Kitachi stood beside her and, to her disgust, touched her, fingered her, as if she were a toy. 'Where is your husband, Mrs Cairns?'

She wanted to defy him, to swear at him, to tell him to do his worst. But she could not, because of Marion. 'I do not know,' she whispered.

Then she knew pain, such as she had never known before. A searing agony which spread across her naked

254

buttocks and seeped through to her groin. She realised she had been struck by a bamboo cane.

Kitachi smiled at her. 'Where is your husband?' he asked again.

Margaret gasped, and tears rolled down her cheeks. But she knew she was going to tell him; she could not bear the thought of being struck by the cane again.

'He is in Singapore, you bastard,' she whispered. 'Where you can't get at him. But he can get at you!'

'Cane her,' Kitachi told Kano. 'Cane her till she bleeds.' He changed to English. 'But I am going to Singapore, Mrs Cairns,' he said. 'Soon. I will find your husband there.'

The news of the sinking of the *Prince of Wales* and *Repulse* hit Singapore like a solid shock wave.

The war had already arrived; on the first night the air raid sirens wailed and Japanese bombers appeared over the city. Although long-prepared blackout regulations were immediately put into force, very few people obeyed them; Singapore still glowed with life. Out of the sparkling incandescence searchlight beams clawed up into the sky and one or two anti-aircraft guns fired. No bomber was hit, and the few bombs dropped did little damage. It was a token exchange of shots on each side.

The sinking of the two great ships, however, was no token. Somehow it felt more devastating than the destruction of the American battle fleet in Pearl Harbor; the people of Singapore had actually met and entertained those gallant men who had drowned in the Gulf of Siam.

Worst of all, the disaster signalled a total Japanese superiority, on the sea, in the air, and on the land; already news was being received of retreats – 'strategic withdrawals', as they were described – in the north of Malaysia.

There was no news at all from Hong Kong, save that Kowloon had been abandoned and that fighting was taking

255

place on the island itself. All physical communication between Singapore and the northern colony had been cut.

And now Malaysia was fighting for its life. The bombing of Singapore continued, but it was desultory; the Japanese directed their efforts further north, where they were gaining ground every day, without opposition. To the people of Singapore, the most difficult aspect of the war to accept was the way the small RAF contingent, their defenders, deemed sufficient before the outbreak of hostilities to turn back any assailants, had been wiped from the sky in almost their first encounter with the Japanese Zeroes.

The Lees did their best to comfort Larry. But there was not much they could say or do, save remind him that as civilians Margaret and Marion could only be interned, by all the rules of war. But Larry remembered Kitachi's threat, and did not sleep.

He could only think, I should be there. I am separated from my wife and child, and from the men with whom I have worked and trained, at the greatest crisis in all our lives. I should be there.

It was Delaney who came to his rescue.

'You're a captain in the Volunteers, Larry. We'd be glad to have you serve here.'

'Fighting the Japs?'

'The Volunteers are strictly a defensive force,' Delaney said. 'It's our job to keep the home fires burning while the regulars do the fighting. We'll fight the Japs if they turn up at the other end of the causeway, however unlikely that may be. But there's one hell of a lot to do, beginning with rounding up subversives.'

Larry realised that Delaney could have had an ulterior motive in recruiting him.

'We are encountering a good deal of resistance from the locals,' the policeman explained to the Volunteer officers. 'We need all the labour we can get. The thing is, no-one even thought Singapore would have to be defended from the land. The experts didn't think any invading army would ever be able to come down the Malay Peninsula.

256

Well, we have no proof as yet that the Japanese can. But orders from General Percival are that defences are to be built along the north shore of the island, facing Johore. For that we need local labour. But they aren't volunteering, and they're resisting all attempts to enlist them. We need a lead from the top, from the Chinese top. It's up to people like the Chungs to show us that they are on our side. Or we're going to have to assume they are on the Japanese side.'

He took Larry aside after the meeting. 'You don't have to do this, Larry, but if anyone can influence Chung Kai, it's you. And if you can't, well, in view of what I have on file, I'm going to have to lock him up.'

Larry went to the House of Chung, and was shown to Kai's desk. He looked around him in amazement; he had never been in the warehouse before. Kai wore no jacket, although he had a tie on, and was busy checking and signing bills of lading himself, although he was head of the firm.

He stood up to greet Larry, his expression courteous, but revealing no hint of welcome; he stared at Larry's khaki uniform, which left his knees bare, and then at the three pips on his shoulder strap. 'Captain Cairns! Welcome to the House of Chung!' He signalled a secretary to bring a chair, which was placed before the desk.

'I had hoped to speak with you in private,' Larry said.

Kai sat down. 'This is private, Captain Cairns. My people are very busy. They have no time to listen to us.'

Well, Larry thought, if that's how he wants to play it. He was in a mood of white-hot desperation anyway, when he thought of what might be going on in Hong Kong.

'Well, then, Mr Chung,' he said. 'The situation is that the government needs labour. All the labour it can get.'

'For what purpose?' Kai asked.

'To build defences for this island.'

'But the government has been building defences for the past four years. Singapore is impregnable.'

Oh, you bastard, Larry thought. No doubt Kai was smiling behind that calm mask.

'Singapore is impregnable to assault from the sea,' he said evenly. 'Unfortunately it is very vulnerable to assault across the Strait of Johore. The Strait is less than a mile wide in some places.'

'But the Japanese are hundreds of miles away,' Kai protested. 'There is a whole British and Australian army between them and Johore.'

'Nevertheless, we must prepare for every possible eventuality. We must assume that the Japanese may manage to get a force through to Johore.'

'There is only one causeway,' Kai pointed out. 'Once that is blown up, Singapore is totally cut off.'

'We happen to be fighting a bold and ruthless enemy. If there is any possible way of getting across, even after the destruction of the causeway, the Japanese will find it. We have got to make sure that there is no weak spot. Thus we need the labour.'

'I will certainly hold a meeting of my staff and see how many wish to volunteer,' Kai said.

'That is not the point. I am speaking of thousands, not a dozen.'

'I do not employ thousands.'

He was being deliberately obtuse.

'What we want from you, Mr Chung, is a lead. You are an important man in this community. If you will go on the radio and appeal to your people to volunteer, every able-bodied man – and any able-bodied woman, come to that – it would be a great help to the war effort.'

'Will these volunteers be paid?'

'Well . . . yes, I should think so.'

'But not very much?'

'Mr Chung,' Larry said, keeping his temper with some difficulty. 'We are fighting a war. A war of survival.'

'No, no, Captain Cairns,' Kai said. '*You* are fighting a war of survival. Not us. And it is not even a war for the survival of Great Britain. It is a war for the survival of an anachronism called the British Empire. Now you are asking me to ask my people voluntarily to enslave themselves, to perpetuate your empire. I do not feel I can

258

do this. Those who wish your empire to survive will undoubtedly volunteer. Those who do not, will not. It would be very wrong for me to attempt to coerce them.'

'Because you personally have no wish to see the Empire survive.' Larry spoke through gritted teeth.

'My feelings are my own affair, Captain Cairns.'

Larry pointed at him. 'I have said we are fighting a war of survival, Chung. I mean just that. If you are not prepared to assist us, then you may find that those who are not whole-heartedly on our side will be regarded as being whole-heartedly against us.'

Kai bowed his head. 'You would be committing a very grave injustice, Captain Cairns. And you would not be gaining any more "volunteers" for your building project.'

'Then that's that,' Delaney said. 'We'll settle his hash, once and for all. And his beastly brothers.'

'You won't trouble the women, I hope,' Larry said, thinking of the dignified Chung Su.

'I'm not here to arrest women, unless they definitely turn nasty.' Delaney grinned. 'I'm not even going to touch Lan Kuei, much as I'd like to. She's doing too good a job entertaining the troops.'

He presented his long-accumulated evidence to the Governor, and obtained the necessary warrants.

'The arrests will be made immediately before dawn,' he told his men. 'This is a police matter, but if the Volunteers wish to take part . . .'

'I will arrest Kai,' Larry said. It was the only way he could be sure his old friend wasn't beaten up; the policemen were mainly Malays, and had no love for the Chinese, especially those Chinese who had become wealthy.

He was given a police sergeant and four men, as well as six Volunteers, just in case there was trouble. They were all armed with rifles and bayonets, and Larry wore his service revolver.

They assembled at four in the morning at Police Headquarters. There were a dozen groups, for not only the Chungs were being arrested.

259

Delaney gave the word, and they drove off in their wagons. Larry had the wagon parked at the entrance to the Chungs' drive, and sent two policemen and three Volunteers along the fence to the rear of the property. Then he commanded his men to cut the gate open.

This was easily done; there was apparently no alarm system. But he knew there were dogs, even if they were kennelled at night. He waited for fifteen minutes to give his circling force time to get through their fence, then they got back into the truck and drove as fast as possible up the drive, screaming to a stop at the front steps.

Dogs barked and people shouted. Larry was out of the truck and up the front steps, the policemen at his heels, before the brake was on. The Volunteers remained with the truck, rifles ready.

Larry dashed across the front verandah and threw his shoulder against the door. It didn't give, and he gathered himself together for another onslaught, when it opened.

Chung Kai stood there, wearing a mauve dressing gown.

He gazed at Larry, and the policemen. 'You only had to ring the bell,' he said.

Larry felt about six inches tall. But he gritted his teeth. 'I have a warrant here for your arrest,' he said.

Kai raised his eyebrows. 'On what grounds.'

'Subversion, and treasonable correspondence with the enemy. Please remember that anything you say may be taken down and used in evidence against you.'

'Then I will say nothing. Except that you must be crazy. Am I to come with you now?'

'Yes.'

'Am I allowed to dress?'

Larry hesitated. But he had no wish to humiliate Kai. 'Yes. But I will have to be with you.'

Kai shrugged, and went back into the house. Larry followed, while the sergeant and the policemen took their places by the door.

Servants peered at them from inner doorways. And

260

Chung Su stood outside the bedroom. She also wore a dressing gown.

She gazed at Larry. 'I had supposed you to be our friend, Captain Cairns.'

'I would like to be, believe me, Mrs Chung. But I also have my duty to perform.'

Kai went into the bedroom, and Larry followed him. The bed was rumpled and smelt of perfume and sweat. Kai took off his dressing gown and pulled on pants and a shirt.

'You will have to bring me a change of clothing,' he told Su, who stood in the doorway. 'And some food. I don't suppose they feed one very well in Changi.'

'Perhaps I am to be arrested myself,' she remarked.

'You will not be arrested, Mrs Chung,' Larry assured her.

'Will I be allowed to visit my husband in Changi?'

'Your husband is not going to gaol, Mrs Chung. He is going to a detention centre. It will be in Changi, yes, but he will not be confined with ordinary criminals. And yes, you will be allowed to visit him.'

Kai was dressed and waiting. He went to the door; his twin sons were in the corridor. They were eight years old now, and they stared curiously at the policemen and Volunteers, and their weapons.

'What is happening, Papa?' one asked. 'Why are all these policemen here?'

'They have come to arrest me,' Kai told them. 'They think I wish the Japanese to win this war.'

The boys stared at Larry, and his revolver, with wide eyes.

They went downstairs to join the Sergeant.

'I am sorry about this, Mrs Chung,' Larry said. 'Believe me. But there is a war on. All we wanted from your husband was some co-operation. But he refused it.'

Chung Su said nothing, but her eyes were like flint.

As Kai had predicted, arresting various local leaders for non-cooperation did not bring the Chinese and Malays hurrying forward to volunteer their help. But in many ways, Larry thought, this was the government's own fault. For while they desperately needed to improve their defences on the north coast of the island, they also refused to disclose to the native population the true facts of what was happening on the mainland, the repeated defeats and 'strategic withdrawals' being carried out by the British and Australian forces. As a result no-one other than a privileged few had any idea of how serious the situation was, and the general feeling was of business as usual.

One of those who knew, as he was a personal friend of Sir Shenton Thomas, the Governor, was Ronald Lees.

'They don't seem able to stop them,' he muttered. 'It's incredible. Imperial troops, being driven from pillar to post by a bunch of little yellow buggers.'

Cables were arriving from the Ansteys in England wanting to know what was happening to Margaret and Larry and Marion. These became quite hysterical when Larry replied that he was in Singapore but had no idea what had happened to Margaret.

It had been going to be a grim Christmas in any event, but Boxing Day was the grimmest within everyone's memory: news arrived that Hong Kong had surrendered.

'Well, at least the fighting's stopped,' Joan said.

As Larry had been out helping the police and, more recently, supervising the building of the fortifications with what labour force had been assembled, and as she had taken up her duties as an auxiliary nurse, they had seen little of each other during the past fortnight. But Larry could not doubt there was a good deal of emotion still simmering beneath that normally placid exterior.

Only a week later news arrived of what had happened when Hong Kong fell. Lees handed the news sheet, which was highly confidential, to Larry without a word; his face was quite pale.

Larry felt the blood pounding in his veins.

'Wounded bayoneted in their beds,' Roly Payne muttered as he read in turn. 'Nurses raped with their hands tied behind their backs . . .'

'That's only the report of the Argentine consul,' Lees snapped. 'It doesn't have to be true.'

'He was there.' Larry turned away and stood at the window, looking down at the harbour.

'Anyway, Meggy wouldn't have been involved,' Lees said.

'Meg was a nurse,' Larry said, his voice harsh, and went down the stairs. He took the car and drove over to the east beach. Petrol rationing was in full force, but no one attempted to stop him.

He parked the car and looked out across the sand at the shimmering water. This beach meant so many things to him. But even the beach was no longer as he remembered it; two armed Volunteers patrolled up and down, their boots scuffing the sand.

He wondered if anything would ever be as he remembered it again.

The New Year brought no alleviation of the growing catastrophe that was the British position in South East Asia.

Not even government censorship could suppress news of the fall of Kuala Lumpur on 12 January. Censorship did, however, curb on-the-spot reports of what happened there, the burning of the rubber stocks, the looting of the great department stores, the total breakdown of civilisation.

'My God,' Lees groaned. 'If that should happen here . . .'

Now at last thoughts were being turned to the evacuation of non-essential personnel, mainly women and children, from Singapore. Immediately there was a tremendous to-do as everyone who was not actually in uniform claimed a place on one of the few ships to get in; no one was guaranteeing any of them would get out again.

'You must go, of course, my dear,' Lees told Lizzie. 'And you, Joan.'

'I'm not going anywhere, Pa,' Joan declared. 'I have a job to do here.'

'My dear girl, think of Hong Kong.' He gulped, and gave Larry a guilty glance.

'This isn't Hong Kong,' Joan insisted. 'This is Singapore. Singapore is impregnable, right? We're going to fight to the last man. And the last woman,' she added defiantly. 'And we'll win.'

Lizzie wouldn't leave without Joan, but there were few others in that frame of mind. From all accounts, the scenes at the dockside were pretty grim. But Larry had nothing to do with them. He and his Volunteer company were assigned the north shore, and here they made themselves at home, digging shelter trenches, mounting their machine guns, gazing across the water at the thickly-forested coast of Johore.

He only visited the Lees at weekends, and there were only two of those before the ultimate disaster arrived. Every day following the fall of Kuala Lumpur, troops streamed back across the causeway, dejected and depressed. They had fearful tales to tell, mostly of atrocities, of prisoners being used for bayonet practice, of the way the Japanese seemed able to move silently through the jungle and appear to the rear of any position, of the unending defeat.

Larry didn't like to think of the effect they were having on morale, but there was little time to worry about that. On 30 January he and his men heard the skirl of pipes, and out of the trees marched some two hundred men of the Argyll and Sutherland Highlanders, the very last British troops on the soil of the Malayan peninsula.

Behind their piper they marched across the causeway to a welcome rest. Within an hour the causeway was blown up.

Singapore was again an island, and about to stand siege.

CHAPTER 11
The Catastrophe

The following day Larry found himself crouching in a shelter trench with his men, and listening to a broadcast by General Percival:

'The battle for Malaya has come to an end and the battle of Singapore is started. For more than two months our troops have fought the enemy on the mainland. The enemy has had the advantage of great superiority and considerable freedom of movement by sea.

'Our task has been both to impose losses on the enemy and to gain time to enable forces of the Allies to be concentrated for this struggle in the Far East.

'Today we stand beleaguered in our island fortress until help can come, as assuredly it will come. This we are determined to do. In carrying out this task we want the active help of every man and woman in the fortress.

'There is work for all to do. Any enemy who sets foot in the fortress must be dealt with immediately. The enemy within our gates must be ruthlessly weeded out. There must be no more loose talk and rumour-mongering. Our duty is clear. With firm resolve and fixed determination we shall win through.'

Larry switched off the set.

'Pity he didn't make a speech like that two months ago,' remarked Lieutenant Parton.

Larry contemplated the jungle across the strait, only a thousand yards away. There was no sound from over there, no sign of the enemy. Yet everyone knew the Japanese were there. It was only a matter of time.

It came as something of a shock to him to realise that he had never killed a man. But how he wanted to kill one now, anyone wearing a green uniform.

* * *

265

That same day the Volunteers were pulled out. The north shore of the island was now the front line, and was to be defended by regular troops: the Third Corps under General Heath, and the Australians under General Gordon Bennett; both forces were augmented by various Indian brigades. The Volunteers passed them marching up as they marched down to Singapore, and did not like what they saw. The regulars were either exhausted escapees from the jungle battles in Malaya, or fresh troops straight from England or India with absolutely no experience of warfare.

The Volunteers, together with two Malayan infantry brigades and the fortress troops, were placed under the command of Major-General Simmons and assigned to guarding the south shore. It had been decided that there was little chance of the Japanese attacking from the sea, a sad waste of all the time and money which had gone into fortifying the harbour. The Volunteers were placed in charge of the dock area, as far from any risk of fighting as possible.

'That's what they think of our capability,' Parton growled. 'Well, at least we're close to home.'

The air raids had now reached a new intensity, and the city was being bombed daily. There were no shelters, and people were told to use the open sewers when the bombs started to fall. There seemed little to choose between being blown up or being suffocated, but at least the gas masks which had been issued came in handy. There was only one air force squadron left to defend the city; the pilots worked heroically, but they had no chance against such overwhelming numbers.

The native population seemed utterly stunned, not only at what was happening to them, but at the apparent inability of the British, for so long the most powerful people in the world, to defend either the city or themselves.

To everyone's relief, there was no rioting or general civil unrest, but the Chinese and Malays were taking note of the British ineptitude, and the anxiety of so many of their bosses to get off the island; they were unlikely to forget these days, no matter what the outcome of the war.

Meanwhile the 'fortress' waited, for there was still no sign of the Japanese. General Wavell, Supreme Allied Commander in South East Asia, flew in to see the situation for himself, and the Volunteers were called upon to provide a guard of honour. The General, a tall spare man with a grim expression, marched quickly down the ranks: he had a lot to do. That evening there was a reception at Government House to which several of the Volunteer officers were invited, Larry among them.

Here he met not only Wavell, but for the first time, General Percival. The army commander had a remote look in his eyes as Wavell chatted, asking questions about equipment and training.

'Don't forget,' he said, 'if every one of you kills one Jap, we must win this battle; we have more troops in Singapore than they can possibly mount an assault with.' He smiled. 'Two would be even better.'

He glanced at Percival, but the general was looking more remote than ever, and for an instant a peculiar expression flitted across Wavell's face.

In that moment, Larry knew that Singapore was lost.

Next day he obtained a twelve hour pass and went up to the house; Hammond and Teng's offices were closed, since there was no longer any business as all shipping was carrying either men or materiel. Also, the building had been struck by a bomb; the Managing Director's office was wrecked, and the famous chair in which many had for so long anticipated sitting had disintegrated. Mrs Lu had been in her office when the bomb landed – she had insisted on going there every day to deal with largely non-existent correspondence – and there was nothing of her left. Ronald Lees had nearly collapsed with distress.

Larry found his boss still virtually in a state of shock.

'What's going to happen, Larry? What's going to happen?'

'We're going to fight, Ronald. You do realise, I hope,

that if the Japanese get across, this house is soon going to be in the front line?'

'But they can't get across, can they? I mean, we've been told that's impossible.'

'If they do, I'd take Elizabeth and move into Singapore itself.'

'But it's sheer hell down there.'

'That's nothing to the hell there'll be up here if the Japanese get here.'

He then went up to the Chung mansion; everyone knew that Bukit Timah, and the main road leading down into Singapore, was going to be a key point, both for attack and defence, and troops were digging trenches and emplacing guns in the once-beautiful garden.

Chung Su sat on the front verandah with her little boys, and watched the destruction; in the house the servants were packing up the furniture and cutlery and crockery, the paintings and the decorated screens.

Su's eyes were cold as she gazed at Larry.

'I am sorry about this,' he said. 'But it is necessary.'

'Of course, Captain Cairns. Everything is necessary.'

'Where are you going to go? To one of your sisters-in-law?' All the Chung brothers had been arrested with Kai.

'I shall go to the go-down, Captain Cairns. I believe it will be safer there. For the boys.'

He nodded; that seemed as good an idea as any. 'Is your husband well?'

'He is as well as can be expected, Captain. He looks forward to being released.'

Kai would only be released, in the near future, by the Japanese. So what did she really think, and hope? The Japanese had murdered her mother and father. But now they might be seen as possible rescuers of her husband.

'I hope that may soon be possible, Mrs Chung,' he said, and left.

He had the strangest urge to go and see Lan, curious to know how she was responding to this unthinkable situation, but he decided against it, went to the hospital instead, and found Joan. As there had been no fighting for several days the initial emergency had somewhat settled down, and she was able to obtain a six-hour pass from Bob Sharples.

Larry took her to dinner at Raffles. The bombing had temporarily ceased, and the waiters were doing their best. So were the chefs; the place was quite crowded. It was remarkable how much good food and drink was available.

They gazed at each other by the light of the candle; there was no electricity as a bomb had severed the mains.

'I'm so scared,' Joan said.

'Snap.'

'You, Larry?'

'Why not? A man can be just as afraid as a woman. It's just his business not to show it.'

She chewed slowly for some time. Then she said, 'Can they take Singapore, Larry?'

It was his turn to chew in silence.

'Pa says General Wavell told him there are eighty thousand armed men on the island,' Joan said. 'And that there can't be eighty thousand Japanese in Malaya. He says there is no chance of their taking Singapore.'

He said nothing.

'But you don't agree?'

Larry sighed. 'There have been a lot of battles won at odds of more than three to one. It's a matter of morale, Joan. Our people don't have any left. What's more, I don't believe the high command has any left, either.'

'Oh, God. Larry . . .' she put down her knife and fork. 'Will it be like Hong Kong?'

'We must pray not.'

'Larry . . . I'm a virgin.'

He stared at her, thinking: what difference would not being a virgin make to the horror of what is going to happen to her?

What does it matter, she was thinking. I don't even know if Margaret is alive or dead. If she is alive, she

269

would have been at the hospital, and she will have been raped with her hands tied behind her back.

And that is going to happen to me.

Their thoughts were interrupted by the air raid siren.

The maître d'hotel, Peter Fung, hurried up. 'You best take shelter, Mr Cairns, Miss Lees.'

Joan stretched her hand across the table to Larry. 'We'll stay right here, Peter.'

Peter looked alarmed.

'You go off, Peter,' Larry told him. 'We'll sit here until you come back to serve the dessert.'

Peter left to join all the other waiters and dinner guests, who clattered down the stairs as the bombs began to fall.

'All alone in Raffles,' Joan said. 'There's an experience I'd never expected.'

The crumps and deeper bangs came closer, punctuated by the sharper reports of the anti-aircraft batteries. They listened to distant cheering.

'They must have got one of the buggers,' Larry said.

They went out on to the terrace. It was raining. They stood watching the searchlights reflecting off the low clouds, every so often illuminating one of the green-painted fighter bombers, looking almost black in the darkness.

'If we're going to die,' Joan said. 'I would like to live, just once.'

They gazed into each other's eyes and, as with Lan that first day, he knew what was going to happen. And for all his earlier revulsion at the very idea, now he wanted to make her happy, perhaps because she wanted it so very badly.

They went back inside.

'I'm soaked,' she said, looking at the water dripping off her uniform on to the floor.

'So perhaps we'd better take these off, for a while.'

They went upstairs, hand in hand. Larry thought of the Götterdämerung, the twilight of the gods. He had come to look on Singapore, after fourteen years, as his own city. Now it was being remorselessly destroyed as his family, his business and his dreams of sitting in the Managing Director's chair had all been destroyed.

As Joan had said, there was nothing left to do but live, up to the very last moment.

Joan was actually a very attractive woman. She might be too tall and too thin, but as he remembered from that night at the beach she had a strong, muscular body and very good legs.

And she was eager. He hoped that he had done something for her; certainly she had been good for him.

But neither Joan nor any other woman could remove the constant aching void in his heart, or the cold anger in his brain. He remembered thinking before the war, with juvenile satisfaction, that he was ruthless enough to be a success in business. He had not known the meaning of the word. Now he wanted only to fight, or die.

And he was not being given the opportunity. So, as in business, as in love, he would make the opportunity on his own. He now knew that Singapore would not fight to the last man, the last bullet. He had seen it in Percival's face. The fortress would be defended by all the rules of conventional warfare, and when defence was no longer practical, it would be surrendered to the Japanese.

But he would not accept that surrender. Of that he was determined. He would fight for life. He would fight for the right to fight the Japanese, for Margaret and Marion, perhaps even for Joan.

When he left her, he went to see a Malayan fisherman, with whom he had played cricket in the old days. He had a plan.

He regained his command at dawn. The rain had cleared but there was still a lot of cloud, which mingled with the smoke columns rising from the bombed city.

'Were you in that one?' Parton asked.

'I got wet,' Larry agreed.

He thought of Joan, back at the hospital now. She

271

would have at least one bright memory to take with her, wherever she was going.

'Listen,' Parton said.

There was a huge amount of noise from the north.

'They're trying to cross,' Larry said. 'Christ, to be up there!'

His men were impatient too, as they prowled the waterfront in impotent anxiety. Bad news began to come in very rapidly. The Japanese had got across in several places, and on Bukit Timah the Commonwealth forces were falling back.

'Then that's it,' Parton said gloomily. He took his revolver from its holster and spun the chambers. 'Looks as if I may get to use this thing, after all.'

They awaited a summons to move up to the front, but none came; they were still not considered battleworthy. Larry recalled Wavell's words, that if each of them took just one Japanese soldier with them . . . but Percival was still attempting to fight by the book, a book the enemy had torn up years ago.

Roly Payne, who commanded the adjacent company, came over to see them.

'Looks pretty grim,' Larry said.

'Don't you believe it,' Roly said. 'We have them now.'

'Have we? How?'

'I've just heard, from someone who knows, that a vast British amphibious force is about to land in the north, at Penang. It will cut across the peninsula and leave the Japanese armies down here absolutely stranded. They'll be pulling out any day now.'

Larry looked at him, one eyebrow raised.

Roly flushed. 'It came from a very good source.'

'Then believe it,' Larry said. 'It'll make you feel better.'

Roly shook his head and went back to his men.

For the next five days the Japanese kept up an unremitting pressure, and the Commonwealth forces were driven steadily back. The Malayan brigades were called up to

272

defend Bukit Timah, leaving only the Volunteers to guard the harbour.

Conditions in Singapore itself were unlike anything Larry had envisaged in his worst nightmares. There was no electricity and very little water. Although there were close on a million people in the city, there was no labour: everyone was sheltering from the bombs and shells. Those who had been killed in the bombing lay unburied in the streets; the air became filled with a dreadful miasma, the stench of humanity, living and dead.

Even though there was still surprisingly little unrest, orders came to place the city under martial law. Looters were to be shot on sight. The police force having virtually disintegrated, the Volunteers took up the task of patrolling the streets. Sure enough, on their very first night, Larry's patrol spotted some youths breaking into a store on Orchard Street.

Larry shouted at them to halt, but they ran off.

'Bring them down,' he told his men.

The volunteers opened fire, and he fired as well.

Two of the boys fell. Both were dead, hit several times. Two of the wounds were caused by point-four-five revolver bullets.

'Good shooting, sir,' remarked his sergeant.

So I have at last killed a man, Larry thought. But he was only a boy, and not my enemy.

That same night, when the Japanese planes flew over, instead of bombing they dropped leaflets calling upon the garrison to surrender.

Next day, the long-prepared plan for the evacuation of key personnel was put into force. Some eighty ships, of varying sizes but all very small, had been accumulated, and to these came everyone who had any claim to be worth saving, and a good number who hadn't.

Air Vice-Marshal Pulford, the deputy commander, and Rear Admiral Spooner, the naval commander, were going; there was obviously no point in leaving more top brass than was necessary to be captured with the now obviously-lost fortress.

Business leaders and their wives were also being taken out; among them were Ronald and Lizzie Lees.

They shook hands with Larry, then hugged him.

'We'll meet again,' Lees promised him. 'When the time comes to put all this together again.'

'When those little yellow devils have been smashed,' Lizzie added fiercely.

'Where's Joan?'' Larry asked.

Lizzie sighed, her shoulders sagging. 'She wouldn't come. Said her duty was to stay here.'

Quite a few nurses were being evacuated, but quite a few were remaining. Larry would have liked to get up to the hospital to see Joan, but he couldn't leave the dockside, where there were some angry confrontations between the locals and the evacuees; no Chinese or Malays were being allowed on the ships.

At dusk the little armada motored out of the harbour, making for the supposed safety of the Dutch islands. Larry watched them go, his brain racing. He had made plans of his own, but couldn't implement them until he was released from duty.

That same night, all officers who could be spared were summoned to a meeting with General Percival.

'I want you all to understand the situation,' he said. 'We are still maintaining our lines in the vicinity of Bukit Timah, and I believe we could do so indefinitely, had we sufficient of the sinews of war at our disposal. Unfortunately, we are running short of both ammunition and petrol.

'Far worse, however, is the civilian situation. I am informed by His Excellency that there have been some thirty-five thousand civilian casualties. This is unacceptable. In addition, since the Japanese have captured most of our reservoirs, we have only sufficient water for another twenty four hours. After that time, Sir Shenton Thomas is afraid that all civilisation in Singapore may break down,

274

and that we may have to contend with a racial war within the city as well as one without.'

He obviously hasn't been into the city recently, Larry thought; civilisation had broken down several days ago, but there had been no sign of any racial war.

'In all these circumstances, and notwithstanding the messages of encouragement I have received from General Wavell and indeed from the Prime Minister,' Percival went on, 'I have come to the conclusion that to prolong the struggle can only cost lives, without serving any useful purpose as regards the winning of this war. I therefore intend to send out a white flag to General Yamashita at dawn on Sunday.'

He paused, and looked over the tense faces before him. 'I, we, all of us, will of course be bound by the terms of the surrender. I will do my utmost to obtain adequate terms, but I cannot be hopeful about this. The best I can anticipate is that I may be able to avoid a massacre such as took place in Hong Kong. Now, regular officers will of course remain with their units. It is their duty to do so. You men of the Volunteers, who have worked so hard and so well for the defence of your city, come into a different category. As of this minute, you and your men are disbanded. Those of you who wish to rejoin your families, to return to your homes, are now entitled to do so. I recommend that you get rid of both your uniforms and your weapons; you will probably receive better treatment from the Japanese if you are civilians.

'Those of you who wish to take some other form of action are welcome to do so, for the next twenty four hours. You will keep such intentions to yourself, of course, except insofar as it may be necessary to inform a possible assistant.

'You will inform your men of my decisions and instruct them to act accordingly.

'I wish to thank you all for everything you have done. I only regret that your efforts have not been rewarded with success. Thank you.'

275

He saluted, and the Volunteers responded. Then he shook hands with each man in turn.

'Some show,' Parton said. 'What are you going to do, Larry?'

'I have an idea,' Larry said, and went in search of Roly.

'So there it is,' Roly said. 'Do you reckon we'll be interned, or told to get on with it?'

'I doubt we'll be told to get on with it,' Larry said. 'The Japanese won't want any of us around. Roly . . . I'm getting out.'

Roly raised his eyebrows. 'Just how do you propose to do that?'

'I've thought about it. In fact I've thought about nothing else for the past week. I've bought myself a small prahu, and she's stuffed with water and food. I'm going to sail out. Tonight.'

Roly's eyebrows seemed to rise higher yet. 'Sail where? Sumatra?'

'In the first instance. But I'd hope to do better than that. What's wrong with India?'

'You're absolutely bonkers, old boy. Sail a prahu to India?'

'It's been done before.'

'Maybe. But for every one which made it, a thousand were lost.'

'It beats standing here waiting to be kicked in the gut by a Jap.'

'We don't know that's going to happen. Larry, look, I know you're in a pretty upset frame of mind, but what you're proposing is just suicide. If you don't die of thirst or starvation, the Japs will get you. Once Singapore falls, their planes are going to have the freedom of the skies. They'll blow apart everything that moves on the water.'

'You really think they'll waste bullets or bombs on a derelict Malay prahu?'

'They will when they spot a white man in it.'

'But they won't spot a white man in it. I told you, I've thought it out. If any plane appears, we nip over the side,

attached by ropes, and stay under the hull until they leave
again.'

'We?'

'I was hoping you'd come with me.'

Roly gaped at him.

'We *can* make it, Roly,' Larry said. 'I know we can.'

Roly shook his head. 'Sorry, old boy. I'm not in the
suicide stakes. I intend to die in my bed.'

Larry gazed at him for some seconds, then he shrugged.
'I wish you joy of it.'

Roly held out his hand. 'I'll wish you every success.
But . . . I don't imagine we'll be seeing each other again.'

Larry was very disappointed. He knew just how dangerous his idea was, and he knew it would be easier if there
were two of them to give each other encouragement and
physical assistance, than for one man alone.

But he also had no doubt that even to die of thirst or
starvation, or be overwhelmed by a big sea, would be
preferable to being a Japanese prisoner.

He prepared the boat, checked his provisions. There
were four jerrycans of water, which he calculated could
be made to last three weeks, and sufficient biscuit, with
an assortment of tinned vegetables and some vitamin tab-
lets, for the same time. If he was going to be on his own,
then he had twice as long. And he had no doubt that he
could obtain more water while coasting up Sumatra, while
with the prevailing wind out of the east he thought he
had a good chance of reaching Burma.

When all was ready, he went up to the hospital. Leaving
Joan behind was the only thing he regretted about sneak-
ing away.

'I've come to say goodbye,' he told her.

Her face was pale, her eyes red-rimmed with lack of
sleep, and her uniform was filthy. The growl of the guns
was very close, and often the whine of bullets or the
crump of an exploding shell penetrated the hospital itself;
the Japanese were only a few hundred yards away.

'Yes,' she said. 'Sister told us they'll probably segregate

the men and women after the surrender.' She gave a twisted grin. 'If there's any screwing to be done the Japs will want to do it for themselves.'

'Oh, Joan . . .' he held her hands. 'I'm getting out.'

She frowned. 'How? Where?'

'I'd better not tell you. But I know it can be done.'

She stared at him. 'Larry . . . take me with you, please!'

'It's incredibly dangerous!'

'Isn't staying here going to be incredibly dangerous?'

He bit his lip. To have her with him; that would be all the support he would need. He had no fears for either her courage or her stamina.

'If you really want to . . .' he tried a grin. 'Roly Payne thinks I'm committing suicide.'

'I can't think of anyone I'd rather commit suicide with, Larry. When do we leave?'

'In one hour, if you can make it.'

'Oh, I can make it all right,' she assured him. 'Just let me have a word with Bob Sharples.'

A white flag was sent out from Singapore on the morning of Sunday, 15th February, 1942. The Japanese refused to discuss any terms save unconditional surrender which the British were forced to accept, but fighting went on until the official cease fire at eight thirty that night.

By then the catastrophe Joan had dreaded became reality. On Saturday the Japanese broke into the Queen Alexandra Hospital and, as in Hong Kong, massacred both patients and staff.

In Singapore itself, orders went out to the Royal Engineers to destroy every drop of alcohol in the city, and a million and a half bottles were smashed to prevent them falling into the hands of the Japanese.

Then, at eight thirty, the firing died. The troops in the front line were taken by surprise; they knew they were holding their own, and they could not believe that the white flag had been hoisted. They stared at each other with hollow and bitter eyes.

The civilians gradually emerged from where they had been sheltering from the bombardments, relieved that they were still alive, fearful of what would happen next.

They had good reason to be. After a miserable night, they watched the Japanese soldiers marching into their city, knew that they had entered a new era, one of harsh repression and sudden death.

The soldiers were disarmed and herded into makeshift camps. The English civilians were rounded up and herded into the padang of the Singapore Cricket Club, clutching whatever small possessions they had been able to gather. Incongruously, they endeavoured to avoid walking on the pitch. They made a pitiful sight, their erstwhile power vanished, their future bleak. Even if they could congratulate themselves on having escaped the rape and wholesale murder of Hong Kong, they now knew that they were on their way, on foot, to a Japanese internment camp.

Colonel Kitachi Tano entered the city that afternoon. He went straight to Changi Prison, but the Chinese internees had already been released.

He found Chung Kai in the main go-down belonging to the House of Chung, where Chung Su and the boys had been living ever since the Japanese had crossed the strait. It had not been possible to have a bath, but Kai was looking remarkably spruce after his ordeal.

Kitachi bowed. 'Chung Kai, my old friend,' he said. He shook hands, and then bowed to Chung Su. 'It is a great relief to see that you have survived unharmed.'

'The British did not ill treat me,' Kai said. 'They were fighting for their lives, for their honour. I cannot blame them.'

'Bah,' Kitachi said. 'Their honour? They have no honour. They have surrendered, eighty thousand men. Do you know how many we brought against them? Sixty thousand. How can such men have honour?'

'They wished to save the civilian population,' Chung Su ventured.

'With respect, Mrs Chung, in wars it is always the

civilian population which suffers. Soldiers should be made of sterner stuff than these people. Now, Chung Kai, there is a great deal to be done.' He looked around at the huge warehouse, stuffed with goods which the Chungs had been unable to ship; even the latex, which was normally stored outside, now filled the air with its stench. It was also crowded with Chinese staff. The warehouse had only been slightly damaged and the Chung employees had instinctively used it as a shelter once their homes had been destroyed. 'I have spoken of you to General Yamashita, and he looks forward to meeting you as soon as the city is fully under control. Then you will not only resume business, but you will take over, assisted by a Japanese adviser.' Kitachi grinned. 'Myself.'

Kai made no reply. Like everyone else in Singapore, he had been dumbfounded by the speed and completeness of the British collapse. Singapore was immutably British; it had been British since 1819. Every institution, every law, every street, every paving stone, every house, was based on British tradition. Even the cars drove on the left.

It was inconceivable for Singapore not to be British. Of course he had dreamed of independence, but a measured, negotiated independence, in which the British institutions would remain, modified to suit the needs of the ruling Chinese – he had never envisaged the Malays ruling themselves – providing the continuity of civilisation which would allow the new nation to advance and prosper. He had never shared his father's dream of independence under the aegis of the Japanese.

In fact, he had never really been able to imagine the British being defeated. As he had left the internment wing of the prison, and saw the burning buildings, the cratered roads, the unburied bodies, he had inhaled the stench of decaying corpses. And he had gazed across the Cricket Club padang at the white people being assembled there, driven by the kicks and rifle butts of their captors. And he had had a sensation that he had died and been born again, in hell.

But a hell through which he, and Su and the children, could apparently walk unharmed.

'My house is wrecked,' he said.

'I know,' Kitachi said. 'The British attempted to use it as a fortress. They are guilty of almost every crime imaginable. But your house will be rebuilt, Chung Kai; you have my word. Now, there is something I wish to do, before anything. I wish to see Larry Cairns. You knew he was in Singapore?'

'Yes, Kai said.

'Well, I hope he has not been killed. Will you come with me to find him? You will enjoy watching him crawl. I will make him crawl to you, too. And then you may beat him, if you choose, for what he did to your sister.'

'I have no desire to see Larry Cairns again,' Chung Kai said.

Kitachi thought he would never understand the Chinese. A supine race, their day was a thousand years in the past.

He went to the padang, had the white men paraded in front of him. But Larry was not amongst them.

Roly Payne was, however: Kitachi remembered him. He had Roly taken out of the crowd and marched to the house the kempei-tai had appropriated as their headquarters.

'Where is Cairns?' he asked.

'I have no idea,' Roly said, and gasped as one of the two soldiers standing behind him hit him in the kidneys with a rubber truncheon. He all but fell, kept his feet with a tremendous effort.

'You will address me as "sir",' Kitachi told him. 'And you will bow whenever you speak to me. Bow.'

Roly hesitated, then gave a brief nod, and gasped again as he was struck again. Tears of pain filled his eyes.

'It is necessary to bow very low,' Kitachi told him. 'I am a very superior person. Bow.'

Roly took a deep, pain-filled breath, and bowed until he was nearly parallel with the floor.

'Excellent,' Kitachi said. 'You learn fast, Mr Payne. Straighten.'

Roly obeyed.

'Now tell me where Larry Cairns is to be found.'

'I do not know, sir,' Roly said, and bowed.

'I am told he served with the Volunteers. You served with the Volunteers. Therefore you served together.'

Roly bowed; the pain in his back was beginning to recede. 'That is true, sir. But two nights ago we were disbanded and told to rejoin our families. I do not know where Cairns went. I think he may have gone up to the hospital.'

'I will have the hospital checked,' Kitachi said.

Roly bowed. 'Or he could be hiding in Singapore . . . sir.'

'If he is in Singapore, and is not in the padang, he is dead,' Kitachi pointed out. 'But I do not think he is dead. If he were, I think you would have known. I do not think he is at the hospital, either. I think you know where he is, Mr Payne. Tell me where he is.'

Roly bowed. 'I have no idea, sir.'

'Beat him,' he said in Japanese. 'Beat him until he is insensible. Beat him!'

The rubber truncheon began to swing. After the third blow, Roly fell to the floor.

General Yamashita was a short, irritable man, who did not seem the least elated by his astounding victory. He barked orders at his secretaries, walked to the window to look down at the city, which was being cleaned up by British prisoners-of-war under the guard and the whips of Japanese soldiers, then returned to bark more orders and instructions.

His greeting to Kai was brief and stern.

'There is a war on, Mr Chung,' he said. 'And Singapore remains in the front line. Martial law will continue, and I will expect you, and the other leaders of the community, to see that the populace not only obeys these laws but gets back to work as soon as possible. Anyone found breaking any of my laws will be executed. Impress this on your people.'

Chung Kai could not stop himself asking, 'Does this include me?'

Yamashita glared at him. 'It includes everybody, Mr Chung. You are dismissed.'

Kitachi followed Kai outside. 'You should not have asked that. Now you have offended the general.'

'Well,' Kai said, 'the general offended me. How can he threaten to execute my people? The British at least never did that.'

'The British have been defeated,' Kitachi pointed out. 'You should remember that.'

'I will,' Kai promised. 'Did you find Larry Cairns?'

'He has disappeared,' Kitachi spat. 'No one will tell me where he is.' Not even Roly Payne, he thought, even though he had been beaten until blood poured out of his mouth and his rectum, until he died. 'I think he has left Singapore, stolen away like a thief in the night. But no matter. I have his wife and child. They can do the suffering.'

'Perhaps one day Larry will come back,' Kai said, 'looking for you.'

Kitachi glared.

'Then you will have the whole family,' Kai pointed out. 'Is that not what you wish?'

Kitachi couldn't make up his mind whether the little rat was poking fun at him or not. He snorted, and went off to the Bamboo Curtain.

He could work off his anger on Lan Kuei.

Sailing due west, Larry and Joan made Tanjungbalai, some twenty five miles from Singapore, by dawn. The prahu, twenty four foot, double-ended and Bermuda-rigged with a long bowsprit, and a little shelter cabin aft, proved a most comfortable sea-boat: even Joan was reassured after a few hours. At first light, Larry dropped the sails and coasted into the beach, where they anchored in as shallow water as possible, in the shade of the trees.

The exhilaration of leaving the falling fortress had stayed with them throughout the hours of darkness. They had looked back at the glare of the fires rising above the city; they had listened to the cracks of rifles, and the deeper reports of artillery coming from Bukit Timah. The hill itself had loomed, darker even than the night. It alone would be the same after Singapore had fallen.

Joan had wondered aloud about her parents, wondering if they had managed to make good their escape to Australia.

Larry thought about nothing save reaching India, and being sent once more against the Japanese. He had a rifle and bayonet as well as his revolver in the prahu, but did not suppose he would have to use them on the journey. Yet he wanted to kill. And kill and kill and kill, until he was himself killed, or reunited with Margaret and Marion.

Ashore, they found fresh water. Larry climbed a coconut tree and also managed to catch a fish, which they cooked over a little fire.

'Do you know,' Joan said, 'if it wasn't for all that has happened, I would be happy.'

They made love on the sand, almost in desperation, and Larry thought that, for a little while, removed from the chaos and carnage of Singapore, he could have been happy too.

It was Saturday, 14 February.

Tanjungbalai was all but deserted. It was evening before a fisherman approached through the trees, and stared at the white people on the beach. Larry pointed the rifle at him and he went away again.

They left immediately. They had seen no planes over the Straits of Malacca all day; the Japanese were too concerned with conquering Singapore.

During the night they made a good fifty miles, and put in to Sungaikabung the following evening. Now they were some seventy miles from Singapore, with no means of knowing what was happening there.

'I think we're going to make it,' Joan said, happily.

It took them eleven nights to work their way up the Sumatran coast. Larry stuck to his plan of sailing from dusk to dawn, keeping well offshore to avoid rocks, and putting in with the first light.

They saw no Japanese activity, save for planes flying high over Sumatra during the day. But those could have been the RAF; they could not tell.

Larry guessed the Japanese had better things to do further south. He had originally toyed with the idea of sailing down to Batavia, but rejected it. He had guessed that would be the way the Japanese would take, and after what he had seen in Singapore he had little faith in the ability of the scratch army of Dutch, British, Americans and Australians to withstand the enemy for very long.

They sat on the beach at Sabang, the island off the northernmost tip of Sumatra, and studied Larry's map.

'This is our first big one,' he told Joan. 'It's about a hundred and thirty miles of open sea between here and Great Nicobar. That will take us about a day and a half. Okay?'

'You're the skipper,' she reminded him.

Fourteen days of enforced intimacy had given them total confidence in each other, and in their venture. They had hardly touched their supplies, and they were just thirty-six hours away from safety.

He studied the sky, wishing he had paid more attention to weather lore in the past. There were scattered clouds to the west overhead and, some heavier stuff to the east. That could well be rain, gathering over the mountains of Malaysia. He had no idea if it would come out to sea, or whether it would be dangerous if it did. He didn't see why it should be: the prahu was a well-found boat.

Anyway, there was surely greater risk in remaining in Sumatra.

They put out at dusk, as usual, and sailed steadily just west of north, using Larry's compass. It was 28 February,

1942, and a bright night; the sea was no more than slightly choppy in the fresh breeze. And the breeze was propelling them on.

At dawn the sun rose out of a red and angry sky. Larry made no comment, but he could only hope the weather would delay another twenty four hours.

Joan did not appear to notice the clouds in the east at all. She sat in the bow and fluffed out her hair. 'This'll be our first daytime trip,' she said. 'I think I'll sunbathe.'

They breakfasted, then she stripped off and lay on one of the thwarts, legs dangling over the side. Sailing in the Indian Ocean in daylight was a new experience for both of them. Presumably there had been marine life all around them in the Straits, but they had not seen it. Now they were besieged by flying fish, and surrounded by dolphins.

They even saw the sharper, more sinister fin of a shark, but it kept its distance.

Larry watched the clouds, which rose slowly. There was going to be rain at least, in the not too distant future. But with every hour they were getting nearer their goal.

It was just after lunch that they saw the planes, three of them, high in the eastern sky.

'Now's the time for our survival drill,' Larry said.

They tied the ropes round their waists and went over the side.

'I just hope that shark isn't still around,' Joan said.

'He isn't,' Larry assured her, optimistically.

They allowed the prahu to tow them along while they watched the planes, did not go beneath the hull until the aircraft started to wheel out of the sky. They were indeed Japanese, and they swooped quite low over the little boat. But as Larry had calculated, they saw no reason to waste either bullets or bombs on such a derelict target. After a few passes they flew away again, south towards Sumatra.

'Whee!' Joan panted, as she climbed back on board. 'I was scared. Tell me about Nicobar, Larry.'

'It belongs to India. There'll be English officials there. From Nicobar we'll get to the Andamans, and from the

Andamans we'll get to India. We're just about there, Joan.'

'Then I'll get on with my tan,' she said, and looked up. 'Bother!'

Clouds were obliterating the sun.

Larry calculated they had done about half the journey. There were only sixty-odd miles to go. But at four knots, which was the best he could coax out of the prahu, that meant fifteen hours.

Soon there came a steady drizzle, which increased into a downpour. The wind dropped completely.

'Not much point in getting dressed,' Joan remarked, as the huge drops bounced off her skin. 'There's going to be a lot of it.'

The clouds were ominously black, and covered the whole sky now, thinning only far to the west. And still there was no wind.

Larry remembered the old aphorism he had heard in Hong Kong: When the wind comes before the rain, soon you will make sail again; but when the rain comes before the wind, then your sheets and halyards mind.

'Put the rope on again,' he said.

'Eh? Whatever for?'

'Because I think we're going to need to be strapped in. I'd get dressed, if I were you, or you'll get rope burn. Tie the rope tightly round your waist and make sure it's secured to the thwart.'

She gazed at him, then up at the sky. 'Is it going to be bad?'

'I don't know,' he said. 'I've never been in a real storm at sea, except in a liner. We don't want to take any chances.'

She obeyed him, then came to sit aft with him, beside the tiller, while they had a meal and drank some water.

Larry was aware of being unutterably tired, both physically and mentally. He had been at the helm since six o'clock the previous evening, eighteen hours. Yet he had not been afraid of the thirty-six hour stretch he had known was necessary to reach Great Nicobar. It was his brain

287

which had suddenly become exhausted. To have come so far, escaped so much, then to run into bad weather . . .

Rain was now filling the bottom of the boat, and he set Joan to bailing. Then he became aware that its drops were hitting the side of his face, and that the sail was filling. The prahu began to race through the water.

The wind was not strong as yet, and the rain had the effect of completely calming the sea.

'Whee!' Joan shouted. 'I never knew this thing could travel so fast.'

'Neither did I,' Larry muttered, hanging on to the tiller for dear life.

The wind increased dramatically; water came slopping over the gunwales; Joan went on bailing with all her strength. Although it was early afternoon, the darkness was pitch black.

Then the darkness was split by a sizzling bolt of lightning, accompanied by an enormous explosion of thunder directly above their heads.

Joan screamed, and cowered in the bottom of the boat.

The first lightning flash was followed by others, in such rapid succession that the day became a whirling kaleidoscope of dark and light. The thunder was continuous, and almost blotted out thought.

The wind was now tearing at the little craft, threatening to roll it over, and the seas were already more than six feet from trough to crest. Larry instinctively turned the prahu away from the storm, running west. But she was going far too fast, threatening to pitchpole stern over bow. Joan was incapable of doing anything, and he dared not leave the tiller. He pulled out his knife and slashed the sheets controlling the sail. Instantly it flew away from the mast, hung horizontally for a few minutes, and then disappeared altogether.

Minutes later, the foresail tore away.

Without the sails the prahu was more manageable, for a while. But the seas were getting bigger all the time, huge walls of dark blue topped with foaming white crests. Larry could hear the roaring behind him as they came up, and wrestled with the tiller to keep the prahu directly in front of them. Despite the rain and the cold, sweat poured down his face and chest.

Never had he known such a physical ordeal combined with such physical danger, and such physical fear, too. Indeed he realised that he had never in his comfortable, secure life, ever faced a physical ordeal at all, compared with this. The longest innings, the wildest drive in a car, even crouching in a sewer watching bombs falling all about him, had been child's play beside facing the full strength of an angry ocean.

Yet at the same time he experienced a kind of exultation, that he was still alive, that he was doing battle with the greatest elemental force in nature and giving as good as he got.

Then he heard the greatest roar of all, and looked up at some twenty feet of solid water, rising high above the little boat, its curling crest about to overbalance and come down directly on them.

'Hold on!' he shouted unnecessarily; they were both holding on for dear life.

The wave surged on, and picked up the prahu. Larry had a sensation of losing all control of the helm, and then of flying through the air. He was brought up with a jerk as the rope round his waist tightened, then pitched forward again as it broke. Instinctively he threw out his arms and clutched at the mast, hugging his body against the wood, hearing it snap just above his head, but holding on with all his strength.

He was engulfed in raging water, the prahu had turned upside down. Rivers of pain ran up and down his arms, and filled his lungs as well, as water pressed against his face. Then he was in the air again, briefly, before being rolled over again. This happened several times; he lost track of how often.

For hours, his body was belaboured by wind and rain as he continued to cling to his stump of a mast. He never knew for how long the storm continued, only gradually became aware that there was less noise, that the turmoil had subsided.

Slowly, fearfully, he released the mast and sat up. The waves were still high, but they were not breaking, and though the wind was fresh, it was also warm. The thunder and lightning had departed, and there was even a trace of starlight visible high above him.

And the prahu still floated, waterlogged and mastless. He had survived.

He crawled aft. 'Joan,' he said. 'Joan, where are you?'

But like the jerrycans of water, the carefully-stowed pack of food, the rifle and the revolver and the bayonet and the cartridges, Joan Lees had disappeared.

CHAPTER 12
The Losers

Margaret felt her chest constrict in utter terror as she heard the shout.

'Cairns! Cairns to the gate.'

All of the women lived in an atmosphere of terror, but she had most to be afraid of.

Although it was more than two months ago she could remember Christmas Day as if it were yesterday.

She could remember hanging from the rafters of her own verandah while the cane slashed into her flesh, blow after blow, and while Kitachi Tano swam slowly up and down in her pool, watching.

She could remember Marion screaming, and the captain, Kano, slapping her face to make her be quiet, so violently the girl had been knocked almost senseless.

When the caning had stopped, the pain seemed to intensify. Kitachi had come to stand in front of her, and finger her, and say, 'I will send for you again, when I have captured your husband. I wish you to watch me cut off his head.'

Amazingly, after that she had been allowed to find herself and Marion some clothes, and they had even been fed before being marched down the hill to join the other women. Nothing had been done about her bleeding back and buttocks, but she understood that it was no part of Kitachi's plan to let her die, at least not until Larry had been captured and executed.

She looked back at her house, blinking back the tears, at Mansur standing to attention on the verandah, afraid even to say goodbye in case he offended his new masters. Kitachi had driven off, so the soldiers were in sole command. They had already raped all the girls, including poor Maline. But was Maline really a victim, or had she been an accomplice? Was Mansur secretly smiling as he watched his erstwhile mistress, beaten and bloody, stumbling down the drive with her weeping daughter, driven by the laughing Japanese.

Could she ever come back?

She knew she was living through history. And that history was terrible to live through. She had never realised that before. She was well-read; she knew her Homer, her Defoe, her Marlowe. It had all seemed vaguely romantic – the sack of Troy, with the women being shared out amongst the victorious Greeks; the sack of Magdeburg, with the Imperialists herding the women into the churches to be raped; the deliberate savagery of Tamburlaine . . . it had never occurred to her to wonder how all those myriad women, victims of men at war, had felt.

Now she knew. The only thing, apart from Marion, that kept her upright and walking was a feeling of kinship with those women and their suffering. The women of Troy probably had no more thought of war and violent death than the women of Singapore had. Yet they had died, and horribly. Margaret was going to live. And so was Marion, no matter what had happened to them. Hatred would keep them alive, and a consuming desire for revenge.

Gasping and stumbling in the hot afternoon sun, they had been reunited with the other women. Janet Ogilvy had burst into tears; she had not expected to see Margaret again.

They had been marched on to the ferry and sent to the mainland, to a camp. On the way they had passed some of the male civilians, on their way to a separate camp. Margaret thought she saw Peter Firth; she couldn't be sure. She was only relieved that she and Marion were two of the most securely-dressed of the women, in slacks and shirts, and laced tennis shoes; for all her agony and misery she had thought carefully about what they would wear, and what they would take with them. That precious bundle was clutched in her arms; aspirin, toothpaste, lipstick, even a razor. Did she really mean to shave her legs?

But most important of all, she and Marion each had two changes of clothing. No other woman was so fortunate.

Life in the camp, which would have been totally unacceptable a fortnight before, was almost pleasant compared with their experiences in Hong Kong.

They were made to bow whenever they were addressed by a Japanese, or sought to address one. Some of the women found this difficult to do properly, and were caned. But even the sight of naked female flesh exposed to the abuse and laughter of the soldiers had become quite commonplace within a week.

They learned to eat food they would not have offered to their dogs, and to drink water thick with dirt and slime.

Thus they had learned to live with almost continuous dysentery, but suffering this debilitating and humiliating illness in front of strange women, and little brown men, soon ceased to be of much importance.

They had learned to sleep forty in a room not much bigger than a box-room, on the floor, where every conceivable type of insect crawled over them, bit them, infested them. And they learned to wash themselves, a little piece of their bodies every day, without soap and without ever actually undressing. The stench was vile.

They had learned to survive. Survival was possible; providing they bowed correctly and did not have hysterics, they were not beaten. Nor were their quarters invaded by lusting Japanese. How could any Japanese, a member of the cleanest nation on earth, wish to assault any of these filthy, ragged, stinking scarecrows?

They had learned to close their minds, not to think of anything outside the camp, of anything that had been or might one day be; that would be to go mad. Life was a matter of existing from one minute to the next, of praying for night during the heat of the day, or praying for day during the stench of the night.

But they also learned to live with fear, because they

knew that, however disinterested their guards might be, their lives were at the mercy of the commandant. They had no right of appeal, no claim even to mercy. They were the vanquished.

Thus rivers of sheer panic ran down Margaret's spine as she heard her name being called in that curiously staccato fashion.

She was sitting next to Janet, but Janet instinctively moved a few inches further away. They were closer friends than ever, now. The two women and Marion slept in a huddle together, seeking mutual sustenance, mutual protection. But as they could not protect each other against the Japanese, it was better to dissociate oneself from the person about to be punished. Margaret did not blame Janet for this; she would have done the same.

And no one doubted that she was about to be punished, though for what no one knew.

Wearily she shambled to the gate, and bowed to the sergeant. The sergeant was actually a kindly little man, who wore steel-rimmed spectacles and who, if he had to cane the women, did so with an air of resignation, as though to say: this is all your own fault, not mine.

'Report to the commandant,' he said.

Margaret swallowed. She was not even to be caned. She could not imagine what she had done, but it must be something pretty terrible. To be sent for by the commandant himself sounded like execution.

Oddly, it didn't really matter, except for the thought of abandoning Marion.

She bowed before the commandant's desk, then stood straight again. She had only ever seen the colonel from a distance. Now he looked her up and down, briefly.

'You are to leave Hong Kong,' he said. 'You are to go to Singapore.'

She goggled at him.

'I do not know the reason for this,' the colonel said. 'It is an order. There is a ship leaving for Singapore tonight. You will be on it.'

Oh, my God, Margaret thought, remembering Kitachi's

threat; they've captured Larry. And I am to witness his execution.

The colonel was staring at her. 'Do you not wish to go to Singapore, Mrs Cairns? I understood it was your home.'

Margaret licked her lips. 'Yes, sir,' she said. If she was going, she was going. And besides, would she not want to be at Larry's side when he died?

'Am I allowed to take my daughter, honourable colonel?'

'Of course.' The colonel tapped the paper on his desk. 'It says that she is to go too.'

Throughout the six weeks following the surrender of Singapore the Japanese gained victory after victory. Four days after the surrender – the greatest defeat ever suffered by the British – Japanese bombers devastated Port Darwin in Northern Australia; that same day they landed on the island of Bali and defeated an Allied naval squadron in a fierce battle, while Japanese submarines began to play havoc with Allied shipping in the Java Sea.

On 21 February the British withdrew across the Sittang River in Burma in the face of Japanese advances; two nights later a Japanese submarine shelled the California coast.

Between 27 February and 1 March, in the Battle of the Java Sea, the remnants of the Allied Far Eastern Fleet were destroyed; four days later the Dutch evacuated Batavia, which was immediately occupied by the Japanese.

On 8 March the Japanese occupied Rangoon and landed in New Guinea; the following day the Allied forces in Java, sixty thousand men, surrendered.

On 23 March the Japanese landed on the Andaman Islands, and on 5 April Japanese carrier-launched planes attacked Colombo in Ceylon. The Rising Sun now shone over all the Indian Ocean.

General Yamashita glared at the Chinese and Malays gathered in his office. He always glared at people. He looked as if he hated all the world.

'As of today,' he said. 'There is no more Singapore. It is now Shonan. Remember this. Shonan. It means, Light of the South. Anyone using the word Singapore from now on will be punished.'

He glared at them. 'One of the waiters in the Raffles Hotel has been discovered attempting to make contact with the civilian prisoners in Changi Gaol. This is strictly forbidden. This man . . .' he looked down at the paper on his desk, '. . . Peter Fung, will be executed by decapitation. The sentence will be carried out this afternoon.'

His audience remained silent, utterly stunned.

'With respect, honourable general . . .' Chung Kai was the first to recover. 'You cannot execute a man simply for breaking a rule.'

Yamashita turned the full force of the glare on Kai. 'Are you questioning my decision, Mr Chung?'

'Well . . .' Kai licked his lips. 'Yes, Your Excellency. We were given to understand that the Japanese forces would come here to liberate us from the British.'

'We have done this,' Kitachi said.

'And now you are going to start executing us?'

'Did the British never execute a Chinese or a Malay?' Kitachi demanded.

'For murder.'

'And for treason. Communicating with an enemy in time of war is treason.'

'But we are not at war. *We*,' Kai emphasised, 'are not at war. If Peter has made a mistake, then I will tell him of it. He will not do so again.'

Yamashita glared at him. 'He will certainly not do so again, Mr Chung, because he will be decapitated at four o'clock this afternoon.'

'I most strongly protest, honourable general.'

'You may do so,' Yamashita agreed. 'Next, it has been decided that Shonan will provide its quota of comfort girls to accompany our armies in Burma and in the invasion of India.'

'Comfort girls, honourable general?' asked Chung Cheong.

'Girls who will bring comfort to the soldiers,' Kitachi explained.

'You mean prostitutes?'

'I mean comfort girls. The girls will be young and healthy. They will be medically examined before being sent to Burma. They will be paid well. I have a list here of probable selections. We will go through it together.'

Chung Kai and his brother exchanged glances.

'Again I must protest, honourable general,' Kai said. 'You intend to prostitute our young women, and send them into the jungle?'

'You may protest, Mr Chung,' Yamashita said again. 'But I would advise you not to make a habit of it. Dismissed.'

Kitachi followed them outside. 'You will make the general angry, one of these days, Chung Kai,' he said. 'And then not even my friendship will be able to help you.'

'Your friendship?' Chung Kai said bitterly. 'You have lied to us, Colonel Kitachi. You promised us that you would come here and liberate us from the British. What you have done is impose a military dictatorship upon us and our people.'

Kitachi's face stiffened. 'You have insulted a Japanese officer. If I choose not to take offence, it is because I respect the memory of your father. But I will not be so tolerant in the future. As for your protests, whether you like it or not, Chung Kai, we are at war. When the war is over, when we have secured what we require, then it will be possible to talk about independence for Malaya. Until then you are bound by the rules of bushido as much as any front-line soldier. Remember this.'

Chung Kai walked up from the gateway to his house; the Japanese had requisitioned his Rolls Royce, and in any event there was no petrol.

Nor were there any gates, and the tennis court was a vast hole in the ground where a bomb had fallen.

The gardens too had fallen into ruin, and the swimming

pool was green with algae as he had been unable to procure any chlorine since the war had started.

The house had been damaged both by bombs and by bullets, and part of the roof was missing. Kitachi had promised him that it would be repaired as soon as possible, but that had not yet happened. In any case, when Kitachi made that promise they had all been the best of friends.

Now he did not suppose it would ever happen.

But the house was habitable, and he was alive, and as favoured as any Chinese or Malay, as were his wife and children.

Chung Su was waiting for him on the verandah, as she always waited for him to come home. She was still the chic and perfectly-groomed woman he had fallen in love with, for all that nowadays she had to hand pump all the water for the household, and also did all the cooking. She had a drink ready for him – the Japanese were using so much labour in rebuilding the harbour and fortifications that the Chungs were down to one servant – and as she gave it to him she marked the lines of exhaustion and anger on his face.

'Tell me,' she said, and sat beside him on the cane settee.

'They are executing Peter Fung this afternoon.'

'For what?'

'For attempting to communicate with one of the prisoners in Changi. It is barbarous.'

'They are a barbarous people.'

'And they are going to round up as many young girls as they can find and send them off to the army in Burma, to comfort the troops. Can you believe it?'

'Yes,' Chung Su said. 'What are you going to do?'

Kai drank deeply, and sighed.

'What can I do?'

Su did not reply for several moments. Then she said, 'Do you believe the Japanese will win this war?'

'They have already won it.'

'You are wrong. They have only just begun it. And they will lose it.'

298

Kai gave her a startled glance, then looked to left and right to make sure there was no one within earshot. Such a statement came under the heading of treason. . . .

'How can you say such a thing?'

'Because I have been to America. I lived there for three years; I know the people. The Japanese may believe that they have dealt America a mortal blow at Pearl Harbor, but I tell you, it is nothing more than a pin-prick to the Americans. They will build a fleet, enlist such an army, as the world has never seen. And they will smash Japan into nothing.'

'You are talking nonsense.'

'Then let me ask you two questions, Kai. Do you know how many machine tools were in use in Japan, before the war started?'

'How should I know that?'

'There were sixty-seven thousand. Now, do you know how many machine tools were in use in the United States, before the war started?'

He gazed at her. 'Twice that number?'

'There were nine hundred and forty thousand, Kai.'

'How do you know these things?'

'The information is available. If each side has been able to double that capacity since the war, the American superiority is increased from fourteen times to twenty eight. And the Americans will have far more than doubled their potential. All of those tools, Kai, are going to be turned to war production.'

Kai moved restlessly. 'Then you may be right. But will there be time? Kitachi tells me that as soon as the Dutch East Indies are cleaned up, the Japanese intend to take over New Guinea, and even perhaps parts of Australia. They will have created an impregnable bastion, against which the Allies will batter themselves in vain.'

'They cannot do it, Kai. How can Japan wage war in China, in India, in Australia, in the Pacific Islands, and against the United States, all at the same time? It is not possible. They do not have the resources; they do not have the men. They are going to lose this war as surely as the sun is going to rise tomorrow morning. And they already know this.'

Kai frowned at her, disbelievingly.

'Oh, they do. Their hope is to force a stalemate peace, behind that bastion you spoke of. Only, the Americans will never make peace. Neither will the British. They will reclaim what they have lost, no matter how long it takes, no matter what it costs.'

'But they will never come back to Singapore. I mean, Shonan.'

'They will come back to Singapore, Kai. Your father was wrong to trust the Japanese, to believe in them. If you do so now you will be doubly wrong. The British locked you up, because they did not trust you. When they return, they will trust you even less. Unless before then you have proved to them that you are a man to trust.'

'You are saying there will never be an independent Malaya.'

'I am saying it will not come about because of this war. I believe it will only be achieved by working with the British to win the war, and then seeking recognition.'

Kai got up, walked to the verandah rail, and looked out at the garden. He was only thirty seven; Su was only thirty five. They still had a long time to live. He would like to live his life in this house.

He turned to face her. 'How can I work with the British? They are no longer here.'

'Anyone who opposes the Japanese, and can prove that he has done so, will be considered as working for the British when the war is over.'

'To oppose the Japanese will be terribly dangerous, for you as well as for me. And for the boys.'

Chung Su's face was composed. 'Only if you are found out,' she said quietly. 'Come and sit down, and let me tell you what you must do.'

All Singapore was astounded when the kempei-tai carried out a series of raids, rounding up young women. The Malays, being Muslims, practised even stricter moral codes than the Chinese. Now they watched helplessly as their daughters were manhandled into trucks and driven off to police headquarters.

It was exhausting work, and by the time Kitachi got to the Bamboo Curtain that evening he was worn out. He and his men had been apprehensive all day, in case the anger and distress of the girls' families should boil over into organised violence.

Lan Kuei was waiting for him, as she had waited for him every evening since the occupation of the city. She was no longer available for ordinary commerce; she was reserved for Colonel Kitachi, and any of his friends he might care to send to her.

These included General Yamashita.

At Kitachi's insistence she had become more than a prostitute; she was now a geisha. She served food and drink to her 'guests', and included singing and music in her repertoire; these were not difficult for her as she had learned to do both as a girl.

In return, she was handsomely paid. She had been given a car and unlimited petrol, and could drive wherever she chose in Singapore, smiling at the people who stared at her so enviously. She had done all she had set out to do, before the war; she had become wealthy enough to retire if she chose; she had driven her parents to early graves and her brothers and sister to distraction. She was now entering upon a new and higher phase of her life, in which all things seemed possible.

And it was all the doing of Kitachi Tano. It amazed her to recall that once, a dozen years ago, she had thoroughly disliked this man; now it distressed her to see him depressed.

'Why did you not just apply to me, my Tano?' she asked, stroking his brow as his head nestled on her naked breast. 'My girls would have been happy to serve you.'

'Your girls are needed here,' he said, and lay back, his eyes closed. 'Those others . . . they became hysterical. But it is done. My people will beat some sense into them.'

'Of course,' Lan Kuei said.

301

'It is possible to beat sense into anyone. Even your brother.'

'My brother?'

'He began by obstructing us, refusing co-operation. He protested, all the time, that we were enslaving his people. His people! Ha! I had much in mind for Chung Kai, Lan. Much. And he was jeopardising it all.'

'He is a weakling,' Lan Kuei said. 'And that wife of his, ugh!'

'She has insulted you?' Kitachi opened his eyes.

'She has never addressed a word to me,' Lan Kuei said. 'It is the way she looks at me, whenever we see each other on the street.' She smiled, and tickled his nose. 'There is nothing for you to be angry about. Once she drove in a car and I walked. Now I drive in the car and she walks. I am content with this arrangement. But you must not let Kai upset you, Tano. He is a little man.'

Kitachi studied her face. 'Do you hate him?'

Lan Kuei frowned. 'Why should I do that?'

'Because he did not take your side over Cairns.'

'He had no choice. You would have had no choice, Tano.'

'Perhaps you are right. Anyway, as I was saying, Chung Kai has suddenly come to his senses. So have his brothers. They are now giving us whole-hearted co-operation. It is a great relief to me. I think I will have Kai appointed mayor of Shonan.'

They made love, but Lan was preoccupied. It did not sound like Kai to perform such a *volte-face*. Even less did it sound like the husband of Chung Su. But it was Kitachi's business, not hers.

When it was over Kitachi lit a cigarette.

'Tell me about Cairns.'

Lan Kuei's face twisted. Kitachi raised himself on his elbow to look at her.

'Tell me.'

'I was young. He was handsome. He was a friend of my brother's. I fell in love. He rejected me to marry a white woman. It is a simple tale.'

'Do you hate him, now?'

Lan Kuei considered. 'Why should I hate him?'

'Suppose I told you he was dead?'

'You know this?'

'It is certain. We have discovered that he fled Singapore two days before it fell, with a woman, Joan Lees.'

Lan Kuei made a peculiar little hissing sound.

'When our men got to Sumatra,' Kitachi went on, 'we discovered that he and this woman reached there, sailing a small prahu, and that they coasted up to the north and then set sail for the Nicobar Islands.'

'Then you have captured them?'

'No. They never reached there. The day after they left Sumatra, there was a fierce storm. The weather was far too severe for a small prahu. It seems certain that they were drowned. In fact, the body of a naked white woman was washed up on Great Nicobar three days later. She could not be identified, of course, even had they had any idea who she might be; the body was badly torn up by sharks and decomposition. But in my opinion it was certainly this Lees woman. Did you know her? She was the daughter of the Managing Director of Hammond and Teng.'

'We did not move in the same circles,' Lan Kuei reminded him, drily.

'Well, her parents are dead too. The ship on which they were trying to escape was sunk by one of our submarines. There were no survivors. It seems certain that Cairns has also drowned.'

Lan Kuei said nothing.

'It is a great pity,' Kitachi said. 'I have never told you, but Cairns betrayed me.'

Lan Kuei turned her head.

'Oh, yes,' Kitachi said. 'No less than he betrayed you. He gave me to understand that he was my friend, that he believed in the aims of Japan, that he was willing to work with me. Because of this, I gave him considerable help. When I asked for some back, he refused it. What is more, he had me expelled from Singapore.'

Lan Kuei gazed up at her crimson and gold ceiling. She would never have believed Larry Cairns had that much determination.

'That is why I am sorry he is dead,' Kitachi said. 'He made me look a fool to my superiors. I would have liked to tear his balls from his body before I cut off his head. Now he is dead. But I have his wife and child.'

Lan Kuei's head turned again.

Kitachi smiled. 'Do you not hate Margaret Cairns?'

Lan Kuei considered.

'Yes,' she said after a few minutes. 'I think I hate Margaret Cairns.'

Kitachi's smile widened. 'She is on her way to Singapore. I have sent for her. She will go to the women's camp on the mainland, she and her daughter. But before she goes there, we will visit her, you and I. Would you like that, my Little Orchid?'

Lan Kuei nodded. 'Yes,' she said. 'I would like that.'

It was only fifteen months since Margaret had last been in Singapore, yet she felt a stranger.

From a distance it looked the same. The steamer negotiated the Dragon's Teeth, and the swell of the sea slowly subsided. She looked at a familiar skyline, the houses and high-rises, the church steeples, and the bulk of Bukit Timah rising beyond. She put her arm round Marion's shoulders. Whatever lay ahead of them, they were coming home.

'Will Daddy be here?' Marion asked.

Margaret hugged her tighter still. The voyage, which had taken three days, had been like a luxury cruise after the internment camp. They had been left on the after well-deck, only occasionally watched by a guard. It had not seemed to occur to anyone that they might seek a way out of their misery by jumping over the rail; or perhaps no one had cared.

But then, it had not occurred to her either, after the first couple of hours. It had simply been too pleasant to sit in the sun, to look at smiling faces rather than harsh ones – the Japanese sailors were happy men – to be fed decent food and have clean water to drink, and to have Marion all to herself.

Marion's resilience never failed to amaze her; she did not think she would have survived so much so well when she had been ten years old. Perhaps she could take some of the credit for Marion's strength; that was a comforting thought. But she did not know for certain how deeply that strength penetrated – and it was not something she dare investigate.

Marion could smile, and even laugh, and make a joke about the gut ache which was hardly ever absent. Presumably she too had shut her mind to the past and the future. But there were things buried in her subconscious which had to surface one day. She had been raped and sexually maltreated; she had watched her mother whipped; she had seen the whole edifice of the society into which she had been born and from which she had never been separated ripped apart and trampled in the mud.

Perhaps these did not matter so much, so long as she retained her family. But soon she would not even do that.

'I don't know if Daddy will be here, darling,' Margaret said. 'We must just wait and see.'

It was as the ship approached the harbour that the feeling of strangeness began. One of the first things Margaret had always looked for was the Hammond and Teng office block; now she gazed at a roofless, windowless ruin.

One of the first things any visitor to Singapore had always been immediately aware of was the numerous flags, the Union Jacks on the buildings, the White Ensigns on whichever warships happened to be in port; now there were nothing but Rising Suns.

Japanese sailors wore white tropical kit, just like the British, and they were every bit as smart; but they were little brown men instead of big red men. Their voices were high and staccato, their movements quick and jerky. All of these things she had become used to in Hong Kong, and in the internment camp, but in Singapore they seemed utterly incongruous.

She had never stepped off a ship at this dockside save immediately to enter a Rolls or the Armstrong Siddeley. Now she and Marion were pushed along the dock by their guard.

There was not a white face to be seen. She wondered if any of the crowd of curious Malays and Chinese remembered her. But they would remember a tall, slender, elegant woman, her auburn hair crisply cut and waved, her pale skin carefully sheltered from the sun by a broad hat, veil, and gloves, her frock freshly laundered and pressed, high-heeled sandals, flawless silk stockings. They would surely not recognise this emaciated and shambling figure in torn and filthy khaki, bare-footed, hair straggling below her shoulders, her complexion a sun-torn reddish-brown, clutching the hand of an equally scruffy child.

No doubt they had seen many white women reduced to such extremity in the past few months. But how she dreaded a shout of recognition, and the laughter that would follow.

There was none. Instead they made their way to the east of the town. She suddenly wondered whether or not her lovely bungalow was still standing, whether she might be allowed to see it. Instead, after a long, exhausting walk in the noonday sun, she saw looming above her the walls of Changi Prison.

She had never been in Changi before.

'Do you know, I have never been here before,' Lan Kuei remarked, as the staff car drew up at the gates of Changi Prison.

'That is a surprising admission, for a whore,' Kitachi said.

Lan Kuei knew better than to take offence. She understood that Tano was nervous, working himself up to be brutal. She had long since discerned that although he felt it necessary to act the samurai whenever possible, since

306

he venerated his ancestors and the laws of bushido, it was, most of the time, an act.

She understood, too, that this was because he had never actually faced an enemy in battle. He had always inhabited a murky world of secrecy and underhand dealings. Of course, he had killed – he had boasted to her of it – but his victims had always been trussed and helpless.

He doubted his own courage.

Even now, he had to screw up that courage to face a woman he had already humiliated and all but destroyed.

Lan Kuei felt sorry for her lover, but she also felt contempt for him, as she felt contempt for all men.

The guards bowed, the gates were opened, and Kitachi escorted Lan Kuei inside. She was wearing Western-style clothes today, partly because Kitachi liked her to in public, and partly because she wanted to humiliate Margaret Cairns on her own account. She had no need to screw up any actual hatred for the woman who had so irrevocably altered the course of her life; she had always hated her.

Thus she wore a silk dress, stockings and high-heeled shoes, her hair loose but flawlessly brushed into a high sheen beneath a picture hat, and a good deal of expensive jewellery. She exuded fragrance and health and confidence, smiled at the Japanese soldiers, who smiled back. They knew who she was; every man of them dreamed of one day gaining admittance to that crimson and gold bedroom.

Lan Kuei enjoyed the thought of men dreaming about her.

Kitachi and an officer exchanged words; Japanese was a language Lan Kuei had never troubled to learn.

They were escorted down a corridor to a line of cells filled with people, both Chinese and Malay, who looked the very picture of dejection.

'They are awaiting execution,' Kitachi told her.

Lan Kuei was astonished. She had no idea this was going on.

'What is their crime?' she asked.

'They have been identified as Communists,' Kitachi said.

'Is that a crime?' Lan Kuei asked, ingenuously.

'It is the most serious of all crimes,' Kitachi said, seriously.

The grille at the end was opened, and Lan Kuei saw a woman and a young girl. Margaret Cairns rose to her feet as they approached, and, recognising Kitachi, backed against the wall of the cell, clutching the girl to her. At the sight of the kempei-tai colonel, the girl started to cry.

Neither spared Lan Kuei more than a glance; she realised they had no idea who she was.

Kitachi stepped inside, gestured Lan Kuei to accompany him. The guard bowed and waited in the corridor.

'What do you think of her now?' Kitachi asked.

For the first time Margaret looked at Lan Kuei. Then she turned back to Kitachi. 'Where is my husband?' she asked.

'At the bottom of the sea, or in a shark's belly,' Kitachi told her.

Margaret's head jerked, and Marion stopped crying, shocked into silence. Then she began again, soundlessly; huge tears just spilled from her eyes and rolled down her cheeks.

'So I will have to make do with you,' Kitachi said. 'And her.' He stepped towards Margaret, drove his fingers into her hair, and pulled her forward. 'When I'm ready, it is your pretty white neck that I will cut from these shoulders.'

Lan Kuei thought of all those people along the corridor, waiting to have their heads cut off. Then, much to her own surprise, she said, 'Do not torment her. Either execute her, or leave her alone.'

Kitachi turned his head in surprise, but he released Margaret. 'Would you not like to cut off her head?'

'No,' Lan Kuei said.

Kitachi smiled. 'This is Lan Kuei, Mrs Cairns. Once

she was known as Chung Lan. She was your husband's mistress, before he threw her over to marry you.'

Margaret gasped.

'So she hates you,' Kitachi went on. 'Is that not natural? Tell me what you would like to do to her, Lan Kuei. Would you like to have her stripped so that you can flog her?'

Lan Kuei stared at Margaret, and Margaret stared back. The little girl was Larry's child, Lan Kuei thought. I hate him. I *must* hate him.

But he is dead, and these filthy, emaciated, ragged relics are only pitiful. She had come to torment this woman, to make her rue the day she was born. Now, suddenly, she only wanted to get out of this prison, where she could so easily have been herself.

'No,' she said. 'She has suffered enough. Leave her to her grief.'

The truck stopped, and Margaret and Marion were told to get out. They scrambled down into the dust, and hastily bowed to the officer at the gate.

He pointed, and they walked through the wooden uprights.

For the past three days they had been living in a kind of never-never land, trying to assimilate what had happened to them, or rather, what had not happened to them.

As if it mattered: Larry was dead.

The sight of Kitachi, even though Margaret knew it must have been he who sent for them, had paralysed her, as had the realisation that the woman with him, so elegant, so sophisticated, was Larry's former mistress. She had understood, too, that the woman held the power of life and death over her and Marion.

As if it mattered; Larry was dead.

But the woman had not wanted to harm her. More, she had either persuaded or shamed Kitachi into not harming them himself at least for the time being. He had simply left.

Then they had waited for him to return, hardly daring

to hope that he might not. But he had not, and they had been fed and exercised like any other prisoner.

Yet their guards still carried out the orders of their superiors. Every afternoon at least one man or woman was decapitated, sometimes several.

Margaret and Marion never actually witnessed any of the executions; they only saw the ground stained with blood where the victims had been forced to kneel. And once one of the guards walked past their cell window carrying a woman's head by the hair, mouth gaping, eyes staring, swinging it as she might once have swung her handbag.

Margaret was almost relieved that she could still feel nauseated by such a sight. All that she had seen and heard and smelt and experienced in Hong Kong was already merged into a general nightmare. Details had been eliminated, feelings dulled.

If Kitachi ever carried out his threat, her head would one day be carried as carelessly as that.

As if it mattered; Larry was dead.

But Kitachi had gone away, and after three days in Changi they had been put in this truck and driven north. They had taken the Bukit Timah Road, and from the open tailgate Margaret had been able to make out both the Hammond house and her own. They still stood, looking relatively undamaged. People were living in them; she could see children, presumably the children of Japanese officers.

The pain of the knowledge that she would never see Larry again never grew less. But she shed no tears, and neither did Marion. It was a matter of survival. They had to live through it and perhaps, one day, avenge.

They were driven across the restored causeway and into Johore, leaving the main road to plunge into the jungle. Eventually, they arrived at their destination.

The camp was very large, because it was actually two camps divided by a wire fence; the perimeter was sealed by a similar fence. On the far side of the fence from her were men.

She was surprised at this, and taken aback when a large number of the men clustered at the fence to call out to her. Their skin was burned red, and they looked terribly emaciated. They were all wearing ragged shorts, and several of them wore bush hats with one side pinned up. She heard shouts of 'Hello, Sheila!' They were Australians!

She glanced anxiously at the guard, but he ignored the Australians, so she thought she better had too.

Marion clutched her hand.

A gate opened in the wire, and she was pushed through it, into a group of staring women. For a moment she didn't recognise any of them; they were much more kempt in appearance than those she had left behind in Hong Kong. She was glad her clothes had stood up to the rigours of life in the camp in China, and proud that after all they had gone through, she and Marion at least looked no worse than these women did.

'Margaret Cairns!' Molly Sharples came running to embrace her, then Mavis Norton and others of her old friends.

Margaret wept to see them again. What a homecoming!

'Where's Joan?' she asked Mavis.

'We don't know. She was at the hospital when the Japs broke in, that's all we know. They killed everybody.'

'No,' Molly said. 'She left the night before. I know, because Bob gave her permission . . .'

'Tell me,' Margaret begged.

'He gave her permission to try to escape. On a small boat . . .'

'With Larry,' Margaret finished for her.

'Oh, Margaret! I'm sorry!'

Margaret forced a smile. 'I'm not upset. I just hope they made it.'

She decided against telling them that Joan must have drowned with Larry. They had enough on their minds.

Almost every day it rained, so heavily that Larry had only to turn his face up to the sky and open his mouth.

The rain kept him alive in other ways as well; the clouds

shut out the sun, which at other times scorched down from a glaringly blue-white sky, so fiercely that he could almost feel his flesh burning.

With the rain, more often than not, came the wind, and then the sea. The waves would break right across the drifting, dismasted prahu, half-filling the hull with water, which kept him cool.

He had long discounted any chance of the waterlogged boat sinking. Not that he would have cared if it did.

There was no means of tracking time, even had he wanted to; more often than not he was only semi-conscious. He was aware of darkness, and he was aware of light; he preferred the darkness.

His brain was filled with a succession of strange images, visions from his past, visions perhaps of his future as the hunger pains wore off and he became light-headed. He conversed with his mother and father, looked around himself carefully at the placing of the cricket field before taking strike, hurled quoits past Chung Kai's smiling face at Brian Anstey's head, kissed Margaret's suspenders and was told to stop it because it was disgusting, kissed Ayesha's mouth, and served tennis balls endlessly to an always-laughing Lan.

And he dreamed of fighting Kitachi Tano. Sometimes he was armed, sometimes not. Kitachi was unarmed, and never in uniform – Larry had never seen Kitachi in uniform. And Kitachi was always menacing, always the victor.

He wanted to face Kitachi once, before he died, and discover if that was the truth.

The prahu was often buffeted by the waves, sudden smacks which made the little craft tremble from stem to stern. Larry no longer noticed them. He didn't notice the slightly heavier bump as the submarine nosed up to him.

But he heard the voices, seeming to come from far away, and speaking English.

He thought he had died, although he found it strange

that anyone, angel or devil, should use words like, 'Holy Jesus Christ! He's alive.'

CHAPTER 13
The Road Back

Throughout April the Japanese advance continued.

On 9 April, the American/Filipino army in Bataan surrendered, leaving only the fortress island of Corregidor holding out in the entire south-east of Asia; on the same day a devastating raid by carrier-borne planes on the naval base of Trincomalee in Ceylon sank an aircraft carrier and several other warships and forced the British to withdraw their ships to Bombay.

On 17 April, the retreating British set fire to the Yenangyaung oilfields in Burma. Twelve days later the Japanese cut the Burma Road at Leshio, sweeping aside the Chinese army which was supposed to be guarding the British left flank.

On 2 May the Japanese entered Mandalay, and on 6 May Corregidor was forced to surrender after a Japanese shell blew up its ammunition reserves.

On 15 May, the remnants of the British army evacuated Burma, and crossed the border into India. The initial stage of the Japanese plan of conquest had been completed.

Only General Tojo and Admiral Yamamoto, the architects of the most amazing series of victories in Japanese history, knew enough to be worried.

In the midst of their continuing triumphs, on 18 April, sixteen United States Air Force heavy bombers – Mitchell B Twenty-Fives – had managed to bomb Tokyo itself. It had been a suicide mission, as everyone recognised. The bombers had been flown from the deck of a carrier, at maximum range, and those not shot down had crash-landed in China. The damage done had been minimal.

But it was a certain indication that, however often they

might be defeated, the Americans were not yet ready to make peace.

And then, in the first week of May, even while the surrender of Corregidor was being trumpeted to the world, was fought the Battle of the Coral Sea.

Unique in that it was the first naval conflict in history in which the opposing fleets never exchanged gunfire, it could only just be claimed as another victory: for the loss of one light carrier, *Shohu*, the Japanese sank a large American carrier, *Lexington*, and thought they might well have sunk another, *Yorktown*. Thus a victory was proclaimed.

But the battle had caused the Japanese invasion fleet bound for Port Moresby in New Guinea, to turn back. It was the first check to the Japanese advance since the war had begun, and the momentum lost there was never to be regained.

Only Tojo and Yamamoto understood this. To the world at large, Japan in mid-May 1942 stood triumphant amidst the wreckage of South East Asia and the western Pacific.

For Larry Cairns, life slowly took on a recognisable shape.

When he had first asked, 'Where am I?' he had not really been interested in the answer. Speaking, from a parched throat and through cracked lips, had been the most painful thing he had ever experienced, at least until his sunburned skin started to hurt.

In any event, the reply, 'On board *Seadrift*,' had meant nothing to him.

'I want to fight the Japanese,' he muttered, and went into a coma.

For the next week he was only dimly aware of being alive. The old familiar sounds, the rustle of the sea, the feel of it slapping his face as it broke over the gunwale, the whining of the wind, the patter of the rain, the rumble of thunder, were all gone. In their place was continual semi-darkness, continual noise, and the most annoying difficulty in breathing.

315

There was also someone who tried to dribble liquid down his throat from time to time. He found that annoying.

'I want to fight the Japanese,' he told them. But they didn't pay any attention.

When next he asked, 'Where am I?' it was because people were lifting him from where he had been lying. His skin was still nothing but half-healed burn scars, and he screamed with pain.

Then he was in the open air, under a blue sky, the sounds of humanity all around him.

'You're in Bombay,' someone said.

'I have friends . . .' he began, then stopped. Speaking was still painful, and for the life of him he couldn't remember if the Ansteys were still there or not.

Anyway, he didn't want to see the Ansteys. That would mean telling them about Margaret.

'I want to fight the Japanese,' he said.

There was a good deal more pain as his dressings were removed at the hospital. But then there were soothing creams and smiling white-clad nurses, English girls, all volunteered for duty to help the war effort.

They couldn't understand when he gazed at them and wept.

'He's in a most terribly depressed condition,' Sister told the doctor.

The doctor, who wore a little moustache and looked amazingly like photographs Larry had seen of Adolf Hitler, visited him twice a day, checked his pulse, raised his eyelids to peer into his eyes, made notes.

This was irritating, so every day Larry said, 'Look here, old man, I am perfectly fit. All I want to do is fight the Japanese.'

But like everyone else the doctor ignored him, until one day he raised his head with a start and stared at him. 'Good God,' he remarked. 'Good God!'

The fellow appeared to be as mad as a March hare.

'Do you know, those are the first coherent words you've spoken?' the doctor asked.

'Oh, for God's sake, I've been telling you for days.'

'Weeks,' the doctor said. 'And you haven't said anything intelligible, beyond "where am I", and that was only just decipherable. Just how long were you adrift in that prahu?'

'How the hell should I know?' Larry asked. 'What's the date?'

'Today is Sunday, 5 April.'

'Good God!' He had lost five weeks from his life. 'We left Sumatra on 28 February. When was I picked up?'

'March 13. You drifted for two weeks, without food or water? What kept you alive?'

'I had water,' Larry told him. 'It rained every day. As for what kept me alive, I suppose you could say . . . hatred.'

'You say you left Sumatra at the end of February. May I ask what you were doing there?'

'Escaping from Singapore.'

'By Jove! And you made it! Do you know, we have no idea what your name is?'

'Cairns,' Larry said. 'Lawrence Desmond Cairns.'

The doctor frowned at him. 'Lawrence Cairns? There's something familiar . . . my God, you're Brian Anstey's son-in-law!'

'Yes,' Larry answered.

'But . . .' the doctor obviously didn't know how to frame the next question.

'Margaret is either dead or in a Japanese prison camp,' Larry told him. 'With my daughter. They were in Hong Kong. I happened to be in Singapore when it all happened. Now, doc, all I want is to be given a uniform and a gun and given a chance to shoot a few Japs. I don't care what unit I'm with.'

'Hm,' the doctor said. 'Hm. Well, we'll see what we can do. But first, old man, you have to get well again. That's going to take some time. But there are damned few men who could have experienced what you did, and lived.'

He went away, but Larry heard him say to Sister in what he supposed was a whisper, 'Larry Cairns, by God. There's a turn-up for the books. I think we may have psychological problems with this one, Sister.'

Chung Kai was more nervous than ever before in his life, as he waited in the dark in the Johore jungle. The Japanese still imposed a curfew and, since he had been whole-heartedly assisting General Yamashita and Colonel Kitachi to impose their will upon Singapore, and had thus become one of the most privileged members of the community – his warehouses were constantly filled with rubber and tin awaiting shipment to Japan – with both a car, a second-hand Ford with unlimited petrol, and a pass to go where he chose, he knew he would have a rough time if he were found lurking here in this remote place. He had told the causeway guards he was going to Johore in order to complete some business the next day.

What made him even more nervous was that it was all Su's idea. She had made the initial contacts – how, he did not know and was afraid to ask – and arranged the meeting. She would have come herself, if he had let her. But she had been content to let him take command. She remembered the dashing young man with the rifle and bandolier who had rescued her from the Japanese in 1931. She would never know how afraid he had been then. So he could not let her know how afraid he was now, of the very idea of what she was driving him to do.

He was not a man of action. He was a thinker, a planner, not a plotter. He did not think he had done a dishonest thing in his life, save pretend to Su that he had the courage he lacked. Now he was paying the penalty of that dishonesty.

A twig snapped and he jumped, desperately tried to get his breathing under control; if it was important to maintain a facade of calm courage to Su, how much more important would it be to these men.

318

Three of them came moving through the trees, no doubt, they thought, with expert silence. Perhaps they hadn't heard the snapping of their own twig.

'The night is dark,' one of them said.

Feeling a considerable fool, Kai relied, 'But it is not cold.'

He sometimes thought Su read too many detective and spy stories.

'I am Diem Chi,' the man said.

That was what bothered him most, Kai thought; his fellow conspirators weren't even Chinese, but from Vietnam, the most virulent anti-Chinese nation in the world.

They were also, as Su had warned him, Communists. Su was a most pragmatic woman. He felt like Dr Faustus, dealing with the devil.

'I am Chung Kai,' he said.

'We know this,' Diem said.

Kai watched the two other men move to either side of him; he didn't like the look of them at all. And both were armed, with revolvers as well as the Malay kris.

Diem saw his expression in the gloom. 'We are careful men,' he said. 'We need to be. You work with the Japanese.'

'I have no choice, if I am to be of any use to you.'

'This we understand,' Diem said. 'But *you* must understand, if you betray our cause we will kill you.'

'Your cause is my cause, as long as it is against the Japanese,' Kai said.

'Why is this?' Diem asked. 'They have executed my people. They have not executed yours.'

'Your people are my people, if they come from Singapore,' Kai told him.

Diem said nothing for several seconds. Then he said, 'We require dynamite.'

'For what purpose?'

'With dynamite it is possible to cause explosions.' Diem might have been speaking to a small child.

'I cannot supply dynamite unless I know the precise purpose for which it is to be used.'

319

Kai wasn't sure that he could supply dynamite in any event; He held a considerable stock, hidden beneath the floor of his warehouse the moment war had been declared to conceal it from the British, but with no fixed plan in mind.

He and Chung Cheong had buried it in the warehouse late one night in December. None of his staff had commented on its disappearance; they were all too loyal to the House of Chung. But even so, digging it up again would involve a considerable risk.

'You will have to trust us,' Diem told him. 'Suppose you are betrayed and questioned by the kempei-tai? You would not be able to withstand their questioning. It is better for you not to know.'

'But if you are taken, you will be able to betray me,' Kai pointed out.

'It is necessary to trust each other,' Diem said. 'I will not be taken.'

Of course, Kai thought, he was a Vietnamese bandit who had spent his entire life blowing up French troops or murdering them in the dark, and hadn't been caught.

But what he was saying made a certain amount of sense. It was best that only the perpetrators of the deed know about it.

'I will get you the dynamite,' he said.

'Eight sticks.'

'Eight? What are you going to blow up, the causeway? And how shall I get them to you?'

'You will bring them here,' Diem said.

'You expect me to drive across the causeway with eight sticks of dynamite in my car?'

'As you did tonight, you will go to Johore on business. You make the journey every week, the Japanese know this. Even if you are stopped, your car will not be searched. Eight sticks,' Diem repeated. 'Bring them here, in one week's time.'

As soon as Singapore could be considered absorbed into the Japanese empire, Kitachi Tano determined to implement a plan which had been slowly taking shape in his mind for some time.

In a strange way, the fall of Singapore had brought his life to a full stop. Everything had fallen flat.

He had been working for the capture of this British bastion for fifteen years. His entire life had been devoted to that single objective and when, from time to time, he had despaired of ever bringing it about, he had despaired to the point of contemplating seppuku. He was not a man who could accept failure.

Then for the last half-dozen years, the capture of the city – which he knew had to be preceded by the fall of Hong Kong – had taken on a personal angle. For with it would fall the man who had betrayed him, Larry Cairns.

Cairns had not been in Hong Kong, and the woman and the girl had suddenly lost their appeal. The woman had been filthy and afraid, and anyway she had already been used by others. The girl had merely been afraid. He felt no pity for them; they had belonged to the master race for too long. Their sudden fall from power, their dejection and humiliation, made them seem so pitiful, hardly worthy opponents.

Yet he had still been angry enough to want to slice his sword through their white necks, after suitably tormenting them. That too had fallen flat, with Lan Kuei.

He had been certain that Lan Kuei, of all people, would hate Margaret Cairns even more than he did. And she had felt pity! A weak emotion. Worse, she had made him feel shame, an emotion entirely at odds with the code of bushido.

He thought, not for the first time, that he would never understand the Chinese mentality, if he lived to be a hundred.

He did not really want to visit the crimson and gold bedroom any more, though he still did so; there was a matter of prestige involved.

And now he knew that Larry Cairns was dead, his life, like a tumbling stream become a placid river, was simply boring. He had been given Singapore to police, his reward

321

for his many years of service there. This was a compliment, he knew; a sign of General Tojo's approval – and Tojo was now openly the most powerful man in Japan. But it meant that he was stuck here, while the Japanese army and navy continued to roll forward in every direction. More than ever was he cut off from the one thing he most feared and desired: the chance to discover whether he was truly a fighting man.

There was not even any real police work to be done any more. He had quickly and ruthlessly eliminated the Communist and subversive elements in the city. True, there were one or two of the scum still at large, but they would soon be taken and beheaded.

He had even got those foolish Chung brothers to understand who were the masters now. They had knuckled under, and were the most docile of servants. Well, that aspect of Chinese mentality he could understand. They were not called the Jews of Asia for nothing. The Chungs were making money hand over fist, accumulating and shipping rubber and tin from Singapore to Tokyo. Their prices were exorbitant, but Yamashita paid them without demur.

Yamashita was not interested in money. Neither was Kitachi. Only power mattered in this world. And he and Yamashita shared that power.

But power, without anything on which to exercise it, was like sweeping the empty air with a long sword; it wasted energy to no purpose. Therefore, if he was to be frustrated for the foreseeable future, he was determined that he would at least also be happy. So he had written to Aiwa.

'You will love Singapore. It has not the charm of Osaka, but it has a very real beauty of its own, and a climate which is unbeatable. I can hardly wait for you to join me.'

She had demurred briefly, reluctant to leave the house she was keeping for his return. But he had persuaded her she would like the house he had for her in Singapore even more. It had belonged to Larry Cairns.

And now the moment had arrived. He felt more excited

than he had since the day he had landed in Hong Kong. He put on his best uniform, and was about to leave for the dock when Kano arrived, looking hot and bothered.

Kano bowed, somewhat perfunctorily. 'There has been an explosion, honourable colonel.'

Kitachi frowned at him. 'What do you mean?'

'An army convoy drove over a booby trap, just north of the causeway. The leading truck was blown to pieces. Twelve men are dead.'

Kitachi's frown deepened. 'When did this happen?'

'This morning, just before dawn, honourable colonel.'

'And I am only just being informed?'

'There was panic.' Kano's tone was contemptuous; like most of the kempei-tai, he had a low regard for the regulars. 'They thought they were being attacked by British who had somehow managed to land in Johore. Can you imagine, honourable colonel? So they conducted a battle for some time, with trees, before they realised there was no one there. I have the car waiting, honourable colonel.'

Kitachi considered, briefly. 'My sister arrives in fifteen minutes,' he said. 'I must meet her. You go out there, Kano, and see what has happened. Bring me all the information you can.'

'Shall I take prisoners?'

'Report to me first. I will decide then.'

He went down the steps, got into his car. It was of course possible that there had just been an accident; army convoys always carried massive amounts of explosives with them. If it was not an accident . . . well, he would have to be brutal about it. But he was not in the mood today, not with Aiwa arriving.

Major Briggs wore horn-rimmed glasses on a very long hooked nose, which made him look rather like an extremely old owl, and a disgruntled owl at that. This was not his first visit to the hospital.

'Well, old man,' he said. 'Dr Frazer tells me you're just about fit again.'

'I've been fit for weeks,' Larry growled.

He sat in a cane rocking-chair on the hospital verandah and looked out at Back Bay, and seethed. It was the end of May, and he had now been in hospital over two months. He understood that it had been a long haul back; he had had second-degree burns – his eyebrows had quite disappeared and were just starting to grow back again, while his hair had bleached almost white – and his skin was still mottled brown and white. He had also been suffering from extreme malnutrition.

But his naturally strong constitution had played its part, and two weeks ago he had been nearly back to his normal weight, while the recurring headaches had ceased and, as he had been encouraged by Frazer and Sister to take all the exercise possible, the press-ups and weight lifting he had indulged in had restored his muscles as well.

But he was still being kept here.

The reason was, he knew, that no one knew what to do with him. Technically he should either be sent home or to the last remaining Hammond and Teng Office, in Calcutta.

But he had refused to go to Calcutta, and he had refused to be sent home. 'I want to be enlisted,' he insisted. 'I want to fight the Japanese.'

He was, after all, Larry Cairns. His arrival in Bombay, especially the circumstances of his arrival, had caused a sensation. The newspapers had insisted on interviewing him and photographing him. His escape from Singapore was front page news. But there had also been a new spate of telegrams from the Ansteys, asking about Margaret. He didn't know how to reply to those.

Fortunately, people had felt the necessity to do something to humour him and his weird ambition, hence Briggs's visit.

'I'm afraid, well, you've no military training,' was Briggs's opening gambit.

'Balls. I've spent four years in the Volunteer Corps. That must be at least equal to five years in the Territorials.'

'You are also somewhat old . . .'

'Old?' Larry shouted. 'I'm thirty-five!'

'That's old, to start,' Briggs pointed out. 'And then you are a married man with a family . . .'

'I don't know that. For God's sake, man, can't you see that's why I have to fight?'

Briggs had understood that, and had gone away. He had come back, asked some more questions, and gone away again. Now he filled his pipe with great care. 'I've been through the lot, I've spoken with Alexander, Wavell, Slim, you name it. I even mentioned the matter to the Viceroy. None of them is keen on enlisting you as a regular private. And you must realise you can't just be commissioned, not without proper training.'

'I do realise that. All I want to be is a private.'

'Yes, well . . . in view of your knowledge of the Far East they'd be very happy to employ you in intelligence.'

'No, thank you.'

'I know. You want to fight. Well, hm . . . there's a bloke just come out who wants to meet you.'

'Oh, yes.'

'There's something hush-hush about his being here; I don't have any details. But it's something to do with the Burmese jungle. I suppose you know a lot about jungles and things?'

'Of course,' Larry lied, without batting an eyelid.

'Well . . . I'm not promising anything, mind. . . . the real reason this chap wants to meet you is that he's very keen on cricket. But he does happen to be in Bombay, and there's a possibility – I won't say more than that – that he might be interested in employing you. I'll bring him along tomorrow, shall I?'

'That would be very decent of you,' Larry said. 'What's his name?'

'Wingate,' Briggs told him. 'Orde Wingate. He's a brigadier.'

'Mr Cairns,' Wingate said. 'I have been hearing quite a lot about you.'

They shook hands. There could be no greater difference

325

in appearance than between the major and the brigadier. Where Briggs wore flawless khaki tunic and breeches, suitably-adorned cap, gleaming crowns on his epaulets, Wingate wore a bush tunic and shorts, no identifying badges at all, and a solar topee, high-domed rather than flattened like the one Larry had first used in Singapore. This one looked like a relic from the Battle of Omdurman in 1897.

He had piercing blue eyes, and a compelling presence.

'Well,' Briggs said brightly. 'I'll leave you to talk.'

Wingate sat down. 'Playing any cricket?'

'I've had a couple of knocks.'

'Saw Bradman's triple hundred at Leeds in 'thirty-four. Missed Hutton's at the Oval. Palestine. Damned boring.'

'So I've heard,' Larry said.

'Palestine as well. Arabs. Don't like Arabs.'

'I don't know any, Brigadier.'

'Had their day. A thousand years ago.' Wingate brooded for several seconds, while Larry waited as patiently as he could.

'Never can tell when the buggers are going to sneak up behind you,' Wingate commented. 'Like the Japs, eh?'

'Yes.'

'Two can play at that game,' Wingate remarked. 'Tell me about your escape from Singapore.'

'I bought a native boat and sailed out.'

'Just like that. Brilliant. Alone?'

'I had a companion,' Larry said. 'She drowned, in the storm that scuppered us.'

Wingate nodded. 'Grim. So now you want to fight. At your age?'

'I'm younger than you,' Larry pointed out.

Wingate grinned, the somewhat tight features relaxed. 'I've been in the army all my life. You've sat behind a desk.'

'Care to try some Indian wrestling?' Larry asked.

'So you're fit. But it's a matter of discipline, training, *esprit de corps* . . . You obviously have guts, and endurance, and determination. And you hate the Japanese. I need men like you. I'm told you know the jungle.'

'I don't, really. I only said that to get this interview. But I'm not afraid of it.'

'No, I shouldn't think you are.' Wingate went into another of his brown studies. 'What's your appraisal of the military situation?'

'I don't know much about it, but it doesn't sound too good.'

'Right. The Japanese are massing themselves to invade India. Oh, Slim is confident he can hold them. But there's the moral factor. Too many of our fellows have that creeping-up-behind feeling whenever they engage the enemy. Too often they're right. Makes no sense. Ever been to Japan?'

'No.'

'Well, there's no jungle up there. Perhaps some of their troops trained in Indo-China, but not many. Yet they're not afraid of going in. Our chaps are. They feel the jungle is hostile. It is. But it's hostile to the enemy as well. If they can tackle it, so can we.'

'Yes,' Larry said.

'Men with guts. Men with determination. Men with the will to kill or be killed.'

'Yes,' Larry said again, heartbeat quickening.

'But how, they ask me,' Wingate said. 'Simple, really.' He pointed at an aircraft circling Bombay before coming in to land. 'Those are the answer. Those are the secret of this war.'

'We don't have enough,' Larry said.

'We have,' Wingate said. 'Only a couple of days ago Harris sent a thousand bombers into Germany on a single raid. Maybe we don't have enough here at the moment, but we have enough for our purpose. Aircraft aren't of use only for bombing, you know. In my opinion that's the least important of their uses. It's the ability to move men and matériel over great distances, quickly and at short notice, that's their true métier. And then supplying the men afterwards.'

327

Suddenly he was totally animated, leaning forward, eyes glowing. 'I've been given permission to carry the fight to the enemy, Cairns. A grand cavalry raid, if you like, only we won't ride round his flanks, we'll drop in on him. I call it Long Range Penetration. And we can stay as long as we like, because we'll be supplied from the air.

'It'll be tough. It'll be the jungle. We may surprise the enemy, but they won't stay surprised long. There'll be no coming back out until I say so. I need men with guts.'

Larry felt a glow spreading through his body.

'You'll have to measure up,' Wingate told him. 'Only the best can take it.'

'Just give me the chance,' Larry said.

Now began the most exhilarating period of Larry's life, as well as the most exhausting.

There were not many volunteers in the training camp. Instead Wingate was given a battalion of Gurkhas and a battalion of British troops, and told to organise his force for Operation Longcloth out of this material. His plan was to create eight columns, four of Gurkhas and four of British, who would operate independently and yet be able to coalesce as and when necessary. He did not intend to stay behind the enemy lines for more than six weeks. 'That's as long as any man will be able to stand it,' he told his officers.

The Gurkhas were naturals for such an operation. They knew jungles and they were masters of the stealthy attack; their endurance was remarkable.

The British were quite the reverse. They were the 13th King's Liverpool Regiment, straight out from England; Wingate had been hoping for battle-hardened veterans. The trouble was that, while Wingate had the ear of Wavell and, it was rumoured, of Prime Minister Churchill, he was regarded as an upstart and, worse, a man who did not believe in orthodox military matters, by the staff. Their attitude was that he should, as they all had to do continually, make the best of what material was to hand instead of looking for perfection.

Wingate knew that for the sort of campaign he was planning, only perfection would do. But he did make the best of what he was given.

His troops were city-bred men from the offices of Liverpool and Glasgow and Manchester, who had been employed solely on garrison duty, soft-bodied and lazy-minded, archetypal non-combat-soldiers. They did not like India; they did not like the food; and they did not like Wingate's training methods. They did not like the weight of the equipment each man, including officers, had to carry at all times, which consisted of a large pack containing personal belongings, two grenades, ammunition for automatics and Bren guns, mess tins, and five days' American 'K' rations, a total weight of some seventy five pounds.

But they did not lack courage. They ran until they dropped, bayoneted sacks until their arms seemed about to fall off, spent hours too long in the sun, ate scanty rations, climbed trees, bridged fast-flowing rivers, walked in the jungle barefoot to get them accustomed to snakes and leeches and spiders. And they began to fall sick.

Soon seventy per cent were on the sick list.

'They aren't really ill,' said the medical CO. 'They're just playing the old army game: when the going gets tough, report sick.'

'Right,' Wingate said. 'We'll put a stop to that.'

He issued orders that any man appearing on sick parade without a serious reason would be punished. Minor ailments were to be treated by platoon commanders, something they would have to do anyway once the campaign began. Officers were also required to carry out daily inspection of the men's stools, to determine which of them actually did have dysentery.

There was considerable grumbling but Wingate's spirit was, at last, getting to them.

The fall-out was enormous; it included the battalion commander and over two hundred of his men. This caused a rearrangement of the original plan, and the eight columns became seven: four Gurkha and three British.

* * *

Larry found the initial going as tough as anyone. Yet he was basically far fitter than the troops straight out from England; he had spent much of his life in the tropics and in the open air, and was therefore less prone to sun-induced ailments; and he had the personal stimulus not only of his desire to avenge Margaret and Marion, but of knowing that he was famous for his escape from Singapore – Wingate often used him as a spur to the laggards.

His Volunteer training proving adequate, together with his stamina and determination, he was commissioned intelligence officer in one of the Gurkha columns, to his great satisfaction.

By then the marauding force, officially the Long Range Penetration Group, had been nick-named the Chindits. This was actually a misnomer; Wingate had misinterpreted the Burmese word for lion, which is *chinthe*. But the Chindwin was the river they were going to have to cross to get into Burma, and Chindit was at least easier to pronounce.

The training, and the organisation of both the penetration and the campaign to follow, took far longer than anyone had imagined; it was not until Valentine's Day 1943, that the expedition began.

By then a great deal had happened in the Pacific. Even while Wingate and Larry were having their first meeting, the American and Japanese fleets had clashed in the Battle of Midway, which resulted in the sinking of four Japanese carriers, and the ending of their hopes, not only of expanding their empire, but even of holding on to their extended perimeter of islands.

In New Guinea, American and Australian counter-attacks brought the advance to a halt, and proved for the first time that 'white' troops could hold their own as well as any in the jungle.

The most stirring events took place in the Solomons, at the very limit of the Japanese perimeter, where American marines landed on the island of Guadalcanal and, after several months of fierce fighting in which both sides rushed reinforcements to the little island and engaged in several bloody sea battles, forced the Japanese to evacuate.

These were all great and heartening Allied successes, but no one supposed they meant that the end of the war against Japan was in sight.

Certainly the Japanese rank and file and their commanders did not feel discouraged. They accepted that they had attempted to expand too fast, but they still held a vast number of fortified island bases in the Pacific, against which the Allies would surely batter themselves in vain. They still held most of New Guinea and all the Philippines, as well as the entire Dutch East Indies and British Malaysia and Burma. Thus protected and supplied, Japan could exist forever, growing stronger. Even the carriers so catastrophically lost at Midway could be replaced, and all the time the Allies were expending men and *matériel* on a prodigal scale. Soon enough they would come to the peace table and accept that Japan had established her Greater East Asia Prosperity Sphere.

If they did not, there were means of making them. General Ishida's veteran troops crouched along the Burmese border, ready for the invasion of India. With them was the Indian National Army of Subhas Chandra Bose, many of them recruited from amongst the Indians who had been forced to lay down their arms in Singapore. Subhas Bose and his Japanese allies had no doubt that once they streamed through Assam towards the Ganges, all India would rise in their support, and the British Empire would, to all intents and purposes, come to an end.

The original idea had been that the Chindits would be part of a diversionary attack which would complement a general British and Indian counter-attack against the Japanese forces in Burma, a pre-emptive strike which would put the Japanese invasion of India back for months, if not for ever. However, plans for the main assault fell through, for a variety of reasons, sheer lack of men and vehicles being one of the most important; equally, hopes

331

of an amphibious strike on the Arakan coast foundered for lack of landing craft, all of which were required for Europe or the Pacific islands.

The question then arose as to what to do with the Chindits. If they went in alone, would they serve any useful purpose?

Major General Irwin, Wingate's immediate superior, felt they were likely to be chopped to bits by the Japanese, and for a while it seemed as if the expedition would be called off. But Wingate fought passionately to be let loose. 'We have trained for six months,' he told the generals. 'I have honed this brigade to a fine edge. My men are keyed up and ready to go. If they are put off now, you may as well disband us, and accept that all that time, effort and money have been wasted, because we are going to fall apart.'

As usual Wavell, who as supreme commander had the last word, was prepared to listen to his brilliant protégé, but even he hesitated, and asked the opinion of the American Lieutenant-General Somervell of the Army Air Force: his planes would be dropping the supplies to the column. 'General, if I were you, I'd just let 'em roll,' the American replied.

Wingate was elated, and issued a long Order of the Day to his men.

'The battle,' he said, 'is not always to the strong, nor the race to the swift. Victory in war cannot be counted on, but what can be counted on is that we shall go forward determined to do what we can to bring this war to an end which we believe best for our friends and comrades-in-arms, without boastfulness or forgetting our duty, resolved to do the right so far as we can see the right.'

It was not exactly Churchillian prose, but the men needed no further encouragement; some of them were in tears.

The columns crossed the Chindwin individually; each had a separate assignment. Larry's Gurkhas, commanded by

332

Major Lowther, were directed to a bridge some seventy miles inside Burma, which formed part of a vital road link. The contingent consisted of three companies, a total of some three hundred men. One of the company commanders was a demolitions expert.

The going was tough from the very beginning, but so severe had their training been that pouring rain, scanty food, mosquitoes and leeches, and long exhausting marches, seemed all in the day's work.

Even snakes, including pythons twelve feet long, hardly caused comment. The Gurkhas were of course used to snakes, and Larry had seen enough of them in Singapore not to be afraid of them.

What was awe-inspiring was the immensity of the jungle across which they were operating. Burma was roughly the size of France, and consisted of endless ranges of hills bisected by deep, narrow river valleys through which the water flowed with the speed of an express train. And every square inch was covered with the thickest forest of trees, rising from matted undergrowth, that could be imagined.

They seldom saw either sun or moon because of the tree screen, and operated by compass, following map co-ordinates as they made first for their 'drop' zone.

'Five will get you ten there's nothing there,' quipped Lieutenant Bruce Allay, A Company.

But when they reached the zone, they found a huge pile of supplies waiting for them, including fresh food and ammunition. As they had not yet seen a single Japanese the ammunition wasn't needed; they buried it to be picked up on their way back. But the food was most welcome.

By now they were encountering Burmese, who stared at these somewhat ragged, khaki-clad invaders in consternation. Larry had been taught Urdu – the universal language of the Indian army and a sort of pidgin for the whole sub-continent – as part of his training to be an intelligence officer, and was able to carry on a limited conversation. The natives were able to inform Lowther that there were a considerable number of Japanese in the area, and this was confirmed by various wireless messages picked up from the other columns, some of whom had been heavily engaged. At least one had been virtually destroyed; the survivors had returned across the Chindwin.

What to do with the Burmese was a considerable problem. Presumably, when next the Japanese came along, they would be informed of the presence of a British column in their midst. But the people couldn't just be executed or imprisoned. Lowther decided to hurry on.

A week later they found themselves crouching among the trees on a steep escarpment above the bridge.

'It's deserted,' muttered Captain Legge, in disbelief.

Lowther continued to watch the road through his binoculars. 'It is, dammit,' he said. 'All right, Legge; take your company down there to cover you, set the explosives, and get back here.'

'Yes, sir.' Legge snapped. 'Allay, follow me.'

Allay signalled his men, and the Gurkhas ran down the slope.

'Captain Moss, unlimber the machine guns and cover the road,' Lowther said. 'Captain Bridgeman, take your company to the far side of the hill and cover our rear.'

'Yes, sir,' the captain said, and hurried off.

Moss gave the orders to his subalterns and they set up the four machine guns and posted their men amidst the trees. As Intelligence Officer Larry had no command, he took his place in the middle of the position with the wireless set and operators.

It was just on ten in the morning, and the jungle was still steaming damp. The sun was rising steadily above the trees to the east, having only cleared the surrounding hills half an hour before; on the hillside the trees were thin enough for it to be clearly visible. Above, the sky was blue, dotted with puffy white clouds. It was an incredibly peaceful scene.

The jungle-covered escarpment on which Larry knelt looked down on the beaten earth road which wound its way through the trees like a snake, clinging to the valley below; the land rose again immediately on the far side. Immediately beneath them, the river, a deep, fast-running tributary of the Irrawaddy some thirty yards wide, intersected the road. There was the bridge; Legge and his men were busily setting their charges. They were making no noise that could be heard up the hill, and indeed the only sounds were the humming of insects and the occasional slither of a lizard.

Then one of the Gurkha sergeants cocked his head.

'What is it?' demanded Lowther.

'Vehicles, sir.'

They all listened, and gradually the distant growl became apparent.

'I thought it was too good to last,' Lowther commented, and turned his glasses on Legge. The wiring was still not completed. 'Very well, Captain Moss. We will have to check those fellows until the bridge is blown. Hold your fire until I give the word.'

'Yes, sir,' Moss said.

Larry discovered that he was quite tense. He was about to go into battle – for the first time.

Slowly the noise grew; it sounded like an entire convoy of trucks approaching.

Surely Legge could hear them! But he was continuing his work with deliberate determination; he did not intend to make a balls-up simply because the enemy was approaching.

If only he'd hurry, Larry thought, they would be able to melt away into the jungle without the Japanese ever discovering them. He found his palms were sweating, and wondered if he was afraid.

At last! Legge stood up, and waved his men back. But as he did so the first vehicle came round the corner. It was a tank.

There was a man standing in the cupola, and Larry saw him reach for his radio mike.

Lowther saw him too. 'Open fire!' he snapped.

The machine guns burst into a deadly racket, and the remainder of the Gurkhas also opened fire with their rifles and Brens. The tank continued to advance, and behind it came another. The lead tank's guns moved to and fro once or twice, and now it fired at the demolition party, who were running for the trees, scattering them like rag dolls.

Legge, who was slowly and carefully unwinding his wire, still had not moved.

The second tank elevated its sights and sent a shell crashing into the trees. This fell wide and there were no casualties.

'Keep firing,' Lowther commanded. 'Cairns, get down there and see what's holding Legge up.'

'Yes, sir,' Larry acknowledged, and began pushing his way through the undergrowth.

Above him the rifles cracked and the machine guns rattled, but they weren't doing much damage, and he was concerned that only two Japanese vehicles had emerged. He was quite sure there were more; so what the hell were they doing?

The second shot from the second tank came much closer, and a tree came crashing down trapping several men.

Larry reached the bottom of the slope, some six feet above the road, just as Captain Legge threw himself into the nearside bushes, where his men were crouching. There were distressingly few of them: the road was covered with little khaki heaps, some lying still, others writhing in agony.

The survivors were returning fire at the tanks as best they could. They were all doomed; but they didn't seem to know it. Larry watched Legge unhurriedly attach the wires, and stand up to depress the plunger. Then he saw that the captain's jacket was stained with blood. Immediately he was hit again, spun round, and crashed to the ground.

Instantly one of his men seized the plunger, and thrust it down.

There was a huge roar, and a cloud of smoke and dust. Steel girders rose into the air and crashed down again, splashing into the water.

The men uttered a cheer, but as they did so there was a fresh burst of firing, and several more fell. Allay looked up and saw him.

'What the hell are you doing here?' he bawled. He was bleeding from the left arm.

'The old man . . .' Larry didn't know what to say.

'Tell him to get the hell out of it,' Allay snapped. 'We'll cover the retreat.'

Larry hesitated; a tremendous outburst of firing came from above him. He looked round wildly and saw a line of Japanese infantry coming over the hillside half a mile to his right; warned by the leading tanks, the infantry had disembarked from their trucks and now flanked the invaders.

Major Lowther had leapt to his feet and was waving frantically: 'Pull out,' he shouted. 'Pull out and make contact with Wingate. Pull . . .' he fell forward on his face.

Captain Moss jumped up to take command. 'Fall back,' he commanded. 'Fall . . .' and he too went over like a puppet whose strings have been cut.

Larry licked his lips, looked left and right. Bridgeman, as ordered, had withdrawn his company to the other side of the ridge, and was out of sight, but there was firing coming from there as well. Legge's company was down the hill, firing at the tanks. Larry reckoned his job was to see if Lowther was dead or alive and obtain some orders.

He scrambled up the hill and found the major, gasping blood.

'Not good, sahib,' the Gurkha wireless operator said.

'Cairns,' Lowther gasped. 'Get the men out. Get the . . .'

He gurgled and his head slumped.

Larry drew a long breath. 'Get your equipment back to Captain Bridgeman,' he said.

He looked up the hill, to where Moss's men were falling back of their own accord, driven by a withering fire from the Japanese. He stood up, searching for one of the company lieutenants. But he could not see them. Except for

Allay on the road and Bridgeman's command round the hill, he was the only officer left alive.

And he had never commanded troops in battle in his life!

His instincts were to tell his men to run like hell, and join them. But he could not; he was now their commanding officer.

'We'll make a fighting retreat, Sergeant-Major Bopal,' he said, amazed at the calmness of his voice. 'Detail a squad to carry out the wounded. Keep those machine guns firing. Two to the hillside.'

He was surrounded by noise, the beauty of the morning destroyed forever. The tank cannon boomed, and the trees crackled; the rifle and machine gun fire was continuous. From the hillside there came the shrill cries of the advancing Japanese, accompanied by the blaring of a bugle, of all things. They were moving more cautiously now, having suffered several casualties, and still being uncertain as to the exact location and strength of the opposing force.

Firing was still going on further down the hill. Larry hated the thought of leaving Allay and his gallant men, but he had been given a definite command by his dead major.

Most of his own men had started stealing back into the trees, carrying their wounded, even though Wingate had issued orders that seriously wounded could not be withdrawn. The Japanese were now very close; Larry estimated there had to be at least a thousand of them, and he now had less than a hundred. There was no time to dismantle the machine guns.

'Smash them,' he commanded, and his men obeyed. Then they too disappeared into the jungle.

The next few weeks were very like the week Larry spent in the boat; he did not suppose he could have survived but for that earlier experience. And this time he had his command to save.

He had anticipated that as they withdrew along the brow of the hill they would encounter Captain Bridgeman, and unite to form a solid retreating force. But clearly Bridgeman was equally heavily engaged. Larry directed his men towards the sound of firing, and arrived at the little ravine which split the hill, beyond which Bridgeman had established his position, just in time to see the Gurkhas overrun by several hundred Japanese, yelling as they charged with fixed bayonets.

Larry had never even seen a battle before. He found himself paralysed with horror.

Equally horrifying was his inability to decide what to do. He could not get his men across the ravine in time to help Bridgeman's company. He could not fire on the Japanese without hitting the Gurkhas. And behind him was another battalion of Japanese, screaming for blood – and still blowing their bloody bugle!

He looked at Sergeant-Major Bopal for guidance.

The little man screwed up his already-tight brown face. 'We have orders from the major to withdraw, sir. Captain Bridgeman will do the same, if he can disengage.'

'Withdraw where?' Larry asked in desperation.

'We must cross the road, sir. And the river.'

Larry realised the sergeant-major was right; the only alternative was surrender. He pointed, and his men flowed down the slope. The retreat was orderly and the Gurkhas kept up a steady fire into the advancing Japanese. They reached the edge of the road and he shouted, 'Go!'

They broke into the open and ran for the jungle on the far side. The tanks had time only to fire once each, but even so several men fell. Panting, Larry plunged down the bank into the water, and saw some of Bridgeman's men also falling back. To his great relief, he also saw the captain, waving wildly. 'Pull back,' he shouted. 'Pull back.'

The Gurkhas flung themselves into the river. It roared about them, plucked at them; one man was swept from his feet and went tumbling away, arms and legs waving futilely. Another stepped into a hole deeper than his own height and, weighed down by his equipment, could not get out again. But most got across and scrambled into the jungle followed by the cannon fire of the tanks, the shells bursting against the trees and bringing branches and leaves showering down.

The Japanese infantry were pausing to regroup, and the Gurkhas were able to do the same. And Larry was at last able to make his way to Bridgeman, whose tunic was soaked in blood. His men were standing around anxiously.

'Pryce-Smith and Evans, both dead,' the captain muttered. 'Where's Moss?'

'Dead, sir.'

'And his subalterns?'

'Also dead, I think, sir.'

Bridgeman summoned a ghastly grin. 'If they're not here, they're dead. Look.' He pointed back across the river.

The men stared in horror. The Japanese were not only regrouping. They were propping up wounded Gurkhas against the trees, then running at them with bayonets, uttering shrill cries. One or two of the Gurkhas raised their arms in feeble attempts to ward off certain death: they all died.

Larry felt physically sick.

'You're in command, Cairns,' Bridgeman said. 'Get the hell out of here. Make for the drop zone and replenish, and make contact with Wingate if you can. Haste, now.'

'I can't leave you here, sir.'

'You can. And you damned well will.' Bridgeman held a grenade in his hand. 'No Jap is going to trouble me, Sailor.' This was the nickname given Larry by his fellow officers, because of his escape from Singapore. 'Now go.'

During his time as manager of the Hong Kong branch of Hammond and Teng, Larry had found the making of decisions and the giving of orders easy, and had carried that training into his brief career as a Volunteer officer. But he had never had the burden of knowing that every decision carried the implication of survival or disaster, life or death.

His first task was to disengage from the enemy. This

fortunately, proved simple enough. The Japanese, having disposed of their prisoners, paused to tend their own wounded, to inspect the Gurkha position and to see if anything could be done about the bridge. Larry and his men hurried back through the forest, waded across another stream, and then paused for breath.

It was noon, and the sun was high, but the forest was again quiet, save for the panting of the men.

Larry held a roll call, and discovered that he was in command of one hundred and thirty four men, of whom twenty seven were hurt, eight of them badly. He and the sergeants did what they could, binding their wounds and giving them water, but obviously carrying them much farther was out of the question.

'We'll stay here, sir,' one of the wounded privates said. 'We can cover your retreat.'

Larry chewed his lip.

Sergeant-Major Bopal shrugged and said, 'It is the only way, sir.'

The men were given a rifle each, and twenty rounds of ammunition and a hand grenade. Then Larry saluted them, and led his men past them as a final farewell. Each of the Gurkhas in turn saluted his comrades, and disappeared into the jungle.

It was some two hours later that they heard a brief crackle of rifle fire, followed by the dull thuds of grenades. The Japanese were not very far behind them.

They were short of ammunition, and Larry knew that his first duty was to follow Bridgeman's instructions and return to the dump zone to dig up the supplies they had left there; he knew that there should also have been another drop of food and medical supplies since they had last been there. But a direct return march was out of the question; next day they reconnoitered a large Japanese force directly between them and the dump, and had to withdraw to the north in the hope of circling round the enemy.

When they had not seen any Japanese for two days,

Larry tried to raise one of the other columns by radio, and managed to make contact with Wingate himself. He reported the situation, that he was the only officer left, and that his men were suffering severely from lack of food, but that he hoped to make it to the dump in another few days.

'Forget that,' Wingate ordered. 'The Japanese have found it, and are waiting for you. Head north west, and make for coordinates S3 and K4. There you will find some supplies. I'm afraid it's about forty miles from your present position, through fairly heavy country. But it's your best hope of coming out.'

Larry gulped. 'Yes, sir. And after we've reached the dump?'

'Return across the Chindwin. You have done all you were sent to do.'

They set off immediately but, as Wingate had said, the going was very rough. They came down from the hills and into the thickest jungle any of them had ever seen, where every step had to be hacked, and often they were wading waist deep through swamps. To add to their misery the rain started again and fell without cessation, so that it was quite impossible to get dry or to light any fires. What food they had – and they were now down to biscuits and a few tins – had to be eaten cold.

Even the Gurkhas began to fall sick. Several of the men already had malaria, and Larry had quite run out of quinine. Small wounds sustained on the march attracted insects and festered in the damp. The slightly wounded who had marched all the way from the bridge did not heal, but suffered intensely. Caring for these men was slowing up the entire column, and on the third day, when they were still some twenty miles from the dump, Larry knew he had to make a decision.

'Sergeant-Major Bopal,' he said. 'I wish you to assemble all the fit men, and call for twenty volunteers. When you have them, you will take command of the remainder and push on as fast as you can for the dump. There you will wait for the rest of us. If we are not with you in a week, you have my permission to withdraw across the Chindwin.'

Bopal saluted. 'Permission to volunteer, sir.'

'No, Sergeant-Major. I need you to command the advance party.'

'That is your duty, sir. I will bring in the sick.'

'I have given you an order, Sergeant Major. I expect it to be carried out.'

The Sergeant-Major stood to attention, then went to find his volunteers.

Larry drew his revolver, and thumbed the chambers. He still hadn't actually killed a Japanese, to his knowledge; during the fight on the hill he had only had the time to send off a couple of rounds.

But maybe he'd have the chance now.

CHAPTER 14
The Victors

'This is special meal,' announced Sergeant Kimishira. 'Very special meal. Your ladies eat, eh?'

The women stared in amazement at the huge soup bowls from which the guards were ladling the stew.

The bowls were the same as were always used to dispense the watery gruel which, with a few bamboo shoots, was their staple diet; but the food waiting to be dumped on their tin plates contained meat and rice.

'You not eat too much, eh?' Kimishira advised, smiling at them. 'Then you get sick. Not good to get sick.'

This was a jovial, laughing Kimishira.

'It's some kind of trap,' Molly Sharples muttered.

Molly had replaced Janet Ogilvy as Margaret and Marion's closest friend. What had happened to poor Janet did not bear consideration; presumably she was either dead or struggling to stay alive in a camp on mainland China.

It was not possible to think, either, about what would happen after the war. Everyone's thoughts had to concentrate upon living from day to day, from minute to minute, while daily growing weaker from lack of food and proper exercise, from lack of proper sanitation and proper medication, from mosquito bites and ant bites, from drinking filthy water, from continuous stomach upsets, from ticks and fleas, from being scorched by the sun in the dry season and being unable to get dry when it rained.

Margaret thought she would have gone mad without Marion, even though she still cursed herself whenever she thought that she could have left the girl in England, where she would now be living with her grandparents, healthy and happy, unaware that there was such misery in the world.

Instead, Marion was aware only of misery. Her courage was enormous. She never spoke of her ordeal with Kita-chi, she never complained. Only sometimes she wept, silently, great tears seeming to overflow from her eyes and roll down her cheeks.

It was heartbreaking to watch her thin legs, the skin drawn tight over her rib cage, her hollow cheeks.

It was even more heartbreaking to think that she should be living a normal, carefree childhood, with pretty clothes and good food, progressing through school with friends of her own age, when all she had were unthinkable thoughts and the ragged garments in which she stood. Even if they survived – and the secret of that lay in reminding oneself every day that one had survived yester-day, was surviving today, and therefore might very well survive tomorrow – Marion's mind would surely be scarred forever.

Yet Margaret and Marion were luckier than most; they also had a friend. Friends were necessary, because some of the women occasionally became desperate, and would attempt to steal the very few personal belongings there still were in the camp. Molly and Margaret shared the bond of widowhood, as far as they knew.

They shared another common bond, the bungalow. They would discuss it by the hour, as they sat picking nits from each other's hair, considering changes here and there, designing extensions, choosing new furniture, just as they took turns at telling Marion stories, remembered from the books they had read. Thus they made up a trio, a little island of love and understanding in the midst of the sea of misery and distrust in which they floated.

They scarcely felt able to involve themselves in the lives of the other women. Even at mealtimes, where so many of the women jostled and pushed, the three of them tended to hang back. There was always something left.

But today, the sight of the meat stew drove them for-ward to take their part in the scrum, reaching out their bowls to be filled, while Kimishira beamed at them. Marion was pushed from behind and went stumbling, cannoning into the sergeant himself.

Everyone froze except Marion, who hastily picked herself up, and cowered against Margaret, trembling. Marion was twelve now, and knew what happened to anyone who dared touch a Japanese.

'Oh, God!' Margaret whispered. Since coming to this camp they had kept out of trouble, keeping to themselves, obeying every command like puppets on a string, bowing as low as necessary, clinging only to their essential selves amid the humiliation.

But now . . .

But Kimishira smiled, and went on dishing out stew. 'Girl is clumsy,' he remarked to Margaret.

Margaret could not believe their luck. Marion was sitting beside her, eating her food; she had not been dragged off and flogged, as everyone had expected.

'Something must be happening,' Molly suggested. Then she looked up. 'Oh, Lord! Here he comes.'

Kimishira was walking slowly down the line of seated women. 'Ladies will wash, when food is finished,' he said. 'Ladies should wish to be clean. Ladies will wash.' He paused to smile at Marion.

They discovered the reason for his solicitude and for the good food that afternoon, when the Commandant entered the compound, accompanied by two men and two women, Europeans wearing clean, well-cut clothes such as the women could scarcely remember.

Margaret and Janet and Marion desperately straightened their rags and brushed their hair. One of the Red Cross representatives came up to them.

'May I ask your name?' the woman asked Margaret. She had a slight accent, and was very blonde; Margaret supposed she was either Swiss or Swedish.

'Margaret Cairns.'

The woman looked down the list she carried. 'And this is your daughter, Marion? Yes. And you are . . . ?'

'Molly Sharples,'

The woman checked her list. 'You are the wife of a doctor in Singapore?'

'I was. My husband was killed in the assault on the Queen Alexandra Hospital.'

'No, no, Mrs Sharples. I saw him a week ago,' the woman said. 'He is well.'

Molly burst into tears.

'Oh, God, thank you,' she sobbed. 'I had heard nothing . . . it's been more than a year. I thought he was dead.'

'He was wounded, when Singapore fell,' the woman said briskly. 'He recovered. Now tell me, both of you, are you well treated?'

They looked round; Kimishira was within earshot.

'As well as can be expected,' Margaret said, looking her straight in the eye, trying to convey some of the terror in which they lived. But the woman was writing busily.

'I have seen the food with which you are fed,' the woman said. 'Is this satisfactory?'

Margaret opened her mouth. Her eyes met Molly's. Kimishira had moved closer.

'The food is satisfactory,' Molly said.

'It looked very good,' the woman remarked. 'And you are in good health?'

'Yes,' Margaret said baldly.

'That is very good. Now, I am sure you have messages for your husbands. If you give them to me I will endeavour to see that they are delivered.'

Margaret took a deep breath. 'My husband is dead.'

The woman frowned at her list. 'You are Mrs Margaret Cairns? Mrs Lawrence Cairns? Your husband was employed by Hammond and Teng?'

'Yes,' Margaret said, scarcely daring to believe her ears.

'Did you not know he escaped from Singapore?'

'And was drowned,' Margaret whispered.

'No, no, Mrs Cairns,' the woman said, almost as though she was irritated with these foolish, hysterical women who kept imagining their husbands were dead. 'Your husband

347

was picked up by a British submarine. He is now serving with the British army in India.'

Margaret fainted.

'She'll be all right. Really she will,' Molly assured Marion. Several of the woman, aided by the Swiss Red Cross representative, had carried her into the shade and laid her down. Even Kimishira helped, disturbed that one of his prisoners should reveal such weakness.

Marion felt a great leaping in her chest at the thought that Daddy might still be alive, but it was Mummy on whom she had come to rely as the fount of their joint strength.

Marion did not remember a great deal about her early childhood; it was not that she had forgotten, it was merely that her memory was unwilling to recapture that period of her life. She had been unhappy, not in herself, but because Mummy and Daddy had been so clearly unhappy. Why this should have been so, she had no idea, and they had never been anything else but unfailingly kind to her, but she had been aware of their joint misery.

All of that had changed after her fourth birthday, and after they had moved to Hong Kong. Hong Kong had been a sheer delight, with Mummy and Daddy smiling all the time, and everyone happy.

Then had come that catastrophic day in 1941. The whole month of December had been one long catastrophe, beginning with the terrible agony in her stomach, the anxious faces looking down at her, the sudden drift into oblivion . . . and the awakening to yet more nausea and pain.

Then she had slowly got better, day by day, and had looked forward to going home for Christmas.

Her life had then been torn apart by noise and explosions and screams. Mummy had had her taken home, but that had been worse than if she had stayed in the hospital, Marion was sure. From the house she could look down at the smoke and the destruction in the town, and know that somewhere in there was her mother. She had cried herself to sleep each night, and when the firing had at last stopped she had been unable to believe her ears.

Mansur had then told her to go to her room and lock herself in and not open the door for anyone. She had been annoyed at that. In Mummy and Daddy's absence Mansur had acted as though he were her father. Although he was always kind, he was also very bossy. She had gone to her room, but when she heard the car in the drive she had not been able to resist coming downstairs.

She still had no clear idea what had happened to her. She remembered the Japanese officer calling on Mummy and Daddy before the war, surely he was a friend. Certainly he had laughed and joked as if he had been a friend, but while he had been laughing he had been doing the strangest things to her. He had pulled down her knickers, and when she had protested – no-one had ever done that to her before – he had slapped her bottom, still laughing. Then he had taken down his own pants, and frightened her before hurting her quite badly.

With the pain she had been aware of humiliation, without quite understanding why. Mummy had never spoken to her about sex before, and she had not yet begun to menstruate. Indeed she hadn't started yet. Malnutrition and illness had prevented it. Many of the older women in the camp had stopped having periods altogether.

Worst of all that day had been when Mummy had come home, and been undressed, and beaten till she bled. Marion had known only hatred for the smiling man then, just as she had known that one day Daddy would punish him for what he was doing. Mummy must have known the same, for she had never flinched, and afterwards she had held Margaret close and told her that indeed the laughing man would be punished.

But then had come the news that Daddy was dead.

It had come at a time when the horror of that day in Hong Kong had itself been submerged in the overwhelming misery of their existence. Marion was sure that neither she nor Mummy had ever harmed anybody – so why were they being punished so terribly?

Yet again Mummy had never flinched. When the laughing man told them of Daddy's death, they both wept. And she had asked Mummy, 'Does this mean that the laughing man won't be punished after all?'

Mummy had hugged her and said, 'He'll be punished, darling. I swear it. If I have to do it myself.'

Mummy was so strong and so brave, and so determined. But she wouldn't talk about what had happened to her that Christmas Day in 1941. 'When you are older,' she had promised. But she always talked of other things, of how happy they would be when it was all over. Marion found it difficult to believe it ever would be over.

Her life had become one long struggle with hunger and heat and dirt. She began to wonder whether she had ever really lived in a house which had a swimming pool in which to cool off, soft sheets to sink into at night, toys and books and lovely food. Now she was poor and dirty and weak and ill, and covered in sores which never seemed to get better.

But Daddy was alive! And the laughing man would certainly be punished! Marion knelt down beside her mother and took her hand.

'Do wake up, Mummy,' she begged. 'It's all going to be all right, now.'

Margaret smiled.

'The situation is intolerable,' declared General Yamashita, concentrating all his ferocity in the gaze he was directing at his kempei-tai commander. 'There have now been twelve bomb outrages in Singapore and Johore in the last year. That is one per month, Colonel Kitachi. Why have they not been stopped?'

'My men are doing their best, honourable General,' Kitachi protested. 'But there are great difficulties. These outrages are certainly being carried out by Chinese. Communists, I would say. Perhaps we made a mistake in executing so many of them when we first came here. Perhaps it would have been more subtle to lull them into a false sense of security, then we would have been able to round up more of them than we did. As it is, those who survived my initial purge managed to go underground, and are only now emerging.'

'I am not interested in your mistakes, Kitachi,' the general told him. 'I want this sabotage stopped.'

'We are making progress, honourable General,' Kitachi said. 'In the past year we have killed seven of these thugs.'

'Why did you kill them, before they could give you the information you need to get at the leaders?'

'They will not let themselves be captured alive, honourable General. They kill themselves when they are cornered. As for the others, the jungles of Johore are very thick. It is very difficult to follow them with success.'

'Kitachi,' Yamashita said. 'You are a fool.'

Kitachi stiffened, his face flushed with anger.

'You spend your time chasing people after they have committed a crime, in a country which they know better than you, and where they can always be sure of shelter. That is a complete waste of time. You must go straight to the root.'

'But, honourable General, I have not yet found the root.'

'Explosives, man. They are using explosives. Now, you tell me that there have been no losses from our own supplies. Therefore they are obtaining explosives from another source. Find that source. It should not be difficult. There cannot be very much dynamite left in Shonan. It should all have been rounded up long ago; it must all be rounded up now. And you must regard everyone who has access to dynamite with suspicion.'

Kitachi remained at attention.

Yamashita wagged his finger. 'I have heard that you are growing soft, Kitachi. I have heard that since your sister has come to Shonan to keep house for you, you are spending too little time at work and too much time at home. I am not interested in your private life, Kitachi. That is between you and your ancestors. But I will have these acts of sabotage stopped. Or I will seek a new chief of police from Tokyo. Dismissed.'

351

Kitachi bowed.

He seethed with anger. He had never been spoken to like that in his life before. To think that once he could have had the general immediately reprimanded . . .

But things had changed since those days. The army now ruled Japan, and no one dared oppose them, not even the kempei-tai. Kitachi, and all of his fellows, had assumed that when their old commander Tojo became prime minister, their power would grow even more. That had not happened. Tojo, as prime minister, had as much interest as his predecessors in keeping the kempei-tai under control. Tojo had given himself entirely to the army. The kempei-tai had become nothing more than an appendage.

Thus he, Kitachi, could be insulted, treated like a delinquent schoolboy!

He got out of his car – he had taken to driving himself and had entirely dispensed with a chauffeur – and stamped up the steps to his bungalow, still simmering with rage. But the rage evaporated as he saw Aiwa waiting for him on the verandah.

He thought she grew more beautiful and more desirable with every year. That she was forbidden fruit only made her the more attractive.

His visits to the Bamboo Curtain, nowadays, were strictly for the purpose of introducing visiting army officers to Lan Kuei, whose fame had now spread throughout South East Asia. She no longer played any part in his desires, his life.

Aiwa had, as he had anticipated, been delighted with the bungalow, indeed with all Shonan. The difference in climate, in the way of life, and above all in the way the houses were built, all entranced her. The Cairns' bungalow was a constant source of delight to her. She had never lived in so many rooms; she had never seen permanent beds; she had never walked on thick rugs rather than tatami mats; she had never known walls which one could bang without making the whole house tremble. She even enjoyed Malay cuisine.

Only in the matter of baths was Western civilisation wholly deficient. The tubs were too small for two people, and it was absurd that one lay instead of sitting upright; this was decidedly unhealthy for the back.

There were no public baths at all.

But if she had found Western civilisation on the whole interesting and exciting, Aiwa had no intention of becoming westernised, in the way the Chinese ladies of Shonan had done. Thus she still wore a kimono, and still put her hair up in a vast chignon secured with a huge ivory pin whenever she appeared in public; and she still wore white socks and white slippers.

She bowed low as her brother came up the steps.

'There is trouble?' she asked.

'Yamashita is always trouble,' Kitachi growled, and went inside, where the tea was waiting. 'It is these Communist bomb outrages. They are hindering the war effort. But I will stamp them out.'

Aiwa had even learned to sit in chairs rather than on a cushion on the floor, but she still brought up her feet beneath her kimono to sit on the settee. She did not ask any questions. Her brother seldom discussed his work, or his relations with his fellow officers. He would tell her whatever he wished her to know.

'I am tired,' Kitachi said. 'We will have an early dinner, and then go to bed.'

Aiwa bowed her head. 'We are invited out to dinner.'

'Where?'

'At the house of Chung Kai and Chung Su. I told you of it.'

'Yes,' Kitachi said.

'You said we should go, because Chung Kai is a leader of the Chinese community here.'

'Yes,' Kitachi said again. 'Yes, we should go.'

Chung Su had bloomed as Shonan's leading hostess. She had abandoned her fashionable Western style clothes in favour of flowing gowns and, having allowed her hair to grow, wore it, for entertaining, in a Japanese-style chignon. This enhanced her bold features, her strong mouth and jaw.

She had, it seemed, overcome her hatred of all things Japanese, and her meal included both Chinese and Japanese dishes; she had provided tempura and duck, as well as plum wine and green tea.

There was also sake, but the men drank scotch whisky.

Kitachi knew Aiwa enjoyed these gatherings where women and men sat down together, and discussed serious as well as frivolous topics. At first she had been very shy, had listened rather than offer any opinions herself. But over the year she had been in Shonan she had slowly blossomed; this evening she was more than usually animated. It was all so different from the secluded life she had led in Japan.

Kitachi spoke little. He was thinking, and besides, he was angry with the entire army and had no desire to converse amiably with the two officers and their wives who were the other guests. Instead he studied the Chung brothers, Kai and Cheong, and their wives.

After their initial opposition to the Japanese takeover, which had been understandable, they had become most co-operative; thus they had been given the facilities to restore their home, and the Bukit Timah mansion was again a place of beauty and peace, with a full staff of servants. Because they had encouraged their people to accept Japanese rule, and Japanese ways, all Shonan had become a happy, peaceful place again.

Except for these Communist outrages.

Kitachi wondered what the women thought of them, how much they knew of them. Chung Han he discounted: she was a pretty, feather-brained creature. But Chung Su . . . he could still remember the hatred with which she had addressed him, twelve years ago. Now she smiled at him, and pretended to admire him and everything he stood for. Could a woman change so completely?

She was a woman who exuded strength, as well as being

highly attractive. He thought he would dearly love to have her all to himself, at kempei-tai headquarters. He enjoyed breaking strong-willed women, especially when they were attractive. Margaret Cairns had been a disappointment to him. Her strength had been that of an angry cat, easily reduced to abject surrender by a few blows.

Kitachi had never discussed the bomb outrages with Chung Kai. He knew that Kai hated Communism and all it stood for. How could he do otherwise, when the Communists, if they ever attained power, would strip him of everything he owned? And he did not wish Kai ever to feel that the Japanese needed him or anyone else to run Shonan successfully.

But now he needed to use every weapon he possessed. He went on to the verandah to smoke an after-dinner cigar – another Western habit which he found pleasant – and Kai followed him, understanding that his father's old friend wished a private chat.

'I need your co-operation,' Kitachi said.

Kai bowed. 'You have but to ask.'

'These Communist outrages,' Kitachi said. 'They must be stopped. I am having great success in catching these men, but there always seem to be more waiting to take their places. This is intolerable.'

'Yes,' Kai agreed. 'It is bad for business.'

'Exactly. Now I am determined to take tough measures. I know these people are being supported and supplied by certain members of the community. Certain members of your Chinese community, Chung Kai. I am asking you to find out who these people are, and give me their names.'

'For you to torture and then execute them,' Kai remarked quietly.

'They are traitors, and undoubtedly Communists. And as we have agreed, they are bad for business. Most important, I would like you to find out if there are any hidden stores of dynamite in Shonan. These people seem to have an unlimited supply of explosives. This also we must stop.'

'I will do my best,' Chung Kai said.

355

'Good. I knew you would co-operate. It would be best for all if you were to find out what I wish to know, because if you do not, I am going to take hostages and force these scoundrels out into the open. I also mean to implement a house-to-house search of all Shonan. These methods will be unpleasant for your people.'

'Very unpleasant,' Kai agreed.

'But I mean to find that dynamite. I look forward to hearing from you very soon. Now, shall we rejoin the ladies?'

'If you wish. By the way,' Chung Kai said, as they returned to the doorway. 'I am sure you must be pleased that the Red Cross have given your camp a clean bill of health.'

'But of course,' Kitachi said. 'What else could they do?'

'Quite. Did you speak with them?'

'No, no. It would not have been right. Then some scoundrel somewhere would have said I was trying to influence their report.'

'Quite,' Kai said again. 'I spoke with them, at a reception. They told me something very interesting. Do you remember Larry Cairns?'

The breath hissed in Kitachi's nostrils. 'I remember him. He debauched your sister.'

'Yes,' Kai said. 'I had believed him dead.'

'He is dead,' Kitachi said.

'Apparently he is not. The Red Cross people told me that he actually survived that storm off Sumatra, and was picked up by a British submarine. He is now serving with the British army in India. I find that very interesting. Don't you?' He turned away as Kitachi again hissed his anger.

'Well, that is that,' Chung Kai said, getting into bed beside his wife. 'I must get rid of the remaining dynamite, and I must have a meeting with Diem and tell him that the sabotage campaign has got to stop.'

'You cannot,' Su said.

'Su,' Kai said. 'Kitachi means business. He is going to

356

take hostages, and if that produces no results, he is going to execute them. He may execute them anyway.' He sighed. 'I knew it had to come to this.'

'We are fighting a war,' Su said. 'We may not wear uniform, and we may not carry guns, but it is none the less a war. And we are being successful.'

'You think so? The Japanese are winning this war. Those officers tonight told us that their army is about to invade India. That will be the end of the British.'

'The Japanese cannot win this war. How often do I have to tell you this? And I am being proved right. One of their wives told me that there is much concern over the defeats in the ocean. The Americans are advancing steadily, taking island after island. I do not believe the Japanese will succeed in their invasion of India. As for us, I was speaking with Kitachi's sister tonight. She told me that her brother is very worried and upset about these bomb attacks, that he has told her it is a serious matter, destructive to the war effort. You cannot abandon them now, Kai. It would be a betrayal of your people.'

Kai sighed again. It was difficult to resist Su with her hair loose on her shoulders like a shawl, eyes sparkling and alight with determination. She was his backbone.

'And the hostages?' he asked.

'They must take their chances,' Su declared.

'I hope they are going to feel the same way,' Kai said. 'I must move the dynamite. Kitachi is also speaking of a house-to-house search in Singapore. He will certainly start with the go-downs.'

'That is right,' Su agreed. 'Move it here, and we will bury it in the grounds.'

'That will be very dangerous. I had thought of handing it all over to Diem.'

'Moving it here will be less dangerous than leaving it in the warehouse. As for handing it over to Diem, that would be crazy. Surely we decided that long ago.'

How calmly she weighed the odds, made her decisions. Did she feel no fear at all?

'But what about us? If Kitachi is so determined to stamp

357

out the sabotage, and either slaughters enough people, or offers enough rewards, someone may betray us.'

'That is a chance we also have to take,' Su said, as calmly as ever. 'But we will not stop just because of the risk.'

Kai accepted her decision, as he accepted her decisions in most things. But he was determined that she should not be involved, and sent her and the boys to Chung Cheong's house for the weekend. They would stay with Chung Han and her two daughters while the dynamite was moved; he would in any event need Chung Cheong to help him.

The danger of what he had to do appalled him, even with the support of Su's courage. He had always been afraid of handling the explosives; from the very start had wanted to give them all to Diem and bow out of the conspiracy. Su had explained that he could not do so. By retaining the stock under his own hand, as it were, he would also retain some control over what the Communists might plan to do, but more important, he was also thus indispensable to them. Were he to cease to be their supplier, they might, if the going got rough, hand him over to the kempei-tai.

If Kitachi was considering some kind of house-to-house search for explosives, then his secret store had to be removed from the House of Chung immediately.

There was only one person he could trust absolutely, apart from Su, and that was Chung Cheong. Cheong had been part of the conspiracy from early on, and had been more even enthusiastic than Kai about co-operating with the Communists.

Next morning Kai put the situation to his brother.

Cheong thought for a few moments, then nodded. 'It will certainly have to be moved. How much of it is left?'

'About a hundred sticks.'

'It will be difficult, moving it.'

'Yet it must be done. We will remain behind after the staff goes home this evening, as we usually do when taking out the dynamite. We will take out all hundred sticks, in our briefcases.'

'They will not fit.'

'This afternoon I will bring a slightly larger case when I return from breakfast. It will hold two thirds. You will take the rest. We will take them to my house, and hide them there.'

'You will conceal a hundred sticks of dynamite in your house? What will Su say? Han would have hysterics at the very idea.'

'It is Su's idea,' Kai said. 'It is her idea that we should continue in this operation. We will bury the dynamite in the garden.'

'When do you next meet with Diem?' Cheong asked.

'In a week's time.'

'If I were you I would give him all the dynamite then.'

Kai shook his head. 'I do not think that would be a good idea. The dynamite will be safe at the house.'

That afternoon, when he returned from his midday meal – known as breakfast although it corresponded with a European lunch – driving the old Ford which the Japanese had allowed him to buy on the black market, he brought, as he had promised, a larger case than usual. None of his staff made any comment; they were too loyal to question what their employer might do.

He remained at his desk, checking invoices, until all the staff had bidden him goodnight and left. Then it was only a matter of waiting for Cheong, who handled the dockside end of the business.

Cheong arrived at a quarter to six. In half an hour it would be dark. By that time they should both be home, because although they had the necessary passes to break the curfew, they would most certainly be stopped. They hardly exchanged a word of greeting, but went immediately to where the dynamite was concealed and carefully took out stick after stick, and packed them into the two suitcases.

'I have told Chung Han that I will be spending the night with you,' Chung Cheong said.

359

Kai nodded, concentrating on wrapping each stick in a fresh piece of paper so that it could not sweat against the next. Then he closed and locked the suitcase. Cheong closed his briefcase in turn, and sighed with relief.

'I feel like a very large scotch,' Cheong said. His face glistened with sweat.

'You shall have a very large scotch, as soon as we get home,' Kai promised him. He picked up the suitcase, turned to the door, and was arrested by a knock.

Chung Cheong nearly dropped his valise.

Kai placed the suitcase on the floor beside the desk, and went to the door of the warehouse. He unlocked it. Kitachi stood outside.

For a moment Kai's knees all but knocked, and he could not speak, his throat was dry. But there were no kempei-tai soldiers behind the colonel; nor was there anyone in his car, which waited on the street.

'I saw the lights on,' Kitachi said.

Kai licked his lips. 'Sometimes it is necessary to work late. I was hastening, to be home before the curfew.'

'I will escort you home. Will you not invite me in?'

'Of course.' Kai stepped aside, forcing himself to remain entirely calm, as Su would have done. He wished he could say the same of his brother. Chung Cheong stood trying to conceal his briefcase on the table behind him.

'I wish to know if you have had any ideas regarding our conversation of last night,' Kitachi said.

'I have had ideas, of course,' Kai said. 'But I have not yet had the time to make any investigations.'

'Then you must make haste; this is an urgent matter.' Kitachi appeared to notice Cheong for the first time.

Cheong nodded, while Kai closed and locked the street door.

'You look like a conspirator,' Kitachi commented.

Cheong gulped, and Kitachi stared at his sweating face, then looked at Kai.

'You have told your brother of our conversation?'

'Of course. I did not know it was confidential.'

'It was confidential. Your brother seems afraid.'

360

'He is concerned about repercussions, honourable Colonel,' Kai said. Cheong was clearly beyond speaking.

Kitachi pointed. 'I will arrest him, for a start.'

'He is not involved, honourable Colonel.'

'Not involved? He is the guiltiest-looking man I have ever seen.' Kitachi reached for his pocket, took out a whistle.

Kai acted instinctively. He picked up a chair and swung it with all his force. It struck Kitachi across the back of his head, and he fell to his knees with a grunt.

Kai hit him again, and this time the Japanese slumped to the floor, unconscious.

Cheong sat down on the table. He looked about to faint.

'It had to happen, I suppose.' Kai was surprised at his own calmness. 'We must hurry.'

'Hurry?' Cheong gasped. 'Hurry where?'

'We have our passes for crossing the causeway. We will do so now, then abandon the car and go into the jungles of Johore. That is where Diem hides out. We will contact him. We will have to live with the Communists.'

'Until when?'

Kai hesitated. 'Until Japan is defeated. Su is certain this will be soon.'

Chung Su!

Cheong had the same thought. 'But our wives and children!'

'They must leave at once.' Kai picked up the telephone, gave the number. 'Han? It is Kai. Listen to me very carefully. It is imperative that you and Su and the children go immediately to Bukit Timah. Cheong and I will meet you there in fifteen minutes. Please understand that there is no time to be lost.'

'What is happening?' Chung Han asked.

'I cannot tell you over the telephone,' Kai said. 'Su will explain it to you. I can only ask you both to do as I say. Fifteen minutes.'

He hung up.

'He is going to wake up in a minute.' Chung Cheong

picked up Kai's paperknife, a miniature samurai sword. 'I should cut his throat.'

'No,' Kai said. He had never killed anyone in his life.

'But he will follow us.'

'And if we kill him, do you not suppose Captain Kano will follow us?'

'Then let us take him with us, as a hostage.'

'Do not be crazy,' Kai snapped. 'He is a samurai. He would tell his people to shoot rather than be disgraced by helping us escape.'

Cheong hesitated, the picture of indecision. 'At least let us take his car,' he said.

'No,' Kai said firmly. 'That would attract attention to us. Help me tie him up.'

They fetched some rope from the storeroom and between them trussed Kitachi hand and foot, then gagged him. The colonel's eyes were open, and he was staring at him with an expression of such malevolence Kai almost thought Cheong might be right. But it would be cold-blooded murder. Kai might supply the means of killing to Diem and his friends, but he had never actually pressed the plunger. As for killing Kitachi, a man whom he had entertained in his own house, that would damn him forever.

'We will leave the car where it is, and the lights on in here,' Kai said. 'Everyone will assume he is in here speaking with me, and that will give us all the start we need. Now let us hurry.

'I hope we will not meet again, Colonel,' he said, and followed Cheong to the inner door; this led to the garage, which opened on to the next street. Five minutes later they were driving away from the warehouse as fast as they dared. The time was twenty past six.

They reached the house in twenty minutes, having been briefly stopped by a Japanese patrol. But Kai's car was well known, and there were no questions.

Kai stopped the car and looked at his watch. It was a

quarter to seven. There was no sign of the women and children.

'We are committing suicide,' Cheong moaned, a quarter of an hour later. 'They are not coming.'

Kai telephoned Chung Cheong's house again.

'The mistress left here ten minutes ago,' the maid said. 'With Mistress Chung Su and the children. She said they were going out to dinner, Mr Kai.'

'Thank you,' Kai said. Ten minutes ago! He had telephoned Chung Han at ten past six. They had delayed their departure for nearly an hour. Why? Still, it should not take them more than fifteen minutes to drive across Singapore.

Seven fifteen.

'They are not coming,' Cheong said again. 'We are going to die. They are going to chop off our heads. Kai, the women will be quite safe. They know nothing of what we are doing. The Japanese will have nothing against them. They will question them, and they will say they were told to meet us here. But they were delayed, and we were not here.'

Kai chewed his lip.

'They will more likely die in the jungle,' Cheong said. 'Han is very delicate.'

To leave Su behind . . . but this was what she had always told him to do, were there ever an emergency. Like Cheong, she insisted that no-one could assume she was involved in her husband's machinations. After all, it was not expected of any Chinese woman so to be involved.

Kai had to admit that Cheong was right. The women did not know anything more than that they had been told to meet their husbands, with the children: they could very well all have been going out to dinner. Once Kitachi was free, it would take only one telephone call to seal the causeway. And Kitachi would be out for revenge against the Chungs, who had tricked and humiliated him. Kai's skin crawled at the thought.

'You're right,' he said finally. 'We must leave. Diem

will be able to get word to Su and Han, tell them where we have gone. They can join us later, if they choose.'

They hurriedly drove down to the road, turning left to the causeway. Kai looked back at his house for the last time.

Su and the boys would be safe. He had to believe that, or he might as well hand himself over to Kitachi with no further struggle.

As was usual kempei-tai practice, for Kitachi was a cautious man, Kano had accompanied him to the Chung warehouse, in a separate car, which he had parked around the corner. From there he could maintain surveillance of the next street without being noticed himself, readily available should his colonel blow his whistle.

At first it seemed that there was nothing out of the ordinary at the Chungs. The colonel entered the warehouse at five to six and the minutes ticked away. It was twenty five to seven when Kano began to worry.

Earlier he had heard the sound of a car in the street behind the warehouse, and thought nothing of it. Now it suddenly became important.

He went to the warehouse and tried the door. It was locked. Kitachi's car was still waiting. There was no sound from inside the warehouse, save for a faint drumming.

Kano tried to see through the windows, but the blinds were drawn. He decided to wait for another fifteen minutes; he did not believe the Chung brothers would be so crazy as to harm a kempei-tai colonel. And he knew how ill-tempered Kitachi could be if interrupted: Kitachi had been ill-tempered all day.

By seven o'clock, he was determined to act. By now the city was absolutely dead; the curfew had taken effect. Kano blew his whistle, and a few minutes later a patrol of soldiers arrived.

'Break down this door,' Kano ordered.

It took them several minutes; the door was made of Burma teak, and securely fastened. But at last they burst into the warehouse, and found Kitachi, his heels drumming furiously on the floor. Hastily Kano untied the gag and cut the bonds. Kitachi gasped. 'Chung Kai! Have him arrested. Have the causeway closed. Quickly!'

Kano seized the telephone. He first called the kempei-tai headquarters and ordered the Chung house to be surrounded and sealed pending the arrival of the colonel and himself; people were to be allowed in, but no one was to be allowed out. Then he called the causeway guards.

'The causeway will be closed immediately, honourable Captain,' said the lieutenant in command.

Kano was about to hang up, when he was struck by a thought. 'Has any car recently crossed over?'

'Yes, honourable Captain. The car belonging to Chung Kai, the merchant. He and his brother Chung Cheong were on their way to Johore, on business, they said. They had a pass.' He hesitated as Kano made no comment. 'They make this journey regularly, honourable Captain, in the evening after business. They spend the next day in Johore, and return to Shonan in the evening.'

Kitachi heard the conversation.

'The fool! Tell him to give chase,' he growled, making for the door. 'Tell him to catch those men, or I will have his stripes. Then come with me to that accursed house.'

Chung Han was in a very excited state when she put down the telephone; Su had never been sure how much Chung Cheong confided in his wife, but clearly she had her suspicions.

'That was Kai,' Han panted. 'He said we must leave here at once, and go to Bukit Timah. Why should we do that, Su? It will mean breaking the curfew.'

Su was instantly apprehensive. What could have gone wrong?

'We have our passes,' she said. 'If Kai says we must go to Bukit Timah, then we must go.'

'With the children? We will be stopped. I know we will be stopped.'

'Of course we will be stopped,' Su explained, keeping her own panic in check. 'But we have our passes. And we must go. And if Kai says we must take the children, then it is a serious matter. Come on, we must hurry.'

Han caught her arm as she left the room in search of the children. 'Tell me what is happening.'

'I am sure Kai and Cheong will tell you, as soon as we get to Bukit Timah,' she said, trying to keep calm. All of her life she had endeavoured to keep calm. She prided herself that she had even kept calm while her parents were being murdered.

But if Kai wanted them all, then he could only be going to flee . . . something terrible must have happened. A huge lump seemed to be forming in her stomach.

But she quietly disengaged herself from Han and went to the children; they were in an inner room playing marbles; Han and Cheong's daughters were only a little older than the twins.

'We are all going out,' she said. 'Come along now. We must hurry, or we'll be late.'

They stared at her, and she almost stamped her foot.

'Hurry,' she said again.

Han had followed her. 'What must we take?' she asked. 'Did Kai say to take anything?'

'No.'

'Then we will not take anything. Come on, children.' She got them to their feet, began shepherding them to the door.

'Then we will be coming back here?' Han asked.

'I don't know,' Su said.

The question got the girls agitated, and they began asking questions of their own.

The butler appeared in the doorway. 'Is something wrong, madam?' he asked.

'Nothing is wrong,' Su said quickly. 'We have decided to take the children out to dinner, that is all.'

The butler looked disbelieving, and none too pleased; he knew how grand a dinner Han had ordered.

Han gulped. 'Yes,' she said. 'Yes. We have decided to go out.'

The butler bowed.

'He will be suspicious,' Han hissed.

'It doesn't matter, as long as we get out of here,' Su said. 'Please let's go, Han.'

They went down to the garage, and the children got into Han's car. Much as Su would have preferred to drive herself, she decided she had better continue being patient.

Han got behind the wheel, started the engine, and then switched it off again.

'What is the matter?' Su asked, trying to keep from shouting.

'I must take my jewellery. I cannot leave without my jewellery.'

'Are we going away, Mummy?' asked one of the girls.

'Where?' asked the other.

'I don't know,' Han said, bursting into tears. 'But I must get my jewellery.'

She got out of the car and ran upstairs.

'My dolls,' said one of the girls.

'My paints,' said the other.

They both scrambled out and ran after their mother.

'What is happening, Mummy?' asked the twins.

'Nothing,' Su said. 'Oh, God, nothing.'

She was very tempted to get behind the wheel and drive off, but she couldn't abandon Han and the girls. So she went back upstairs as well, and tried to hurry them up. But it was a slow business, as each one remembered something else that simply had to be taken.

It was ten to seven before they finally drove out of the yard. Ten minutes later they saw a Japanese patrol. Chung Han screamed and threw both hands into the air. Desperately Su reached across to grab the wheel, but already the car was off the road. A moment later it was sliding down the parapet into the ditch.

No one was hurt, but Han continued to scream, and immediately they were surrounded by Japanese soldiers.

The soldiers were actually very helpful, once they had inspected the passes with their flashlights. They pushed and pulled and got the car back on to the road.

'You drive carefully, now,' warned the sergeant, who spoke English.

'I will drive now,' Su announced.

Han got out from behind the wheel without demur; she seemed to have collapsed entirely.

Su drove up to the house. The gates were open. That was to be expected. But Kai's car was not to be seen.

She had a tremendous urge to scream herself. Instead she said, 'This is because of the time we took.' She got out of the car and ran up the steps.

'Where are you going?' Han cried.

'To see if there is a message.'

But the servants only knew that Chung Kai and Chung Cheong had come to the house, waited about half an hour, and then left again.

'Half an hour,' Su muttered. They had been so close.

She went back to the car, trying to make up her mind what to do. Presumably they had been betrayed or found out. Thus Kai and Cheong were fleeing to Diem in the jungles of Johore. And they were supposed to do the same.

But the thought of taking the children, much less Han, into the jungle with a bunch of Communists was horrifying.

'What are we going to do?' Han also got out of the car.

Before Su could reply, she knew the decision had been made for them: several cars were driving through the gateway, and at the same time Japanese soldiers emerged out of the garden; the house was surrounded.

'Arrest those women,' Kitachi said.

Han gasped and shrank against Su. The little girls started to cry.

'And the children,' Kitachi commanded. 'Take them to headquarters.'

Su's brain seemed to have frozen. She wanted to protest, but she knew that if she opened her mouth she was going to beg, and she was determined not to do that.

Hands grasped her arms and she was bundled forward. She knew a flicker of relief that she was wearing trousers tonight, but she did not suppose they were going to be all that much protection.

This could not truly be happening, not to her, Chung Su, wife of Singapore's wealthiest merchant, daughter of Mukden's wealthiest merchant, friend of Marshal Chang Hsueh-liang . . . but her father was dead, and Marshal Chang Hsueh-liang was fighting for his life in the mountains.

And, oh God, where was Chung Kai?

She was pushed into the back of Kitachi's car, between two Japanese soldiers, who stared at her but did not touch her until they reached the kempei-tai building, when they bundled her out, punching and kicking her and pulling her arms and clothing. Apparently they did this as a matter of course; it was nearly eight o'clock by now and there was no one on the streets to see.

The building was full of people jabbering at each other in Japanese. She had picked up a few words of the language since the Occupation and didn't like what she heard.

She was shown into a room with a desk and three chairs. Instinctively she sank on to one of the chairs, and her head jerked as a guard struck her across the arm with a rubber truncheon. The pain was exquisite, and she leapt to her feet again.

'You stand,' the guard said.

She stood, and waited, and listened to other noises, stamping feet, high pitched laughter . . . someone screaming. She was sure it was either Han or one of the girls, and discovered that her fingers were clenched into fists so tight that her nails were eating into her palm.

What good was calmness going to do her now?

Kitachi came in, followed by Kano.

Kitachi glared at her. 'Your husband has been trying to make a fool of me,' he said.

Su returned his stare. 'I would say he succeeded, Colonel.'

Kano glanced nervously at his superior, obviously expecting an outburst of rage.

But Kitachi kept his temper. 'I am going to destroy

369

you, woman,' he said. 'I am going to enjoy doing that. Tell me where your husband has gone.'

'I would expect him to have gone into the jungles of Johore,' Su replied.

'To join his friends, the Communists?'

'To look for friends, perhaps.'

'Tell me why he felt it necessary to assault me and flee.'

'You will have to ask him that.'

'Do not prevaricate, woman. You were fleeing to join him.'

'I was attempting to join him. I am his wife.'

'Thus you know his secrets.'

'I know nothing of my husband's business,' Su said. 'He instructed me to meet him at the house, and I went there. But I was late. I do not know what he intended to do.'

Kitachi then gave some orders in Japanese. Before Su could catch her breath the men had seized her arms and dragged her to the door. She lost her balance and fell, and they dragged her through the doorway and along the corridor, banging her hips and legs as they did so.

'I can walk,' she shouted. 'I can walk.'

They dragged her down the corridor and into another room, larger than the first. There were several more men there, who descended on her. She was pulled to her feet while they tore at her clothing. In a matter of seconds she was naked.

Too breathless even to protest, Su was carried to an iron bar, some three and a half feet from the floor. Across this her body was draped, while men busied themselves securing her ankles to rings at the foot of the bar's uprights, which were several feet apart, so that her legs were spread. Then her head was pushed right down on the other side, and her wrists secured beside her ankles, leaving her utterly helpless, and utterly exposed, her buttocks highest, her hair brushing the floor, and blood rushing to her head.

She saw booted feet, and realised Kitachi had joined them.

'Bring them here,' he commanded.

More feet. Little Lo and Little Kai. Oh, God, she thought.

'Mama!' Lo shouted.

'Your mama is going to talk to you,' Kitachi promised. He spoke to his men in Japanese, and Su was shown the cane, a thin length of bamboo, bound with wire to prevent it splitting.

I am going to suffer, she thought. I am going to be in agony.

A table was brought and one of the soldiers climbed on to it. He was handed the whip.

He glanced at Kitachi, and Kitachi nodded.

Su and her sons screamed together.

Diem brought the news to the Chungs, as they sat around the campfire deep in the Johore jungle.

Communist scouts kept watch a mile away, looking out for any sign of Japanese penetration. But the Japanese, who had penetrated the jungle so easily to turn the British and Australian positions at the end of 1941, had no great desire to plunge into these swamps and forests in search of men who knew them better than they did. In the jungle Kai thought that were it not for the absence of Su and the boys, and the incessant irritation of the mosquitoes, he might even learn to be happy. He had asked Diem to discover if his family was well, and if it might be possible to get a message to them.

Diem's face was sombre, and he watched the Chungs carefully as he spoke. He was contemptuous of them, these men who had only ever held a pen, and who until a few nights ago had not known what it was to be in peril of their lives. Now he wondered how they would take what he had to tell them.

'Your women were arrested the night you left,' he said.

'Han was arrested?' Chung Cheong was aghast. 'My daughters?'

'Yes,' Diem said.

'What has happened to them?' Kai asked, quietly.

371

'They were taken to kempei-tai headquarters,' Diem told him. 'And have not been seen since. But my people have learned that terrible screams were heard that night. You must prepare yourselves for the worst, Chung Cheong, Chung Kai.'

Tears rolled down Chung Cheong's face. 'My Han,' he moaned. 'My girls.'

Kai remained expressionless, except for a slight tic at the corners of his mouth; it might almost have been a hardening of the muscles.

'You have weapons,' he said to Diem. 'But you have given none to us. I have brought you a hundred sticks of dynamite, Diem Chi, with which to kill Japanese. Will you not give me one of your weapons in return?'

'To kill yourself?' Diem sneered.

Kai stood up. 'To kill Japanese,' he said.

General Wavell himself conducted the investiture. It was a grand occasion, with a guard of honour and a band. A crowd of notables and their wives, bright with coloured frocks and saris, hummed and rustled, pointing out their relatives or acquaintances.

The war, leeches and snakes, rain and mosquitoes, mud and filth, seemed very far away. Larry wore clean khaki, his bush hat set squarely on his head and tightly strapped beneath his chin, his boots and belts polished to a high sheen; a sword hung at his side in a leather scabbard.

'For conduct in the best traditions of the British army, in that you took command of your column on the death of your senior officers, and led it to safety, fighting several rearguard actions with the enemy in conditions of extreme danger and difficulty, the Military Cross,' the Field Marshal said, and pinned the ribbon on the breast of Larry's tunic.

Then he shook hands. 'Singapore seems a long way away now, Cairns,' he remarked. Clearly he remembered their meeting at Government House in February 1941.

'Not long enough, sir,' Larry replied.

Wavell smiled. 'You'll get back there, Captain,' he said. 'We all will, God willing.'

He saluted, and Larry returned the salute, and stepped back into line.

His comrades were jubilant, none more so than Wingate. 'Now this beggar Slim wants to seduce you into the regulars,' he remarked.

Larry had not met General Slim before, but he recognised him instantly from his photographs; the thrusting jaw, the tight lips, the intense face, were all exactly as pictured.

'I am going to need men who know the jungle, and who aren't afraid of the enemy, when I start my advance into Burma,' the commander of the 14th Army said. 'Men like you, Cairns.'

'I would be delighted to serve with you, sir,' Larry said. 'And I will . . . providing that General Wingate is not going to lead any more Chindit expeditions.'

Wingate grinned. He still wore the beard he had grown in the jungle months before, although Larry had shaved his off. 'Oh, I shall be doing that, Cairns. You may count on that. And you're going to be on my staff.'

The Chindits had been withdrawn from the jungle in April, after the six weeks dictated by Wingate as the maximum he expected his men to stand in such extreme conditions.

Their exploits, when released to the press, had aroused tremendous enthusiasm. Here were British and Indian troops, for so long derided as being unable to meet the Japanese in the jungle with any hope of success, carrying the fight to the enemy, and apparently triumphing.

Larry knew that his medal was as much a result of that publicity – which Wingate felt was important to the future of his brainchild – and the consequent euphoria, as to any military prowess on his part; if His Majesty's Government had awarded an MC to every subordinate commander who had led his men to safety during the retreat through

Burma they would have run out of the things in very short order.

Not that he wasn't proud of both his medal and the way he had earned it. On that horrendous retreat he had been blooded, more than once, had himself fired a shuddering Bren gun into the face of a screaming enemy only a few yards away, had used the bayonet on another. He had been wounded twice, superficially if painfully; but he had brought the rearguard to safety, and himself to fame.

It was an experience to remember with pride for the rest of his life. And he had struck a blow for Margaret and Marion.

But Larry also knew – knowledge that was shared only by a few senior officers – that for all the cheering the expedition had been a military failure.

The Chindits had suffered more than a thousand casualties – more than a third of their total force, and in return had accomplished very little. A few bridges blown – easily repaired – and a few Japanese regiments disrupted to chase the marauders, seemed very little reward for such heavy losses.

Even more important, the evidences of Japanese strength Wingate and his men brought back convinced Wavell that there was no hope of launching a successful invasion of Burma until considerably more men and matériel could be accumulated, and this simply could not be done before the monsoon would put an end to campaigning for several months. So the long awaited advance had to be postponed until the end of 1944.

Actually, both Larry and the High Command were at once right and wrong, although they could not know it then. The Japanese were indeed in such strength in Burma that the British needed more troops than were then available to dislodge them, but Wingate's raid had disturbed them far more than was apparent, with the result that their own plans for invading India were postponed by a year, and this was to prove a godsend.

Throughout the remainder of 1943, therefore, both

374

sides gathered strength. The Japanese were further distracted by the Chinese invasion of North Burma, led by the redoubtable American General 'Vinegar Joe' Stilwell, who was disgusted with the British procrastination and said so. Stilwell was desperate to re-open the Burma Road, for although American aircraft were now regularly flying over the Hump, as they called the Himalayas, carrying supplies to the beleaguered Chinese in Chungking, they really could not take in sufficient matériel for the maintenance of a vigorous defence, and the Chinese had suffered several severe defeats.

All this time the Americans were inching steadily forward in the Pacific as well as, with the Australians, gaining ground in New Guinea, and by the end of the year they were poised to attack New Britain and the great naval base of Rabaul. Yet despite these distractions, such intelligence as came out of Burma left no doubt that Field Marshal Count Terauchi, supreme commander of all Japanese forces in South East Asia, was preparing for the invasion of India which had been Japan's ambition since the summer of 1942. To do this, it was said, he had accumulated an army of a hundred thousand veteran troops, under the command of General Mutaguchi Renya.

Stopping such a force was going to be a desperate business, and before the end of the year Wingate was told to prepare another Chindit raid to disrupt the Japanese preparations.

Known as Operation Thursday, it was to be an altogether more ambitious project. Wingate, now a major-general, was given no less than six brigades, collectively known as the Third Indian Division, but in fact retaining the designation of the Long Range Penetration Group and the nickname of Chindits.

These were to be split up into columns, as before, but only one was going to march in across the Chindwin; the others were to be flown by the American Air Force into specially selected sites and landed by glider.

This was to be no hit-and-run raid, like Longcloth. Wingate's orders were not only to disrupt the enemy on a large scale, but also to provide assistance to Stilwell's Sino-American force, still battling its way slowly south, its goal the communications centre of Myitkyina. To do this he had developed a new concept. He intended to establish a fortress, known as The Stronghold, in the jungle, upon which the columns could fall back and concentrate when they had completed their raids, and which could be constantly replenished by air to withstand any Japanese onslaughts. It would be a painful thorn in the Japanese side.

'Nothing like it has ever been done before,' Wingate told his officers. 'We are simply going to drop out of the skies behind the Japanese engaged with Stilwell, and establish ourselves in an impregnable position. The enemy will have to do something about us, and that will relieve the pressure on the Chinese.'

'How do we get back, sir?' someone asked.

'We don't, this time.' Wingate surveyed the faces; only a very small proportion of them were, like Larry, veterans of the earlier raid. 'We wait for the rest of the army to join us.'

He then went on to expand his concept in one of his remarkable Orders of the Day:

OBJECT OF THE STRONGHOLD

The Stronghold is a machan (Hindustani for platform) overlooking a kid tied up to entice the Japanese tiger.

The Stronghold is an asylum for Long Range Penetration Group wounded.

The Stronghold is a magazine for stores.

The Stronghold is a defended air-strip.

The Stronghold is an administrative centre for loyal inhabitants.

The Stronghold is an orbit round which columns of the Brigade circulate. It is suitably placed with reference to the main objective of the Brigade.

The Stronghold is a base for light planes operating with columns on the main objective.

The motto of the Stronghold is NO SURRENDER.

★ ★ ★

376

The training was every bit as vigorous and tough as in the previous year, and the fall out was again heavy. But at the end of the day the Chindits were again a hard, eager fighting force, ready to take on the world.

Larry was happy once again to be going to war. The news, from the Swiss Red Cross, that Margaret and Marion were both alive and well in a Japanese internment camp in Malaya had made him happier than he had been for three years. However, the fact that they had been transferred from Hong Kong to Malaya struck him as sinister. He knew that Colonel Kitachi Tano was commander of the kempei-tai in Malaya, with his headquarters in Singapore, and an impressive list of atrocities to his credit. If Kitachi had been responsible for transferring Margaret and Marion from Hong Kong to Johore, then every day that was wasted seemed like an eternity.

Larry had been promoted captain and, as promised, given a place on Wingate's staff. Since Operation Longcloth, the two men had become good friends. Larry welcomed his appointment; as Wingate's aide-de-camp he would be in the very heart of things.

Thus he was present when, the day before they were due to fly, a reconnaissance team brought in photographs of one of the principal 'drop' areas, selected because it was a considerable clearing in the forest, code-named Piccadilly. Now it had been covered with logs of wood.

There was an immediate high-level conference to determine whether the site had been deliberately blocked, which would suggest that the Japanese had prior information on the coming campaign, or if it was merely a stroke of bad luck. General Slim himself flew in to hear the views of the Chindit commanders. Naturally Wingate was all for going on, even if Piccadilly was useless as a landing area. And since he was supported by Brigadier Michael Calvert who was to have commanded the Piccadilly landing as well as another known as Broadway, permission was given to go ahead.

'Stop, start, stop, start, just like the last time,' Wingate growled. 'But now we're off.'

★ ★ ★

377

There were mistakes and confusions, and one or two tragic errors, such as when gliders were put down in the midst of Japanese forces. But the Japanese were again taken completely by surprise. They had never actually worked out what was behind the first Chindit raid, or how many men had been involved. And once the United States Engineers, commanded by Lieutenant Brockett, got to work with their bulldozers to create proper airstrips, the operation grew in intensity. Planes – Dakotas – flew non-stop to and fro ferrying a total of nine thousand men and well over a thousand mules. By 11 March the drops had been completed and Wingate could issue an Order of the Day telling his men that 'This is a moment to live in history!'

Many, principally amongst his superiors, felt that he went overboard with his rhetoric. But Larry knew exactly what he meant.

Once Thursday was launched, Divisional Headquarters were moved forward, firstly to Imphal, a delightful spot in the Naga Hills near the Burmese border, and then to Comilla. Here Wingate had the operation more under his hand, as it were, and it was as well that he did, for after the initial success of getting the Chindits in, things were not going altogether according to plan.

Calvert's men, deep in enemy territory, were meeting severe resistance; reports came in of old-fashioned bayonet charges and hand-to-hand fighting, even with swords; a namesake of Larry's, Lieutenant Cairns of the South Staffordshires, was awarded a posthumous Victoria Cross following one of these mêlées.

More serious were the problems encountered by the column sent across the Chindwin on foot, commanded by Brigadier Bernard Fergusson who, like Larry and Calvert, was a veteran of the first raid. This powerful force, some four thousand men, had as its target an area north of the railhead at Indaw, where The Stronghold was to be set up in accordance with Wingate's requirements: closely wooded and broken country, an area which could be cleared and levelled for use by the Dakotas, neighbouring friendly villages and an inexhaustible and uncontaminated supply of water.

The chosen area was codenamed Aberdeen, and it lay on high ground some distance to the east of the Chindwin valley.

The march got into trouble from the start. The country was horrendously difficult, and the weather quite remarkably bad. In this sense, the British decision not to go into Burma in force until after the monsoon was justified. Progress, therefore, was slow. Wireless communications were also poor, and headquarters could not always know the exact whereabouts of the force.

Meanwhile news began to come in that the Japanese had been alerted and were reinforcing Indaw itself, which they could quite easily do by rail. This would have put them in the heart of the Chindits' operations, rather than vice versa.

Being on the staff was tremendously interesting, but it could also be intensely frustrating, as Larry now discovered. Instead of being out there with a column and a definite objective, able to radio back to HQ for instructions, he found himself the recipient of such messages, often contradictory and backed up with insufficient information for him to give the general any coherent summary of what was happening in that area.

Wingate realised that Indaw had to be captured, and quickly, or the Japanese might bring sufficient force to bear to destroy his Group before The Stronghold could be set up. He therefore ordered Fergusson, as soon as Aberdeen was secure, to advance on the railhead.

Then came more confusion. Fergusson assumed, with good reason, that Indaw had priority, and that he would be supported by all the Chindits in the area; this specifically meant the 14th Brigade, commanded by Brigadier Ian Brodie, situated to Fergusson's left. But Wingate had already ordered Brodie to move south-west against the Japanese lines of communication – Indaw lay south-east.

With messages racing back and forth, orders and counter orders blistering the air, and the weather steadily getting worse as rain teemed down accompanied by recurring thunderstorms, Wingate realised that his entire operation was in danger of foundering in one enormous snafu.

'I'm going to have to go in myself and sort things out,' he announced. Actually, like all his staff, he was itching to see action.

He selected those officers who were to go with him. To Larry's chagrin he was not amongst them.

'You help Tulloch mind the hut, Larry,' Wingate said. 'Expect me back in about forty eight hours.' Brigadier Derek Tulloch was his Chief of Staff.

'Yes, sir,' Larry said. He was seething, but there was nothing to be done.

He went outside and found the RAF weather officer, Flight Lieutenant Bonnor, and Lieutenant Hodges, the United States Air Force pilot who flew the Mitchell B–25 loaned to Wingate for his personal use.

'When are you off?' asked Bonnor.

'I'm not off. I'm staying,' Larry said bitterly.

'Well, you could be the lucky one. It's ten tenth cloud up there, and clouds so thick you could walk on them. You going to tell the old man about it, Lieutenant?'

Hodges surveyed the sky. 'Reckon I'd better. Looks like I might not be able to find where he wants to set down.'

He went inside, and Bonnor and Larry took shelter from the steady rain beneath the porch of the headquarters building.

Hodges returned ten minutes later. 'He says go. So I guess that's it. See you guys.'

He trudged off into the rain to find his machine and crew.

Wingate came out a moment later, followed by his staff. He was well wrapped up, and well armed too.

'I'll call you when we're down,' he told Larry. 'Should be two or three hours.'

Larry saluted, and the little party disappeared into the rain.

Bonner and Larry watched the Mitchell's engines roar

into life, and the huge machine taxi down to the end of the runway. Within seconds of leaving the ground it had vanished into the low cloud, but they heard it for several seconds before the sound died.

Then it was just a matter of waiting for the General's call. Three hours passed without a summons. Larry went along to communications, where he found Bonnor prowling up and down behind the operators.

'Should've got there by now,' he grumbled.

It was not till dusk that they received the message. The Mitchell had crashed on the side of a hill, and all on board were dead.

CHAPTER 15
Those Who Came Home

Wingate's death meant the end of the Chindit operation, both in plan and in spirit. After some hesitation, Slim chose as his successor Brigadier Lentaigne. Calvert might have been a better choice, as he understood Wingate's ideas better than the more orthodox Lentaigne, who was in command of one of the Chindit columns.

In any event Lentaigne's orders were to forget the Long Range Penetration plan and link up with Stilwell's Sino-Americans, who were still battling their way towards Myitkyina. The Chindits were placed under the command of Stilwell, who had no understanding of what Wingate had tried to achieve. He regarded the Chindits as an undisciplined mob, and even resented being given them. In any event he immediately turned them into ordinary line infantry, and a few months later the remnants were withdrawn for rest and recuperation in India, unhappy and exhausted.

All of this might have happened anyway, whether Wingate had lived or died, because only two days after Operation Thursday had begun, on 7 March, 1944, the Japanese invasion of India – Operation U-Go – commenced.

This had been expected, in view of the large numbers of men known to have been accumulated by Mutaguchi, but not while the monsoon was still raging, nor had British Intelligence properly estimated the strength of the Japanese. As before, the regulars were bedevilled by the speed and ferocity of the Japanese onslaught, which repeated all the familiar infiltration and terror tactics that had been so successful in Malaya.

Like all of Wingate's personal staff, Larry was left

somewhat out on a limb by the general's death. Lentaigne had his own people and his own ideas. Larry wired Slim, and asked if there was still a place for him with the regulars.

The reply came back promptly: REPORT RICHARDS AT KOHIMA.

This was rather disappointing. Larry had no more idea than anyone else where the Japanese were; few people even understood that the long expected invasion had actually started.

What he did know was that Colonel Hugh Richards had been in command of one of the Chindit columns, and had been hastily pulled out when it was discovered that he was fifty years old, ten years older than British Army regulations allowed any officer to be when serving in the field. Larry knew and liked the man, and had a high respect for his toughness of both mind and body, but in the circumstances, if Richards had been sent to Kohima it was obviously because Slim did not anticipate any severe fighting in that area.

There was no choice but to obey orders, and Larry arrived in Kohima on 31 March, having been flown to Dimapur and taken the road south from there.

This road followed the border between India and Burma, and as it was the only good surface for miles, it was of vital importance for the reinforcement and replenishment of the frontier positions south of the railhead at Dimapur, which was the main supply centre. Thus, when Larry's driver pointed out Kohima, Larry realised that this little hill village – several thousand feet up in the mountains – could be of enormous strategic importance. It was an obvious natural stronghold; and whoever held it would control the supply road.

Richards was delighted to receive another Chindit officer as his Chief of Staff. The two men sat on the verandah of the Deputy-Commissioner's house, situated on a spur to the north of the village, high above the road which looped right round the little hill.

Beyond was jungle, and to every side, despite Kohima

being several thousand feet above sea level, was very thick jungle indeed.

'I'll take you on a tour of inspection tomorrow morning,' Richards said. 'But I can tell you that we really have no more than garrison troops here: a battalion of the Assam regiment, a Native State battalion, which frankly I don't rate very highly, and some platoons of the Assam Rifles. They're good chaps, but their name says it all as regards weapons; rifles and a few machine guns. And of all of those, a good third are in hospital with various ailments.' He brooded for a few moments. 'I actually had a battalion of the West Yorks here last week, but they were ordered off again.'

'So what do you think of the situation?' Larry asked.

'Well, from the reports I've been receiving, it seems clear that the Japs' main effort is going to be directed at Imphal, well south of us. This makes sense; if they can take Imphal, the plain to the west is all theirs. You could say: next stop Calcutta. However, they *must* know that Slim is expecting them and is prepared to defend Imphal to the last. And it's possible that Mutaguchi may make it his business to cut Imphal off from Dimapur, and prevent men and matériel getting through to reinforce the garrison. If he decides to do that, then the obvious place for him to cut the road is right here.'

'I spotted that coming in,' Larry agreed. 'Put a few thousand well-supplied Japs on this hilltop and they could be a bloody nuisance.'

'That could be the understatement of the year. So I reckon it's up to us to beat them to it, when it comes to turning Kohima into a fortress. I've already chosen some possible dispositions. We'll look at them tomorrow.'

They walked over the terrain the next day. From the south the ground undulated gently upwards, while the road clung to the shallow valley, which accounted for the loop. Richards had marked several positions which were already being entrenched and fortified as much as possible. South of the road was DIS Hill; immediately north of it was FSD Hill. At the bottom of the steeper slope up to

384

the administration centre was a third position, marked as Kuki Piquet. Above this, and behind the Commissioner's bungalow and some other houses once occupied by British planters, was Garrison Hill, which was the dominating feature. The whole hill was thickly wooded.

'If I could lay my hands on some barbed wire I'd feel a lot better,' Richards confessed. 'But apparently there isn't any in Dimapur. So we must do the best with what we have. Garrison Hill provides us with a sort of keep, if we were to be attacked in overwhelming force.' He grinned. 'We must hope it won't come to that.'

But next day arrived a message from GHQ: ELEMENTS IDENTIFIED IN JAPANESE FORCE MOVING NORTH OF IMPHAL MAKE IT POSSIBLE ENTIRE THIRTY FIRST DIVISION ADVANCING IN YOUR DIRECTION STOP ESTIMATED STRENGTH FIFTEEN THOUSAND MEN STOP PLEASE ADVISE DISPOSITIONS.

Richards passed the paper to Larry without a word.

'Holy Jesus Christ!' Larry commented.

Richards was already writing on his pad: REQUIRE EXPLICIT ORDERS AND REINFORCEMENTS.

The reply came back briskly: POSITION MUST BE HELD TO THE LAST MAN STOP NO SUBSTANTIAL TROOPS AVAILABLE BETWEEN KOHIMA AND INDIA SAVE FOR ONE SIX ONE BRIGADE STOP AM MOVING THESE TO YOU NOW STOP GOOD LUCK SLIM.

'Well, that's good news at any rate,' Richards remarked. 'You and I will have to take a back seat when Brigadier Warren gets here, Larry. But meanwhile we'll put ourselves in the best possible defensive posture.'

They placed the men themselves, and checked their weapons. They might have no heavy equipment, but they were at least armed with Bren guns, sighted to fire point-three-oh-three bullets to a range of two thousand yards, with a theoretical firing rate of five hundred rounds a minute. The magazine only held twenty-eight cartridges,

385

however, which meant that the gunner had to be accompanied always by an aide, who not only whipped one of the curved magazines out and thrust another in every four or five seconds, but would also change the air-cooled barrel whenever it became too hot. The Bren was a most efficient weapon as Larry well knew, having used it with the Chindits, but he also realised that the coming engagement would largely be a close combat one as well.

The huge, thick trees and tangled undergrowth which stretched away from the road to the south limited visibility to fifty yards at most. On the other hand, it would also slow up the Japanese.

And 161 Brigade was coming to their aid. The odds – one brigade and Richards' motley command against a full veteran Japanese division – would still be great, but it could only be a matter of twenty-four, or at most forty-eight hours, before their position became a really strong one.

The following day, some Naga tribesmen arrived with the information that the Japanese units were not far away.

'We need the earliest possible information on the enemy's whereabouts,' Richards told his officers. 'I want a reconnaissance to the south.'

Larry immediately volunteered; since Wingate's death he had been desperate to regain physical contact with the enemy. But Richards vetoed that.

'You're on the staff,' he pointed out.

A company of the Assam Rifles was sent out, with instructions to move cautiously south through the jungle, establish contact with the enemy, and then fall back with all speed; the Japanese were still thought to be several days away.

When the patrol had moved out, the garrison waited, gazing anxiously up the road towards Dimapur, from which direction the brigade was expected.

That same afternoon they heard shots, and Richards put every man on the alert. It was dusk when the remnants of the reconnaissance company staggered in.

'Japs,' said their English lieutenant, Caldwell. 'In considerable force.'

'Only a day's march?' Richards was astounded.

'All around, sir. Every bloody place.'

He had lost several men, and several more were wounded.

That meant the Japanese were advancing twice as fast as anyone had thought possible.

'Where the hell is Brigade?' Richards growled.

That night, shells began to fall in and around the village.

'Those are seventy fives,' Larry said.

'Against machine guns,' Richards answered grimly.

For the moment the firing was inaccurate, but close enough to frighten inexperienced troops. Next morning Larry was greeted by a furious lieutenant-colonel. 'The beggars have run off!'

'What? Who?'

'My Native State Battalion. Can you believe it? I'm down to officers and NCOs!'

They reported to Richards.

'Poor devils,' the CO commented. 'They'll be cut to pieces in the bush. Never mind, Brigade will be here today.'

That very morning the Fourth Battalion of the Royal West Kent Regiment arrived, some five hundred men, together with the Twentieth Mountain Battery of the Indian Artillery.

Richards and Larry saluted as the regulars marched in.

'Now we have an army,' Richards said. 'With more to come.'

But the West Kents' lieutenant-colonel, Laverty, was not optimistic. 'We had to fight our way in here,' he told them. 'The Japs are round to the north as well.'

Larry immediately got on the wireless to Brigade HQ. Brigadier Warren was aware of the situation, but could do nothing about it. 'I'm afraid we're under orders to remain here and prevent any incursion to the north of your position,' came the reply. 'Whatever happens the enemy must not be allowed to reach the supply dumps at Dimapur. You must do the best with what you have. We shall maintain our position as close to you as possible, and if there is any sign of the enemy pulling out we shall come down to your relief. We will, in any event, give you all the artillery support we can, and you will be supplied as necessary by air. Report your positions hourly.'

Richards stood on the verandah, his hands on his hips. He was the senior officer present and therefore retained his command, but instead of a brigade and his own people, he now had just over three thousand men, of whom only about half were actually fit for duty.

'Right,' he told them. 'General Sato – I believe he commands their Thirty-First Division – will have about fifteen thousand. I just want you to know this. We need to take ten of his for every one of ours.'

Larry was reminded of his chat with Wavell and Percival at Government House in Singapore in 1942. The difference was that Richards meant what he said.

As he had planned to do from the beginning, Larry evacuated his staff from the Deputy-Commissioner's bungalow and set up a command position on Garrison Hill, with an artillery emplacement in front of it. He then walked round the perimeter. The defenders had now been pulled back across the road, thus leaving a brief open space which the Japanese would have to cross to get at them; this had been carefully sighted and enfiladed as far as possible for the maximum fire power.

Above the road the bungalows provided some cover, but up the hill, between the bungalows and Garrison Hill, was a considerable open space occupied by, of all things, a tennis court with a little pavilion. The area reminded him painfully of the Chungs' mansion; also it was definitely a weak spot in their defences.

'If it were a bit larger, we could develop it as an airstrip,' Richards commented. 'As it is . . .' he gave orders for shelter trenches to be dug on either side of the court, and then with Larry worked out a fire-plan for here as well.

'If they get this far they'll be just about home and dry,' Larry commented.

'Like hell they will,' Richards said. 'Home base is the top of that hill . . . with the last of our men dead. That includes you and me, Cairns.'

Then it was simply a matter of waiting, as dusk fell eerily. The artillery bombardment continued, but in a desultory fashion. The Japanese were still unsure of the exact position and strength of the garrison. It was uncanny to gaze at the wall of trees and know that out there, perhaps only a few hundred yards away, were fifteen thousand fanatical and totally merciless enemy soldiers.

That evening, Larry was down in the Deputy-Commissioner's bungalow chatting with the commander, Captain Lawrie, when they heard the first call.

'Hey, Johnnie, let me in. Let me in, man, the Japs are right behind me.'

'Douse that lamp,' Lawrie snapped, while a ripple went through the men who hurriedly took their positions at the windows.

The West Kents were jungle veterans, and were not going to be taken in by any tricks. But the bungalow next door was held by a company of the Assam Rifles, and Larry hurried over there to find Caldwell in a state of some agitation.

'It could be one of our chaps,' he muttered, 'just finding his way back.'

'It isn't,' Larry told him.

Caldwell gritted his teeth. Even in the darkness the sweat could be seen gleaming on his face, and his men were equally jumpy.

The calls continued well into night, but the British officers had their men well in hand and there were no replies.

The artillery fire also stopped, and the night was hideously quiet except for the buzzing of cicadas and, incongruously, the occasional roar of a distant tiger. It was utterly dark, because although the night sky was clear the stars were invisible behind the branch and leaf canopy which overhung the houses.

Soon after midnight, when Larry was just considering returning up the hill for a few hours' sleep, a shot rang out. It was impossible to tell where it came from or where the bullet went, but instantly several of the Indian troops returned fire.

'Cease fire!' Larry snapped. 'Cease fire, for God's sake.'

'But they're shooting at us!' Caldwell gasped.

'No, they're not. They're just shooting, hoping for a reply like that. Now they have you pin-pointed.'

He decided to stay with the frightened men, and used the field telephone to talk to Richards, to ask if some reinforcements could be sent down.

'Can't be done,' the Colonel replied tersely. 'They must hold with what they have. We have no idea where the Jap onslaught will come, and I must keep my reserve companies of the West Kents to plug any gaps. But you have my permission to stay there for a bit and give Caldwell a hand.'

'Thanks,' Larry said.

He looked at his watch. It was past three. There had been several other isolated shots, but these had not been answered. The Japanese would literally be attacking in the dark if they came now. He reckoned, and hoped, they would probe a bit more.

When the attack came he was as surprised as everyone else. One moment the bungalow was silent save for the odd cough or scrape of a boot on the floor, the next it was a mass of screaming, shouting men, behind whom the inevitable bugles were blasting the morning.

The Japanese had approached the perimeter in great strength, and crossed the road, totally unseen.

'Fire!' Caldwell bellowed, and his men obeyed. But then the enemy were in their midst, thrusting with their bayonets, and swinging their rifle butts. In the darkness it was next to impossible to tell friend from foe, and the once-attractive little house became a pit of hell.

Larry fired his revolver at one yellow face, side-stepped

a bayonet thrust, swung his left arm to catch the man a blow on the side of the head and tumble him over, and bumped into Caldwell just as the lieutenant fell, a bayonet in his chest.

There was no chance to discover whether he was dead or only wounded. Larry was being forced back by the weight of bodies, snarling, shrieking, wailing; he was surrounded by steel, gagging on cordite fumes. And the Indian riflemen were already fleeing.

His revolver clicked on an empty chamber and he could do nothing more. He had been pushed into the kitchen by the melée. Desperately he hurled himself at the jalousied window and went straight through, landing on his hands and knees. He regained his feet and ran for the trees, about twenty yards away. Something exploded in his face and he fell, more from surprise than having been hit.

'Don't shoot,' he snapped. 'It's Larry Cairns.'

A moment later he had been pulled to safety by a sergeant of the West Kents, and gasped for breath while the regulars fired volley after volley to accompany the chatter of their Brens.

The Japanese had also driven the West Kents from the Deputy-Commissioner's bungalow, although there the retreat had been more orderly. The enemy now paused to regroup, but the respite was only brief. With full daylight they surged on again, regardless of the casualties inflicted by the Brens and machine guns, and the West Kents and Indians were forced back by sheer weight of numbers.

Larry had by then returned up the hill to report on the situation to Richards, who immediately ordered a counter-attack. This was successfully carried out, and the Japanese were tumbled back out of the bungalows, fighting desperately. They were even occupying the cookhouse ovens as strong points. The perimeter was thus re-established, though the houses were now in flames and uninhabitable, while the Japanese lapped round the British position and came up the hill at the tennis court.

'They can't come any closer than that,' Richards said.

'From now on we die where we stand.' Which is exactly what the British and Indians proceeded to do.

The next week became an unending nightmare of noise and terror and sudden death. The Japanese attacked again and again, sometimes during the day, sometimes at night. They forced their way right up to the trenches, and the defenders were compelled to withdraw yet again, but only across the tennis court. The Japanese then occupied the trenches on the south side, so that the opposing forces faced each other at a distance of hardly twenty yards, utterly exhausted, yet both as filled with fight as ever. The defence was now assisted by the deadly accuracy of the Indian Mountain Battery, firing at close range and often delivering its barrage only a few feet in front of the British and Indian position.

As promised, planes came over to drop supplies for the garrison, but with the perimeter now so shrunk it was inevitable that a lot of these should fall into Japanese hands. 13 April was the most disastrous day of the siege, which had already then been going on for five days: an entire drop drifted down the hillside into Japanese hands. On this day too the enemy artillery finally got the range of the hospital, and began shelling it with deadly accuracy. There were well over a thousand men inside, and the slaughter was immense.

The command post was shelled often enough, but the Japanese were not exactly sure where it was, and although from time to time some of their more fanatical men burst right through the British troops and charged up the hill, they were always killed by revolver fire from Richards and Larry and the wireless operators.

Of course washing and shaving were out of the question; eating was a matter of snatching a bite from time to time, sleeping a matter of a quick ten minutes' kip between attacks.

Moving the wounded was impossible once the hospital had been hit; they lay where they fell, given what field dressings and analgesics were available.

Kohima turned into a vast cesspool, in which decaying bodies and human excreta vied as the most pungent and repulsive odours, in which men fought, with fists and teeth as much as with rifle and bayonet, and cursed, and screamed, and moaned and prayed, and died.

But Kohima held. Further south Imphal was also holding, and the Japanese were sustaining enormous casualties. At last the command post picked up a message from Brigade: the Japanese were retreating, and a rescue column was on its way.

Next morning binoculars were turned to the north, and at last the convoy, spearheaded by tanks, could be seen moving along the road. The Japanese had been defeated.

> When you go home
> Tell them of us and say
> For their to-morrow
> We gave our today.
>
> Inscription on the graves at Kohima.

The Japanese failure at Imphal and Kohima was more than merely the repulse of U-Go and the saving of India, vital as these were. It marked the end of Japanese dominance in South East Asia. Mutaguchi's army of veterans was now hurled back, suffering in the process sixty-five thousand casualties, mostly from disease. Yet the retreat, harried by the Allied air forces as well as ground troops, was always orderly, and no-one doubted that a lot of hard fighting remained to be done before Burma could be reclaimed.

It was not actually until November that the British army crossed the Chindwin in strength. With them, now on Slim's staff, went Major Lawrence Cairns, DSO, MC.

Although Japanese resistance continued fiercely, progress was steady, and by the end of January 1945 the Burma Road had been reopened. Before Slim's Fourteenth Army lay the Irrawaddy, and the primary goals of Mandalay and Meiktila, the gateways to Rangoon.

The end was in sight. But would they be in time, Larry wondered, or were they already too late?

The arrival of new inmates always provoked a flurry of interest in the internment camp: the women went to the fence to see who was coming.

They moved slowly, like people just awakened from a long sleep. In fact, most of them were half asleep all the time, their bodies worn down by emaciation and exhaustion; meals such as they had had just before the visit of the Red Cross were hardly even memories now.

Their clothes hung in rags from their shoulders and hips; their feet were bare and a mess of festering sores, as were their heads.

Many of them had died during the three years they had been in this camp. Many more were clearly going to die, unless they were rescued soon.

But rescue seemed impossible. They had no news from the outside world, save of Japanese victories. They could only use what mental energy they still possessed to attempt to work things out for themselves. The fact that their rations had been halved might have been Japanese callousness; the fact that the guards' rations had also been cut indicated that all was not going quite as well as their captors pretended.

But there was no suggestion that the British were returning to Malaya, or would ever do so.

However, arrivals from the outside world might have some news, some knowledge of what was really happening.

To Margaret's disappointment, the new arrivals were all Chinese: two women and four children, two boys and two girls. They were in a bad state. One of the women wept all the time, the other walked with a limp. They had clearly once been prosperous; they wore the rags of good clothes and, apart from their grief and the cuts and bruises inflicted by the kempei-tai, they looked quite fit and well-fed.

There was a crisis immediately on their arrival, when

the boys were dragged away to the male camp. The weeping woman just stood there, but the injured woman protested and was struck across the face. She fell to her knees, but did not cry out.

The boys were marched away.

Margaret returned to Marion and Molly.

The euphoria of knowing that Larry was alive had long disappeared into memory; that had been eighteen months ago. The Red Cross had been back again to see them a few months before, but this time they had no news of Larry except that he was serving with the army, somewhere in eastern India. There was no way of knowing if he was still alive, nor of knowing if she and Marion would still be alive when he finally came for them.

They kept themselves as fit as they possibly could. Unlike most of the other women, Margaret made Marion and Molly join her in taking exercise every day. They forced their wasted muscles to carry them round and round the compound for as long as they could before they collapsed with spinning heads and black spots before their eyes.

They had avoided madness, and they had avoided any serious disease, although of course they all had malaria which every couple of weeks would plunge them into a terrifying ague, which in their weakened state could easily prove fatal.

And they tried to believe in the inevitability of their rescue, although with every day this belief grew more and more difficult to sustain.

Margaret did not think there was any possibility that the two Chinese women would have any news of Larry, but Molly was anxious for news of Bob, and she went over to join the throng around the new arrivals.

She returned in a state of high excitement. 'You won't believe this,' she said, 'but those women are Chung Kai's wife and sister-in-law. You remember Chung Kai, Meg? He was once Singapore's biggest merchant, after Hammond and Teng.'

'I remember Chung Kai,' Margaret said, although she had never met him.

But she had met his sister. And she remembered too much about her. She could not be sure whether or not Chung Lan had saved her from a whipping, or worse, in Changi. If she had, it would have been an act of contempt. And even though Larry's affair with her had happened before their marriage, and her anger was the reaction of a stupid, petty-minded woman, still she felt a resentment, amounting to hatred, of Chung Lan. This resentment extended – Margaret couldn't help it – to all the Chungs, even their wives and children, undeserving as they were.

And she knew that Chung Kai and Larry had been enemies for years.

'Why has he fallen out with the Japanese?'

'Apparently he's been working against them for years, since the fall of Singapore. He and his brother Cheong have been masterminding sabotage attacks and all manner of things, in both Johore and Singapore Island.'

Margaret wondered if Lan Kuei knew about that. But if Lan Kuei knew, then surely Kitachi knew as well.

Was it possible that Lan Kuei had betrayed her own brothers?

'They don't know what went wrong,' Molly was saying. 'But the whole thing exploded a couple of months ago. Chung Kai and Chung Cheong made their escape into the jungle. As far as Chung Han and Chung Su know they are still alive.

'And guess what, they say that the Japanese are being beaten from pillar to post in the Pacific, and are retreating everywhere.'

'Are they retreating in Burma?'

'Well . . . they didn't know about that.'

'How can you believe anything they say?' Margaret asked scornfully. 'They were nothing but collaborators.'

'But Chung Su . . . she's been most horribly tortured. They wouldn't tell me what they did to her, but she can hardly walk.'

'I don't see what she's got to complain about,' Margaret

said, bitterly, thinking of Marion's rape and her own flogging.

'Oh, Meg! They're in the same boat as us. And they used to know Larry. Wouldn't you like to talk with them?'

'No,' Margaret said. She didn't think she could bring herself to speak to people whom she regarded as somehow being responsible, even if indirectly, for everything that had happened to her, and her family.

She didn't believe what they had said about the Japanese defeats, because she was afraid to. Anyway, wars were a matter of retreats and advances; there was no point in becoming euphoric about a few American victories. It was here in South East Asia that her future lay, if she had a future.

Everyone in the camp was most sympathetic towards Chung Su, because she had been tortured by the Japanese. None of them knew that Margaret had been raped and beaten by the Japanese, because she hadn't told them. Everyone seemed to know what had happened in Hong Kong, but because she hadn't moaned about her misfortunes they somehow supposed that she had swanned through the whole dreadful episode unscathed. For the first time, she felt bitter about that.

More than ever, Margaret began to turn in on herself. She told herself she could no longer even count Molly as a friend. And Marion was as bad as the rest, sitting with the Chinese women and listening to their misfortunes. She did not know if Marion told them of her own rape or not, but at thirteen she was at an impressionable age, eager to listen to other people's adventures; it was one of the catastrophes of her life that the only adventures she could listen to were so dreadful.

But it hurt Margaret to think that even her own child had betrayed her.

It was about a month after the arrival of the Chung women that Molly was taken ill.

All the women, and the men in the adjacent camp,

397

suffered from dysentery more or less continuously; lack of good food and any proper sanitation accounted for that. The miracle was that cholera had not set in long before it did.

And Molly was not a young woman; she had kept going only because of her indomitable spirit. When she was too weak to use the latrine trench she was clearly very ill: she had always been a stickler for the niceties.

The women carried out a well-rehearsed drill. Cases of serious illness had to be reported to the Commandant. Then, some time afterwards, an army doctor would come and examine the victim. Sometimes, very occasionally, there would be a dose of medicine. More often there was a kick in the ribs and a command to get up and bow on pain of a beating. And sometimes the patient would be removed on a stretcher.

Quite a few of the women presumed Molly would be taken to hospital and given proper treatment; Margaret suspected that the sick were taken outside the camp and buried, possibly while still alive. But she kept that opinion to herself.

Molly's condition was reported to Sergeant Kimishira and thence to the Colonel, and the next day a doctor appeared. By then Molly's condition was much worse, and two other women who had slept near her were also affected. They had no control over their bowels; they were too weak to move, and they cried out for water all the time.

The atmosphere was so foetid it could almost have been cut with a knife. The doctor stood in the door of the tent, trying to hold his breath and listened to the description of the symptoms, then hurried for the gate, which was promptly locked and double-locked.

It was Marion who went to the gate to protest. 'Mrs Sharples needs help, Sergeant Kimishira,' she said.

'You must help her,' Kimishira said. 'The doctor cannot do so. He cannot help any of you now. You must help yourselves.'

'But . . . what do you mean? Has she got the plague or something?'

'The plague,' Kimishira said. 'Yes, the plague. Mrs Sharples has cholera.'

When Marion told them, the women stared at each other in appalled silence for several seconds. Then some screamed. Others just slumped to the ground in horror.

There was cholera in the camp, and the Japanese had sealed it off. They would either die or they would recover, but their guards would not consider allowing the dread disease to spread.

That evening their food was thrown over the fence; no guard entered the gate.

'Mummy,' Marion said. 'You've got to do something.'

'Why?' Margaret asked. 'Why me?'

'Because you're the only one who can. You're the toughest one here. All the others are just crying. But they'll listen to you. If you don't do something, we're going to die. And I don't want to die!' Marion wept. 'Not before Daddy comes!'

Margaret knew she was just being bloody-minded. For the past three years, she had blindly believed that as long as she kept to herself she would survive. No matter what happened to the others, their misfortunes would not touch her or Marion. But now Molly was mortally ill, and death threatened every one of them.

Keeping to oneself would not stop cholera running rampant in the crowded camp. Margaret stood up and surveyed the compound. Already the stench of the disease was worse than the usual smell of the camp.

You must do something, Marion had said. But surely nothing could be done about cholera, without medicine, except stop it spreading. And how could that be done, in the limited confines of the compound?

Only by being utterly ruthless.

She clapped her hands. 'All right!' she shouted. 'We've been told to get on with it and solve this problem ourselves. Gather round and I'll tell you how we'll do it.'

399

They stared at her as if she was mad. One or two swore at her.

'Do you want to die?' she shouted at them. 'Do you all want to die?'

Still they muttered and stared.

Then Chung Su got up and came over to her. 'Tell us what you want us to do, Mrs Cairns.'

Margaret could only thank God that it was the dry season. She went to the gate and negotiated with Kimishira for some matches and a large cooking pot. He demurred at first, but then listened when she explained what she had to do.

'Just remember, Mrs Cairns,' he said, 'that if there is a big fire, you will all burn.'

Margaret then put the women to work, using Marion and Chung Su as her aides. Those who already had cholera were carried from the hut and placed against the far fence. Those who were not yet affected but were too weak to be of much help were gathered in another group, as far as possible from the first.

The remainder – even Chung Han and her daughters, who were in hysterics – were put to work emptying all the huts, save for the diseased one, and accumulating the scanty remaining belongings. Once she had the matches, Margaret built a stack of dried leaves and branches beneath the diseased hut and set fire to it.

It went up in a gush of flame and smoke, and even the Commandant came out of his office to look at it. The men in the adjacent compound also came to look. They too had the disease and had been sealed in.

Margaret left some of the women to keep an eye on the flames, armed with blankets to beat them out if they showed signs of spreading. The others she set to digging a pit in the earth, and in it she built another fire. Over this she suspended the cooking pot, and emptied all the water containers into it.

'No one is to drink any water until it is boiled,' she told them.

It could all so easily have been done long ago. But the Japanese would surely not have co-operated until they, too, were threatened.

That had been the easy part. Margaret was now left with the business of caring for the sick, and disposing of the dead.

Molly was the first of these. She had started to eat her own tongue. There was nothing anyone could do about her after that, save prise her jaws apart with pieces of stick. Margaret wept, and prayed for her friend to die, and eventually she did.

Molly had been well-liked in Singapore, and her death distressed her many friends in the camp. 'Where can we bury her?' one of them asked.

'We can't,' Margaret said harshly.

The woman simply gaped.

'The body must be burnt,' Margaret told her. 'All her clothes must be burnt.'

Margaret called Marion and Su, and between them they lifted the poor emaciated body and carried it to the still-burning hut.

'Do you wish to pray?' Su asked.

'Afterwards,' Margaret said. She knew she would not have the resolution to go through with it if she hesitated.

They threw the body on to the fire. Then Margaret and Su and some of the other women knelt in silence for a few minutes.

'I did not know you were a Christian,' Margaret said to Su.

'I am not a very good Christian,' Su replied. 'Mrs Cairns, will you help me pray for my boys?'

Margaret hadn't considered what it must be like to be separated from one's children. She had Marion close to her. And if Marion died, it would be in her mother's arms. But Su's sons had no-one to look after them. Their mother might never see them again.

She was suddenly overwhelmed by an unfamiliar feeling

401

of compassion for the woman. She took Su's hand. 'Yes,' she said. 'Yes, I will.'

The body took a long time to be consumed, because they had no petrol. And soon it was joined by others.

Cholera is a disease where the victim quite literally rots while still alive.

Margaret was reminded of her time in the hospital in Hong Kong, only now she was Sister. The sick had to be tended and cleaned, their voracious thirst for water satisfied as much as possible, while the fires had to be kept stoked and fed and the water boiled.

And there was also the strain of worrying who might next be taken ill. Margaret never worried for herself; she was indeed the strongest woman in the camp. But she was terrified for Marion. However, the child worked as hard as anyone, and seemed to gain a new lease of life each day.

Even more than Marion, however, she came to rely on Chung Su, who took over the care of the Chinese and Malays, much to Margaret's relief. Unlike her sister-in-law, who remained a constant bundle of hysterics, Su was calm and forceful, nearly as strong as Margaret herself.

They talked little about anything except the disease, and yet an inevitable intimacy grew between them. Margaret's heart gave a great lurch one day when Su keeled over with gripes in her stomach.

'Oh, my God,' she said.

'It is fate,' Su said, trying to prevent her face from grimacing with pain.

Margaret felt a wave of despair wash over her. She had long forgotten that this woman was the wife of her husband's enemy, the sister-in-law of her own bitterest enemy.

Su had all the courage in the world. How much, Margaret only realised when she undressed her to wash her, and saw the terrible scars on her thighs and between her legs, even on the vagina itself.

'Yes,' Chung Su said. 'That was done by a man named Kitachi Tano. He is an enemy of my family.'

'Kitachi!' Margaret exclaimed. 'A colonel in the kempei-tai?'

'Do you know this man?' Chung Su asked.

'He whipped me too. And he raped my daughter.'

Chung Su said nothing, but reached out, squeezed her hand. Margaret burst into tears, and folded the Chinese woman in her arms.

'You will live, if you are determined to do so,' she said. 'You *will* live, Chung Su.'

'I *must* live,' Chung Su whispered. 'My boys . . . my husband . . . I must live. I cannot let them kill me now. Will my boys live, Mrs Cairns?'

Margaret hugged her tighter still.

'Ah, Colonel,' said General Abe. 'Come in. Come in.'

Kitachi entered the office and bowed. Ever since Abe's appointment to Singapore command he had been nervous, wondering how much the general remembered, or even knew, of that incident on the Korean border so many years ago. But Abe either knew or remembered nothing, it seemed. Out of the corner of his eye he could see the general also bowing. Abe was an officer of the old school, not in the least like Yamashita; it was gratifying to know that Yamashita, now commanding in the Philippines, was having the pants beaten off him by the Americans.

The two men straightened at the same moment.

'It is a sad world,' Abe observed.

'But the Empire will survive,' Kitachi said.

He genuinely believed this, for all the unrelieved series of disastrous defeats suffered by the Imperial army over the past year.

'Of course,' Abe said, with less certainty. 'Sit down, Colonel. I have some news for you, news which I know you have long been awaiting.'

Kitachi sat down.

'Things are bad in Burma,' Abe said. 'Frankly, they are a shambles. Our armies are disintegrating. Oh, they're fighting to the last man, but being driven from pillar to post. There is even talk that Mandalay may fall before long.'

Kitachi said nothing. He knew of the news from Burma, and was perfectly confident that a counter-attack would soon be launched which would again drive the British back across the Chindwin. He did not see how it could affect him.

'And now Colonel Kawabe has been killed,' Abe said.

Kawabe had commanded the kempei-tai with the Burma Army.

'So I have recommended you to fill his place,' Abe said.

Kitachi stared at him in total disbelief.

'I can see that you are dumbfounded,' Abe went on. 'I can believe that. I can understand that you had almost given up hope of being given a combat post. And I know, from your record, how much you have always desired such a post. My heart bleeds for you. That is why I seized the opportunity.'

You blithering idiot, Kitachi wanted to shout. You want me to leave Shonan, and Aiwa, and go into the jungle to rot? You cretin! I once entered in my record that I desired a combat posting above anything else, but that was ten years ago!

'Honourable General,' he said. 'I do not know what to say. You have granted my dearest wish. I have spent my life dreaming of achieving such an ambition. But to leave Shonan, while these Communist scoundrels, that villain Chung Kai and his equally dastardly brother Chung Cheong, are still at large . . . to do so would lie heavy on my conscience.'

'You have had bad luck with Chung Kai and Chung Cheong, and the Communists,' Abe remarked, drily. 'A change of air may bring you greater success.'

'But my replacement here . . . he will not know the people, the conditions . . .'

'Oh, he will, Colonel. He will. Your replacement is to be Kano Ishiburi.'

'Kano?' Kitachi was astonished. 'But Kano is my aide. If I go into the jungle, Kano will accompany me.'

'I think the time has come for Colonel Kano to stand on his own feet, Colonel.'

'*Colonel* Kano?'

'I am promoting him as of today. The commander of the kempei-tai in Shonan must be a colonel.'

Kitachi gulped. 'But Kano has risen from the ranks, honourable General. He is not a samurai. He . . .'

'Is a reliable and conscientious man. Now, I know you have a lot to do, Colonel,' Abe said. 'You leave for the front at dawn tomorrow.'

Kitachi stumbled up the steps of the Cairns' bungalow, threw himself into a chair.

Aiwa, rising from her bow, took one look at his face and decided to abandon the tea she had so carefully prepared. She mixed him a scotch and soda instead.

'What has happened?'

Kitachi told her.

'Is it not what you have always wanted?' she asked.

'Of course I do not want to be sent into the jungle!' he shouted. 'I do not want to be killed, or die of malaria or dysentery. I want to stay here with you. Do you not wish me to stay here with you?'

Aiwa bowed her head. She was totally confused. She *did* wish Tano to stay with her, but not at the cost of his honour. And the only honour for a Japanese soldier lay in fighting for the Emperor.

Her embarrassment was saved by the arrival of Kano. He bounced up the steps. 'Honourable Colonel . . .'

'I have heard,' Kitachi said. 'My congratulations, honourable Colonel.' The wretched man did not even own two swords, would probably not know how to commit seppuku.

'I am deeply honoured, honourable Colonel, to be asked to take your place. But how I envy you, being given a fighting post. I wish we could change places.'

Kitachi glared at him, drank some whisky.

405

'Well,' he growled. 'Before I disappear into the jungle, I am going to go down to the internment camp and chop off a few heads. The Cairns woman, for a start. And then that Chung bitch who defied me until she fainted.'

'I would not concern yourself, honourable Colonel,' Kano said. 'There is cholera in that camp. It is not expected that any of the women will survive.'

'I want you in Mandalay,' Major General Tanaka Nubuo told Kitachi. 'We are expecting a heavy enemy assault there in the near future, and frankly the troops are a mess. Get up there and knock some backbone into them, even if you have to shoot a few.'

Kitachi Tano bowed. He was in the mood to do just that. His journey from Singapore to Rangoon, and thence up the east bank of the Irrawaddy, had been a terrifying eye-opener. He had been strafed by American fighter-bombers, and he had watched the Japanese army disintegrate.

The men lacked neither courage nor morale. They were as willing and eager to fight as ever. But they were riddled with disease, much of it brought on by malnutrition, and their brains had equally been riddled by a growing consciousness of British superiority in men and matériel and – worst of all – British equality in guts and determination. Were these the same people they had chased out of Burma in 1942 with scarcely any effort?

Kitachi had had no idea things were so bad.

In Mandalay he found a division, the Fifteenth, dug in, and their commander, Major-General Yamamoto Seiei – no relation to the famous admiral – prepared to fight to the last man. However, Yamamoto was deeply downcast.

'We stand and fight because we have been ordered to do so,' he told Kitachi. 'This is the first message sent to me.'

Kitachi read: 15 DIVISION WILL DEFEND MANDALAY TO THE LAST MAN.

'I asked for confirmation,' Yamamoto said, 'and got this, if you can understand it.'

Kitachi read: FIGHTING TO THE LAST MAN IS FROM THE POINT OF VIEW OF COMMAND THE VERY WORST OPTION.

'I queried the meaning of that,' Yamamoto said. 'And got this.'

Kitachi read the third piece of paper: LITERALLY WHAT IT SAYS.

'What did you do then?' Kitachi asked.

'I signalled, LEAVE IT TO US.'

Kitachi gulped. He certainly hadn't come up here to die in some muddy trench.

'And that is what we are going to do,' Yamamoto told him. 'Here, I have written out a little poem, and had it distributed amongst the troops. You may as well have a copy.'

Kitachi read:

> For their sovereign
> Our warriors will fall
> Defending to the end
> This town of Mandalay.

'Very nice,' he said. He felt sick.

Mandalay was situated on the plain of the Irrawaddy, and had been built, less than a century before, as the capital of Upper Burma. Behind the city, the land rose steeply into high, wooded mountains. In front of it, at a distance of no more than fifty miles, the land rose again, into the high hills separating Burma from India – the hills in which nestled Imphal and Kohima. The Irrawaddy made an S-bend to the west and then south immediately below Mandalay, before continuing down its four-hundred-mile valley to Rangoon and the Indian Ocean.

Situated where it was, Mandalay was the key to control of the Upper Irrawaddy, and therefore the key to any British advance down the river on Rangoon. It had been strategically important ever since its foundation in 1858, and had been the last Burmese stronghold captured by the British when they annexed the country; it had not in fact fallen until 1885.

But the British had come to stay, as they supposed, forever; they had built the massive Fort Dufferin to dominate both city and river. Some two thousand yards square, with walls which thinned from thirty feet at the bottom to twelve feet at the top, twenty-three feet above the ground, and surrounded by a seventy-five-yard wide lotus-filled moat, it reminded Kitachi of Osaka Castle, on a smaller scale. Inside it were barracks and offices, also King Thibaw's palace and even a polo ground.

Certainly it was a good place from which to undertake a desperate defence, even if Kitachi doubted it would stand up to a modern artillery bombardment.

Mandalay was also the centre of the Buddhist religion in Burma, and contained no less than seven hundred and thirty pagodas in and about the city. One of these, the Maha Mya Muni, or Arakan Pagoda, contained a brass Buddha twelve feet high. The whole area was covered in Buddhist relics. Just across the river, outside the town of Sagaing, was the huge pagoda which contained one hundred and twenty Buddhas in alcoves round its base. Kitachi was advised against going across to look at it, because no one knew where the enemy actually were on the west bank, and the great Ava Bridge was a twisted mass of red girders, having been blown up by the British during their retreat in 1942, and never rebuilt.

Using his glasses, however, he could see the dome of the temple, which was shaped like a woman's breast; the story was that when the architect asked the reigning queen what was the best shape for such a dome, she had uncovered her breast and asked if he could possibly improve on that!

Kitachi sighed, and thought of Aiwa. Then he went to look at the brass statue, and thought it was a tragedy that so much beautiful history was about to be destroyed.

But he was more interested in their chances of holding the place, and allowed himself to be slightly reassured by the broad Irrawaddy flowing past the city; Yamamoto had fortified a prominent bluff, just above the right-angle turn to the west. The defences looked strong.

Even so, everyone thought that the British were stronger.

'Nothing stops their advance, honourable Colonel,' said Captain Yoshida, who had been in command of the kempei-tai pending his arrival. 'We are told they have already crossed the river, both above and below us.'

'We want to go home,' said Chin Lu. She was the spokeswoman for the comfort girls in the city. 'We are doing no good here. The men are too tired to fuck. And too frightened.'

Kitachi remembered her from Singapore, screaming as she had been dragged from her home. She had been a virgin then, her parents had claimed. Now she was a hardened professional. She even looked well, if entirely lacking make-up and wearing a very ragged and soiled dress.

'You will leave here when I leave here,' he told her. 'Not a minute before. As for being frightened, you and I, Yoshida, will weed out the cowards and deal with them. Mandalay is to be held to the last man.'

Or at least, he thought to himself, the last soldier. There was no point in fighting to the last comfort girl, or to the last member of the kempei-tai.

'Welcome, Major Cairns. Uncle Bill wants to have a first hand account of what is going on, is that it?'

Major-General Pete Rees was a somewhat sad-faced man who looked as if he had just walked through the Burmese jungle, which he literally had. He was a distinguished soldier, who had fought in North Africa, but it had been his conduct of the recent campaign in command of the Nineteenth Indian Division which had made his reputation.

His had been the most difficult role to play in the campaign which Slim had carried out with the brilliance which justifiably earned him the reputation of being the best English general of the entire war. When the Fourteenth Army crossed the Chindwin in December, they were surprised by the paucity of the resistance offered by the Japanese. As it was well known that there were still a large number of veteran soldiers at the disposal of Lieutenant-General Kimura, who had taken over from the defeated Mutaguchi, this could only mean that he was concentrating his forces for a massive counter-attack, and the obvious time and place to launch this would be while the Commonwealth forces were endeavouring to cross the Irrawaddy.

Slim therefore made a bold decision. He appeared to continue his original advance towards the river north of Mandalay, but secretly directed the bulk of his forces, the Thirty-Third Corps, to the south, where they made the crossing virtually unopposed.

The troops left to carry out the original advance, and made to look like the entire army by a stream of radio directives every day, had been the Nineteenth Indian Division. They had been therefore only the bait of a trap, but Rees had driven his men, and their officers, with such determination that they too forced their way across the river north of Mandalay as originally planned, in the teeth of an expected savage counter-attack by Kimura's forces.

His reward for that brilliant feat of arms had been the taking of Mandalay, which now lay before him.

'The old man is interested in your decision not to call up air strikes to blast the defenders, sir,' Larry said.

'That would be rather a shame, don't you think?' Rees asked. 'This is an historic city. Besides, I think it would be counter-productive. The enemy are dug in, so far as we can tell. We are going to have to winkle them out in any event. So I think we are just going to have to get on with it. I do want air strikes, low-level bombing and machine guns, on Fort Dufferin. But they must be accurate. There will be no general obliteration of the city.'

'Yes, sir. Thirty Three Corps will be moving two divisions up from the south to assist. But they won't attack the city itself.'

Rees nodded. 'That suits me very well. Well, major, are you returning to GHQ, or staying here?'

'General Slim suggested I stay, sir, if you have no objection, until after the fall of the city. He thought I might be able to pick up some information as to Japanese plans for the defence of Rangoon from any prisoners we might take.'

'If we take any prisoners,' Rees observed. 'Well, major, let's get this show moving.'

The noise was tremendous as the Commonwealth forces moved into the northern suburbs of the city.

Standing on the battlements of Fort Dufferin with binoculars, Kitachi could make out Gurkhas and Indian and British soldiers, using automatic weapons together with rifles, blanketing the houses with fire as they moved forward. They were met with determined resistance for a while, and the area became smothered in smoke and dust. But then Kitachi saw groups of men starting to steal back through the houses towards the city itself.

He wiped sweat from his forehead. This was not altogether because of fear; like just about everyone else, he had contracted malaria, and there was no medicine left. It was also very hot. And the battle was not going well.

In fact, the battle was lost. Perhaps it had been lost from the beginning. He had done his best, had lectured the men, had weeded out the grumblers and put them on fatigue duty. He had even, as Tanaka had suggested, shot three of them. They had fought well, but the numbers brought against them had simply been too great.

Now the planes returned, swooping low out of the sky, their machine guns chattering. Kitachi hurried down the steps to the shelter of his office, leaving the anti-aircraft gunners to do what they could. The entire fort shook to the *crump crump* of the bombs, dropped from very low levels as the RAF avoided striking the city itself.

Yoshida regarded his chief with an impassive face, and Kitachi pulled himself together and put away his sodden handkerchief. 'It is the heat,' he explained.

411

Yoshida made no comment; he knew that Mandalay was a good deal cooler than Singapore.

Had it been like this in Singapore during the Japanese onslaught? Kitachi wondered. No wonder those people had been too shocked to think clearly when he had entered the city.

He went to find Yamamoto, who was in his control room, radio microphone in hand, giving orders in every direction, while aides hurried to and fro.

'We are in an impossible situation,' Kitachi told him.

'Oh, quite,' Yamamoto agreed. 'But I have good news for you. GHQ has rescinded its "last man" order. We are to launch a final counter-attack on Nineteenth Division, and then pull out. Apparently there are more British troops south of us, and behind us, so we are no longer serving any useful purpose here.'

'But . . . if they are behind us, how can we pull out?'

'That is up to us. We will make it. I am certainly not going to surrender. And I strongly advise you against doing so, Colonel. You are kempei-tai. The British will hang you, for certain.'

'If we are pulling out anyway,' Kitachi said. 'I request permission to leave now.'

Yamamoto shrugged, 'Suit yourself.'

Kitachi summoned Yoshida. 'Assemble your men. We are moving out. You and I will wear red badges, as regular infantry. Oh, and bring the comfort girls as well.'

'Moving out, honourable Colonel?' Yoshida was astounded.

'I have given you an order,' Kitachi growled.

He strapped on his two swords, checked his revolver. He had still not engaged in battle. Certainly he had never supposed that a battle would be anything like this, a relentless advance of dust and smoke and bullets and bayonets. There could be no glory in dying anonymously in such chaos. A man should meet his enemy, face to face in the bright sun, where everyone would see his courage. Then he would give as good as he got.

412

The girls were excited. 'About time,' Chin Lu remarked. 'A girl could get shot in here.'

'A girl can get whipped at any time,' Kitachi reminded her. But there was no time for that now.

They left by means of an old dry moat which lay beneath the existing one and made their way in a crouching crawl through the drains, right out of the city. They stumbled through sewage and one of the girls screamed when she trod on a rat. Kitachi boxed her ears; he felt like screaming himself.

But at last they emerged into daylight, and paused in the trees to look back at the city, the clouds of dust and smoke, the fighter bombers wheeling above the fortress.

'Brave men,' Yoshida commented. 'We should be with them.'

'We have our duty to perform,' Kitachi snapped. 'Move out.'

'In which direction, honourable Colonel?'

'East. Due east.'

'Due east will take us into the mountains, honourable Colonel,' Yoshida queried. 'That is difficult country, and we have only rations for three days. We will never cross the mountains.'

'If we go south we will run into the British,' Kitachi told him. 'They are all round us, except in the east. We will go east. We will find food, and we will cross the mountains.'

Wearily they hefted their packs and went into the trees. There were eighteen of them: eleven members of the kempei-tai and seven girls. Every one had malaria.

Yamamoto pulled out the remnants of his battered division two days later, and Rees's men occupied the town.

There were only dead or dying Japanese to be found. Larry did what he could, but few of the dying soldiers wanted to talk. However, eventually he found a lieutenant, who had lost his leg and had some chance of surviving, and who did not like the kempei-tai.

'Who was the kempei-tai commander in the city?' he asked through his interpreter.

'Colonel Kitachi Tano.'

Larry frowned. 'But surely Colonel Kitachi is in Singapore.'

'He was sent here,' the lieutenant insisted.

'Then where is he now?'

'He left, two days ago. With his people. And a gaggle of comfort girls.'

Larry hurried off to find Rees.

'They'll get their come-uppance, eventually,' the General said. 'They're not going to stop us now.'

'I want Kitachi, sir,' Larry said. 'From all accounts he has a string of atrocities a mile long to his name in Singapore. I want him to go back there and stand trial.'

'Then get him,' Rees said. 'If you can. It's between you and Uncle Bill Slim if you get your head shot off.'

'We must keep moving, honourable Colonel,' Yoshida begged. In three days they had covered not more than ten miles. The one roadway was very steep, and neither Kitachi nor the girls were in good physical shape. Then they had to leave the road and hide in the jungle whenever British or American planes flew over, which they did regularly, strafing the retreating troops. The road was littered with dead and dying men.

They had been overtaken by the hurrying army, who had no time to spare for them; every man knew that the kempei-tai had pulled out first. Not even the trucks laden with wounded had stopped for them, no matter how hard they waved.

'Bastards!' Kitachi swore. He had taken off his boots, and was sitting by the roadside, rubbing his feet. 'They could have taken us in those trucks.'

'Those were wounded and sick, honourable Colonel.'

'Are we not sick?' Kitachi painfully pulled on his boots again and stood up. 'Come along. Move out.'

Chin Lu remained sitting. 'I can go no further. I will sit here.'

'And starve?'

'I will wait for the British. They cannot be far away.'

'The British will rape you.'

'So what? I'm a whore. You made me a whore, honourable Colonel.'

'I should cut off your head,' Kitachi spat at her.

Chin Lu shrugged, and began looking for bush ticks. They were all covered in bush ticks.

'But I won't,' Kitachi said. 'Because after they have raped you, the British will hang you as a traitor.'

Chin Lu shrugged again, and popped a tick between her thumb nails.

Larry had no doubt that Kitachi would go east. Any kempei-tai commander would risk forest and mountain rather than be taken alive by the British to be tried as a war criminal. So he commandeered a jeep, gained permission to enlist four Gurkhas, who were happy to accompany Larry Cairns anywhere. They remembered how he had brought a Gurkha column out of the jungle two years before.

He understood that what he was doing was dangerous, but he was also accompanied by the column sent by Rees to harry the retreating Japanese, while the RAF were overhead nearly all the time.

He knew he was close when he came upon the comfort girl Chin Lu, sitting with her back against a tree. She smiled at him, and the men with him.

'Are you going to rape me?' she asked.

He was amazed to hear good English. 'Who are you?'

'I am Chin Lu. I remember you, Mr Cairns. From Singapore.'

'But . . . what the devil are you doing here?'

'I was sent here to comfort the troops. I was sent here by Kitachi. Then he came too; isn't that amusing?'

'Where is he?'

'They left here yesterday. They cannot be far. They are

415

travelling very slowly. You will want to catch Kitachi, Mr Cairns. He boasts of how he flogged your wife, and raped her daughter.'

'Yes I'd heard about that,' Larry said through gritted teeth. 'I have a debt to settle with your Colonel Kitachi.' He signalled his men back into the jeep.

'Aren't you going to rape me or hang me, Mr Cairns?' Chin Lu asked, wrily.

'There's a medical team behind me,' Larry said. 'Stay here and they'll find you.'

'Will they rape me?'

'I should think they'll put you to bed, at least,' Larry said, and drove away.

Every so often Kitachi would burst into song. He knew he was delirious quite a lot of the time. His skin was burning, and the top of his head lifted off and then dropped again with a resounding crash with every step he took. Often he found himself lying on the ground without any idea how he had got there.

He was dying of malaria!

And no-one seemed to care. When he fell down they stood around and waited impatiently for him to get up again. They never tried to help him.

But this time, when he struggled to his feet, they did not even resume walking up the steeply-climbing road, which was now nothing more than a track. The rest of the army had long since left him behind, and the forest close at hand was quiet; there was a great deal of noise in the not too far distance.

'There is no more food, honourable Colonel,' Yoshida said.

Kitachi blinked at him. Yoshida was obviously as delirious as himself; he couldn't remember having eaten anything since leaving Mandalay. No doubt that accounted for the way legs kept giving away.

'We cannot go on, honourable Colonel,' Yoshida said. 'The men wish to turn back and surrender.'

'Soldiers of His Imperial Majesty do not surrender,'

Kitachi said. 'And soldiers of the kempei-tai *cannot* surrender.'

'We are wearing red badges,' Yoshida said. 'We will surrender as infantrymen.'

'You are a coward and a disgrace to the uniform you wear,' Kitachi growled. 'Do you not think the girls will betray you?'

'It was your idea to bring the girls, honourable Colonel. May I suggest that we dispose of them?'

He was speaking Japanese, but the girls knew enough to understand him; they screamed, and huddled together.

Kitachi blinked at them in turn. However much he had wanted to, he had never actually cut off a woman's head. He had had it done, but had never been present. He had dreamed of cutting of Margaret Cairns' head, and Chung Su's, but he had always known he would never even be able to watch it.

'Leave the girls with me,' he said. 'Go on, clear off.'

Yoshida hesitated. 'What will you do?'

'I am going to die as a Japanese officer should.' His hand dropped to the hilt of his long sword.

'That is the honourable way, honourable Colonel. But you must have a second. I will stay and be your second.'

Kitachi knew Yoshida just wanted him out of the way, as quickly as possible, so that the rest of them could surrender. But he also knew that the captain was right: he had to have a second to strike off his head the moment he had made the belly cut, or he would die in agony.

'Are we to remain, honourable Colonel?' asked the sergeant.

Yoshida looked at his men. There was no doubt what they wanted to do.

'Take us with you,' begged one of the girls. 'We will not betray you.'

'The colonel has decided that you will stay with him,' Yoshida said. 'You must obey. If you attempt to follow my men you will be shot. You have permission to withdraw, sergeant.'

'Clear off,' Kitachi said.

The men saluted, then marched down the path and were soon lost to sight. The girls continued to huddle together. If they no longer feared the colonel because of his illness, they certainly feared the captain, who was just as well armed, with revolver and two swords.

'We must make haste,' Yoshida said.

He himself unfastened Kitachi's pack, and took out the kimono. Then he removed his colonel's weapons, and helped him to undress.

The girls watched in fascination.

'There is no water for purification,' Yoshida said sadly.

'Then I will do without.'

Naked, Kitachi felt better than he had since leaving Mandalay. Besides, it was good to have made a decision. Now he must have the strength, of mind as well as body, to go through with it.

Slowly he put on the kimono, leaving it open. Then he sat down, cross-legged, on the ground.

Yoshida bowed, and presented the short sword.

Kitachi took it, drew it from its scabbard, tested the blade; it was as sharp as a razor.

At last understanding what was to happen, the girls shuddered.

Yoshida drew the long sword from its scabbard, and tested the blade in turn. Satisfied, he took his position behind the Colonel, feet spread, body tensed, both hands wrapped round the hilt. Like every Japanese officer he knew the duties of a second. When the principal had plunged the short sword into his belly, and pulled it across to tear open his intestines and leave himself mortally wounded, he would throw out his left hand. As he did so, it was the duty of the second to strike off his head; once the principal had behaved with honour, it was not fitting that he should suffer a moment more agony than necessary.

But the head had to be struck off with a single blow. Yoshida was nervous. If only the Colonel wouldn't take such a time to compose himself!

Every principal was allowed several minutes, to commune with himself, to pray if he chose, to prepare himself for his sudden violent exit from the world. But Kitachi had been communing for nearly a quarter of an hour.

And now Yoshida could hear an engine, drawing closer; a four-wheeled drive vehicle was coming up the track.

He had no wish to be found in the company of Kitachi Tano, and he wanted time to despatch the comfort girls before the British caught up with him.

'Honourable Colonel,' he said. 'It is time.'

Kitachi ignored him. He was thinking of Aiwa, of her soft arms, her softer breasts, her tight little thighs and buttocks. No man had been so blessed as himself during this past year. It had been the happiest year of his life.

Aiwa was going to grieve when she heard of his death.

The jeep was very close. Yoshida went so far as to tap Kitachi on the shoulder. 'Honourable Colonel . . .'

Kitachi raised his head, gazed at the jeep as it came round the bend in the road and scraped to a halt. Indian soldiers wearing bush hats rather than turbans leapt out of it, their rifles levelled. With them was a white officer, also wearing khaki and a bush hat, who carried a drawn revolver.

'Surrender, Kitachi!'

Larry Cairns! Kitachi blinked to make sure. But it was Larry Cairns.

'The colonel is about to commit seppuku, sir,' Yoshida said. Like most kempei-tai officers, he had been taught English. 'You cannot interrupt him now. When he has finished, I will surrender.'

Larry slowly lowered his revolver.

Kitachi continued to gaze at him. Larry Cairns, he thought. After fourteen years of bedevilling him, Cairns would be a witness to his death.

He had never swung his long sword in battle. As a samurai, he was a failure. Only seppuku was left to him, to save his honour, or to swing his sword in battle, just once before he died.

Kitachi Tano leapt to his feet, and uttered a huge roar. Yoshida was too dumbfounded to protest or resist as Kitachi tore the long sword from his hands, uttered a mighty shout of 'Banzai!' and charged the jeep.

Larry Cairns raised his right hand and shot the charging figure through the head.

Since her brother's departure Aiwa had kept very much to herself, accepting no invitations. Kano, who knew all Kitachi's secrets, was well aware that brother and sister had been lovers. He held no pronounced moral views on the matter. But Aiwa was a beautiful woman, and as he had taken Kitachi's place in the crimson and gold bedroom of Lan Kuei, so he dreamed of taking Kitachi's place in Aiwa's bed as well.

He had known that he had no chance of that while Kitachi lived. But now . . .

His head was bowed. 'Colonel Kitachi died with the greatest honour, sword in hand, charging the enemy,' he said. 'He was my friend, more than my superior. I will grieve his loss, for the rest of my life.'

'I thank you, honourable Colonel,' Aiwa said, very softly.

'If I can ever be of assistance . . .' Kano ventured.

'I thank you again,' Aiwa said.

'With your permission, I will call again tomorrow,' Kano said.

'I will expect you,' Aiwa said.

Kano was jubilant. She was a lonely woman, and she had accepted his advance. After all, she would need a man to replace her brother.

He could hardly wait for the next morning. But when he got there, he found the servants distraught. Aiwa had performed the ritual form of suicide permitted to Japanese women, by stabbing herself in the throat.

Mandalay fell on 21 March 1945, and the advance on Rangoon commenced. The Japanese had had enough in Burma. When, on 2 May, Wing-Commander Saunders of the RAF flew low over the city, he saw nothing but freed prisoners-of-war. So he landed, and he and his mechanic formally took possession of the city.

For the Japanese it was a mad struggle to regain French Indo-China and Malaysia, where they hoped a stand might still be made. But within a month of the fall of Rangoon, the Americans had secured the island of Iwo Jima as the climax of their spectacular three-year Pacific counter-offensive, and the mainland of Japan was exposed to round-the-clock bombing.

Then on 6 August, the atom bomb was dropped on Hiroshima, and eight days later, after the similar destruction of Nagasaki, Japan surrendered.

The news was immediately flashed to all Japanese commands throughout Asia and the Pacific. In many cases it was disbelieved; Japan had never surrendered to anyone in all her history. Even when those generals who demanded confirmation received it, there were units which were not informed and which, when informed, flatly refused to accept it.

The civilian populations in the conquered areas were even less informed, and more bemused.

By the middle of August it seemed clear that the cholera epidemic had run its course. Thirty three women and eight children had died. Amongst them was Chung Lo. His mother was still too weak to move, but she had survived and would live. Marion went to the fence to find out from the Australians what had happened, and spoke with Chung Kai junior. She was able to tell Chung Su that she still had one son.

Still it was necessary to maintain precautions, to keep the fires going, keep boiling the water; they could pay little attention to what the Japanese were doing. Then one day no food was thrown over the fence. Margaret went to the gate to shout for Kimishira, and to her consternation discovered that it was unlocked.

She just stood there for several minutes, unable to accept such a miracle. The Rising Sun still flew over the Japanese barracks and offices, situated some hundred yards away, but there was no-one in sight.

She called for Marion, who came running.

'Do you think it's a trap?'

Then they saw that the men's gate was also unlocked, for the Australians were cautiously emerging. Ten minutes later the camps were an explosion of joyous screams and shouts as the inmates embraced each other, tears as Chung Kai junior was led to his mother.

The Australians rampaged through the Japanese barracks, pulling down the flag, hunting for any living creature.

They found nothing, and no food.

'What are we going to do?' Margaret asked Major Lowry, happy to hand over command at last.

'I think we must stay here, Mrs Cairns. I know it'll be tough, but I'll have my men out hunting for grub. At least we're visible from the air here. If we try to get down to Singapore on foot, we could run into real trouble. Anyway . . .' he gestured at the pitifully emaciated inmates. 'I'm not sure a lot of these could make it.'

Margaret knew he was right, but the thought of having to stay here, with the funeral pyre slowly dying, while they continued to starve dispirited her. Then the next day an RAF plane flew low over them and, when they all shouted and waved, waggled its wings.

Next day a much larger plane appeared, and dropped several parachutes with food and medical supplies.

'We're going to live!' Marion screamed. 'We're going to live!'

Margaret smiled at her, though her heart was heavy. There was no way of asking the machines if Larry had survived.

Three days later they heard shots in the jungle. A motley collection of men emerged from the trees, Malays and Chinese, brandishing weapons and firing into the air.

'My God, if those are bandits . . .' Lowry said, wondering if his men would be able to offer any protection to the women.

But the men stopped at the gates, and only two came in.

Chung Han uttered a tremendous scream, and ran straight into her husband's arms.

Chung Su was too weak to do the same. Could this filthy, ferocious creature really be her husband?

He wore a bush hat and a khaki bush tunic over a loin cloth, and carried a rifle, and there were two bandoliers of cartridges slung across his shoulders. A revolver hung on one hip and a kris on the other.

'Kai?' she whispered. 'Is it really you?'

He knelt beside her and held her close.

She told him about Chung Lo, and he held his surviving son tight in his other arm.

'We have come to take you to Singapore,' he said.

'All of us?'

Chung Kai stood up; the white women were clustered at a distance. 'All of *us*,' he said, pointedly.

Chung Su held his hand. 'I would not have survived without them, without Mrs Cairns.'

'Mrs Cairns?'

Margaret came forward. 'Hello, Mr Chung.'

'This is my friend Margaret,' Chung Su said. 'She saved my life.'

'I think my people and I should be given facilities to leave Shonan, honourable General,' Colonel Kano said.

'That is not possible,' General Abe told him. 'All Japanese forces have been commanded to remain where they are.'

'Honourable General, the British will hang us.'

'That is a risk we all have to take, Colonel. If you are afraid of it, there is another way out. But until you decide to take it, it is your duty to remain here and preserve law and order. The people are starting to understand what has happened. Soon there could be rioting.'

'Then you will have to use your men to preserve order, honourable General.'

'I have given orders that no Japanese soldier is to fire on any civilian,' Abe told him. 'I expect order to be kept by the kempei-tai. After all, Kano,' he said with a smile. 'Does it matter which crime you are hanged for? There are so many.'

Kano bowed, and left the office. He had not really expected any sympathy from Abe, who had always hated the kempei-tai.

He went to the Bamboo Curtain. My Lai was alone in the bar, drinking gin. She was all of sixty now, but beneath the powder and the paint she looked much older.

'Where is Ahmed?' Kano asked.

'He has left. All my girls have left.'

'Lan Kuei has left?' Kano was horrified.

'Lan Kuei is my partner,' My Lai said.

Kano breathed a sigh of relief and went along the corridor to the crimson and gold room.

Lan Kuei sat in her chair reading a book; she was a voracious reader. She put it down when he entered.

'My Kano,' she said. 'You have come to take me away?'

Kano sat on the bed, the picture of dejection. 'They will not even let me leave,' he said.

'Then you are doomed.'

'Yes. It is a question of when.'

Lan Kuei thought quickly. Obviously she did not want Kano here when the British arrived; there would be too much to do and she did not want to be seen to be associated with a kempei-tai officer.

'Let us make love, Kano,' she said. 'For the last time.'

Afterwards they lay in each others' arms, and listened to a rush of noise, swelling above the sound of their own breathing.

Lan Kuei sat up. 'That sounds like a storm. But the sky was clear earlier.'

'It is a storm,' Kano told her. 'Of people.'

She turned her head sharply.

Kano smiled. 'Your people have found out about the surrender.'

'But . . .' she listened to the sound of breaking glass and shattering wood. 'Why are they doing that?'

'They are looking for Japanese soldiers. Especially members of the kempei-tai.'

'Then you must leave. Now!' She hopped out of bed, began gathering up his clothes.

'But I am comfortable here,' Kano said.

Lan Kuei glared at him.

'I am also safest here.'

'Safest . . .' the noise was very close, and she could identify some of the shouted words.

'Lan Kuei!'

'Chinese bitch!'

'Japanese whore!'

Down the corridor, My Lai's scream was drowned in a fresh outbreak of shattering glass and wood.

'You must protect me!' Lan Kuei said to Kano.

'Pass me my revolver,' Kano said.

Lan's hands were trembling as she gave him the gun. She stared at the doorway, undecided whether to dress or not. For she was Lan Kuei, the most beautiful as well as the most desirable woman in Singapore. No one was going to harm Lan Kuei when they could bed her instead. If necessary she'd screw every last man of the mob.

The bedroom door burst open; the men rushed in and stopped abruptly. Every member of the mob had dreamed of one day entering this sanctuary. Lan Kuei stared back, panting now. Then she was startled by an explosion. She turned her head sharply, and nearly retched.

Kano had put the revolver barrel into his mouth and pulled the trigger; the entire top of his head had been blown off.

She turned back to look at the mob, gasped as they reached for her.

'No,' she shouted. 'Wait! You want me? I will come to you, one at a time. I will . . .'

She was forced through the door, hands clutching at

every part of her body as she was half pushed, half dragged along the corridor. She was surrounded by cruel faces, laughter and obscenities.

Vaguely she realised that the bar was a shambles; My Lai had disappeared. Then she was at the head of the stairs, and she saw the rope.

For the first time in her life, Lan Kuei screamed.

The rope was already secured to the bannister. Now the other end was tied round her neck.

'No,' she begged. 'No. I will give you anything you wish. Please . . .

But they lifted her body over the stair well, held her for a moment, then dropped her.

She writhed and kicked for several seconds, surrounded by a cloud of swirling black hair.

Margaret had stood all day on the front verandah of her bungalow, watching for the staff car. She almost stopped breathing as she watched the tall figure in the khaki uniform, with bush hat and revolver, getting out. She saw the crowns on his shoulder straps, the medal ribbons above his right breast pocket, the deeply sun-browned skin.

Was this really her husband?

He came to her. 'Margaret,' he said. 'Oh, Margaret.'

Was this very thin but strongly muscled woman with the ruined complexion and the freshly washed but surprisingly long red hair, and the utterly fearless look in her eye, really his wife?

Then she was in his arms, held close.

After a long minute he held her away. 'Are you all right?'

'I'm a little thinner than when last you saw me. But I'm putting on a pound a day.'

'Oh, my darling.'

'Look who's here too.'

His jaw sagged.

In December 1941 he had left a ten-year-old girl. Now he gazed at a fourteen-year-old young woman.

426

'Hello, Dad,' Marion said.

'The house is in amazingly good condition,' Margaret told him. 'You'll never guess who lived here during the occupation. Kitachi, with his sister.'

'Kitachi! You know he's dead?'

'I heard. Did he commit suicide? His sister killed herself.'

'I shot him,' Larry said. 'For you and Marion.'

There was a moment's silence. Margaret would have to get used to living with a man who had killed, time and again. But so would a great many women.

'I'm glad you shot him, Dad,' Marion said.

Larry squeezed her hand.

'There's a telegram for you,' Margaret said. 'It came two days ago.'

Larry scanned the words: KINDLY ASSUME POSITION MANAGING DIRECTOR ON RECEIPT THIS INTIMATION STOP PLEASE ADVISE AS SOON AS POSSIBLE REQUIREMENTS TO REESTABLISH HAMMOND AND TENG ON PAYING BASIS STOP CONFIRM STOP DIRECTORS LONDON.

'There are lots of others,' she said. 'Mumsy and Pa. . . . oh, lots.'

'Is anyone left? Roly?'

'He died. The kempei-tai beat him. You'll have to start from scratch.' She smiled. 'You'll have to buy a new chair.'

'Margaret . . . all those bastards are going to hang. Those who survived.'

'Yes,' she said. 'Mumsy thinks I should go home, and take Marion.'

'I think she's absolutely right. I'm afraid I'll have to stay here . . .'

'Then I'm staying too,' she said. 'There's a lot to be done.'

'And me,' Marion said firmly.

Larry was glad they wanted to stay. He had been separated from his wife and daughter for so long that he could

427

not bear to lose them again. He wanted time to get to know them again.

'Anyway,' Margaret went on, 'my friends are here. Oh, by the way, Bob Sharples is coming to dinner. So are Chung Kai and Chung Su.'

Larry frowned at her. 'Chung Kai and Chung Su?'

'I told you, my friends are here.'

After dinner, Chung Kai and Larry went out onto the verandah with their cigars.

'So you're a hero,' Larry commented.

'So are you.'

'What happened to Diem Chi?'

'He's still around. He could be a problem. Revolution, mayhem, murder: that's his way of life.'

'But right now he's a hero too,' Larry observed. 'So we can't touch him.'

'Yes.' Chung Kai said.

There were a few moments of silence, then Chung Kai said, 'I am going into politics.'

'Ah.'

'It is something I have long wanted to do. Now I have the opportunity. Everyone knows and respects Chung Kai.'

'Oh, quite. And my brief is to re-establish Hammond and Teng.'

'So we will be rivals again.' Chung Kai gave a quick smile. 'My brief is to seek independence for Malaysia.'

'And the best of luck.'

'Will you oppose me?'

'I'm not in politics, Kai. Thank God.' Larry took a deep breath. 'Kai, I heard about Lan. I am most terribly sorry.'

'She deserved it.'

'But she would never have been in that position, but for me. If you knew how that lies on my conscience . . . It always will.'

'Is there a man alive who does not have some shameful act on his conscience, even if it is a secret to him alone?

428

I abandoned Su to be tortured by the kempei-tai. That is something I can never forget. But there is no use looking back. We both have a lot to do. It would be very pleasant if we could be friends, and work in harness rather than in opposition.'

Larry grinned, and held out his hand.